The Seer Awakening

Uriah Rowland

Chapter 1

With a strangled cry and panicked breath, Travis Williams awakened. Desperately fighting the sheets that threatened to strangle him, he fell out of bed, landing with jarring force against the carpeted floor of his bedroom—first with his right shoulder, then his head. His lower half hit something soft, which promptly yipped and jumped aside. He had landed, at least in part, on the dog.

"Sorry, Starkey." Travis mumbled, bringing his hand up to his face to rub at his eyes. Starkey was quickly at his side, licking the back of his hand and arm with enthusiasm; all was forgiven. Travis pushed the dog away and remained on the floor, eyes closed, trying with all his might to calm his breathing and extinguish the evil from his mind. But it was still there, always there.

After several minutes, he managed to sit up and give himself a mental slap. Rubbing the back of his shoulder with his left hand, he listened to the quiet house, as he had learned to do. Life experiences told him to listen before he moved; before he did anything. In the foster homes growing up, not listening before you entered a room or crawled out of bed would often end in pain, especially in the homes where the foster parents were less than stable.

He listened, but all he heard was the shower running down the hall. His brother, Randy, was already up, no doubt preparing for work. Travis glanced at the clock; it was a little after six thirty in the morning. He had ample time to get to Susanville in time to save Aaron's life.

He picked himself up off the floor and went to the dresser. Shedding off his boxer shorts and throwing them in the hamper, he grabbed out a new pair, then dressed in jeans and a black t-shirt, his usual apparel. Unlike most young men his age, his room was spotless and relatively bare. One twin bed in the middle of the room, one desk in front of the one window, the top very clean, with only one lone pencil left sitting out, and a dresser and hamper next to the closet door. The floor was clean and vacuumed, and in a few minutes, the bed would be made. No photographs adorned the walls. Travis had nobody to take pictures of. There was only one person in his past he wanted to remember, but she was still far too painful to even think about, let alone look at a photograph.

He walked down the hall, past the closed bathroom door and into the living room. He turned on the computer, and while it was booting up, he went to the kitchen and grabbed a beer from the fridge. Despite the fact that he had only just turned twenty-one, Travis had been a solid one beer a day drinker since the age of sixteen. He knew it was an unhealthy habit, but it was necessary to preserve his sanity.

Back at the computer, he opened up a browser. Starkey came and sat down beside him, and he absentmindedly scratched the dog behind the ear. He had found the black, germen shepherd type dog two years before in San Francisco. The pup had been shivering behind a dumpster, so small that he could fit in one of Travis' hands, so young that his eyes weren't open yet. Travis had taken the pup home and bottle fed him for a month, thinking the entire time that the pup was going to die. But he hadn't, and now, he was as large as the average germen shepherd, healthy, and a great partner in crime.

He had named the pup Starkey because he had been going through a Beatles phase at the time and Starkey seemed to like the drums. The abandoned puppy had tugged at his heart; Travis himself had been found in much the same way. Not behind a dumpster, of course, but in a river. A fly fisherman had found him clinging to a bush, barely alive, in some river in Northern California when he was around twelve years old. Revived briefly at the hospital, Travis had been told he had only said two things before slipping into a three-month long coma: his name was Travis, and he had been asking for his sister. Upon waking from the coma, Travis had no memory of his former life; his slate had been wiped completely clean.

He could still feed himself, still write, walk, draw, and tested into a very high math and reading level. The only thing affected by his apparent trauma was his memory. A massive search had ensued to find his identity, and Travis' likeness had been cross-referenced with thousands of missing person's cases, but none of them had panned out. Nobody had ever come forward to claim him. Eventually, Travis had been given the last name Williams and been placed in the foster care system.

He heard the shower shut off and took a quick chug of his beer. Randy would disapprove of him starting off this early, but he doubted his brother would make a fight of it today. Randy didn't like alcohol for obvious reasons. After all, if Travis' story was tragic, Randy's story was a fucking nightmare.

When Randy had been seven years old, his father, a mean alcoholic, had beaten his mother to death with a full beer bottle. At the time, Randy was hiding in the closet under a coat with his hands clasped firmly over his ears. That was where the police found him some twelve hours later, still in the closet, still with his hands over his ears.

The two of them had met in a foster home when they were both twelve years old and had become fast friends. At the time, Randy was a quiet, reclusive kid with no steady friends and a bitterness that even a hardened veteran could admire. Travis, just out of the hospital, had no idea who he was but had seen a kindred spirit in the quiet boy. By the time they left that first foster home nine months later, their friendship was solid, and both of them benefited immensely from it. Randy came out of his shell and began to smile and laugh again, even began playing sports, and Travis was actually acting like a normal kid. It was for this reason that their respective social workers made the commitment to keep them together.

The bathroom door opened, and Randy stepped out, wearing jeans with a shirt thrown over one shoulder, humming a song by

Green Day. Tall at three inches over six foot with dirty blond hair which he liked to keep short and the type of farmers tan that only a construction worker could get, Randy was more handsome with a shirt on. With his shirt on, he looked like a typical American boy. With his shirt off, however, the impressive array of scars that decorated his torso in morbid design was hard to miss.

Randy stopped at the end of the hall, his blue eyes instantly zeroing in on the beer bottle sitting two inches from Travis' left hand. He didn't say anything, though, not today. He could read his foster brother well: the tightness in the neck and shoulders, the rigidness of his back, the vacant look of his eyes. He wasn't going to bring up the beer.

"What's the quickest way to Susanville?" Travis asked.

Randy frowned and walked into the kitchen, which was connected to the living room. "Hmmmm, not sure. From Chico? I don't know, maybe 90? I've never been there."

Travis snorted. "Some Caltrans worker you are. I'll Google map it."

"Hey, I just pave the roads, I don't memorize them," Randy shot back. "What's in Susanville? I heard you thrashing around in there earlier, thought about waking you up, but your aim is getting better." Randy pointed to the diminishing shiner bellow his right eye.

Travis sighed. "Bad one this time. Little boy, his name is Aaron. He's seven. Some guy is going to nab him from the park while his mom is distracted with his little sister. They probably won't find his body for days. The guy, he's already killed six, I think. He keeps souvenirs."

Randy poured himself some orange juice. "Do you need help?"

"Nah." Travis shook his head. "The dude's a coward—pedophiles always are. I can handle this."

"You sure? I can call in; say my back hurts…." Randy began.

"No, I've got this. Besides, one of us needs to keep a job." Travis clicked on the Google bookmark and navigated his way to maps.

"As if you need one," Randy said as he poured himself some cereal.

Travis didn't reply. Nearly two years before, at Randy's insistence, Travis had bought a lotto ticket—the only one he had ever purchased—and had been the sole winner of the jackpot. The initial payout had been substantial at over ten million dollars, and with the yearly installments, Travis wouldn't have to worry about money any time soon.

They had purchased this small two-bedroom house in a low-income neighborhood in Chico, California. Not wanting to draw attention to themselves, there was little about the two brothers that suggested they had more money than they let on. Some of the only objects of value they owned were their two trucks, which were used but still very nice, and an incredibly expensive gaming setup. Everything else, except maybe their clothes, was secondhand, even the furniture which had been purchased from the Salvation Army.

Due to a misplaced guilt over actually winning, Travis had given most of the money away to countless charities and organizations as well as some personal projects of his own. He had given a neighbor close to half a million in order to escape her extremely abusive and controlling boyfriend and to give her and her three children a new life in a new state. Despite his many charitable deeds, Travis still had nearly five million dollars in three separate bank accounts, and the annual payout would keep him well-off for years to come.

"89." Travis said. "I guess that's the fastest route."

"Wow, I was way off." Randy leaned against the counter, eating his cereal. "You probably don't want to take 89, though. There is major road work in three different places, expect a three-hour delay, maybe more. They just sent some of our guys over to help out."

Travis frowned at the computer screen. "I can go over to the five and take it to 44. It goes straight to Susanville. That should get me there with time to spare, especially if I speed." He pushed himself up from the chair and walked into the kitchen. Without thinking, he opened the fridge and grabbed another beer. He hadn't withdrawn the beer more than a few inches when Randy's hand clasped firmly on his arm. Randy didn't say anything; he didn't need to. Travis sighed, put the beer back, and took out the apple juice instead.

"You okay?" Randy asked around a mouth full of cereal.

Travis nodded and stuck a couple pop tarts in the toaster. "Will you please put on a shirt?"

Randy paused with a spoonful of cereal halfway to his mouth. "That bad, huh?" He set his cereal down and pulled his t-shirt over his head. "You're acting weird. Well, weirder than usual," he said as he took his cereal to the couch.

"I just have a feeling is all. It's bothering me."

"A feeling about the pedophile?" Randy asked.

"No, something else, I don't know." Travis took a long drink of his apple juice and tried hard not to think about Randy's scars. He wished his brother had had the good sense to put his shirt on before he left the bathroom. Travis didn't need that reminder, not today.

Travis had only been in the foster home three or four months when the dreams had begun; horrible, terrifying dreams, the kind that no normal child would have. The therapist called them night terrors, but Travis knew they were something else. He knew there was something dark behind them.

But the worst part of the dreams, the part that made his skin crawl, was that his dreams tended to be echoed in the news in the next couple of days. A murder, rape, car accident, or robbery that he had dreamt of would be the breaking news two or three days later, and that scared Travis. He didn't know what he was, but he knew he wasn't normal.

Fear lead him to silence. He didn't tell a soul about what he dreamt of, and when the therapist asked, he would make things up. He buried the horror deep within himself and ignored it. After all, he was a kid; there was nothing he could do. He tried to forget it even happened, but it became harder and harder to ignore, and the knowledge was causing him to retreat more and more within himself. The dreams didn't come every night, not even every week.

Sometimes, he would go months without having one, but they happened often enough.

Then, when he was a few months shy of fourteen, something happened that he couldn't ignore. He dreamt that his foster brother, Randy, had been kidnapped by his estranged father and beaten to death. Travis knew nothing of Randy's past at the time; it wasn't exactly something the other boy advertised. He didn't know what had happened to Randy's mother, and he didn't know that Randy's father had never been found. He assumed Randy was just another orphan, and Randy never talked about it. But he knew what he had seen that night, and it caused him to sit crying in his bed until dawn.

The next day, when Randy didn't come home after soccer practice, Travis panicked, screaming that "he" was going to kill him. His foster parents, good people at heart, had been somewhat hardened by the chores of their trade. They were used to their charges running away, used to the abused and battered boys that came through their door freaking out. They had seen their share of anxiety attacks, and Randy and Travis hadn't been in that particular home long enough for either of their parents to know that Randy was not the type to run away, or at least not the type to run away without Travis.

They locked Travis in his room to give him time to calm down and called the police about the "runaway." Meanwhile, Travis knew that Randy was out there dying. He paced in his room, crying and punching walls for a half hour until he found a baseball bat lying under one of the beds.

He used the bat to break the window, reached through and unlocked it. Then he was gone, with bat in hand, before either foster parent could come and investigate the noise. He ran the four blocks to an abandoned house where he knew Randy was. By that time, Randy was covered in blood, drifting in and out of consciousness, lying on a sea of broken beer bottles, his father's weapon of choice. The man was drunk, taking a break from beating his innocent son to rant.

Mr. McCully had realized that he was evil, it seemed. The brutal murder of his wife had eaten away at him for all those years, and redemption had finally found him. He was evil, and he needed to die. But if he was evil, then his spawn must be evil as well. Randy must die too, because Randy already knew he was evil. He was an evil demon. In fact, maybe it was even Randy who had beaten poor Mrs. McCully to death? The facts didn't matter, not in the skewed logic of a fractured mind.

Travis had used this rant to sneak into the house and get behind the psycho. He was only fourteen and small for his age, and Mr. McCully was as tall then as Randy was now, heavy set with a beer belly. Travis still didn't know how he had managed to do it. He struck the man as hard as he could in the back, and when the giant fell, he brought the bat down on his head. Travis wasn't strong enough to cause any real damage, but he bought the two of them some time.

Half dragging his friend who could barely move by that time, the two of them managed to get across the street to where a terrified woman let them in, locked the door and called the cops. Mr. McCully was killed a few minutes later, shot by the police while trying to force entrance into the house and finish the job he had started. Randy was rushed to the hospital where he endured two hours of surgery followed by months of physical and mental therapy. The doctors were forced to insert metal rods into his left arm to save it from amputation.

Until this day, Randy was the only one who knew of Travis' sixth sense, though Travis had come very close to telling Sophia. Travis would never forget what his hesitation had cost him, and Randy's scars were a constant reminder of that price.

"Dude!" A balled-up paper towel bounced off his chest, bringing him back into the present. "Spacing much? Your pop tarts are getting cold."

"Oh." Travis grabbed his pop tarts out of the toaster, threw them on a paper towel, and took them to his recliner. "I'll probably get a motel or something somewhere tonight rather than driving all the way home. You and Gwen should do something, have a romantic night."

"Nah." Randy shrugged. "She's working a split at the hospital. Eddy's bachelor party is tonight, but I'm not going if you aren't." He stood up and went to the kitchen to replenish his orange juice.

"Why not?"

"You know what it's like to not drink at a bachelor's party? They won't leave me alone. Everybody turns into an asshole at those things."

"Yeah, I guess you're right," Travis said and took a bite of his first pop tart. Randy was constantly watchful, never drinking or smoking or anything that may sink its teeth into him. Travis honestly didn't know why because Randy did not have his father's addictive personality. In fact, if Travis hadn't seen the resemblance between them with his own eyes, he wouldn't think Randy was related to his father at all. Randy didn't have a drop of monster blood in him despite the constant fear that he did.

Oddly enough, Travis *did* have an addictive personality. It was Randy who had made Travis quit smoking, and it was only Randy's constant vigilance that kept Travis from slipping into alcoholism. They had both smoked weed for maybe a week when they were younger but stopped pretty quickly when one of their foster brothers developed an allergy to cannabis that caused him to break out in the most unpleasant rash any of them had ever seen. The worst drug Travis had ever tried was cocaine, shortly after a car accident had taken somebody he loved. He made the mistake of doing it with an old girlfriend of Randy's, though, and when Randy found out, his reaction was less than understanding. The ensuing fight landed Travis in the hospital and Randy in jail.

"You know, Eddy's sister was asking about you again yesterday," Randy said as if it was an afterthought.

"I thought I told you to tell her I was lazy and an alcoholic."

"You did, but it may have come out something more like he's a nice guy, but he's still not over his last relationship, so take it slow with him."

Travis threw down the paper towel. "Damnit, Randy!"

"Well, I'm worried about you; you've been reclusive for weeks! You are a young, reasonably handsome, rich…."

"You didn't tell her I'm rich, did you?" Travis asked quickly.

"No, she thinks you're an out of work welder who is currently living off your infinitely more awesome brother." He took a drink of his orange juice and winked. "That's a keeper."

"She probably is a keeper, which is why she should stay the hell away from me!" Travis grabbed the TV remote with vengeance, determined to distract himself from this conversation.

"Oh, for the love of….!" Randy began, throwing his arms wide in a gesture of helplessness. "You didn't kill Sophia!"

"If she hadn't been following me…." Travis said, not looking at his brother or the TV.

"Yeah, and if I hadn't left my shoes in the living room where dad could trip over them, mom would still be alive," Randy snapped. "Stop it! This "what if" guilt crap gets us nowhere!"

Travis sighed. "Yeah, you're right." He ran a hand through his messy hair. "I'm just not ready yet, okay? I can't….I'm not ready. Leave me alone about it."

"I've been leaving you alone about it for two years," Randy grumbled. "But yeah, okay. You sure you're okay? You're acting weird?"

"I feel… I feel like something is wrong, kind of the calm before the storm. I feel like something bad is coming." Travis shook his head, looking at the floor. "It's so strong. I'm surprised you can't feel it."

"I'm not a psychic," Randy said.

"But you're human."

"Debatable."

Travis sighed. "You should go; you're going to be late for work."

"Yeah." Randy began to pull on his boots which he routinely left sitting beside the couch. "Lucky we're still working just out of town; it was a pain in the ass when I was getting up at four to drive to site."

Travis nodded. "You should take the gun with you."

Randy paused, one shoe on, and raised an eyebrow at Travis. "Pardon?"

"You should take the gun with you."

"Why?" Randy asked, drawing out the word for emphasis.

"I just have a bad feeling; it will make me feel better if you have it," Travis explained.

"If *I* have it?" Randy finished putting on his shoes. "*You're* the one taking a road trip to have some face to face time with a *serial killer!*"

'Dude's a pedophile. I don't need a gun to deal with him, and to be honest, I would much, much rather do it with my fist. Their kind are always cowardly and pathetic. To use a gun would just be plain lazy, plus, I don't want the police to get confused about who the bad guy is again. It didn't turn out that well last time."

Randy laughed. "That's an understatement!"

"Will you?"

"What?"

"Take the gun."

Randy ground his teeth for a moment, thinking. He was superstitious about guns and thought that even having one invited trouble. Travis did not share his sentiment. "Yeah, okay," Randy agreed. "But I'm leaving it in the truck!"

"Thanks," Travis said. Randy walked into the kitchen and reached up above the cabinets to grab the firearm. Both boys were tall, so this was a convenient place to keep it. It ensured that no child would ever be able to find it accidentally, and the way the cabinets were designed kept it completely hidden. The ammunition was kept in a drawer next to the fridge.

With gun and ammunition in hand, Randy grabbed his Technicolor vest from the coat rack. "If you're heading to the five, you'll be coming right through us. If you seem drunk or out of it or anything that might impair your driving, I will drag you out of that truck myself."

"Duly noted," Travis said. "Get going."

"Yeah, yeah, I know. Watch him for me, Starkey," he said as he headed out the door. A moment later, Travis heard his truck pull out of the drive. Still uneasy, but not sure why, Travis walked down the hall to the bathroom and splashed some water on his face. He needed a shave; he was one of those guys that defiantly had no problem growing facial hair and had started at fourteen. Missing one day of shaving would probably make him look like Charlie Daniels. He shaved quickly, using a manual razor because he didn't like the electric one somebody had given him for Christmas.

After shaving, he studied himself in the mirror. His longish chestnut hair was sticking out at all angles, evidence of his hard night. He had thoughtful eyebrows, the kind that curved and were not too thick or thin, a long strait nose, thin lips, nicely rounded cheekbones, and almond shaped, deep brown eyes. He had broad shoulders and a lean frame, the type you would likely see on a track runner, which Travis had been in high school, and he was slightly shorter than Randy at six-one.

He knew he was good looking, but he didn't quite think of himself as arm candy, which was what Sophia used to call him. *She* had been beautiful, Italian with long black hair, beautiful dark eyes, tanned skin, and a body that had amazed him. He had loved her, loved everything about her. He loved her voice, her humor, her shy laugh, her bleeding heart. He loved the way she fit next to him, the perfect height for him to put his arm around her, as if they had been made for one another. He loved the way she smiled when he slipped the ring on her finger the day they graduated from high school.

He blinked the images out of his mind and forced them down and away. He didn't need to think about that now. Randy was right;

the what ifs in life got them nowhere. He brushed his wild hair down and looked at himself in the mirror one more time, wondering, not for the first time or the last, whose eyes he had gotten, his mother's or his father's.

Stepping out of the bathroom and flicking off the light, he suddenly felt like he wasn't alone in the small house, as if the air had suddenly grown thin and crowded. He quickly glanced at Starkey, but the dog was sleeping at the end of the hall, unbothered by what tormented his master. Taking a deep breath, Travis turned and went down the hall, first checking his room, then Randy's; both were empty, as they should be. Walking back up the hall to the living room seemed suffocating, as if the Norwegian Wood was closing in on him, but he got to the living room safely. It, too, was empty. So was the kitchen. The entire house was empty, but he felt as if somebody were breathing down the back of his neck.

Something was coming; Travis knew it with a certainty that sometimes scared him. Something bad, something dangerous, something…evil, was coming, and he was sure that whatever it was, it was coming for his family. The only family Travis had was Randy, which was why he had insisted on him taking the gun to work.

Being a road construction worker, it made more sense that if something was going to happen to Randy, it would happen as a result of some work-related accident. After all, his job did have a certain degree of danger to it, especially when working on a freeway. But Travis didn't think that was the case. The evil he felt coming was the distinct type of evil that could only be found in humanity. Someone was coming; someone who made his skin crawl.

"Come on, Starkey!" he said, grabbing the map to Susanville from the printer. "Time to go."

Chapter 2

Travis took a bite of his double cheeseburger and chewed slowly, his eyes sweeping the park carefully behind his sunglasses. It was a nice park, but Travis had seldom seen a park that wasn't, with an impressive array of swing sets, slides, teeter-totters, and other things that might entertain a child for a few hours while their parents caught up on reading. It also had a large grassy area where several picnic tables were located. That was where Travis now sat, perched on top of one of them eating a lunch that would probably be the death of him in forty years but tasted worth it.

A clump of pine trees took up one end of the park, just behind the swing set, providing shade so that the metal wouldn't get too hot and a nice place for hide-and-seek and tag. There were also a few more pine trees scattered here and there near the picnic tables, giving them shade as well. It was a nice place, very peaceful, the type of place that most kids would look back on and smile.

Travis doubted Aaron would ever think back on this place and smile, but at least, if Travis did this right, he would have the chance to think back.

Aaron was a brown-haired little boy, who appeared to have an affinity for climbing. He made a beeline for the jungle gym the moment he came through the gate. His little sister, three, with curly brown hair, preferred the slide; she hadn't gotten off of it since they had arrived some fifteen minutes before. She was a cute little girl but clumsy. She had already fallen off the slide three times.

"Hey, Sir?" Travis sat down his hamburger and turned to Aaron, who had escaped the jungle gym to come and investigate Starkey. He was standing about ten feet away, weary of approaching further without Travis' permission. His parents had clearly taught him manners. "Does your dog bite?"

"Yeah, but not you. He loves kids. Go ahead and pet him," Travis said, taking off his sunglasses.

Aaron excitedly rushed forward to pet Starkey.

"It's a big dog! What's its name?" Aaron asked, smiling as Starkey tilted his head so Aaron could pet him better.

"His name his Starkey."

"Weird name." Aaron laughed. "Why did you name him that?"

"He's named after a Beatle."

"Why would you name your dog after a bug?"

Travis had to laugh at that, he liked this kid. "Not that kind of beetle. It was a band back in the way back. Ask your grandparents about them, or your mom might know."

"Oh, okay." He scratched Starkey under the chin. "I really, really want a dog, but my dad says I'm not responsible enough yet. He says that if I keep my room cleaned all summer without having to be told, I'll get one for Christmas."

"Dogs are a big responsibility." Travis nodded. "But I think you could probably handle it."

"Would you tell my dad that?"

Travis laughed again and took a drink of his soda.

"Well, I'll see you later!" Aaron said, giving Starkey one last pat and running off towards the monkey bars.

"Nice kid, huh?" Travis said to Starkey and took another drink of his soda. He finished eating quickly, tossing French fries to Starkey, and watched as the pedophile entered the park and sat down on a bench on the opposite side of the park as the kid's mother sat. At first glance, he didn't look like Satan. There was no red, scaly skin, no long-pointed tail or horns, but Travis knew what he had seen, and he knew that looks were deceiving.

Across the park sat a balding, middle aged man whose brown hair had gone mostly grey, with a round face, a nose that had been broken at least once, and glasses. He wasn't as tall as Travis, probably about five-nine, and was wearing a blue button up shirt, black slacks and loafers. He looked like he had just stepped out of an office building or maybe church, a harmless accountant. There was nothing about him that even hinted that he had murdered several innocent children or even that he was untrustworthy. But that was how real life worked. In real life, the monsters hid in plain sight.

"Come!" he said to Starkey, balling up his trash and throwing it in a can on his way out of the park gate. He walked up the street and down another at an easy pace, hands in his pockets, Starkey moving silently beside him. As he turned the corner, he heard the little girl scream in the park and knew she had fallen off the top of the slide and hurt herself. Her mother would rush to her side and try to comfort her, look for serious injuries, and in that brief time of distraction, Aaron would disappear.

This was the tricky part. He had to let that man forcibly take Aaron from the park, had to let him scare the boy so that blame could be firmly established, enough blame to ensure that the police would search the vehicle. What they found in that vehicle would likely buy the bastard the death penalty.

He turned down a side alley that ran behind several buildings, on which was parked a newer, gold van with a scrape on the passenger side door. Travis walked towards the van, adrenaline already pumping through his veins. He stopped opposite the van and leaned against the back wall of a thrift shop, just around the corner from the alley that ran between the thrift shop and a closed-down bakery. He waited, knowing it wouldn't be long.

It was Starkey who alerted him when the pair entered the alley. Travis ventured a slight peek around the corner. The pedophile was holding Aaron tightly against his chest, one hand clasped firmly over his mouth, the other twisting his arm up behind his back at a painful angle. Aaron had stopped struggling for the most part, probably due to the pain in his arm, and was crying so hard, he was having trouble breathing. The pedophile was saying something to him, most likely threats of what would happen if he screamed or tried to run away.

Travis took a deep breath and turned the corner, walking down the alley as if he had just been taking a stroll, and stopped upon seeing the pair. "What…what's going on here?" Travis stammered, playing his part well. None of this could seem deliberate.

The pedophile quickly sat down Aaron but kept a tight hold on his arm. "My son here took himself to the park without permission; he's throwing a bit of a fit about being grounded," the man said, sounding completely sincere, like a loving, if strict, father.

"Oh," Travis said, beginning to walk again, but then he took a closer look at Aaron. "Wait, you were the kid at the park. You went there with your mom and sister; I saw you show up."

"His mom didn't know I had already told him he needed to clean his room first." The man said smoothly. He was the type that could probably charm the pants off a snake.

But Travis wasn't looking at the pedophile. He was looking at Aaron, who was shaking so severely, it was a miracle he was still standing, he had wet himself and the pedophile still had such a firm grip on his arm, his bone was probably bruising. He was looking at the ground, afraid to even look at Travis lest the pedophile hurt him again.

"Aaron?" They all heard his mother call from the park, and for the first time, something other than confidence flashed in the pedophile's eyes.

"I don't know what's going on here, but I think we should go back and talk to the boy's mother," Travis said, drawing himself up to his full height.

"I think you should just mind your own business!" The man snapped and tried to shove past Travis. It was a bad idea. Travis brought his left fist up to connect with the man's cheek with maximum force, and in the same fluid movement brought his knee up into his stomach. With his right hand, he grabbed Aaron and pulled him away from the falling monster. When the pedophile hit the ground, Travis kicked him three more times, which was probably unnecessary but felt good.

"Aaron!" The boy's mother could be heard, frantic now that she realized her son wasn't in the park. "Aaron where are you!"

The man was down now and wasn't going anywhere, so Travis took a step back and pulled a pair of handcuffs out of his back pocket. "Rrnooo," the man groaned, spitting blood, and reached for Aaron who was now standing beside Starkey. A snarl from the highly intimidating dog, with hackles and fur raised, stopped him, and he collapsed back to the ground with a pathetic whimper.

Travis grabbed the man by the upper arm and dragged him over to a nearby dumpster where he cuffed him securely. The pedophile was crying and whimpering now, refusing to meet Travis' eyes. "Please don't hurt me!" he begged as Travis kneeled in front of him.

"Hurt you? No, I'm not going to hurt you anymore," Travis said coldly. "I'm not going to hurt you like you deserve. I'll leave that to your cell mates, but I promise you this: there is a special corner in hell reserved for people like you."

"Please…." he begged, too ashamed to look at Travis or Aaron; too afraid to look at Starkey.

"I know what you have done," Travis went on, quietly so Aaron wouldn't hear. "And I know what they are going to find in that van when they search. I know about Edward, Michael, Tyler, Samuel, Isaiah, and Shawn. I know what you did to those boys, and you will pay tenfold for what you did to them." Without another word, Travis stood and turned his back to the man. He walked over to Aaron, who had his face buried in Starkey's fur, and picked him up. "You're safe now," he said to him. "Let's get you back to your mom, okay?" Aaron nodded into his shoulder, not saying a word but still crying.

"If you try to move, try to run away, my dog will rip your throat out," he said to the pedophile, and Starkey dutifully moved to stand in front of the man, growling softly.

Travis took Aaron back to the park where his frantic mother had gathered quite a crowd and where the cops had already been called. He led a group of three or four civilians to where the pedophile was handcuffed and told them he had come upon the man dragging the struggling boy towards the van. Then he split, saying he had an outstanding warrant and didn't want to deal with cops, which was his usual excuse.

He left town immediately, barely getting out of the parking lot of the thrift store when the cops arrived. He heard the codes come in through his police scanner and knew that the cops had found what they needed, the parents of six innocent children would finally know who had destroyed their lives.

Travis didn't know why he hadn't been able to help those other six. He guessed it was because those murders had happened in another state, and Travis' awareness tended to be limited by area. They were almost always within the realms of northern California, and once, he had ventured into southern Oregon. His area of impact seemed to be getting larger as he grew, though. When he was younger, it was limited by the town he was in at the time, but as he got older, it grew to the county and then the entire north state. He had never seen something that was too far away for him to stop. There had been times when he hadn't gotten there in time, but this had never been due to distance.

They didn't always come as dreams, of course, though dreams were the most common and most vivid. Sometimes, they came as visions. Travis would merely "check out" for a few minutes, go someplace else. This usually happened when he was playing video games with Randy or eating dinner or goofing off, and seldom happened at a time or place where they would cause serious damage. However, it was for this reason that Travis had totaled his first car.

On top of dreams and visions, Travis also got flashes. These usually came from direct contact with another person and weren't always bad. While helping an elderly woman change a tire once, he had gotten a flash of her when she was a young woman, picking flowers with her two-year-old daughter. Once, when a waitress handed him a bill, he had seen that she was four weeks pregnant and was going to have a boy which she would give his father's name. Another time two children, brother and sister, had shoved past him in a grocery store, and he got a flash of the little girl on her wedding day, while at the same time, he somehow knew that the little boy was going to die in the military.

The flashes, he didn't mind, and he really didn't much mind the visions, either, though they gave him one hell of a headache afterward. Visions were rare, far rarer than anything else. It was the dreams he hated and wished he could avoid. But by this time, he had accepted his lot in life and come to realize it was not a bad lot at all. He got to save lives, which was something. But he also had to constantly live with pure evil invading his mind, which was something else entirely. He had learned to live with it, though, and sometimes, it wasn't so bad.

Chapter 3

It was seven o'clock by the time he got into Redding—a mid-sized city almost exactly halfway between Susanville and home—and got a room at a Motel 6. For some reason, these ventures usually left him exhausted, so he planned on turning in early. He walked across the street with Starkey and picked up a foot-long sub and soda for dinner, then settled down to eat and do some channel surfing. He wasn't that big on television, so he didn't watch it very often. He hated cop shows because he felt they glorified a broken system, hated reality shows because…well…did he need a reason? He didn't really like sitcoms because he couldn't relate, didn't really like to watch the news for obvious reason, which left little else. He did like sci-fi style shows, though, so he settled on an oldy but a goody, *Stargate*.

He was halfway through his sandwich when his phone started vibrating on the bedside table. He picked it up, glanced at the caller I.D., flicked it open and said "Yeah?"

"I just got a dear john voice mail," Randy said.

"Oh, you poor baby. Should I pick up some Ben&Jerry's on the way home?"

"Don't be a jerk. How'd it go with the kid?"

Travis leaned forward in his chair and turned down the TV. "He's scared, will probably need some counseling, but he's going to be fine. The son of a bitch is behind bars at least and will be for the rest of his life."

"You have any trouble with him?"

Travis shook his head, even though Randy couldn't see. "He's a pathetic excuse for a human being. No trouble at all."

"I'm glad the kid's all right."

"Yeah. That sucks about Gwen, I'm sorry."

"I just wish I had seen it coming. I mean, I thought we were pretty good together."

Travis took a bite of his sandwich and talked around a full mouth. "Maybe Gwen got tired of robbing the cradle."

"She was only six years older than me!"

Travis laughed. "Kidding, I'm kidding."

"She said I was too good to her. What the heck is that supposed to mean?"

Travis sighed. "C'mon man, you know you attract battered women. I mean, look how her ex treated her. Then you come along and you're all open doors and flowers and romantic dinners. She probably just panicked, waiting for the other side to show."

"But why? I mean, do jerks really screw them up that bad that they see an abusive husband behind every nice guy?"

"Yeah, probably."

"That's messed up."

"You were good to her, you let her know she deserves to be treated right, got her over being afraid." Travis stood up and threw the sub wrapper in the trash.

"Yeah, you're right. I hope she finds a good guy."

Travis paused. "Seriously? That's it?"

"You said it yourself, she is six years older than me. we are in different places, it's cool."

"Oh, come on, man! Be madder than that!" Travis snapped, suddenly angry.

"Why? We were only serious for what? Three months?"

"Five months."

"Whatever."

Travis began to pace. This was something he hated about Randy: his complete inability to let anybody in. When he was in a relationship, he put all his time and effort into making that girl feel special and beautiful and worthy of love. He was the ultimate romantic, the dream guy, on the outside. But there was a wall around his heart that nobody could break, that he wouldn't let anybody past.

It wasn't that Randy didn't want to love. It was that he couldn't. He didn't know how. He was too used to people leaving him or using him or simply hurting him. There had been plenty of girls he had really liked over the years, but not love. Never love.

Randy didn't even let himself get attached to friends. If any one of them besides Travis were to up and leave, never to be heard from again, he wouldn't bat an eye. Travis had known Randy for as long as he had known anybody, and in all that time, he was positive that he was the only person Randy actually loved, the only one he had ever let past that wall. Sure, Randy was a good guy; he would protect the girls he was with from jerks or perverts, but fight to keep the relationship going? Never. He would just accept it.

Travis had been in love. He had felt it and tasted it and seen it splattered across a freeway. He knew it wasn't normal to find somebody you truly loved at sixteen and to stay with that person and be in love with that person for three years until the day they died. He knew that he was both lucky and unfortunate at the same time to have felt that. He didn't expect Randy to fall in love at twenty-one, but instead wished he *could* fall in love. He wished he could let someone, anyone, in.

"You want to be that way, be that way!" Travis snapped. "But someday, you're going to have to let someone past that wall of yours."

"I let people in!" Randy countered.

"Really? Who, other than me?"

"Momma," Randy said.

"Momma doesn't count."

"Why not?"

"Because she's a little old woman who is 80% saint, 15% angel, and 5% unicorn, and people like that don't count."

Randy was silent for a long time, then sighed. "I…I'm getting better. At the emotional stuff, I mean. It's not like I'm a sociopath, I just…. I know it's not normal."

"Nothing about our lives is normal."

"That's true, but what is really wrong with you?"

"Nothing."

"Bullshit!" Randy stated matter-of-factly.

Travis sat down and rubbed his forehead. "Okay, I just have that feeling again, the same one I had this morning."

"Yeah, you were acting weird then, too."

"Maybe I just need some sleep."

"Go to sleep, then."

"Yeah, I'll take Starkey out one more time first, though," he said, then remembered something. "Oh, make sure you take the gun to work with you again tomorrow."

Randy was silent for about fifteen seconds before speaking. Travis could practically feel his eyes narrowing. "All right! What the hell? Did you see something you're not telling me about?"

"No!" Travis said quickly. "No, it would just make me feel better."

"I'm not sure I believe you."

"Please."

"Okay, but I don't like this."

Travis opened his mouth to reply but was cut off by a knock on the door. "Uh, I gotta go, somebody is at the door."

"All right, see to you tomorrow."

Travis closed his phone and opened the door. "Yeah?" he asked, confronted by a girl who appeared to be around nineteen or twenty.

"Do you own that blue truck right there?" the girl asked, pointing.

"Yep, that one's mine."

"Mind giving me a jump? I have a dead battery."

"Sure." Travis said, holding the door open so Starkey could slip out. The girl was tall at around five-eight, with long, straight hair down to mid back.

"Oh, you have a dog?" she asked, surprised as Starkey trotted off towards the truck.

"Yep. You're not afraid of dogs, are you?"

"No." She shook her head. "I love dogs. What is his name?"

"Starkey," Travis replied, sliding behind the driving wheel and popping the hood. "You got jumper cables? If not, we can use mine."

"I've got some, but they are a bit frayed, so it may be better to use yours," she said, scratching Starkey behind the ears. "Starkey, huh? After Ringo Starr?"

"Yeah!" Travis smiled. "A lot of people wouldn't get that."

She shrugged. "I was raised on the Beatles."

"I take it this little Chevy is yours?" he asked her.

"Yep."

Travis took a moment to study her out of the corner of his eye while hooking the cables up to the battery. She was very average, not too skinny but couldn't be called fat by any stretch of the imagination. Fairly muscular, but not overly so, probably the type of girl who could take care of herself. She had average breast and an average face with a long, straight nose, thin lips, long neck, and chestnut hair almost the same color as Travis'. There was nothing striking about her at all, nothing that stood out, but she was also very pretty in a girl next door kind of way.

Travis wasn't attracted to her, though, and wasn't really sure why. Maybe she just wasn't his type. "I'm Travis, by the way. Travis Williams."

"Laura Nightdale," she said, holding out her hand. Travis realized there was no way to get around shaking it. He took her hand and instantly got a flash of her chasing her big brother along a wooded path when they were children. It was a happy moment, and the overall feeling he got from it was peaceful. He was thankful for that.

"You look really familiar," Laura said.

"Really?" Travis said, distracted.

"I know where I've seen you!" Laura suddenly brightened. "You were in Weed a few months ago!"

"Weed?" Travis leaned back having finished connecting the jumper cables. Weed was a small town up north near Mount Shasta, which was practically Oregon. Yes, he *had* been there a few months before.

"Yeah, you helped get those kids out of that fire!" She was certain now; there was no convincing her it wasn't him. "You and that other guy, the tall, blond one. He was really cute!"

"Yeah, that's me and my brother," Travis admitted reluctantly.

"You two saved those kid's lives. Nobody even knew they were in there," she went on. "But why did you take off so quick?"

"We have issues with cops," Travis said. "All right, start her up."

Laura got in her car and turned it on. It started up without hesitation. "You should let it idle for a few minutes," he advised.

"Thanks, but I'm kind of in a hurry." Laura said, getting out of the car. "It does this all the time; it will be fine now that it's running."

"You sure?" Travis asked as he started to undo the cables.

"Yeah, I'll be fine. It was really nice meeting you, Travis."

"Yeah, nice meeting you too," Travis said.

"And it was awesome of you guys saving those kids like that. Really, you guys should have gotten an award or something."

Travis shrugged. "Drive safe, okay?"

"Yeah, thanks again," she said as she pulled out of the parking space. Travis watched as the car pulled away, increasingly uneasy. He and Randy had only been in Weed for about a half hour. It had been a quick in and out, and nobody should have seen them go into that building. Maybe one or two people saw them bring the kids out, but they had all been workers from the nearby business, all of them older. He didn't know when or how Laura could have seen them and how she could have gotten a good enough look at them to remember several months later.

"That's weird," he said to Starkey, winding up the cables. "That shouldn't have happened."

There was something odd about the whole encounter, he realized as he thought about it. The car had not been there when he had walked across the street to get his sandwich. It had just pulled up and died? That wasn't how batteries worked. Then there was the way she had looked at him after they shook hands. It was like she was expecting something or hoping for something to happen that hadn't.

You're being paranoid, he told himself, trying to shake it off. She was just a girl who didn't know that much about cars. There was no ulterior motive here. Just a chance encounter with a stranger, over just as quickly. Still, he couldn't quite shake the feeling that something was off.

***

The next day, Travis slept in late, which he normally did after an "intervention", as he had come to think of them. He was naturally an early riser. It was rare that he would sleep past nine, but that day, he didn't wake up till nearly noon. He checked out of the hotel early deciding that he would rather take a shower at home, got another sandwich similar to the one the night before, and hit the road. He drove for about an hour before pulling off the main road and heading to a little out of the way picnic area he was familiar with along the Sacramento River.

He sat on the tailgate eating the sandwich and watching Starkey trying in vain to catch a pair of mallards that kept teasing him. The two ducks would swim closer to shore and go back and forth until poor Starkey could take no more and would dive in after them. The ducks would swim off towards the middle of the river, quacking manically, and Starkey would swim out about fifteen feet, realize it was too cold, and head back. In due time, the ducks would circle back, and the pattern would start anew. Each time, Travis laughed, and Starkey looked at him like he was a traitor.

He was happy to see that they had the place to themselves. It was so green here, with thick forest lining both sides of the river and overripe blackberries everywhere. It smelled wonderful, and the sound of the river was peaceful enough to fall asleep to. The river was wide and deep here, perfect for floating, and had an almost slate gray color to it today despite the sun. He loved it here, always had, and it brought back many happy memories. Sophia had first brought him here over two years ago, in the summer between their junior and senior year, and they had come back the week of graduation. That last time, Sophia climbed a tree as high up as she could to see if she could see Mount Shasta; she couldn't. She also asked Travis to marry her, joking, of course, and he had said yes but hadn't been joking. Two months later, he placed the engagement ring he had bought inside her casket.

This place held happy memories, and he was loath to leave. He wasted an hour walking along the trail with Starkey, just breathing in the sheer joy of memory so fresh, he could almost relive it. He could still see her jet black hair shinning in the sun, her dark Italian eyes laughing down at him from an upper branch.

When he circled back towards the truck a little over an hour later, he began to get the uneasy feeling that someone was watching him. The feeling was strong, so overwhelming, it made his skin crawl and seemed to settle over him like a heavy blanket. He didn't know what it was, but it felt like nothing he had encountered before. He stopped several times to look around and listen, but each time, he heard nothing but the familiar sounds of the river, saw nothing out of ordinary. Starkey, who was probably more observant than the average city dwelling dog, didn't seem to notice anything, either. Still, the unnerving feeling followed him all the way back to the truck and out of the picnic area.

His stop at the river cost him, and he didn't pull into his own driveway until nearly seven. He let Starkey wonder into the backyard and closed the gate behind him, then went inside and made a beeline for the fridge, leaving the front door open because the house was stuffy. He soon realized they had no food. It wasn't surprising. Apart from sandwiches, processed, microwavable foods and the odd barbeque, they weren't big on cooking. He glanced at the clock one more time and hit the speed dial on his phone.

"Yeah?" Randy picked up on the third ring.

"Where are you?"

"About fifteen minutes from home. Today sucked. Made me seriously consider my career choice." He sounded tired.

"Sorry. But while your day is sucking, could you run through a drive through on your way home? The fridge is bare." Travis glanced out the kitchen window to see what Starkey was doing.

"Yeah, I guess so. Any preferences?"

"Anything but Taco Bell," Travis said.

"Okay, be there in a bit."

"Thanks." Travis hung up the phone and headed up the hall to the bathroom. He was washing his hands when he heard Starkey going crazy in the backyard, barking and growling up a storm. "Starkey?" he yelled, opening the bathroom door. He paused before stepping out into the hall as that same overwhelming feeling settled over him.

He heard the dog yip and fall silent and began to charge down the hall. "Starkey?" he yelled again.

He had just reached the end of the hall when somebody stepped into the open doorway. Silhouetted, all Travis could make out was the frame of a man roughly the same height as himself, muscular and bulky. "Can I….?" Travis began but stopped when the man raised his left arm and pointed. There was no mistaking the small handgun he held, and Travis could recognize a silencer any day.

In the next moment, Travis was on the floor gasping for breath, having no idea how he had gotten there. His chest hurt with the most unbelievable pain, and something hot and sticky was spreading and dripping down his side. He couldn't breathe, and every attempt to draw in breath brought more blinding pain.

He saw a man standing over him. An older man, but his vision kept going in and out, so he couldn't focus. "It's nothing personal, kid," somebody said from very, very far away, and the man flicked a piece of paper at him.

Travis wasn't scared; he was too confused to be scared. He tried desperately to draw a breath and managed to get just a little oxygen each time. Blindly, he managed to find the terrible, aching hole in his chest. He put his hand over the bullet hole but did not have the strength to apply any kind of pressure. He felt hot blood between his fingers and tried to focus. He needed to calm down, slow his heart, calm the panic, but he was already drifting away.

Somewhere, very far away, Travis understood what was happening. Half of him was lying on the floor at the end of the hall, dying, confused, and desperate. The other half was somewhere else, still there, but not there. That half of him, the half that wasn't dying, could *remember*. That half of him could *remember everything*.

Lying on the floor, so close to slipping away, Travis heard Randy's truck pull into the driveway, heard the gravel crunch under his feet as approached the door. He tried to lift his head but couldn't. He didn't know who had shot him. He didn't know where the man had gone. Was he still in the house? Travis' world was spinning now as darkness seemed to cave in on him. Was Randy going to be shot too? He had to warn his brother but already, everything was so dim.

He heard Randy yell, and a self-serve soda hit the floor. It was the last thing her heard as his world faded. All that was left in the darkness was a tiny pinprick of light, as if he were viewing his life through a pinhole camera. But then even that disappeared, and so did he.

Chapter 4

"Randy?" Randy's head came up suddenly as he realized Gwen had said his name several times. She was leaning down in front of him holding out a small bundle of clothes. "I asked Kevin to bring these in for you. He's a bit larger, but the sweat pants are adjustable, so you should be fine. I thought you should get out of those clothes."

"Yeah," he said groggily, not from being tired but more from the shock. He reached out to take them from her, his movements too slow to seem real. "Thank you, I will."

She frowned at him, noticing the way his eyes didn't seem to be seeing anything. "You don't look good Randy; you should go home and sleep."

He shook his head slowly. "Not home. Blood everywhere. I have to stay here in case...." He trailed off. "I have to be here."

She reached out and took his head in her hands, gently forcing him to look at her. "Listen to me. He is going to make it through this. The bullet didn't go all the way through. There was no exit wound, and he should make it through this. He's strong."

Randy nodded, unconvinced. He took no comfort in the fact that she had been a registered nurse for four years and may know what she was talking about. He had lived through things and seen things that had given him an appreciation of the messed-up. He was not as idealistic as he pretended to be. He knew that good people died with the kind of skewed average that one would expect to find in a Dickens novel. Good people died, especially around him, no matter how much he tried to protect them. The assholes were the ones that lived forever.

He had said that to Sophia once, during one of their infrequent deep conversations while Travis was recuperating from a vision-induced car accident. Sophia had smiled at him and said something he would probably never forget. *Of course, and that's the way it should be. After all, it's the assholes that need a second chance more than most.*

Randy did not have Sophia's faith, though, and he was far too scared to be optimistic. Travis was the only person who gave a damn about him. He had been Randy's best friend and brother for as long as he cared to remember, since those shadow days when he was half a person; too steeped in bitterness and heartache to even want to try to live. Travis had saved him, in more ways than he cared to admit. If he died, Randy knew he would not be able to hold himself together. He was not that strong and never had been.

Gwen said with a sad little smile, "You're a good guy, Randy," then stood up. "You get out of those clothes. It will make you feel better, and after my rounds, I will bring you some food, okay?"

"Thanks," was his only response. She frowned down at him like she wanted to say more but then left. She was a good person, a healer at heart, which was one of things that had first attracted Randy to her, but some things couldn't be helped.

After a few minutes, Randy managed to stand up, his movements sluggish and awkward. He went to the bathroom up the hall, stripped off his blood and dirt soaked jeans and tossed them in the trash. He also pulled off the scrub top one of the male nurses had given him and tossed that in the trash as well.

He got several paper towels wet and used them to scrub his bare legs trying to get the blood off, but no matter how hard he scrubbed, he could still feel it there. He felt like Lady Macbeth in Shakespeare's epic tragedy. *Now here's a spot, and here another....* It was weird, the things you retained from high school. After a few minutes of scrubbing, his skin was bright red but still didn't feel clean. He wondered if it ever would. *Out, out, damn spot!*

He pulled on the sweatpants and tied them tightly around his waist. Kevin, Gwen's brother in law, was a big guy, and Randy, while tall, was not very round. He pulled on the t-shirt as well and glanced at himself in the mirror. It reminded him of living in the foster homes when he was a young child, forced to wear the clothes some older kid had left behind. He normally referred to those days as the shadows days, a saying nobody got besides other people who had gone through the foster care system.

He went back to the waiting room but couldn't bring himself to sit. Instead, he paced back and forth with heavy, rapid steps, rubbing the back of his neck and wishing he had something to punch. He wished he knew who had done this. If he knew who hurt his brother, he would have somebody to direct this anger at. But there was nobody to blame, nobody to track down and hurt.

He thought about going and checking on Starkey but didn't want to leave the hospital. The dog had been tranquilized, presumably by whoever had shot Travis, which apparently said a lot about the shooter. He was currently at a veterinarian clinic somewhere, spending the night. Randy probably couldn't get in to check on him anyway. Still, Travis would be worried about his dog. He loved that dog.

But why wouldn't he? Starkey had given Travis a much-needed anchor when his world had collapsed. Randy had tried, but there was little he could do to make Travis snap out of it. After Sophia had died, Travis spent an entire week in bed, awake, staring at nothing, sometimes crying. He wouldn't eat, wouldn't talk to anybody besides Randy, and even then, he barely said a word. He lost twenty pounds in the first two weeks, didn't sleep at all, and began to look like a skeleton. Two months after her death, he tried cocaine for the first and what was surely the last time.

Randy didn't regret losing his temper, and he would again if Travis proved to be so stupid a second time. They had lost so many foster brothers and sisters over the years to drugs. It was almost a go to for the kids society had forgotten about and was so common in the homes around Sacramento, nobody seemed to bat an eye when another sixteen-year-old foster overdosed. Travis knew this, he knew better, and Randy was not willing to lose another friend to something so pointless.

Still recovering from the injuries Randy had inflicted, Travis had left in the middle of the night, leaving a hurried note about a kidnapping, and returned with a newborn puppy, barely alive. He was determined to save the puppy, as if saving it made up for Sophia being dead. Somehow, in the act of keeping the pup alive and nursing it back to health, Travis begun to heal. Starkey saved Travis from himself; he would be devastated if something happened to that dog.

But Starkey was safe and, from what the vet said, was going to make a full recovery. There was little to divide Randy's attention. His brother had been shot and left for dead, and there was nothing Randy could do about it. Vengeance was out of the question and thus there was no outlet for his anger.

"Are you okay?" A quiet voice asked, and Randy spun around to see a girl standing in the doorway of the waiting room regarding him with quiet interest. She was tall for a girl, with reddish brown hair she had tied back in a bun, and has lovely almond shaped eyes. She had an overall average look to her but at the same time was striking in her own way. Pretty, but not in a fashion model way. Randy thought she was lovely.

"Is anybody pacing in a hospital waiting room okay?" he shot back at her.

She gave a nervous laugh and looked down for a moment, uncomfortable but too concerned about this stranger to walk away and leave him in his misery. "Good point," she said, looking back up at him. "So, who is it? Mom? Dad? Girlfriend?"

"No." Randy shook his head. "My parents are dead, and my girlfriend dumped me. It's my brother. Somebody shot him."

"I'm sorry," she said, taking a few steps farther into the waiting room. "Is he going to be okay?"

"I…." Randy began, but his voice caught in his throat, and he suddenly felt too exhausted to stand. He lowered himself into a nearby chair and buried his head in his hands. "I don't know," he said, on the verge of tears but too unwilling to cry in front of a stranger.

She came in and sat beside him. "What happened?" she asked softly.

Randy leaned back and shook his head, throwing one hand in the air in a helpless gesture. "I came home, and he was on the floor covered in blood. I had just talked to him. He asked me to pick up some food. It must have just happened a few minutes after." Randy shook his head and grinned at her; it wasn't a happy grin but tortured and tired. "And you know the really messed up thing?" Randy went on.

"What?" she asked quietly.

"I was right next to Burger King when he called, and I started to pull into their drive through, but then I thought why am I going here? I hate Burger King. Travis likes it, but there's maybe one thing on the menu I can eat. So I changed my mind and drove another four blocks to Jack in the Box. If I had just gone to Burger King, maybe this wouldn't have happened."

"And maybe you both would be dead," she said, smiling in an annoyingly understanding way. "Travis, is that your brother's name?"

"Yeah." Randy nodded. "I'm Randy, by the way. Randy James." He held out his hand, and she stared at it for a moment, hesitated, then took it. She startled, as if he had shocked her, then smiled at him. "I'm Laura. Your parents gave you two your first names?"

"Actually, my parents gave me the name Randy McCully, but I changed it to my mother's maiden name when I turned eighteen."

"I like James better anyways," she said. "Did your brother change his name too?"

"No." Randy shook his head. "We're not related by blood. We're foster brothers. We've been best friends since we were twelve, and we're kind of each other's only family. He's all I've got; I'd be dead if it weren't for him."

"He means that much to you," Laura said, more an observation than anything else.

"No, I mean I literally would be dead if it weren't for him. When I was fourteen, I was kidnapped by…..some mad man…he tried to beat me to death. Travis saved my life."

"He sounds like a good friend," she said.

"Yeah, and the weird thing is, he always felt guilty about it. I was hurt pretty bad, and he thinks he should have gotten there sooner or something. He likes to beat himself up about things like that. He forgets that he was just a kid too." Randy wasn't sure why he was telling this stranger his life story. Maybe it was the stress of everything coming down on him, but for some reason, he couldn't stop himself from telling her. Something in her eyes made him feel safe, in a way no therapist ever had.

"Tell me about him," she said, and something in her voice made Randy think that she actually really wanted to know about this person. There was an earnestness in her eyes that startled him, a hunger for information that he didn't quite understand.

"What?" he asked nervously. "Do you just roam hospitals in the middle of night looking for somebody who looks like they need to talk?"

She laughed a light, gentle laugh. "No. My friend is in here for some intense chemotherapy, and I promised I would wait with her. She's asleep, though, and I came looking for a vending machine."

"There's one down the hall, but it will steal your money." Randy pointed. "Is your friend going to be alright?"

Laura shrugged. "Cancer. Who can tell? I want to hear more about your brother, though. He seems like a good guy."

"He is," Randy said. "He's incredible. The best person I know. I don't understand why anybody would want to hurt him."

"Some people are just hurters." Laura said quietly, her voice changing tone suddenly, causing Randy's head to jerk up. He wondered who had hurt her to make her sound so hollow.

"He really doesn't need this; he's been through enough," Randy went on, trying to ignore what he had heard in her voice. "He's had a really hard life."

Laura put a hand on his shoulder, bringing him back to the present. "He's going to be fine," she said, and there was a certainty in her voice that made him want to believe her.

"Mr. James?"

Randy jumped, having not heard the police officers approaching, and got to his feet. "Yes?"

"Um, I should get back to my friend," Laura said. She grabbed his hand and squeezed it for a moment. "I'll come back later and check on you if I can."

"Yeah. Thanks, Laura," Randy said as she walked away, then he turned his attention to the police officers. Two of the officers where in uniform, and the third was wearing a faded suit, a detective by the looks of it.

"We have a few questions for you, if you don't mind, Mr. James," the Detective said.

"Call me Randy, please," Randy said. "Mr. James makes me sound like a spy."

"Okay, Randy, I'm Detective Martinez. First off, we've been informed that your roommate is out of surgery and in recovery, but it will still be another couple of hours before you can be allowed to see him."

Randy was so relieved, he almost fainted. The detective noticed. "Er, maybe we should sit?" Once they were seated, he regarded a clipboard he had been holding. "Now, Travis had a small handgun registered to him that was not found in the house…."

****

"I had the gun," Randy said. "It's in my truck, in a lock box under the seat…." Laura had heard enough, and she slowly moved from where she had been listening just around the corner. Travis was going to live; she had expected as much.

She made a speedy exit from the hospital, not wishing to be there any longer than necessary, and went directly to her car, fumbling with the keys. While she was trying to detangle her car keys from her purse, another vehicle pulled into the space beside her. She looked up to see a familiar figure sitting in the driver's seat. She glared at him; anger written on her face.

"You shouldn't be here!" she accused him, moving to stand beside the driver's side window.

"I know, but I had to come," he said. "What did you find out?"

"He's going to live," she said, some of the anger leaking from her voice.

"We already knew that. He wasn't aiming to kill, after all; this whole thing is a trap to draw us out," the man in the car said, his voice tired.

"Which is why you shouldn't be here," she snapped. "This is my fault. I thought he was going to make his move at the motel. I was wrong."

The man nodded. "This one is unpredictable, and Travis is outside of our protection. He knows that."

"So we tell Travis," Laura suggested, not for the first time. "We tell him and bring him back to us."

"We both know that is not an option at this time. But he'll come after Travis again, especially if he continues to practice, which he will."

Laura nodded and couldn't help but look back up at the hospital, knowing there was a chance they would not be able to save this one. "We have another problem," she said.

"What?"

"Randy, he's a….."

"I know," he cut her off. "I've known for quite some time. Let's just pray that the Hunter doesn't."

✳✳✳

"Travis asked me to take it," Randy said, realizing that the truth probably sounded like a hastily put together lie. "He had a bad feeling and wanted me to have it with me. I don't like guns, though, so I left it in the truck. You don't need a warrant; I'll give you the keys if you want to look at it."

"That won't be necessary. We already determined that the firearm that Travis was shot with was not his own. We looked at the bullet just a few minutes ago. We will need to see it eventually, though," the detective said. "Do you have a concealed weapons permit, Randy?"

Randy nodded. "Yes. Travis and I go camping every year, and it just make sense that both of us should have a permit. We like to keep things legal."

"That will be easy enough to check." He wrote down a quick note before looking up at Randy again and squinting his eyes at the right side of Randy's face. "That bruise is almost gone, but I bet it was a nice shiner three or four days ago. What happened?"

Randy hesitated. "It was an accident."

"Your boss told us that you told him Travis punched you." The detective raised a brow.

"Yeah, on accident," Randy said quickly. "He has really bad nightmares sometimes, and I tried to wake him up. I know better, but he was thrashing around so much, I was worried. Anyways, when you wake him up quick like that, you gotta duck because sometimes he comes out of it swinging. He really didn't mean to hit me; it was just a reaction."

The detective nodded and kept taking notes. Randy got the distinct impression that the Detective didn't believe a word he was saying. "Are these nightmares documented at all?" he asked, still writing.

Randy nodded. "Yes, well documented from our time in foster homes. Travis used to go to therapy for them because the county required him to. Then after he won the lottery, he started going to a pricy psychologist, trying to unlock his memory because he thought it would make the nightmares go away. They got worse, though, so he stopped going."

"Do you know the doctor's name?"

Randy thought for a moment. "Nah, I can't remember. He was in downtown, though."

The detective nodded. "Now, has Travis had any contact with anybody claiming to be family recently?"

Randy shook his head. "No."

"Has Travis had any contact from anybody claiming to be family ever?"

Again, Randy shook his head. "No."

"Not even after he won the lottery?"

"No, but we both kept that pretty hush hush, ya know? He claimed the money using an LLC. We left town right after and moved here where nobody knew us. But Travis has never met anybody who claimed to know him, ever. It's like he didn't exist before waking up in the hospital."

"Is it possible that he was contacted and didn't tell you?"

"No!" Randy snapped. "That's not possible at all! There isn't a chance in hell that he wouldn't tell me about something like that!"

"Okay, okay!" The detective held up his hands, not wanting Randy to get upset. He held up the paper on his clipboard and unclipped something from underneath: a small zip locked baggy with a square piece of paper in it. The detective turned the baggy around and held it up for Randy to see. It was a Polaroid photo with the words *At Camp* and a partially rubbed away date on it.

It was a photo of a family sitting around a picnic table: a mother, a father, a little boy and little girl. The little boy was Travis, around eleven or twelve years old. Randy guessed that the photo had been taken just before Travis had wound up in that river. He appeared to be about the same age as he had been when Randy met him.

The mother, who was sitting next to her son, was strikingly pretty with long, curly chestnut hair, almond shaped, dark eyes, and dominant cheekbones. She had a wonderful smile; the type that let you know she was actually happy at the time. She had one hand resting on Travis' shoulder. The father had plain brown hair that was kind of wild, like his son's. He had beady eyes and a small nose, thin lips like Travis. He was broader than Travis, though, solid. He was deeply tan.

The little girl was sitting next to her father and had chestnut hair that was partially obstructing her face. She was the only one not looking at the camera. A few years younger than her brother, she was a scrawny little kid with what looked to be a round face and large ears, wearing a yellow dress and white and pink tennis shoes.

"Have you ever seen this photo before, Mr. James?" The detective asked.

"Where'd you get that?" Randy asked.

"Have you ever seen it before?" The detective asked calmly.

Randy shook his head. "No, no I've never seen it before. Where'd you find it?"

"It was found lying in your hallway near where Travis was shot. It's completely absent of fingerprints which is…highly unusual for a photo. You're sure you have never seen it before?"

"No. You've got to show it to Travis, though. He's got to see it!" Randy insisted.

"We will." The detective put the photo away. "Now, we must ask that you refrain from trying to see Travis until after we have had a chance to talk to him."

"Am I a suspect or something?" Randy asked.

"You are a person of interest at this time." The detective answered honestly. "At the moment, you are the only person on this side of prison that has any motive to harm your foster brother. The fact is, the person who is first on the scene is always considered."

"Motive!" Randy was appalled. "What motive?"

"You're the primary beneficiary in his will. If something were to happen to him, you would become a very rich man," the detective said.

Randy just stared at him for a moment, cold fury sweeping his face. "*What will?*"

Chapter 5

"Who the hell makes a will at twenty years old!" Randy yelled as he paced from one side of the small hospital room to the other, waving his arms in the air like a mad man. "That's like begging somebody to kill you! What the hell were you thinking?"

Travis was amused by his brother's hysterics and was trying very hard to suppress a smile. He was very stiff and sore, and the painkillers flooding his system were making him feel groggy. Other than that, he was feeling pretty good for somebody who had just been shot. "I told them you didn't know about the will," he said quietly.

"And why?" Randy yelled, turning an accusing finger at his brother. "Why would you not tell me about something like that? You make me a primary beneficiary and you don't tell me? You know how suspicious that looks? Of all the stupid…"

"Randolph James!" Gwen was suddenly at Randy's side. She grabbed hold of Randy's arm and jerked him towards the hall. "Half the hospital can hear you yelling!"

"But…" Randy began.

She let go of his arm and grabbed hold of his ear. "I need to have a word with you." She said firmly and pulled him out of the room.

Travis smiled and leaned back against his pillow. The doctor had only just cleared him for visitors twenty minutes ago, and Randy was probably making him regret that decision. A detective had been by to see him earlier that morning to get a statement, and after seeing the photograph they found, Travis had gotten very upset. So upset, in fact, that his blood pressure skyrocketed, and the doctor had given him a sedative.

The detective refused to give him the photo on grounds that it was evidence and almost certainly had been left by whoever attacked Travis in his home. This meant that whoever shot him knew more about his past than he did, which disturbed Travis greatly. He wished he could see the picture again but knew that it was probably impossible.

No matter, he had the scene burned into his memory. He had a family once, a family that loved him. He had come from somewhere. He hadn't realized until now how desperately he wanted that information before, how desperately he needed it. He once had a mother, a father, and a sister; a family. Once upon a time, he had a family.

The people he had seen in that photo did not look like the type that would abandon their son. The woman, whose hand rested protectively on his shoulder, had not abandoned him. They had not left him to drown in some river. They had loved him.

Maybe Travis was leaping to conclusions; after all, he was basing all this information on a photograph. But they looked happy in the photo. *He* looked happy in the photo. He looked loved. Knowing this made all the difference in the world to Travis.

Travis was just beginning to delve into these disturbing thoughts when a tiny, elderly woman suddenly appeared in the doorway. African American with warm sepia skin, she was pushing eighty, and the cornrows in her hair had been gray for well over a decade. She was barely five foot tall and heavily wrinkled from a lifetime of hard work and laughter, a relic of a woman. Despite this, she was still as spry as she had been sixty years ago when she was marching with Martin Luther King.

She caught sight of Travis and smiled so big, her eyes practically vanished. "Travis, my boy! What trouble have you gotten into?"

"Momma," Travis said in greeting with a tired smile.

Momma shuffled into the room, picking up the hem of her brown dress as she came, and kissed him on the cheek before dropping into the chair next to his bed. "Now, what happened?" she asked.

Travis shrugged. "Apparently, somebody doesn't like me."

"Oh," She waved a hand dismissively, "that can't possibly be it."

"I can't really remember much of it. It happened so quickly." Travis closed his eyes for a moment. "How did you find out so fast?"

"Your brother called me last night," she said, glancing at the door. "He was very upset. By the way, who is that lovely young woman lecturing Randy out in the hall?"

"That's Gwen. They were dating up until about three days ago. She's a nurse here," Travis said.

"Oh yes, he told me about her," Momma said. She reached over and rubbed the back of her hand against Travis's cheek affectionately. "You need a shave."

"I wouldn't know," Travis said. He guessed that unseemly facial hair was probably the least of his problems. "How are your kids, Momma?"

"I only have two at the moment. Both boys, brothers. Their mother died when they were young, and they were placed with a family member they never should have been placed with. They are staying with Markus and his wife right now. I'm trying to convince them to adopt the boys," Momma said, not looking at Travis but at her hands in her lap. She did not like hospitals, but Travis wasn't sure why. "They are good boys; they just need a safe place to thrive."

"Well, if they are with you, then they are in the best place possible," Travis said, prompting another smile from the elderly woman.

Randy and Travis had appeared on Momma's doorstep just shy of Randy's sixteenth birthday and entertained little hope that this home would be any different from any of the others. At the time, they had been two bitter and angry boys who had changed foster homes four times in six months. They didn't want to get to know the woman who welcomed them into her home. They didn't want anything to do with her. To them, this new "home" was just a safe place to keep their clothes. It would be no different from the others.

But it had been different. Momma specialized in children who had been extremely emotionally and physically abused, and Randy's background put him right in that category. Momma had given them the first real home either of them could remember and had given them a chance at a real life. What they assumed would be a temporary home turned into much more, and they stayed with her for three years until they turned eighteen and graduated high school. They were grateful for what she had given them, and there was very little that they wouldn't do for her.

Momma knew how important family was. The middle child in a family of six, Momma had been ten when her parents were killed in a train accident. After the deaths of her parents, her siblings were split up for the most part, "farmed out" and shipped off from one family member to another to be used as an extra pair of hands and little more. Very seldom were her sisters and her ever allowed to attend school, and Momma was very proud of her high school diploma, which she had gotten at the age of forty-three.

She married young and left the life of servitude behind for a short while, settling down with her husband and starting a family. As an African American couple in Mississippi in the 1950's, they were poor, but they got by as best as they could. They were happy at the very least.

When the civil rights movement began, Momma (whose real name was Rose) and her husband were among the first to join the ranks. Momma was proud of the fact that she had marched with Martin Luther King, proud of the beatings and hazing she endured in the name of civil liberties. But the price was far too high.

Her husband was arrested after participating in a sit-in at a local restaurant and never made it to the local jail. The police said he ran off, but those people who were arrested with him knew the truth of what happened. His body was found two weeks later, severely beaten. No arrest was ever made.

Momma could not allow her family to be in danger, not even for such a righteous cause. She had packed up her five children and fled as far away as she could possibly get: Northern California. She worked as a single mother, first in the strawberry fields and then as the manager of a grocery store until her back forced her to retire.

By that time, all her children were grown. But Momma was not an idle woman. At sixty years old, she had taken up the mantle of foster mom and hadn't put it down since.

"How are you feeling?" Momma asked, her concern obvious. "I hope that brute didn't hurt you too badly?"

Travis shook his head. "From what the doctor told me, it could have been much, much worse. I'll be in the hospital for another couple of days as a precaution and then I'll have to do some physical therapy for my back. As long as I take it easy, I should make a full recovery."

"And you will, won't you?" Momma asked, giving Travis a stern look.

"I'll do my best," Travis said. Momma gave him a knowing look that said she didn't quite believe him. Often, while living with Momma, Travis had gotten the impression that she knew about his sixth sense. She would give him a look here, let a curfew breach slide there, but never anything concrete enough to convince him. But still, he wondered.

"Well," she said, covering his hand with her own, "I certainly hope you do."

"I really scared Randy," Travis said with regret. "He'll probably make sure I stick to the treatment."

As if on cue, Randy appeared in the doorway, hesitated a moment, then walked in. "I'm supposed to apologize to you. I'm told I was being stupid and insensitive."

"That's as good as it's getting, isn't it?" Travis asked.

"Yep." Randy walked over and kissed Momma on the cheek before flopping down on the other bed in the room which was unoccupied. "I'm sorry I didn't say hi in the hallway, but Gwen still had hold of my ear. Did you know that Travis had a will?"

"Of course!" Momma said. "I witnessed it."

Randy covered his face with his hands for a moment and shook his head. With day-old stubble covering his face and dark circles around the eyes, he looked more like a homeless meth-head than the clean-cut construction worker he was. If Randy looked this bad, Travis wondered how he looked. He hadn't been allowed out of bed yet, and there were no mirrors around. He was sore and stiff all over, had a pounding headache and a dry mouth, but other than that, felt pretty good, all things considered.

"Travis?" Momma squeezed his hand. "Are you okay? Are you in pain?"

Travis realized he had drifted off in thought and quickly shook his head. "No, not physically, at least. The detective showed me a picture, an old Polaroid from when I was a kid, from before…before the river, I guess. They said that the shooter must have left it." Travis pulled on his lower lip for a moment, not really looking at anybody.

"In the picture, I was sitting at a picnic table next to my mom. She had her hand on my shoulder. My dad and my sister were sitting across from us." He looked up to see that Momma was watching him closely. "They looked like they loved me." His voice got suddenly tight, revealing for a moment the emotion he felt. He quickly looked away and blinked several times.

"I wish I could remember them," he said, looking at his foster mom again, voice back to normal. Momma frowned at him, a little annoyed at how quickly he had recovered. She was used to it by now, though. Every battered and bruised kid that had come through her door over the years had been emotionally stunted in one way or another. They were all tough. They all acted like their hardness was their strength.

"You will," she assured him. "Someday, when you're ready."

Travis gave Randy a barely noticeable glance, a quick signal to change the subject which Randy picked up on instantly. He sat up at the edge of the bed and stretched. "So, Momma, how's your mustang running?"

"Oh!" Momma turned to him with an eye-vanishing smile. "It's like a whole new machine now. Thank you so much!"

"I wish you would let me buy you a new one." Travis lay his head back against his pillow.

"Nonsense!" Momma waved the offer away. "Why buy a new one when the old one is running perfectly! Besides, that car is as classic as it gets! Just like me."

"Running perfectly after I spent an entire weekend re-working the transmission, and Travis re-welded the frame," Randy said, jerking a thumb at Travis.

"You did a wonderful job on it! You can hardly tell where that truck hit me now, and it drives like it did when it was new," Momma crooned, proud of her boys. "Travis, I wish you would go back to school and get your welding certificate. You're so good at it."

Travis shrugged and closed his eyes. "Maybe I will."

Momma's phone suddenly began singing loudly from her dress pocket, an old CCR song, startling Travis and making him jump and then wince. "Sorry, dear," Momma said, looking at the caller I.D. "It's social services. I need to take this. I'll be back in a moment." She got up quickly and began moving towards the door. She flipped the phone open when she was halfway there and said in a sweet, grandmotherly voice, "Hello?"

Randy walked over to in the chair Momma had just vacated. "You seem a little jumpy. You okay?" he asked, leaning forward and putting his elbows on the bed, propping his chin up on his closed fist.

Travis tried not to let on that he was beginning to feel worse. The pain meds were probably wearing off. "I was shot in my home, Randy. Yeah, I think it's safe to say I'm a little jumpy."

"Maybe we should get an alarm system. We haven't had one since we moved here. Heck, other than when we're gone, we never even lock the door. Maybe we should think about getting one of those home security thingies with the code and everything," Randy said thoughtfully.

"I left the door open. Wide open," Travis said, shaking his head at his own stupidity. "Starkey was in the backyard. He was my only warning. I didn't even hear a vehicle, and if I did, I probably would have assumed it was you." He closed his eyes again. "I left the door wide open, Randy. *Wide open!*" He opened his eyes and looked at his brother sadly. "A security system can't fix stupid."

Randy had to laugh at that. "I guess you're right. Still, we should think about it."

"Are you and Gwen still broken up?" Travis asked.

Randy nodded. "Yeah, we talked a little about it last night. She knows I don't love her, and she says that it's okay; she just needs something more than what I can give her. You know, like a ring, kids, a lifetime." He shrugged. "We both know I'm not ready for that. She's a wonderful friend, though. I'm glad we're both adult enough to still be friends."

"Yeah, I'm glad too," Travis agreed. "Hey, can you go grab a nurse or something for me? I think the drugs they gave me are wearing off. I'm starting to feel pretty lousy."

"Yeah, sure." Randy hopped up so fast, he made his back crack. "I'll be right back."

It took Randy a few minutes to find a nurse. Luckily, he had gotten to know the hospital pretty well from visiting Gwen. He found a nurse a few stations up the hall and relayed the message. She said somebody would be around shortly.

He had already decided that after telling Travis a nurse was on her way, he was going to go down to the cafeteria and get something to eat. He was starving and hadn't eaten anything since some Doritos earlier that morning. He also desperately needed a shave and a shower and maybe some clothes that fit.

He spotted Momma in a waiting room and decided to ask her if she wanted any food but realized she was still on the phone. If

Momma had taught them anything, it was how to be polite. He leaned against the wall on the other side of the waiting room door and waited for her to finish the conversation.

"He's upset, more upset than he's been in a long time. It's understandable," Momma was saying. Randy wondered if she were talking to *their* social worker, a woman whom he had mixed feelings about.

"He still doesn't remember a thing, even after seeing the photo….no, he'd tell me if he did, and at the very least, he would tell Randy, and Randy would tell me." Momma made an annoyed noise. "Are you sure it was him? I thought you said he was dead."

Randy was uncomfortable now and seriously regretting his decision to stop and wait. "And how do you intend to protect him?" Momma asked angrily. "If that man hurts either of my boys again, I'll track him down myself and….."

Randy had heard enough and was thoroughly freaked out now. He charged down the hall, putting as much distance between Momma and himself as possible. He didn't know what to think or what to do. But Randy was very good at compartmentalizing. It was a survival technique that he had grown adept at. He pushed the questions that he had down and away, tucked back in a nice corner where they could do no harm.

Chapter 6

Two days later, Travis was released from the hospital. Or escaped, as he liked to put it. Sophia's mother and one of her brothers had come to see him, and while he was overjoyed to see them, the whole process had been painful and full of memories that Travis didn't particularly want to relive. The last time he had seen them was at her funeral.

Life slowly got back to normal; Travis went to physical therapy three times a week for his back and began to regain strength. A week after being released from the hospital, Randy officially hid Travis' pain medications and hid them well, only leaving enough out for each day. "There's no way you went through all those that fast taking them on time!"

Two weeks after leaving the hospital, Travis tipped off the police that there was a thirteen-year-old girl about to sneak out to meet her fifteen-year-old internet boyfriend who was in actuality a thirty-six-year-old man. He also sent Randy out in the middle of the night to make sure the cops took the tip seriously.

A month after being released from the hospital, Travis was released from physical therapy and began to jog again and even took Starkey on a few hikes in the woods around Chico. Outwardly, Travis had recovered well and was fine. Inwardly was a different story. He was haunted by the photo he had seen, and his nightmares had gotten worse.

He was relieved when Randy's crew finished the job they were working on and were given three weeks leave before they started on a new project just outside of Willows. It was an excellent excuse to leave town for a while and go camping, something they had done every year since graduating high school.

The two of them packed up their stuff, about four ice chests full of food, and drove up into southern Oregon. There was a campground on the Rogue River where they had camped at the previous year. The campground was beautiful, lush, and green with trees everywhere, and the campsites were far enough apart to give the campers some semblance of privacy.

"Awesome!" Randy said, looking out at the river as he stomped a peg to his tent into the ground. "We've never been able to get this close to the river before. These spots are always taken."

"Yeah," Travis said distractedly. He had gotten a little tangled up while trying to put his tent together and was now looking at the directions with a confused expression on his face. "We had better hope there isn't a flash flood."

"I don't think Oregon is flash flood territory," Randy said snidely.

Travis shrugged. "It can happen." He looked at Randy's tent, then at the bundle on the ground and back at the directions.

"Would you like some help?" Randy asked, enjoying his brother's confusion.

"No," Travis shook his head. "I can do this. I'm not *that* much of a flat-lander."

"Yes you are, we both are. We just hide it well," Randy said as he began tossing stuff into his tent.

"I wish I would have just patched the old one. This new tent is way more complicated," Travis said. For the next ten minutes, he was intent on putting his tent together, which he managed to do without getting himself killed or seriously injured. When he finally got the tent together and looking like the one in the picture, he turned to see Randy standing knee deep in the river reeling in his fishing pole.

"Isn't that cold?" he asked.

"Not really. Feels pretty nice, actually," Randy replied. "I got a bite."

"Cool." Travis kicked off his sandals and put a foot in the water…and then froze as a feeling of absolute terror overcame him. He looked down, felt the cool water swirling around his foot, and suddenly, he *remembered* what it was like to be surrounded in icy cold water that beat against him and sucked the air out of him. He could remember being afraid, not wanting to die, desperately trying to hold on but there was nothing to hold onto, a hand reaching out to him. A hand he couldn't reach because the current had already swept him away.

"Got one!" Randy yelled, jerking back the rod and reeling like mad. Then suddenly, the line went slack. "Awe!" Randy slapped his forehead. "I can't believe it got off the line!" He turned to his brother. "Did you see tha…. are you okay?"

Travis was shivering, and when he looked at Randy, he didn't look like the twenty-one-year-old man he was any more. Instead, he looked like a terrified child. He quickly stepped out of the water and walked backwards several steps. "I…I…" Travis began but was shivering too badly. "I remembered something."

Randy stepped out of the river and set down his pole. "You're shivering. It's like ninety out here." He walked over to his tent and took out his coat, tossing it at Travis. "Here, put this on."

Travis did, then walked over to the picnic table, similar to the one that had been in the Polaroid photograph left by the shooter and sat down. Randy sat down opposite him. "What did you remember? Can you tell me?" he asked calmly.

"Um." Travis began rubbing his arms, still convinced he was freezing. "Um, it was weird. When I put my foot in the water, I suddenly remembered…. I remembered being in icy cold water, fast moving, turbulent, ya know?" He took a deep breath. "I was holding onto something, but it broke, and there wasn't anything else to grab. Somebody reached for me, and I tried to grab their hand, but…I couldn't reach. The current was too fast."

Randy didn't say anything, just waited for Travis to keep talking, sensing that his brother wasn't done. Travis was silent for about thirty seconds. "It was cold, Randy," He said finally. "It was so, so cold. Like the water was filled with snow or something."

Randy thought for a moment. "What time of year did those fly fishermen find you?"

"Late August," Travis said.

"Where was it again? The Klamath?"

Travis shook his head. "No, it was the Salmon River, near the Klamath. I think they run together."

"Is that a very cold river?"

"I don't know," Travis said. "I haven't been there since, and I don't really want to go back, either."

"Maybe you should," Randy suggested. "If you're starting to remember, maybe you should go back, see if you can get anything else. They say things like smells are the strongest things tied to memory; maybe it was the smell of the river and plants that did it. Maybe going back will help."

"Maybe." Travis was rubbing his forehead with the tips of his fingers, messing up his hair. "I honestly don't even want to think about it right now." He wasn't cold anymore, so he shrugged out of Randy's jacket and handed it back. "Thanks."

"You okay?"

Travis took another deep breath. "I'm scared, Randy. It wasn't like I was just remembering it. It's like I was living it, like it was happening right then."

"I know what you mean," Randy said.

Travis shook his head. "No, I don't think you do."

"I do," Randy insisted. "I never told you this before."

That got Travis' attention. He thought Randy told him pretty much everything. Randy rubbed the back of his neck, clearly uncomfortable. "Remember that day when dad got me?" Travis's eyes narrowed, and he nodded. Of course he remembered. It had pretty much been the worst day of his life. Well, that he could remember.

"Well," Randy continued, "I was walking towards the parking lot with my soccer ball under my arm, ya know? And I heard him behind me. I heard him say my name. That's all he said. My name. *Randolph*. In this cool, even voice. The moment I heard his voice, I just froze. I hadn't even seen him yet, but his voice just threw me back there, to the closet that night, and all of the sudden, I was hearing it again, hearing him laughing, hearing Mom screaming. And I just froze. I couldn't move a muscle, I was so afraid." Randy closed his eyes for a moment, trying to block out the image of that dark closet and that abandoned crack house. "It made it so easy for him to grab me. I didn't run, I didn't fight. I just froze. I was fast. Maybe if I ran, I would have gotten away. Maybe if I screamed, the coach would have heard me, or one of the teachers. I should have done something but instead, I did the exact same thing I did in the closet that night: just froze."

"We all have our nightmares, Randy," Travis said softly. "We all have our regrets."

"You wouldn't have hesitated," Randy said. "You wouldn't have frozen."

Travis shook his head. "You don't know that. I froze just now, didn't I? Everybody has their demons. You're stronger than you were then."

"Maybe," Randy said thoughtfully. "It's getting dark pretty fast; we should probably start the barbeque up. Want to cook those steaks or stick with burgers?"

"Let's cook the pork ribs." Travis brightened, standing up. "We can try out that new barbeque sauce I picked up."

"Yeah, okay." Randy stood up too. "I'll cook, you start shucking that corn."

"Sheesh, you burn one dinner, and you lose barbeque privileges," Travis mumbled under his breath.

"You did more than burn it. You almost started a forest fire." Randy laughed "Who doesn't know that you're supposed to open the beans before you put them on the fire?"

"Hey, that was funny, and you know it!" Travis said as he grabbed the corn from one of the ice chests.

"No, but hearing you whine over those burns for a week was," Randy said, then quickly dodged because Travis had thrown one of the corns at him. The serious moment was behind them for the time being, though Travis wouldn't go near the river again for several days, at least not of his own free will.

***

Eight days after Travis' flashback, Randy sat on the edge of the river, watching the stars. It was early morning, and there was no moon. The stars were brilliant, and it was perfect conditions for nigh fishing. There was a slight breeze moving through the reeds next to the water, and on the other side of the river, an owl was hooting. Other than that, there was no sound.

Randy reached into the potato chip bag at his side and withdrew a sun chip, plopping it in his mouth and watching his pole. He had gotten a few bites, but other than that, it had been a quiet night. Travis had gone to sleep a few hours ago, bored, but Randy wasn't sleepy and was determined to catch at least one keeper before this camping trip was over.

Starkey, who had been curled into a ball beside him sleeping, a large, black blotch in the grass, suddenly sat up and perked up his ears. Randy reached over and scratched the dog behind the ears. "What's up? You hear a deer or something, boy?" he asked quietly.

The dog started wagging his tail, and Randy heard the zipper on the tent behind him. "Nature calling or something?" he asked Travis as his brother crawled out of his tent. "Not like you're missing much. I haven't caught anything."

When Travis didn't answer Randy turned to look at him. Travis was standing at the front of his tent wearing boxers and a t-shirt, staring at the water, not moving. One look at his friend and Randy knew Travis wasn't all there. The blank expression on his face made it clear he was sleepwalking.

Randy climbed to his feet and watched Travis closely. As far as he knew, Travis had never walked in his sleep before. He suffered from night terrors often enough and would thrash and occasionally yell but had never done anything like this.

"Travis?" Randy asked, just to be sure.

Travis gave no sign that he had heard his brother and began to walk shakily and slowly towards the river. He stopped a few feet from Randy and blinked several times. "Dad," Travis said, barely over a whisper, though the inflection suggested that Travis probably thought he was yelling it. "Dad, help us."

Starkey began to walk over to Travis and Randy quickly grabbed the dog's collar. He had heard that it was dangerous to wake a sleepwalker, though he didn't really know why. Still, he thought they should keep their distance. He watched his brother with great concern as Travis took three more steps, not even flinching when he left dry land and entered the river.

Though the majority of his face was blank and free of expression, the tightness in his jaw and the intense look in his eyes made it clear that whatever he was dreaming of was traumatic. Travis was terrified of something. "Dad, please, help us."

"Us?" Randy echoed, looking to Starkey for help. The dog didn't feel inclined to elaborate on Travis' psyche, though, so Randy turned his attention back to his brother who had taken another step into the river. Now knee deep in the black water, Travis reached out in front of him with his left hand and made a grabbing gesture. His other hand, Randy now noticed, was loosely clasped at his side as if he were holding somebody's hand.

Travis squeezed the invisible hand a little tighter and took another two steps deeper into the river. "Dad! Dad, help us!" His voice broke on the last word, and he began to take another step deeper into the river.

There was a drop-off; Randy couldn't let him go any farther. He let go of Starkey's collar and rushed into the river, grabbing hold of Travis' arm just as he began to take yet another step. Travis jumped and sucked in a deep breath but didn't appear overly harmed by his sudden entrance into the waking world. He looked down at the water swirling around his thighs, then at the hand firmly clasped around his wrist. He looked up at Randy, extreme confusion on his face.

"This is weird, even for you," Randy said, gently pulling his brother back towards shore. "You're okay." Randy kept his tone light in case Travis had a delayed freak out. "Just take a few steps back, and we'll get out of the river. Come on. You're very close to the drop-off."

Travis looked down at the water again, then back at Randy, and nodded once. Randy led Travis out of the river and didn't let go of his wrist until they were on dry land. "You okay?" he asked Travis, who still appeared to be in a heightened state of confusion, as he picked up his pole and quickly reeled in.

"Yeah." Travis said, staring at the water. "How did I get in the river?"

"You were sleepwalking," Randy said.

Travis shook his head. "I don't sleepwalk."

"Apparently, you do." Randy removed the bait from his hook and threw it into the river, then folded up his pole. "You came out of the tent and made a beeline for the river. You kept talking under your breath."

"What was I saying?" Travis rubbed the back of his neck and looked back towards his tent as if trying to configure the path he had taken.

"Dad, help us," Randy told him "You said it about three times."

"I didn't say anything else?"

"No." Randy turned and walked over to the table to sit down and take off his now soaked tennis shoes. "What's going on with you?"

Travis rubbed at his left eye with the back of his hand, confused and, though he tried to hide it, a little scared. "I don't know. I've never done that before, have I?"

"Not that I know of," Randy said. "Does this have something to do with that photo?"

"Yeah, I think it does." Travis walked over and sat down on the end of the bench next to the table and buried his face in his hands for a moment. "What the hell is happening to me?" he mumbled into his hands. The words were too muffled for Randy to understand, but he got the gist of it. Travis looked up again. "Sorry."

"It's not your fault," Randy said, wringing out his socks. "Not like you planned on taking a midnight stroll into the river. Talk to me, what is going on with you?" Randy's voice was soothing. It was the same way he had talked to younger kids in the foster homes when they would freak out or have panic attacks. Something about Randy had always been able to calm them down and make them feel safe. He had a presence they had always responded to, and Travis found himself beginning to calm.

Travis shook his head. "I don't know, it's like ever since I saw that photo….I can almost remember, Randy. Almost. It's on the tip of my brain. So close; I just can't seem to reach out and grab it." He slammed his fist down on the table in a sudden gesture of anger that was uncharacteristic. "It's so frustrating!"

He turned to Randy. "Everything is getting worse. The dreams, the nightmares, hell, the flashbacks! Everything is getting worse!"

"Maybe you should start going to therapy again," Randy suggested.

Travis glared at him. "No. I don't want to go down that road again."

"Have you thought about going back to the river?"

"I don't know," Travis said and looked away, wanting to avoid the subject.

"Roger and Anthony probably remember where they found you; I bet they can take you back," Randy suggested.

Travis shook his head. "No, Roger died last year, remember? You went to the funeral with me. And Anthony is married and living in Washington now. I haven't seen him since he and Roger took me out to lunch for graduation."

"Oh, yeah," Randy said thoughtfully. "Still, I bet Anthony wouldn't mind."

"I don't want to go back there Randy, and I bet Tony doesn't, either" Travis said. "You know, he told me that finding me in that river traumatized him for life?" Travis laughed nervously. "He was only seventeen, fishing with his grandfather. Next thing he knows, he's carrying a barely alive kid out of a canyon." He shook his head and looked at Randy again. "I don't want to go back there. I don't think I can handle another flashback like the one I had the other day. Maybe it's good I don't remember."

"Maybe." Randy had to agree. "I mean, people do repress memories for a reason."

"Yeah." Travis nodded and stood up. "I'm going back to bed. I think I'll tie the tent flap closed so that doesn't happen again."

"If you want, I can move my tent in front of yours for the night." Randy suggested.

"Yeah," Travis said. "That's probably a good idea." He laughed nervously. "Some camping trip, huh?"

Randy gave him an easy smile. "It could be worse. You still have your eyebrows, so there's that."

Chapter 7

It was an unusually cold night for September in Mount Shasta, California, near the Oregon border. Located in the Eastern Cascades and surrounded by some of the most picturesque landscape in northern California, Mount Shasta was a popular location for tourist. Three major rivers ran near here: the Sacramento, Klamath, and McCloud, providing ample opportunity for fishing and hiking as well as anything else a city slicker would find entertaining in the great outdoors, so long as it didn't get them killed.

Tourist season was almost over, though, and the sudden cold spell had driven all but the most adventurous home. Ski season was not due to start for another few months, and for now, the town was quiet. Shasta Mountain, the volcano from which the town had been named, stood out like a god, majestic and stunning in the cold, clear night. Blinding white with sharp, defined angles, the mountain looked like the tip of a monstrous diamond some deity had shoved deep into the earth long ago. Likewise, on an ice cold night like tonight, the stars appeared to have been multiplied by ten. They were a breathtaking, a million points of twinkling light shining deep within the void.

Shawn McAlister flipped up the collar of his leather jacket as he gazed up at the night sky, trying to provide a little warmth to the back of his neck as he puffed on a cigarette with a gloved hand. He was fairly certain he was the only one out on a night like this, eyeballing the natural beauty of his surroundings. Nobody else was insane enough to endure this cold.

He certainly wasn't insane enough. He would have closed the bar hours ago if he had managed to get rid of Mitch. He took one last, long drag from his cigarette and threw it on the ground, smashing it under one foot. He took one last look at the stars, then turned and headed back inside.

The bar was warm despite the cold outside, and as welcoming as a bar could be. Soft yellow lighting flowed out from the mason jars attached to the ceiling, giving the primarily brown interior a kind of warmth that the heater did not provide. This was not the type of bar that miserable old men came to, to get drunk and hit on loose woman. It was a family establishment where old buddies came to watch football games. They served reasonable dinner specials, and several arcade games in a back room made it a welcoming place for kids. They also had a pool table and an air hockey table as well as a large screen tv and an area designed for watching it. The bar itself took up the far wall.

Shawn walked across the room quickly and took his place behind the bar, grabbing his apron and tying it around his waist again. He glanced at the clock; it was a quarter till midnight. "All right, Mitch, car keys. Hand them over," Shawn said to the one occupant of the bar.

The man sniffled, his eyes nearly swollen shut from all the crying he had done in the last hour, and handed over his car keys without comment. Shawn stuck them in his apron pocket. "Can I get you another?"

Mitch nodded mutely and stared at the bar as Shawn grabbed a shot glass and filled it three fourths of the way up with water and the rest with Jack Daniels. Mitch was already three sheets to the wind; Shawn would have cut him off a while ago if he hadn't felt so sorry for the guy. Plus, he had already called home and made sure it was okay with his wife that he brought Mitch home with him.

Mitch was not a drinker. In fact, most of the time, he was the sober driver, come game night. Shawn had known him for practically his whole life having been good friends with Mitch's younger brother.

He was a good man, a devoted father and husband, the type of friend a friend would like to have.

At six five and two hundred and fifty pounds, Mitch was a gentle giant, a teddy bear, really. He owned and ran a local nursery which he had purchased after retiring from firefighting. Normally, Mitch was one of the happiest people you could ever meet. But not tonight. Tonight, his world had fallen apart.

"How could she have done it? How could they do this to me?" Mitch said, slurring his words badly as he took the shot glass and cupped it with both hands as if it were the only thing tying him to reality. Tonight, Mitch came home after dropping his kids off at their grandmother's to find his wife and best friend in bed together. Their betrayal had broken him. Not a violent man, Mitch had reacted to this revelation by leaving without a word. He just turned and left the house, driving around until he finally landed here, ruining Shawn's hopes of closing early.

"I know it doesn't seem possible right now, but you are going to get through this," Shawn said, leaning against the bar. "You're going to get through this, and things will get better. This is just a low point; you can only go up from here."

Mitch nodded, then began to sob again. He was a loud crier, so loud, in fact, that Shawn almost didn't hear the bell on the door. He turned to see a kid coming through the door who didn't look like he was any older than twenty-two. His cheeks and nose were red, a sure sign that he'd been walking in the cold. The hefty brown jacket he was wearing didn't appear to have kept the night at bay; he was shivering.

The kid was tall. Not as tall as Mitch, but probably taller than Shawn at a little over six foot with longish reddish-brown hair which didn't look like it had been combed. He looked like the kind of kid you would expect to see on a college campus chasing girls, not the kind to show up at an old man's bar at midnight.

"Help you?" Shawn asked.

The kid came closer, and Shawn could see that the young man looked exhausted, like he hadn't slept in a few days. His eyes and skin were clear, though, and when he spoke, it was friendly enough. Shawn doubted he was a drug addict. He was muscular, but not in a body builder way, more like a runner or swimmer, lean and wiry. This fact added to Shawn's judgment that he was not a tweeker. Most drug addicts didn't take very good care of their bodies. Still, as tired as the kid looked, he could probably easily be mistaken as a junkie from across the room.

"Have anything warm to eat?" the kid asked, rubbing his arms to get the circulation back.

"Normally, we stop serving food at ten, but we were pretty dead tonight. I can heat you up some soup. Its clam chowder, you mind?"

"Not at all!" The kid sank into a chair in the corner next to the jukebox. "That sounds wonderful, thank you!"

Shawn came out from behind the bar and approached him. "Can I see some I.D.?"

"I'm not drinking," the kid said.

Shawn shook his head. "Doesn't matter. If you're going to be in the bar this late, I need to see some I.D."

The kid produced a wallet from his coat pocket and opened it to show Shawn his I.D. He was twenty-one, would be twenty-two in a few months. "What are you doing out in the cold tonight, Travis? Not in any trouble, I hope?"

"Nah." Travis shook his head. "I've got a touch of insomnia, thought a walk would help me sleep. I think I need to thaw out a bit, though. Is it always this cold this time of year?"

"God no!" Shawn exclaimed. "You not from around here?"

"Chico," Travis said. "It's still summer there. I'm just in town for," he glanced at Mitch, "business."

"Well, I'll get you that soup. Should thaw you out a bit. Anything to drink?" Shawn asked as he turned and headed back to the bar.

"Anything warm," Travis said.

Shawn went back into the kitchen and dished out some soup which he had stuck in the fridge for the next day. He was technically breaking the rules, but he didn't want the kid to freeze, and they needed the business. Besides, Shawn had been feeling overly protective lately due to his daughter's illness, and the kid reminded him of his little brother who was currently serving in Iraq.

When Shawn brought the soup back to the kid, he seemed overly grateful, like the clam chowder was the best smelling soup in the world. When he took the soup from him, however, something strange happened. Shawn's hand brushed against the kid's, and the kid pulled back suddenly, like he had been shocked. His eyes lost focus for a second, then he smiled and thanked Shawn again. Something about his behavior seemed strangely family to Shawn, but the bartender shrugged it off and headed back over to tend to Mitch, who had stopped crying and was talking to himself again.

The next hour went by slowly with Mitch altering between blubbering, sobbing, staring at the bar and talking about how much he loved his wife in a broken, slurred voice. The kid put some Arrowsmith on the jukebox and sat quietly reading a science fiction book and drinking the coffee that Shawn had brought him. Shawn busied himself with comforting Mitch and preparing the place to close.

At ten till one, Shawn took off his apron and set it on the counter, heading into the bathroom to answer nature's call. He didn't realize his mistake; not until it was too late.

****

Travis looked over the top of his book as Mitch reached across the counter and grabbed the keys, which had fallen out of the apron. Keys in hand, the large man promptly fell off the stool he had been perched on for the past three hours.

Travis doggy-eared his book and calmly stuck it back in his coat pocket as Mitch picked himself up off the floor and stumbled towards the door, running into a table as he went. It took him three tries to open the door. Fourth time was a charm. Travis watched him quietly.

Travis was in no hurry to go back out into the cold. Mitch wasn't going anywhere; Travis had made sure of it when he had removed the battery from his truck an hour before; not an easy job when it was two friggin' degrees outside!

He was exaggerating. It wasn't that cold, but it felt like it. Travis was a wuss when it came to cold. He didn't like it. But he had best get out there before Mitch decided to take off walking and die of exposure.

He put his coat back on, zipped it up, and removed his wallet. He wrote a quick note on a napkin and left several bills on the table before heading out the door after Mitch. He found the drunken man sitting in his truck trying vainly to start it. He looked so confused, it was almost comical.

Travis hugged himself against the cold and trotted across the street to tap on the driver's side window. Mitch jumped and stared at Travis like he was a banshee come to take him away. "Need some help?" Travis asked as he shifted from one foot to another, trying to stay warm.

Mitch opened his door and nearly fell out of the vehicle before righting himself. He gestured hopelessly towards the dash. "It broke," he said, bewildered.

"I'm sure you just left the lights on or something. Where you going? I can give you a ride," Travis suggested.

"Not going nowhere." Mitch slurred his words so badly, Travis had to make an assumption as to the end of the sentence. "Nowhere to go, just going. Going, going, gone. Gone! Gone! Gone!"

"Come on man, it's freezing out here. Let's go back inside, and you can get another drink." Travis was buying time. Mitch was a big man, and while he wasn't violent, Travis didn't think he could stop him if the man had his mind set on leaving. Travis was familiar with a few different forms of martial arts and was usually good in any situation, but not tonight. Tonight, he was exhausted and freezing half to death.

"Truck broke," Mitch said again. There was something about alcohol that made people age in reverse. The more you drank, the younger you acted. This seemed like a pretty ironic observation seeing as Travis was so young himself. Circumstances had aged Travis well past his twenty-one years, and on nights like this, he felt it.

Across the street, the door to the bar suddenly burst open and the bartender rushed out, skidding on the icy sidewalk as he looked around frantically, a half terrified, half angry look on his face. He spotted them and came charging from across the street. "What the hell do you think you're doing, Mitch?" he shouted.

Mitch smiled and waved goofily. "I'm talking to my friend!"

Shawn shoved past Travis and reached into the truck, grabbing the keys out of the ignition. "Son of a bitch!" he growled, mostly to himself. He knew he had made a big mistake leaving the apron on the counter. His mistake could have cost somebody their life.

Only Travis knew how high the cost would have really been.

Mitch looked at his truck with concern. "It won't work. It broke," he said, slurring his words comically.

Shawn sighed and gave Travis an apologetic look. "Sorry about that. Thank you for grabbing him for me."

"It was no problem," Travis said, then startled as Mitch engulfed him in a giant hug. At least he was an affectionate drunk rather than a violent one. Travis had more experience with the violent ones. Still, violent or not, if Travis hadn't intervened, Mitch would still have been a murderer come morning.

Disentangling himself from the affectionate drunk, Travis waved bye to the two men and began to walk off. "Kid!" The bartender called after him, one hand on Mitch's arm, concerned. "You walking far? It's below freezing out here."

"Just up the road. I'll be fine, thanks!" Travis turned and waved back. Shawn looked like he was going to argue with him for a second but then nodded. Shawn was a natural protector, even when it came to complete strangers. He didn't like seeing Travis walking off into the cold alone, but it couldn't be helped.

Shawn led Mitch back across the street to the bar and felt grateful for the warmth that greeted them. He locked the door behind them and flicked off the neon "open" sign. He didn't want any more unexpected visitors and was in a hurry to get home. His wife didn't like him being out so late. These were not his usual weekend hours, but they really needed the extra money, and the owner was trying to give him all the extra hours he could to help out.

Shawn deposited Mitch in a chair next to the door and walked across the room to where the kid had been sitting. He had left his coffee cup and bowl sitting on the table as well as several dollar bills when he had run off chasing Mitch. Shawn didn't want to think about what would have happened if that truck had started. Mitch could barely walk let alone drive. It was a lucky thing the town was so deserted tonight.

Shawn picked up the bills without much thought and shoved the money in his apron pocket, then noticed the note scribbled hastily on a napkin that had been underneath the bills. It read:

For Megan's surgery, she's going to be just fine!

Shawn stared at the note for a moment, eyes narrowing. Megan was his daughter; she was three years old and currently going blind due to a tumor in her left eye. Shawn and his wife didn't have insurance, and they had been trying everything they could think of to raise the money for the surgery but were still several hundred dollars away from the initial payment to insure she even got the surgery.

Still staring at the note, Shawn withdrew the bills from his apron pocket again and realized that they were hundred-dollar bills. In his exhausted and stressed-out state he hadn't even noticed. That kid had left a thousand-dollar tip. For Megan's surgery….

Without hesitation, Shawn shoved the money back into his apron pocket and sprinted across the room towards the door, pausing briefly to unlock it before rushing out into the cold night. He skidded to a halt in the middle of the deserted street and turned full circle, his breath coming out in big puffs of steam.

The kid was gone. There was no sign of him. He had vanished.

Shawn looked up and down the street one more time before turning and heading back into the warmth of the bar. He knew beyond a shadow of a doubt that, for the second time in his life, he had just encountered a Seer.

***

Travis blew into his hands and cupped them over his ears, wishing he hadn't just recently cut his hair. Though his hair was a little longer than the average boy's, it wasn't quite long enough to protect his ears from the cold. He hoped they wouldn't fall off.

He was only a few blocks from the motel, but he stopped at a street corner and waited, shifting from foot to foot and rubbing his ears. He really didn't like being this cold, but he had to appreciate the effect it had on the stars. They really sparkled on a night like this.

Travis blew out a puff of air and watched as the steam hang in the air a little too long before dissipating. He allowed his mind to drift back to the month or so that he and Randy had lived near here when they were fifteen. It hadn't been one of their better foster homes, but not one of the worst, either. Travis couldn't remember what the foster parent's names had been, but he remembered the night the husband had come home stumbling drunk. The smell of alcohol had been thick. Randy was still going to physical therapy from the beating his old man had given him, and he was still due for one more surgery to put another metal rod in his arm. That night in the abandoned house was still very fresh in his memory. At the first smell of alcohol, he freaked out a little, flashing back into a nightmare, and his first instinct was to run. Of course, the moment Randy was out the door, Travis was right behind him. That was the way it worked; they never ran alone. But they hadn't thought it out too well. It was a spur of the moment exodus, and neither of them grabbed a coat.

They ended up lost, walking down the side of some road with several inches of snow coming down. If it wasn't for the kindness of a stranger, they may have both died of exposure that night. It was Travis' first real encounter with cold that he could remember.

And now, he was back here again, freezing his butt off again, and all he wanted was to go to sleep. This had been his second intervention in two days, and he had another one tomorrow. They almost never came in clusters like this, and when they did, they had a profound physical and mental effect. When visions and dreams came together, they left Travis feeling as if he were coming off some dangerous drug. Like an addict going through detox or something. He felt twitchy, groggy, exhausted, and moody.

He wasn't quite there yet, but he would be tomorrow. Three interventions in three days, it was going to be hard on him. He knew he would not be able to leave town right away like he usually did. Tomorrow, after seeing to that house fire, he planned on going back to the motel and sleeping for two days. He looked forward to it.

Out of the corner of his eye, Travis saw a blue minivan turn onto the street some three blocks up. He kept the vehicle in the periphery as it approached traveling at a safe speed. The van pulled up to the stop sign, and the driver's side window rolled down. The man who peered out at Travis looked tired but alert.

"Are you all right, son. It's awfully cold out tonight," the man said quietly.

"Fine sir, I'm just heading back to the motel now," Travis said with a nod and a smile. He wasn't expecting them to stop and was caught a little off guard.

"Do you need a ride?" the man asked. Travis knew what he was thinking. He was thinking there was a good chance Travis was lying, that he didn't have a hotel room because if he did, he would be in it. He was worried that Travis was perhaps a runaway teenager or a transient that hadn't realized it was going to get this cold. He didn't want Travis to freeze to death. After all, he was a police officer. It was his job.

The back windows of the minivan were tinted, so Travis could not see the three children sleeping in the back seat. Amanda, age nine, William, age six, and little Tamara, who was eight months old today. Their mother was sleeping in the passenger seat.

Travis tried not to think what would have happened if he had failed tonight. The father and oldest daughter would have been killed instantly when Mitch's truck hit their vehicle at nearly a hundred miles per hour. The mother would bleed to death while the emergency crew worked to free them from the crushed minivan. Baby Tamara would die of internal trauma at the hospital. William would endure seven hours of surgery and be the only survivor, though he would never walk again.

The father looked out at Travis in concern, not knowing how close he and his family had come to destruction. Mitch would not be able to live with himself for destroying this family and three days after being released from the hospital, he would put a bullet in his brain. So many lives would have been lost.

"No, Sir. I can make it. Thank you, though. Have a good night!" Travis said and turned up the street, walking towards the motel.

The father hesitated, torn between instinct and familiar duty. He pulled away and headed down the opposite street, away from Travis. Once they had turned the corner, Travis put on some speed, sprinting up the road towards his safe, warm motel room. He had always been a good runner, had even gone to state in high school, but running tonight made him feel like he was breathing ice.

He got to the motel room and swiftly kicked Starkey off the bed, wrapping himself up in the warm blankets. He was asleep before his head touched the pillow. He didn't bother to lock the door.

Chapter 8

Randy slammed the door of his truck a little hard as he stepped onto the firmly packed gravel of the driveway, wincing as the window rattled. He was glad to be home after an extra-long day ripping up chunks of pavement and laying new ones down. He was hot and sticky and could swear that he was sweating tar, thinking of nothing more than a shower.

He ran a hand over the top of his forehead and kneeled down beside the truck, tracing the area where that idiot Ken had run into it with the small forklift. The front driver's side door would open, but the back one would not. It would need to be re-welded and bent back into shape for the door to work properly again. Luckily, he knew a welder.

He walked the length of the truck to make sure he knew the full extent of the damage. He drove a full size, four door Toyota which he had upgraded to last year after he landed the Cal-Trans job. He loved this truck and had paid for it completely by himself, without any help from anybody. He was proud of it, and looking at what that reject had done to his baby made him livid.

He pulled his phone out of his pocket and dialed Travis. His brother had been gone for nearly an entire week. Randy didn't blame him. Three interventions in one week was tough. Knowing Travis, he had probably slept the last two days. But Randy needed to know when he was going to be back; his boss didn't want him driving the truck to work on Monday unless it was fixed. It was probably too late to get it into a shop, and if Travis couldn't get the door welded by Monday, he would need to take Travis' truck to work.

The phone rang five times, then went to voice mail; Randy left a message and hung up. He shoved the phone back in his pocket, then grabbed his toolbox out of the back of the truck and pushed open the gate into the backyard. He went directly to the large shed and elbowed open the door, flicking on the light with the edge of the toolbox.

He set the box down next to the door and turned to head back to the house but paused, realizing something was wrong. He turned back to the interior of the shed, scanning from corner to corner. The shed was very clean, which came as no surprise to Randy. Both Travis and he had been somewhat institutionalized by the system they had grown up in. They had been *trained* to be orderly. They washed the dishes the moment after using them, made their beds right after getting up, folded their laundry, and kept their bathroom counters wiped down. Most of the time, they didn't realize they were doing it, but occasionally, one of them tried to make a mess as a way to exert their own free will. Leaving a crumpled paper towel on the counter to prove that they were rebels.

The shed, like the rest of their lives, was ship-shape. The project Travis was currently working on, a steel rose, was clasped firmly in the vice at the edge of the worktable, but all the metal shavings had been brushed off. The rods were arranged according to size and placed on the shelves above Travis' three welding machines, the floors swept, everything organized, everything in its place.

Everything except the crumpled Taco Bell wrapper on the floor under the table.

Randy walked farther into the shed, leaned down, and snatched the wrapper up. He stared at it for a moment, frowning. Travis never ate while working in the shed. Even as clean as he kept the place, there was still a chance that a metal shaving could get into the food. Travis also didn't eat Taco Bell. Randy ate there, but he hadn't in several days, and he wouldn't eat in the shed, either, so why would there be a Taco Bell wrapper on the floor?

He looked back, trying to remember if the door had been open or closed when he walked up. It was possible that it had blown in from outside. The widow across the street occasionally borrowed tools; she could have left the door open when she brought them back. It was nothing to get concerned about.

Randy slid the latch on the shed door closed and carried the taco wrapper with him to the house; he threw it in the outside trash and entered the house through the kitchen door. He needed a shower.

He was halfway through the living room when he caught a flash of movement in the periphery, then something hit him hard on the back of his head causing him to drop to his knees. He hadn't quite comprehended the first hit when the second came, rendering him unconscious.

****

Randy's head was throbbing in time to the song *Renegade* by the *Styx*. The music seemed to come from far away, penetrating his delirium slowly but insistently, drawing him away from his unconscious state to his terrifying reality. Slowly and with great effort, his conscious mind swam upwards through the hazy fog of uncertainty and confusion to find himself tied to the computer chair.

He lifted his head, and the action almost made him pass out again. For a moment, the world spun wildly, then it settled back down again. God, his head hurt. His hands were tied loosely but firmly behind his back and fastened to the computer chair so as to provide for blood circulation but make it impossible for him to break loose. His legs where individually tied to the front legs of the chair, providing for no movement at all. Another rope was across his chest, holding his abdomen in place.

"You boys have an interesting collection of music here," a man said. He appeared to be in his mid-thirties and in really good shape, solid, with biceps to match Randy's, which was saying something. He had short, mouse brown hair, which was thinning a little, creating a dominant widows peak on his forehead. He was very well groomed and clean shaven with beady eyes that watched Randy with a blatant confidence he instantly found disturbing, as if being knocked out and tied to a chair hadn't already done it for him.

The man was wearing dark blue jeans and a red golfing shirt, both of which looked like they had been pressed. His brown loafers also looked like they had been shinned. This was a man who took his appearance very seriously, like he always wanted to make a good first impression. Randy figured that ship had sailed when this jerk had tied him up.

The man was sitting on the arm of the couch going through their CD binder, and as the *Styx* finished *Renegade* and started on *Miss America,* he turned it down a little. "I mean, look at this, it's crazy," he said, indicating the binder. "You have Lynyrd Skynyrd next to Frank Sinatra, Eminem next to Joe Nichols, what is wrong with you boys?" He turned a page and laughed. "Wow, you even have some old school jazz in here! Benny Goodman, huh? I was always a little more partial to Count Basey." He seemed to be enjoying himself.

Security system, Randy thought as he watched the mad-man stop the CD player and change CD's. *Should have gotten the damn security system.*

Then he remembered what Travis had said. *A security system can't fix stupid.*

As the *Goo Goo Dolls* began to sing *Black Balloon,* the stranger came and sat down on the coffee table directly in front of Randy. He leaned forward casually with his elbows on his knees and regarded his hostage with a creepily friendly smile. "I am sorry I had to hit you so hard, Randy, but you're a big guy, and I had to make sure I knocked you out quick. I'm not as fit as I used to be and well, not hitting you hard enough may have just pissed you off, then I may have had to use my gun, and that wouldn't have been pleasant for either of us."

"Who are you?" Randy asked at last, making furious eye contact with his captor.

"Oh, yes, how rude of me," the man laughed at his own insolence and shook his head. "My name is Tim."

Tim? Randy thought. *The evil mastermind's name is Tim?*

"Okay, *Tim*, what do you want?" Randy asked.

"I want to know where Travis is," Tim said. He stood up and began to pace back and forth in front of Randy, waving his hand in the air as he talked. He was shorter than Randy, at maybe 5'9" or 5"10. "See, I've been watching the house for five days now and haven't seen any sign of him. I even spent last night in your shed and still nothing. You must know where he is."

"Why do you want to know where Travis is?" Randy asked calmly.

"Because, Randy, I intend to kill him. Not right away, of course. I intend to use him as bait and then kill him when I'm done with him," he said conversationally, like he was talking about going bowling or something. "See, if I have Travis, those other creatures will come after him, and then I can wipe out the whole lot. Don't give me that look; I'm nothing more than an exterminator. You think that thing is your brother, but you are misinformed."

"I don't think so," Randy said, locking his jaw, the only outward sign of the furry he felt boiling inside of him.

"Where is he?" Tim flashed him that talk show host smile again.

Randy resisted the urge to glance towards the kitchen where he was pretty sure the note Travis had left about going to Mount Shasta was still sitting on the counter next to the microwave. Instead, he made eye contact with Mr. Sunshine. "Go to hell!"

"You don't need to protect him, he's not even human." Tim lost his smile.

"Go to hell," Randy repeated.

Tim sat down on the coffee table again. "Trust me, Randolph, you want to cooperate. I don't want to hurt you, but I will, to get what I need."

"I'm not afraid of you," Randy said truthfully.

Tim actually laughed, then he reached down, picked a paper bag up off the floor and set it on the table beside him. "Oh, I think I know what you're afraid of." He reached into the bag and withdrew a six-pack of Corona, moisture glistening on the outside of the clear glass bottles. At the sight of the beer, Randy's heartbeat sped up and adrenaline began to flood his system. All of the sudden, he was overtaken with an extreme fight or flight response. *You're fine,* he told himself. *You're going to be fine.*

He tried valiantly to keep his breathing even, but he was sure that the psycho had seen the fear flash in his eyes at the first sight of the beer. With a grin, the man said, "Corona was Daddy's beer of choice, was it not, Randy?"

Randy didn't answer. With a satisfied smile, Tim stood and grabbed one of the Coronas out by the neck, smacking the bottle against the palm of his hand. Each impact heightened Randy's anxiety, and his arms and legs began to tremble. He hoped the psycho couldn't see. No matter what, he was not going to tell this bastard where his brother was.

"Now, I'm going to ask you one more time. Where is Travis?" He paused for thirty seconds, giving Randy ample time to answer. Randy stared daggers into him and didn't say a word. Tim sighed, disappointed. "Have it your way, then," he said and swung the beer bottle.

***

Travis' heart was pounding, and his legs were burning as he took in great gulps of air. Beside him, Starkey jogged along happily, not missing a step. They had been running for over an hour now, and the dog looked like he could go all day. Travis was annoyed.

He jogged to a stop and leaned forward with his hands on his knees, watching the panting dog. "You know, that kind of perfection can get annoying," he said and flopped down in the long grass beside the trail. Starkey quickly tried to crawl in his lap, but he pushed the dog away. "You should have been on my track team, boy."

He leaned back, catching his breath, and watched as the river silently moved by at a rapid pace. He thought about jumping in, then remembered how freezing the Sacramento River was. Still, it would probably feel good to get wet. He had slept off the exhaustion for two days from the three successful interventions he had done, but he woke up restless. After a few hours of driving towards home, he had pulled over at a trail head and decided to go for a run. Eight miles later, he wasn't restless anymore.

His heart pounding against the inside of his chest felt good, and so did the exceptionally light feel of his legs. It felt good to run. He had always loved it. He watched Starkey wander over to the river and begin to lap up the cold water happily. Travis laced his fingers behind his head and lay back in the long grass, closing his eyes and feeling the warm September sun on his closed lids. He fell asleep to the sound of the river and birds singing overhead.

He woke up a half hour later when Starkey touched his cold nose to Travis' cheek. Travis laughed and pushed Starkey away as he sat up and rubbed his face. It felt good to relax after such a stressful week, felt good to have a good dream for once. He was glad he had left his phone in the truck.

He needed to get moving, though. He really wanted to spend the night in his own bed tonight, and at this rate, it would be nearly dark by the time he got back to the truck. He got to his feet, took a quick look around, then began a light jog back to the truck, enjoying himself thoroughly.

It was about eight thirty by the time he got back, and he was hungry. He decided he'd find a decent sit-down place somewhere and get something to eat on his way home. His phone was beeping, though. He had a voice mail. He listened to it, then dialed Randy's cell.

***

Tim stepped back and made a disgusted noise, running the back of his hand across his cheek to wipe away the blood splatter. He was probably going to have to throw away this shirt, and it was one of his favorites. His fault, of course. He hadn't expected the boy to cooperate. He should have worn a different shirt.

He dropped the broken beer bottle in the pile with the three others and grabbed a fresh Corona. This newest bottle had sliced the kid pretty good along the side, but Tim doubted the cut was deep enough that he needed to worry about blood loss. He had avoided hitting the kid's head with the bottles, instead using the beer on his abdomen and legs. He wanted to keep Randy awake for as long as possible, so he used his fist on the face and head. The beer bottles could fracture the skull, and that didn't suit Tim's purposes at all.

He really had no qualms against killing the kid. As far as he was concerned, Randy had no right to be alive in the first place. He should have died in that abandoned crack house when he was fourteen. That was what was *supposed* to have happened. That creature had no business screwing with the natural order of things.

As far as Tim was concerned, he was setting things right. Randolph James, formerly Randolph McCully, was supposed to be dead and come morning, he would be. As it was, the boy was already unrecognizable. One side of his face was so swollen, his eye had been completely lost, along with his cheek bone and jaw line. The other side of his face was almost as bad, though he could still see out of that eye. The whole bottom half of his head was covered in blood ,and his shirt was drenched as well. He had probably already lost at least a pint of blood from his nose and mouth alone. He was showing some pretty impressive bruises, especially on his face and arms.

For the most part, Tim was extremely impressed with the young construction worker. The boy hadn't said a word, hadn't cried or screamed for help once. He took the beating with a steady resolve that was admirable. It was as if Randy was sure he was going to make it out of this alive, sure that if he just made it through tonight, he would be okay. Tim grinned. the poor, delusional bastard. Endings were very seldom happy, especially when the Hunter was involved.

He smacked the beer bottle against the balm of his left hand and paced back and forth in front of the kid. "Now, now, now, Randolph, it doesn't have to be like this. Just tell me where dear old Travis is, and this all can be over. You want it to be over, don't you?"

Randy lifted his head with great effort and spit a glob of blood in Tim's general direction. Tim punched him in his already swollen eye, his ring slicing the tender skin easily. "You little bastard!" he screamed, not worrying about anybody overhearing. He had the music turned up pretty loud. "You son of a bitch! Don't you see, you're betraying your own kind! He's not even human!"

To his surprise, Randy chuckled. "Yeah," he said, slurring his words. "*Travis* is the one that looks human right now."

Tim hit him again, this time with the beer bottle on the left side where there was already a dark bruise. "I'm so going to love it when that creature comes home to find you in pieces!"

Then he heard something out of place. He quickly stepped across the room to the CD player and turned down the music. Yes, he could hear it clearly now. It was the Star Wars theme. How very quaint. Tim loved the Star Wars movies. The old ones, of course, not those crappy newer ones.

He stepped back across the room and reached into Randy's pocket, withdrawing the boy's phone. "Well, will you look at that?" Tim grinned and showed Randy the caller I.D. "Travis is calling."

****

"Hello?" Travis felt a cold chill move down his spine, and his grip on the phone suddenly tightened. *That voice!* He knew that voice, but from where?

"Who's this?" he asked, keeping his voice steady despite the panic he felt. In an instant, the gorgeous day had been transformed into something dark and lonely. The setting sun, which had been glorious a moment before, suddenly looked blood red and murderous. Travis began to shake. He feared for Randy's life. It was a monster on the other line, he knew it. A monster that he had met before, in the time before memory. His own personal monster.

"Oh, I think you know who this is, Travis," the man said smugly. Outwardly, he sounded friendly, almost teasing, a lilting, pleasant voice that turned Travis' blood to ice.

Travis took a deep breath. "Where's Randy?"

"He's tied to a chair right now. See, Randy is having a bit of a bad day. I only wanted him to tell me where you are, but he didn't want to cooperate, so I was forced to resort to violence."

Travis began to pace pack and forth in the deserted parking space of the trail head. "Listen, I don't know who the hell you are, but if you hurt my…."

"Oh, it's too late for that," the man cut him off. "I think he's hurt pretty bad; you may want to think about getting him to a hospital."

Travis stopped pacing and took several deep breaths. "What do you want?"

"You, Travis. I want you," the man said, losing the lilting quality of his voice. "You hand yourself over to me, and we can call Randy here an ambulance. And don't think about calling the cops, Travis. See, I *am* a cop. I have a police scanner right here, and I'll know. Then I'll slice Randy's throat with your steak knife. I may even let you listen while he chokes on his own blood."

Travis closed his eyes and rubbed the bridge of his nose. "Okay. But I'm still a couple hours away."

"Let's hope Randy has that long," the man said and hung up on him.

Chapter 9

Travis pulled into Mrs. Hellen's driveway and turned off the lights but left the engine running. Mrs. Hellen was an eighty-year-old widow who Travis and Randy did work for on occasion. This time of night, she would already be asleep and would not notice the truck in her driveway.

Travis got out of the truck and held the door open for Starkey to jump out. The dog stood motionless at his master's side, picking up on Travis' tension. Travis reached under the driver's seat and grabbed out the hefty Mag flashlight he kept there. He hadn't taken a gun with him to Mount Shasta, hadn't needed one, but the flashlight was as good a weapon as he could hope for.

He shoved the flashlight into his belt and grabbed his Swiss Army knife from the glove box. Not for the first time in the last hour, he thought about calling in backup. He had friends, other foster brothers who would come if he asked. But he didn't want to put anybody else in danger.

Travis knew that whoever had been on the other end of that phone would not hesitate to kill Randy and probably would kill him the moment Travis surrendered himself. That man was planning on killing them both tonight. Why, Travis had no idea, but with any luck, that wasn't going to happen.

He rolled down the window of his truck; just in case there was a problem with the door, they would need to make a speedy exit. He did a quick once over to make sure there was nothing else he should bring. He wanted to keep things light. Besides, he already had one of the best weapons in the world: Starkey.

He quietly opened the gate into Mrs. Hellen's backyard, then jumped the back fence into the Jacobson's yard. Starkey was a step behind him, the five-foot fence posing no obstacle to the agile dog. The Jacobson's were a family of five, a widowed father of four. Travis had to be careful here. Two of Mr. Jacobson's daughters were teenagers and he would not react kindly if he thought a boy were trying to sneak into one of their rooms.

The Jacobson house was quiet, though, and soon, Travis and Starkey were in the Smith's backyard. He didn't have to worry about the Smiths causing him any trouble. An old retired couple that would sleep through anything.

Travis crossed the yard quickly and pulled aside a loose board in the high fence so Starkey could get through. He had been meaning to fix this fence for a few months now but was glad he hadn't gotten around to it. Once Starkey was through, Travis slipped through as well and crossed his own backyard at a half crouch, keeping his eyes on the house. Both bedroom lights were off, but the hall light and living room lights were ablaze. Travis was pretty sure his adversary was in the living room where the music was coming from. Travis couldn't make out what kind of music it was, but it was probably loud enough to drown out any cries for help but not loud enough for a noise complaint.

He sidled up to his bedroom window and peered in. His bedroom door was open, and he could see a shadow moving against the hallway wall. Somebody was pacing in the living room. Travis reached into his pocket and pulled out his knife, carefully inserting the blade under the window frame and wiggling it back and forth. Then he put the palms of both hands against the window and pushed up. It didn't budge. He tried again, but still nothing. Then he saw that the window was locked. Now when had he done that?

He moved around the corner to Randy's bedroom window and found that it was open a crack, making his job that much easier. The window slid up easily and quietly, and Travis lifted Starkey and lowered the dog to the bedroom floor where he stood motionless, his ears back and hackles raised, staring at the partially closed bedroom door.

Now that the window was open, Travis could hear that the mad man was listening to one of Travis' favorite songs. He crawled through the window as quietly as possible and moved to the door, glad they both were such clean freaks, he didn't need to turn on a light to avoid tripping over anything.

Starkey was already at the door, sticking his head out into the hallway and growling softly. The dog kept shifting from front paw to front paw, excited. He knew what Travis wanted him to do; he was just waiting for the signal.

Travis crouched beside the dog and pulled the Maglite from his belt, already feeling the adrenaline pumping into his veins. It wasn't the best thought out plan in the world—as a matter of fact, it was hardly a plan at all—but it was what he had and what he was going to roll with. He leaned forward so his head was next to the dog's and whispered, "Attack!"

Starkey was gone so fast, Travis didn't even see him move, streaking down the hallway, a black blur. A split second later, somebody in the living room screamed in surprise and cursed. That was Travis' cue. He sprinted down the hallway, Maglite at the ready, and burst into the living room.

Starkey had the man by the left leg, and already the skin looked shredded. He hadn't fallen yet, though, and he had grabbed a beer bottle, swinging it at the dog full force. He smacked Starkey square on the head as Travis came into the room. The dog yipped and jumped away, only to lunge at the man's other leg. By then, Travis was on him, and he swung the Maglite with full force, noting with satisfaction the surprised look on the intruder's face a moment before the light hit him.

He went down on a knee, and a second hit dropped him completely. He fell face down on the bloody carpet, and Travis used his foot to roll the man over. "Hold!" he ordered Starkey, and the dog instantly moved to put his jaws around the man's throat. He did not bite down, though; he simply held the man to be sure he wasn't faking unconsciousness and growled menacingly.

The pale tan carpet was covered in blood splatter, and when Travis turned to face the rest of the room, he saw why. Randy was tied to the computer chair in the middle of the room, and he was hardly recognizable anymore. He looked much the same as he had that day in the abandoned crack house, black and blue, swollen and all cut up.

Around the chair lay about four broken beer bottles and a couple of intact ones. *Corona.* How the bastard had known to use that brand, Travis didn't know. But he had chosen the best possible way to break Randy. He had somehow known how to tap into that fear.

Travis hated the man. It was a new feeling for him, hatred, and one that he wasn't accustomed to. The fury that rolled through Travis at that moment as he surveyed the damage that son of a bitch had done to his brother surprised him and even scared him a little. He wanted nothing more than to make the man pay. But there was no time for that.

Travis cut Randy's feet free first, then his hands, which fell limply at his sides the moment they were free. Lastly, he cut the blood-soaked rope that was across his brother's chest. Randy fell forward, but Travis pushed him back into the chair.

Tapping his brother on the cheeks, Travis tried to rouse him. "Randy! Come on, man! Wake up! We have to go! Randy! Randy, wake up!"

Randy didn't make a sound, and his skin seemed strangely cold under Travis' hands. An icy feeling moved through Travis, and he felt like cold hands had reached into his chest and clutched his heart. "No," he said to the room at large.

From behind him, he heard the man groan, and Starkey growled and tightened his grip on the man's throat. Travis turned and watched the pair for a few seconds, then turned back to Randy. Both sides of

Randy's neck and face were swollen, but one significantly more than the other. Travis chose the less swollen side to try to find a pulse but couldn't. He picked up his brothers' wrist and pressed two fingers against it, exhaling in relief. He could feel life thumping rhythmically beneath his fingers. Randy was alive.

Behind him, the man groaned again; he was coming to. Travis knew they didn't have much time. He went into the kitchen and filled up a glass with cold water, then came back into the living room and threw the water in Randy's face.

There was surprisingly little reaction, but his head came up about an inch, and his one good eye flickered open. Travis kneeled in front of him and cupped Randy's head in his hands, forcing the other boy to look at him. "Randy! It's me, Travis. Look at me!"

Randy's eye took a little too long to focus on him but finally did, and there was a tiny flash of recognition there. "I need you to run. Can you run?"

Slowly Randy nodded. Travis wasn't convinced, but there really wasn't all that much choice. He looped his arm under Randy's and forcefully pulled his brother to his feet. Randy swayed a bit but managed to stay upright. Travis pushed him towards the door. "Go! I'm parked at Mrs. Hellen's! Get to the truck!"

As Randy stumbled outside, Travis turned full circle in the living room, scanning for anything they may need. He grabbed Randy's wallet off the table but didn't see his car keys anywhere. After seeing the shape Randy was in, he regretted parking so far away. Randy couldn't move very fast, and the psycho on the floor was coming to quickly, judging by Starkey's increased growling.

The man on the floor made a noise that was almost a curse and tried to push Starkey away from him. Starkey growled and tightened his grip. The man stopped moving and held completely still. His eyes were now open. He recognized danger when he saw it, and Starkey was about as dangerous as a man's best friend could get. He wouldn't break the skin of the man's neck, not until Travis told him to, but if the man were to thrash around, well, accidents did happen.

Travis took one last look at his home, then turned and ran out the door. He found Randy at the end of the driveway, leaning over with his hands on his knees, trying very hard to stay upright. Travis grabbed his arm and pulled him forward. "It's not far. C'mon, we need to run."

Randy stumbled into a half-run and nearly fell, but Travis still had a hold of his arm. "Not far, c'mon!" he urged his brother on. Randy nodded and seemed to gather himself up; he began to run clumsily but quickly down the street towards where Travis' truck was parked.

When they were some forty feet from the house Travis turned and yelled at the top of his lungs "Starkey! Release! Come!" He didn't wait to see if the dog was coming or not. He trusted his dog and knew that the animal was well trained.

Ten seconds after he had called off Starkey, Travis heard the door slam into the side of the house, followed by an angry, incoherent yell. The mad man was behind them now, and with the way Randy was running, it wouldn't take much for him to catch up. Thankfully, they were nearly to the truck, and by that time, Starkey was already running beside him. They would make it. . . .

"Oh Shit!" Travis skidded to a stop and stared unbelievingly at Mrs. Hellen's empty driveway. His truck was gone. He had parked it right there, and it was gone. "Oh no, oh god!" Travis smacked his forehead, breathing hard. There was a homicidal maniac behind him, a very injured brother beside him, and his truck had been fucking stolen!

Something zoomed past Travis' ear, and he instinctively ducked to the side.

Make that a homicidal maniac *with a gun* behind them!

Travis didn't dare look. Instead, he pushed Randy into a run again. "Go go go go go!"

They were nearly to the end of the street and without looking back, Travis knew the maniac was closing on them. Their street only had one street light, and it was dark enough to make aiming with a gun very difficult. Starkey had messed up his leg pretty badly, which was probably the only reason he hadn't caught up to them yet, but soon he may be close enough to shoot accurately. Travis was panicking. He didn't know how things could have gone so terribly wrong, and he didn't know how he was going to save Randy or himself.

The sound of screeching tires temporarily distracted him from the danger, and he skidded to a stop, half holding Randy up. Danger was ahead too. A late 80's model blue sedan screeched onto their street, taking the corner at well over sixty miles per hour, and sent gravel flying as it spun around them expertly. If Travis hadn't been terrified, he would have been impressed. It looked like something out of a Tarantino movie as the car came to a stop some ten feet away and the passenger door flew open. "Get in!" the driver yelled to them.

Travis stood still, stunned, as he held onto Randy. "Laura?" he asked.

"Get in!" she screamed as another bullet whizzed past them and into the back door of the car with a *metallic ting*. No choice.

"Go! Get in!" Travis pushed Randy towards the open passenger's door, and he grabbed the handle of the back door and jerked it open. "In!" he yelled to Starkey, who didn't hesitate and dove into the car, his master a split second behind him.

The moment they were in the car, Laura floored it and the car took off, peeling rubber, the momentum shutting both the doors. They left their pursuer in a cloud of smoke and burnt tires.

"Randy, you okay?" Travis asked. When his brother didn't answer, Travis scooted over and reached up between the seats to pull at the lever that would recline Randy's seat. He looked bad, worse than Travis had originally thought. "Randy, talk to me, man."

"I think he passed out," Laura said as she turned to head out of town and floored it again.

"What the hell are you doing?" Travis demanded. "We need to get to a hospital!"

"No hospitals," Laura said calmly. "It will be the first place he'll look."

Travis leaned his head back against the seat, exhausted, and clutched his upper left arm which suddenly hurt like mad. He looked down at it and realized it had been grazed by a bullet. Adrenaline must have kept him from feeling it.

"Who are you?" he asked.

"My name is Laura…." she began.

"That wasn't what I asked, and you know it!" Travis snapped, too tired and scared to play games.

She sighed and made eye contact with him in the rearview mirror. "I'm a Seer," she said. "Like you."

Chapter 10

"Okay, lay him down on the bed," Laura said, holding the door open for Travis, who was carrying Randy fireman style. Travis ducked through the door, careful not to smack Randy's head on the frame.

Travis was acutely aware of how broken Randy felt as he lowered him onto the not quite clean looking bed of the sleazy motel. Outside, they could hear a car alarm going off and a dog barking. This wasn't a good neighborhood, but it was one of the only places you could find that allowed you to pay with cash. Laura had paid for only five hours; she said it was important that they keep moving.

But Randy needed some medical attention, so here they were, smack dab in the ghetto of Sacramento, when they should have just gone to a hospital. Travis could see why they hadn't in Chico, but he didn't understand why they couldn't take Randy *here*. Laura assured him she knew what she was doing, but Travis was skeptical; Randy looked bad.

Travis stepped back from the bed, shut the door to the room and locked all four locks on the door. He also made sure the curtains were drawn securely over the one window. When he turned back towards them, he saw that Laura was cutting Randy's shirt off with a pair of sewing scissors. She was professional enough not to acknowledge the horrific scars across Randy's chest, which impressed Travis. Randy's scars had ruined more than one relationship for him and had brought at least three people to tears..

"I have stitches, but I'm going to need bandages, peroxide, medical tape, and a lot of ice, maybe some cooling pads too, to bring down the swelling," Laura said, not looking at Travis, already attending to a large, swollen and bruised cut across Randy's left pectoral. The cut was deep and was still bleeding. Without turning from her patient, she reached into her coat pocket and held out her car keys to him. "Don't use a debit or credit card. They show up too quick. If they process checks electronically, you best stay away from that too."

Travis sighed. That didn't leave him with very many options. He wasn't in the habit of carrying a lot of cash on him, and going to an ATM would leave a record as easily as any purchase would. He picked up Randy's wallet, which Laura had deposited on the little table in front of the window when she had come in, knowing Randy normally had cash. "Anything else?"

"Yes." Laura nodded. "Medication. He's going to be hurting for a while. Get as much ibuprofen and aspirin as you can, though I'm not sure if it will help him much, the condition he's in."

Travis nodded and left without another word. He waited just outside the door until he heard Laura engage the first lock, then he walked to the car. He was pissed about his truck being stolen, pissed about his brother getting the shit beat out of him, pissed about his house, pissed at the sonofabitch psychopath that had forced them into this situation. He really had too many reasons to be pissed. He forced himself to take several deep breaths.

He turned on the car and pulled out of the driveway as the sun was coming up in the distance. He drove past a Walgreens on the corner and kept driving some thirty blocks into a slightly better neighborhood. He pulled up to an apartment building that was nicer than the ones around it due to the new paint and landscaping that was actually taken care of. Travis took the stairs to the upper floor two at a time and half jogged down the hallway until he came to the second to last apartment on the left and rapped the door as hard as he could.

He waited a full minute, then knocked on the door again; after he had repeated this cycle three times, he finally heard life grumbling within. "All right! Who's got the death wish!" Somebody growled as the door was flung open. Travis was confronted by a large black man, easily as tall as Travis and way more muscular. The man looked like a walking wall, toned to the core, biceps probably as large as Travis' head, and a scowl that would kill a nun. All this was offset by the hot pink, lacy tank top he was wearing on top of his grey sweats.

Since coming out of the closet a year ago, Dwayne strived to make his sexuality as clear as possible, and it seemed that this fact held true even while he was sleeping. Dwayne was the opposite of any stereotype Travis had ever heard about homosexuality. He was buff, he was mean, he hated any kind of music that wasn't rap, and he was proud of the five...or was it six now?...homophobes he had put in the emergency room since coming out. He blinked in surprise as he was confronted with Travis, and his scowl instantly turned into one of concern. "What the fuck happened to you?"

"Long night," Travis said and stepped into the apartment without asking for permission. He pulled the door closed behind him, a fact that was not lost on Dwayne. "Are you in trouble?"

"Yep," Travis said. He sank onto a futon next to the door and buried his head in his hands. "Yeah, I guess you could say that."

"Who the fuck is it?" Dwayne's brother, Damon, yelled from a bedroom down a short hall. "Did you kill the bastard yet!"

"It's Travis," Dwayne hollered back and sat down in a recliner opposite Travis. "What happened? You look like you've been through hell."

"Have," Travis mumbled into his hands as Damon came into the room. Equally as large and toned as his brother, Damon was made even scarier by the white burn scars that decorated one side of his face in a stark contrast against his ebony skin. A parting gift from his abusive father when he was four. The burning was the last memory Damon had of his father. His mother had put a bullet in the man's head two hours later, after coming home from work and seeing what he had done to her boy. She was given twenty-five years for the murder, something the entire community still considered a massive injustice. Self-defense was off the table. She had taken her son to the emergency room, then gone back home, grabbed her gun, and gone from one bar to the next looking for him. It was premeditated, pure and simple.

After their mother's arrest, the twin boys had been placed with their grandmother until she had a stroke. Then they were handed over to the state at age ten, which was where Travis had met them. They, too, had been fostered by Momma. Outside of Randy, Travis could safely say that Dwayne and Damon were two of his best friends.

Damon had only been in the room thirty seconds when he zeroed in on the bullet graze on Travis' arm. "Who shot at you?" he demanded.

"Long story," Travis said, looking up at him. "You still selling?"

"What?"

"Pain meds? Vicodin? Percocet? Anything that would make somebody stop hurting?" Travis elaborated.

"Yeah, but I don't sell to you. Randy is scary persuasive."

Travis laughed. "It's for Randy," he said, and then he told them what happened, leaving out why he was in Mount Shasta. They didn't need to know how much of a freak he was. When Travis got to how messed up Randy was, Dwayne stood up and punched a hole in the wall. Both of them were fiercely devoted to their friends, and the idea that somebody had tortured Randy, who they thought was a saint, made their blood boil.

Damon didn't have his brother's explosive temper. He was more calculating; he thought things through like a chess player. He sat on the futon beside Travis doing an excellent impression of that old sculpture "the thinker".

"So, this chick you're with? She says that this guy wants you dead, probably because of who you are which you're not even sure of, and he has the means to track you?" Damon asked.

"Yeah, that's it," Travis said. He felt relieved to have told somebody about what was going on.

"Hey, Dwayne?" Damon turned to his brother.

"Yeah?"

"When you leaving for San Diego?"

"Tomorrow, why?" Dwayne frowned.

"You're gonna be gone how long?"

"Two weeks."

"Okay," Damon stood up. "Say you take Travis' card with you, stop periodically to get coffee or a bite to eat or something."

"Why?" Dwayne asked. Travis wasn't really following, either.

"Because," Damon turned to Travis with a grin, "that will make it look like Travis here is heading straight for Mexico."

***

Travis had one arm full of a large paper bag and the other carrying a bag of crushed ice, so he had to knock with his elbow. On the other side of the door, he heard Starkey's tail begin to wag. A moment later, he was faced with an angry Laura. "What took you so long?" she asked huffily.

"I went to visit a friend," Travis snapped back, unsure why he was defending himself from this girl whom he didn't know and who was yet to answer any of his questions. "I may have bought us some time."

"What do you mean?" she asked as she snatched up the paper bag and carried it to the bed. Randy already looked much better. She had done a good job cleaning him up. She had washed the blood and dirt off him with a wash rag and had already stitched up most of the larger cuts. She was currently working on a five-inch-long cut on his right shoulder.

Laura dug into the bag and pulled out an ice pack. "Hold this against your face," she said, pressing the pack into Randy's hand and bringing it up to the extremely swollen side of his face.

"Heartless woman!" Randy growled.

"Stop being such a baby," Laura snapped, unremorseful, and went back to her stitching.

Travis came around to the other side of the bed, having not realized that Randy was awake until just then. "How are you doing?" he asked his brother.

"I think I'm having a bad day." Randy slurred his words, but he was still understandable. "I'll live though. The psychological torture may be harder to get over."

"Yeah." Travis sank into a chair beside the bed. "I wonder how he knew to do that? I mean, he said he was a cop, and if that's true, he would have access to records. But since you changed your name, I would think that it would be more difficult to connect the two."

"They have ways of knowing things," Laura said quietly.

"They?" Travis asked.

"Hunters," Laura clarified, glancing up at him once before going back to what she was doing.

"What do they hunt?" Travis was almost afraid of the answer.

"Us," Laura said. "They hunt us."

"He said you aren't human," Randy said quietly.

"What?" Travis leaned forward to hear him better.

"That guy, the lunatic, he said you aren't human," Randy said a little louder.

"I'm not human?" Travis asked no one in particular. A cold chill moved through him. He had always known he was different, but if he wasn't human, what was he?

"You're more than human," Laura said. "So am I." She looked up to see the bewildered look on Travis' face and sighed. "We're human, but we are also more. We are Seers. We see tragedies, one at a time, and through our actions, we curve fate. We shift the balance." She tied off the end of Randy's stitches and cut it with the scissors. Then she began dabbing peroxide onto them with a cotton swab, causing Randy to hiss. "We are ancient. There have been Seers on this planet throughout the expanse of human history, but for the most part, we are legend, mythology, and we like it that way."

She leaned back, set the peroxide down, and pushed her hair behind her ear. "And for as long as there have been Seers, there have been Hunters. Hunters exist to kill Seers. They believe that Seers destroy the natural balance. That we save people who are meant to die, and through the centuries, they have been obliterating us. The last hundred years have been particularly devastating. With the advent of credit scores and social security numbers, computers and record keeping, it has become much harder for us to disappear, and much easier for the Hunters to find us. There are few of us left."

"So…." Travis stood and began to pace. "They try to kill us, and we run? That's the way it works? We don't defend ourselves?"

"There are rules," Laura said. "Rules that have existed for millennia. These rules give Seers a slight advantage, and when they are broken, all hell tends to break loose. This particular Hunter is showing certain disregard for the rules that I find disturbing." She began putting bandages over some of Randy's larger cuts. "Until now, he's just been using you as bait to draw out other Seers. He must have grown impatient, for him to be after you like this."

"What do you mean, using me as bait?" Travis asked.

"He's been watching you for some time, hoping that you will lead him to other Seers. He knew that you were outside of the protection of other Seers, but he also knew that you were too valuable for other Seers to not be keeping tabs on you. You were twenty-one years old by the time the Hunter caught wind of you, which means somebody was covering your tracks. The Hunter knew this. He figured all he had to do was wait. But then he realized that we were onto him and he would have to do something drastic to make us come out. He was planning on making his move at that motel when I showed up. My presence threw him off. He already knows about me, but I'm not twenty yet, so he can't kill me. It's one of the rules. I thought that would be the end of it. But instead, he followed you home and…."

"He shot me," Travis finished.

"He's over being patient now. He wants you. It's very difficult for a Hunter not to kill a Seer once he's onto him or her. Everything in them, their entire being, yearns for the kill. Killing us is their life's work, their primal instinct. He couldn't wait any longer. But then you left, and Randy was his only link to you." She gave Randy an apologetic look. "He was probably planning on using you for the same purpose that he used Randy: bait. He was going to torture you and wait for more Seers to come for you. You surprised him, though."

"How so?"

"You fought back, viciously. That is very uncharacteristic of a Seer. We too have primal instincts, and one of them is to stay as far away from a Hunter as we can. We can sense when they are near, a feeling of something not being right, a calm before a storm, a tension in the air that only we can feel. Our first instinct is to get the heck out of there. You fighting back the way you did, it's not normal Seer behavior. You threw him off. It probably won't happen again. He knows you're different now."

"So…" Travis began. "Is…I mean, how…." He chewed on his lower lip for a moment. "This Hunter, is he the reason why no one came for me after I was found in that river?"

She looked down at the floor and was quiet for a moment. "Most likely," she began. "A Hunter attacked your family….and you somehow escaped, survived, and were able to slip into the system. Hunters are not allowed to kill a Seer under the age of twenty; it's one of the most sacred rules. Seers don't reach full maturity until then. Also, a Hunter is not supposed to attack families, or attack a Seer in his or her home. The Hunter that attacked your family must have been a rogue."

"That's why nobody ever came for me," Travis said softly. "They were all dead."

"Most likely." Laura shrugged. "It's possible that when your loss of memory became apparent, the surviving members of your family allowed you to enter the system as a means to hide you, especially if a Hunter was already onto them. It's also possible that you were the only survivor. All that matters now is that the Hunter has our scent, and it's very hard to lose a Hunter once he's onto us. You mentioned buying us some time when you came in. What did you mean?"

Travis told them about his visit to Dwayne and Damon's place and about Damon's idea of leading a false trail towards Mexico. Laura listened intently, letting him finish before she asked any questions. "And you trust these men?"

"I'd trust them with my life," Travis said confidently.

"You trust them with your money? What is he going to do with the card when he gets to San Diego?" Laura went back to dabbing at Randy's stitches with peroxide.

"Shred it. And of course I trust them with my money! Dwayne has more integrity then just about anybody I know."

"A drug dealer with integrity, huh?" she said, but not in a cynical way. It was more contemplative.

"Damon is the drug dealer." Travis snapped.

Laura blushed. "I'm sorry. I didn't mean to insult your friend."

Travis got the distinct impression that she desperately wanted him to like her, and to his surprise, he realized that he did. There was a certain quality to her that made him want to trust her, an openness that Travis had rarely seen in his life. But she was hiding something from him; he could read it clearly in her eyes. Whatever it was she was hiding, she was afraid of what would happen when he found out.

Randy was looking back and forth between them. He had the look of somebody who had just figured something out. He got the same look when he figured out the end of a movie ten minutes in. "What?" Travis asked him.

Randy shook his head. "Um…nothing." He pulled the ice pack away from his face and gingerly touched the tender skin, wincing. "So…did you get the drugs?"

"Oh, yeah." Travis got Randy a glass of water and shook a pill out of the Ziplock baggy that Damon had given him. *Maybe I should cut it in half?* Travis thought. Randy had a pretty low tolerance for these things. He seldom took pills, not even when he hurt his back, and preferred to suffer through things.

"Just give it to me," Randy said, holding out his hand. His eagerness to take the pill spoke volumes about how much pain he was actually in. Travis didn't argue with him and handed the pill over with the glass of water. Randy had taken a major beating for him; he wasn't going to argue with the guy about over-medicating himself.

"So," Travis said, turning away from Randy, "I'm a Seer? What exactly does that mean?"

"It's not without its perks," Laura said, hoping to give Travis an updraft in this downward spiral.

"Which are?" Travis rubbed his face; he was exhausted.

"Luck favors Seers," Laura said. "If you were to sit down and take a multiple-choice test, without having known any of the information ahead of time, you would probably get eighty percent. My father says that it is the universe's way of taking care of us. Being a Seer takes up a great deal of one's life. It's not as though we can ignore what we see. It's almost physically impossible, and with that being the case, it's hard for us to hold down jobs. The new age and all the technology it offers leaves us at a disadvantage.

"Migrant workers used to be much more common. We could come into town, work a few odd jobs and then keep moving. But those days are gone now. To get a job, you must put down a social security number, have a background check, work experience and what not. This makes it harder for Seers to work, and easier for Hunters to track us.

"But, like I said, luck favors Seers. We are not guaranteed to win in a game of chance, but we are more likely to. At the same time that we are favored, we have an ingrown disposition against gambling. Our instincts tell us not to, which is a survival technique. Hunters know how most Seers make their living, so they keep an eye on large jackpot winners, which may be how he found you."

"I told you it was a bad idea," Travis said to Randy with a sideways glare. Randy ignored his brother's jab.

"Also," Laura went on, "Seers can read personalities. We don't literally see inside people, but we know who to trust and who not to. This, too, is for protection. We can also instantly recognize other members of the Third Kind."

"Third Kind?" Travis asked.

"Other people who are…more than human. It's the term my father uses for us," Laura tried to clarify. "Hunters and Seers are not the only ones. There are also Changers, people who can move between human and animal form. Changers like to blend in with the rest of the world, like us, and they closely guard their secret. Over the last couple hundred years, however, factions have formed among them, almost like mobs, and they have been warring amongst themselves for generations.

"There are also the Flyers, humans adapted for flight. They literally have wings and seldom mix with the general populace because they find it so hard to hide themselves. They live in secret communities, usually at very high elevations up in the mountains, and they do not trust those who are not of the Third Kind. They have every reason to fear humans; they were hunted to near extinction several thousand years ago.

"And then there are the….." Laura began but stopped when Travis held up his hand.

"Stop," Travis said. "Please, just stop. I think my brain just stopped working. This is too much to take in right now. I just…." He stood and looked around the room helplessly. "I need some time to let this sink in." Laura nodded in understanding.

"You guys aren't very creative, are you?" Randy asked sleepily.

"Pardon?" Laura said.

"The guys that see are called Seers, the guys that change are called Changers, the guys that fly are Flyers….Not very creative."

Laura smiled at him adoringly, like he was a very small child who had just said the cutest thing she had ever heard, and patted his hand. "Our Latin names are a little more glamorous, though they mean basically the same thing."

Yeah, Travis thought, *they mean different, not normal…freak.*

Chapter 11

Travis was tapping his foot against the ground impatiently and drumming his fingers against the glass tabletop. Randy had been gone for too long. Something must have gone wrong. He pulled his phone out of his pocket and stared at it for a moment, debating calling his brother.

"Will you stop that?" Laura asked. She was sitting across the table, calmly reading a book as though there was no mad man with a bloodlust after them. "Everything is fine."

"He's been in there a long time," Travis said, leaning back in his chair and staring across the street at the bank.

"He's only been gone twenty minutes, and as stiff and as sore as he is, he's not going to be moving very fast. You act like we're doing something illegal," she said without taking her eyes off her book. Travis hated how indifferent she was to their situation, how calm and collected she always was. He knew she was scared; he could sense that in her. He wished she would show it a little.

Despite how annoyed she made him, Laura was really beginning to grow on Travis. She was a take charge personality, but at the same time could be very sweet and had a wicked sense of humor. His heart wanted to trust her, but his brain had other plans. His brain kept telling him that this girl had shown up out of nowhere the day he was gunned down in his home. Randy had told him she was at the hospital with him that night, and then she had shown up again two days ago, when they were running for their lives. If she was a Seer, like him, all that could be explained, but still, he didn't want to trust her.

His *heart* trusted her, though, and his brain was quickly losing the battle. Randy, Travis knew, already trusted her, but Randy was a pushover. Plus, Randy also thought she was hot. They had discussed her looks the night before while Laura was out picking up some food.

Laura glanced up from her book and pushed her long hair back behind her ear. "There he is," A slight smile of relief lit her face. Travis turned and looked across the street as Randy emerged from the bank. They were sitting outside of a local coffee shop in Willows, California, a small town a few hours north from Sacramento. It was a nice place and a beautiful day, the kind of place that Travis would enjoy if he weren't so tense.

It seemed like half the town had come out today, and there were conversations going on everywhere around them. Very few of the tables of the coffee shop were empty, and almost all of the patrons were outside taking in the sun. Despite the jovial atmosphere, several people halted their conversations to watch as Randy walked by. A few people winced just looking at him.

Randy ignored them, of course. He knew he looked like a train wreck, but cuts healed and bruises faded. He would be back to his handsome self in a few weeks. He pulled up a chair and sat down stiffly. "Wire transfer went through just fine, and I closed the account. They wouldn't give me cash, though, and gave me a weird look when I asked. I laughed it off and said it was a joke. We'll have to go somewhere else to cash the check." He reached back and rubbed his shoulder for a moment. "I think they thought I might have been in some kind of hostage situation. Can't blame them for being cautious. The security guard asked me what had happened about six times." He winced, unable to reach the spot on his shoulder that was bothering him. "I don't like having this much money on us."

"It probably won't last us very long." Laura said. "We need to disappear for a while. I have a plan, somewhere we can go to lay low for a bit." She pushed a large cup across the table towards Randy. "Here, I got you a vanilla frap."

"Where?" Travis asked, noticing how vague she had been.

"Out in the middle of nowhere. How are you guys at roughing it?"

"Define roughing it?" Travis leaned forward. "I mean, are we talking tents and sleeping bags or eating squirrels and wearing skins here?"

She smiled at his joke. "Tents and sleeping bags, but we'll have to carry everything in. It's at least three miles off of any road and isolated."

Travis glanced at Randy. He wasn't up for a three-mile hike, especially weighed down with a pack. "When?" he asked Laura.

Laura, too, glanced at Randy. "A few more days, maybe a week."

Randy was no idiot; he knew they were thinking he wasn't up for it. But he also knew that they were right. He couldn't pull off something like that, especially in steep terrain, in his condition. "Sounds fine to me," Randy said, taking a drink of his vanilla frap.

"We still don't know if your ruse with the debit card worked yet," Laura said, "So we'll need to keep moving. This Hunter is very persistent."

"Do you have much experience with these people? Hunters?" Tavis asked.

Her eyes got distant for a moment, and something dark seemed to settle over her. There were memories she didn't want to remember. Travis had seen the trauma response before in countless foster siblings. He recognized the look. Sometimes, the only way to protect yourself and heal was to push the dark away into the deepest recesses of your soul and never open that door again. He didn't want to push her, but he needed to know.

She looked away. "It doesn't matter."

"Yes, it does" Travis said softly but firmly. "Listen, I know you were probably raised in this world, but all of this is new to me. This guy already tortured my brother and tried to kill me. I want to know what else he is capable of. What people like him are capable of. I don't want any more surprises."

She took a deep breath, not looking at either of them as she spoke. "When I was young my family was attacked by two rogue Hunters. They killed my uncle right in front of my brother and me. They shot him in the head." She closed her eyes. "I didn't even know what had happened at first. The wetness hit me, and I thought my brother had thrown something at me, but it was pieces of my uncle. Blood and…other stuff." She opened her eyes and looked down at her lap, trying to hold back tears.

"We lost my uncle and my brother. My mother was hurt badly, but she survived. My dad says luck was with us that day, but I don't think so. Hunters are not supposed to attack families. My mother isn't even a Seer. My brother and I were underage, but they came after us anyway. Some of them are like that, they just destroy and no one no where is safe. Rogues are the most dangerous kind," She shivered despite the warmth of the day and rubbed her arms.

"I know you weren't raised in this world," she said, finally looking at Travis. "Maybe that's a blessing."

"I'm sorry," Travis said.

She shrugged again. "It was a long time ago."

"I *am* sorry." Travis insisted.

She nodded and graced him with a sad little smile before catching Randy out of the corner of her eye. He was watching her with those piercing blue eyes of his. With half of his face still considerably swollen and discolored, it was very hard to read his expression. His eyes spoke volumes, though, and they were looking right through her. She wondered if he knew what she was hiding.

"That's disgusting," Laura said, turning up her nose as she watched Travis shove a glob of cheese, sour cream, meat, and olive covered tortilla chips into his mouth. She snatched a napkin out of the holder and tossed it across the table at him. He grinned and used the napkin to wipe at his mouth.

"There's no clean way to eat nachos," he said as he snatched up another chip and used it to scoop up some refried beans.

"You can try using a fork?" She took a bite of her salad, holding the fork daintily as if she thought Travis needed a demonstration.

"There are so many things wrong with that sentence, I don't even know where to begin," he said and scooted over a bit so that Randy could sit down beside him. Randy looked at the plate in front of him, which had arrived while he was in the bathroom, and made a noise close to a moan. He picked up part of the club sandwich and made several attempts to take a bite before realizing his face was still too swollen. He picked up a knife to cut it into smaller pieces.

"Do you ever eat anything remotely healthy for you?" Laura asked.

"As a rule, no," Travis said.

"How do you stay in such good shape?"

"I run a lot."

She turned to Randy. "Please tell me you don't share the same death wish."

Randy shrugged and shoved a french-fry in his mouth. Laura rolled her eyes and looked away. "You two are pitiful." She grabbed her coke and took a long drink, then dabbed at her mouth with a napkin. Always so proper, she even had a napkin in her lap. Travis guessed she had a pretty posh upbringing. She was a debutante even if she tried to hide it.

Travis had just opened his mouth to ask if his theory was correct when the waiter walked over to refill their water cups. Travis leaned back and put his hands in his lap, an action that had become second nature to him by this time. He didn't even notice that Laura had done the exact same thing.

Randy noticed, though, and he grinned at the two of them. They had no clue how similar they really were. Travis had developed a kind of dance, a way of movement while in public in order to keep physical contact with strangers at a minimum. Randy had become so used to his brother's behavior, he didn't even notice it anymore. But now, watching the two of them sitting across from each other, the mimicry was obvious. The sociology of Seers; what a concept.

"Dude, what happened to you?" The waiter asked, eyeing Randy.

"Extreme Frisbee. I don't recommend it," Randy said with a straight face.

The waiter started to grin, but then recognition flashed across his face and he said, "You're that guy that they are looking for, aren't you?" He seemed sure now. "Aren't you supposed to be dead?"

The three of them exchanged a concerned look. "Where did you hear that?" Travis asked.

"It was on the news." The waiter pointed towards a tv that was mounted on the corner of the diner. "You may want to look it up."

Travis pulled out his phone as the waiter moved on to the next table. He had been careful not to use it in case the Hunter was tracking them and had disabled his GPS. Now that they had money, he would pick up a burner eventually. He turned off airplane mode and navigated to the local news page.

Yes, it was true. The authorities were looking for them, and one or both of them were presumed dead. That's what happens when you leave your front door wide open with a bloody crime scene in the living room. Their neighbor, Mr. Jacobson, had been rightfully concerned when he had stumbled upon the obvious torture scene.

"What do we do about this?" Travis asked Laura. "We can't have the cops looking for us right now."

"Call Momma," Randy suggested. "She's got a lot of sway. If she tells the police she has heard from us and we are ok, they will listen to her. There has been a steady increase in gang violence for the last several years. Crime is getting bad. They don't have the resources to look into an assault, especially when nobody is pressing charges."

Laura nodded. "That's a good idea. Who is Momma?"

"She's our mom," Randy said. "Or as close to one as we've got."

"We're never going to be able to go home again, are we?" Travis asked, looking at his plate. He had known it was a possibility when they ran, but it hadn't quite hit him until that moment. "Nothing is ever going to be the same again. Our life as we knew it is over."

Laura nodded sadly. "I'm sorry."

Travis rolled his shoulders, trying not to let on how much it bothered him. He had moved so much as a kid. But when he purchased that house, he thought that was it. Never again would he come home to find his clothes in a garbage bag and a social worker waiting. He thought he finally had a true and permanent home.

"It's ok," Randy said quietly, knowing what his brother was feeling all too well. "We've been here before. Fosters don't get to lay down roots."

Chapter 12

Tim Harvey brought the coke he was drinking to his lips and watched the four guys across the room. The Denny's was a big place and relatively crowded and loud. Still, Tim had a keen ear, and he had no trouble following the four men's conversation. One Hispanic with a surprisingly southern accent, two white guys, one with brown hair, one blond, and a huge Black guy. All of them were wearing a uniform of some kind: tan slacks, brown loafers, a deep blue t-shirt. They were eating and talking nonchalantly about work and for the most part, gossiping. They were here in San Diego for some kind of conference and being as it was Friday and the conference was concluding, they were thinking about heading south of the border for a little fun for the weekend.

Tim rolled his eyes and looked away a little disgusted. This was a waste of time, and their conversation was about to make him lose his lunch. He hated the mindless chit chat of the everyday citizens, he hated even interacting with the brain-dead zombies of the world. Did they even know how insignificant they were? He doubted it.

It hadn't taken him long to figure out that he was chasing the four men, and not that creature that had surprised him. At first, he thought it was one of the two white guys using the card, as the two ethnic gentlemen had been in the back seat and never taken a turn driving. It wasn't till they were in the city that he was able to narrow it down to the large black man. He hesitated, though. There had to be a reason why this man was using a debit card that was not his own. He didn't act suspicious, didn't act like it had been stolen, and he only used it for small purchases, which lead Tim to believe that he was purposely leaving a paper trail.

Tim had been well past Las Angeles when he had realized this, but he had followed the men all the way to San Diego, sure that this man knew where Travis Williams was. He was hesitant to confront the man openly. The guy was huge, and Tim was in no hurry to get his arms ripped off. Besides, he was also injured. That damned dog had done a number on his leg. Tim liked dogs, which was why he didn't kill the thing the first time around. He wouldn't make that mistake again.

Though he was still limping, his leg was recovering nicely. Fifty stitches would do that. Still, he needed to take Dwayne off guard, needed to surprise the man. The only question was, could he kill him. If Dwayne had been saved at some point by a Seer, then his life was forfeit. He could kill him at leave and enjoy himself. After all, there was no crime in killing somebody who shouldn't even be alive. But if Dwayne had never been slated for death, if he had never been saved when he was meant to die, then Tim's hands were tied. There was a difference between justice and murder.

He had spent the last day looking into Dwayne's past, which was how he had found the connection between him and Travis. They had spent a year at the same foster home and must have stayed in touch. It made sense, given their mutually tragic backgrounds. Tim looked forward to finding out just how good friends they were.

****

Dwayne threw a ten down on the table and pushed back his chair. "I'll catch you guys at the conference later. I think I'm heading back to the hotel to get some sleep."

"I hear you, man!" Kenny said, stretching. "Five o'clock is way too early to be doing anything. Why the hell they got to start these things so damn early?"

Dwayne shrugged. "Hell if I know! If I had it my way, the sun wouldn't rise till ten at the earliest. See you guys later!" He waved at them and headed for the door. He paused to hold it open for a thirtyish man with thinning brown hair who smiled and thanked him, then walked across the street to the hotel. He hung out outside for a couple of minutes to smoke before going inside, then took the elevator to the third floor where he was staying.

He was standing outside his room, fumbling with his keycard when it happened. A man opened the door across the hall and stepped out into the hallway. Dwayne barely glanced at him and went back to trying to detangle his keycard from his pocket. A split second later, he felt a sharp pain in his arm and pulled away, whipping around to face the man behind him. His first thought was that he had been stabbed, but what faced him was much worse. Instead of holding a knife, the dude was holding a syringe.

"What the fuck is wrong with you, man!" Dwayne demanded, reaching up to rub at his arm and feeling that the needle had broken off in his skin. He pulled it out and looked at it, then looked his attacker up and down. He recognized the guy: it was the one he held the door for. He had to be out of his mind! Dwayne was huge, and this guy stood no chance against him in a fight.

Dwayne vision began to blur, and his whole body felt heavy. He stumbled back against the door. "What…what the fuck did you do to me!" he demanded,, but his voice sounded far away. Then he was on the floor, not remembering how he got there, and the guy that had drugged him was pulling him into the room across the hall before the whole world went black.

***

Dwayne was a big guy, and he had seldom felt as though control of a situation was out of his grasp. He had been a body builder since he was eleven years old, when some of the older kids in the home had started picking on his brother and him. By the time he was fifteen, he was already over six feet tall, and even the gangs had left Damon and himself alone. Being built like a tank, there really wasn't much Dwayne was afraid of.

The gangs of Sacramento hadn't scared him, nor had any of the other bullies he had come across in his short life. In truth, the only man Dwayne had ever been truly afraid of was his psychotic old man. He still had nightmares about the sonofabitch who had doused his brother in lighter fluid because Dwayne had failed to wipe up the water on the bathroom floor after taking a bath. He was glad his mother had ended the man.

Dwayne did not have any trouble admitting he was afraid of his father. What he was not afraid of was the skinny white guy facing him now. So this was the guy who had tortured Randy? That was hard to believe.

Dwayne knew better than to underestimate the man. He could tell the guy was dangerous, but that was okay; so was he. Something about the man seemed off. There was a cynical aspect to his smile, and something about the eyes just seemed wrong, like his expression stopped just behind the pupil. The man's voice and mannerism were outwardly friendly, but when you looked deeper, you saw that the whole act was a facade. This guy was going through the motions of a normal human being, but he wasn't quite making it.

He was sitting on the edge of one of the motel room beds ordering takeout, being polite and smiling even though the person on the other line couldn't see him. He may have even been flirting. Dwayne guessed it was a woman because this guy practically screamed heterosexual. Dwayne was baffled, but he knew this guy scared the hell out of Travis, and Travis did not scare easily. He kept that in mind.

He didn't bother pulling on whatever it was that bound him to the chair. Duct tape, he assumed, the same thing that was over his mouth. Instead, he just sat and watched the guy, waiting for his headache to go away. Whatever the bastard had drugged him with left him with one heck of a headache.

Finally, the guy hung up the phone. He wrote out a check and set it on the bedside table. He was calm—very, very calm. He had done this before.

Once the check was deposited on the bedside table, the guy grabbed another chair and pulled it up to sit directly in front of Dwayne. He pulled Dwayne's wallet out of his pocket and opened it. He held up a debit card and waved it in front of Dwayne's face. "This," he said in that lilting voice of his, "does not belong to you."

Dwayne rolled his eyes. Still duct taped, he didn't have much else he could do to vent his frustration. The guy seemed to perk up a little. "Oh, forgive me, I forgot about the tape." He reached over and savagely ripped it off, taking the top section of Dwayne's lips with it. He winced and worked his jaw, tasting blood.

"So I stole a debit card," Dwayne shrugged. "What's it to you?"

The maniac laughed, a friendly, normal sounding laugh. "You're cute," he said, "but I already know about Travis. I know you're just trying to be a good friend." He leaned forward so his nose was only an inch from Dwayne's. Dwayne debated head butting him but didn't think it would get him anywhere. "But you don't know what he is. You think he's normal, but he's not."

"Buddy, you're delusional if you think Travis Williams is normal." It was Dwayne's turn to laugh.

The man blinked and leaned back. He seemed surprised. "You know what he is." It wasn't a question. "He's a creature, a thing that has no purpose existing other than to break the natural laws. He's an unnatural flaw in the fabric of the world that must be exterminated. He probably even thinks he's human, but he is not."

Dwayne raised an eyebrow. "You got a bad reading by a psychic once, didn't you?" Dwayne leaned forward as much as his bindings allowed, which was only a few inches. "So, what if Travis is psychic? I don't really care. I don't really care if he's human, either. I know a friend when I see one. 'Sides, I figure he's a lot more human than you." Dwayne practically spit the last part at him.

The guy smiled though, undeterred. "Really? How do you figure?"

"The light in your eyes," Dwayne said, "it doesn't quite go all the way to the soul. It stops somewhere in that neutral zone. My old man had the same problem. It's called being a sociopath."

"Ah, your old man. I know a bit about him. I can read his sins in your very being, Dwayne." Something about the way he said it made the hair on the back of his neck stand up. "I'd be careful what I said if I were you. Wouldn't want to make another mistake, would you? After all, when you make mistakes, people get hurt, people get burned."

An icy chill moved through him then. How did this guy know that? How did he know it was Dwayne that their father had been punishing when he lit Damon on fire? Neither brother ever spoke of it, ever. It had been one of their father's favorite forms of torture. *You mess up and I hurt your brother, or I hurt mommy.*

There was no way this sonofabitch could have known that.

"See, I can't kill you, Dwayne. I can hurt you, but I can't kill you. Damon, now that's another story."

"Yeah, I heard you like to hurt people's families." Dwayne said, unimpressed by the bastard's bluff. "But Damon isn't as trusting as Randy, or as stupid. You won't be able to blitz attack him. He'll rip both of your arms off and shove them down your throat!"

"Who said anything about a blitz attack?" Tim grinned. "I could just shoot him, maybe even from Mrs. Ingles' balcony. You have a wonderful view of both bedrooms from there. He wouldn't even know what hit him. He'd be dead before anybody even heard the shot, which is a far cry better than the way he was supposed to die, believe me."

Tim leaned back in the chair and crossed his arms, smiling. "When Damon was sixteen, he got a job at a pawn shop. The hours sucked, but he really wanted a car. Despite those scars on his face, Damon has always been likable, always had a certain air about him that made him attractive. This, and the fact that he was already as big as the *Terminator,* made him catch the eye of a girl named Tosha. She was four years older and running with a local banger named Seid.

Damon was smart, though; he knew that girl was nothing but trouble, and he blew her off every time she flirted with him. It still made Seid mad, though, and one night, when Damon was walking home from work, a drunken Seid stepped out of an alley and stabbed Damon seven times. There were a lot of witnesses, but nobody called 911, they just let him bleed to death. Another dumb black kid got himself killed, who cares?"

Time leaned forward again. "That was what was supposed to happen, what *should* have happened! But instead of going to work that night, Damon was in detention, and his foster mom wouldn't let him go to work. Do you know why he was in detention?" He paused, and when Dwayne didn't say anything, he went on. "He was in detention because he jumped in a fight to help out a buddy. It was so uncharacteristic of Travis to start a fight like that, especially with somebody so much bigger than him. After all, Travis may be 6'1" now, but back then, he was as scrawny as could be. Travis seldom got into fights, but Damon, he lost his temper a lot. Travis knew that Damon wouldn't let that guy pound his buddy's face in, and he knew that Damon would get detention for it. He also knew what was going to happen that night."

Tim stood up so quickly, he toppled the chair, and began to pace, talking with his hands in wild gestures that Dwayne would have found comical under any other circumstance. "See, that's what they do! That's what creatures like Travis do! They save those who are supposed to die! Your brother was supposed to die! Now he's alive, and the world is not how it should be! Everything is out of balance! When people who are supposed to die, live; people who are supposed to live, die! It's wrong! The world will not tolerate the imbalance forever!"

He abruptly grabbed the chair and sat down again, leaning uncomfortably close to Dwayne. "See, there is a delicate balance between the forces of this world, forces you could not begin to understand. That balance holds the planets in their cosmic dance, it holds the tides to their predictable routine, it holds the seasons to their time, and without it, chaos reigns. Rules must be followed. And Seers, creatures like your friend; they have no respect for the rules!" He yelled the last part, snarling so forcefully that spittle landed on Dwayne's face.

Dwayne stared at him for a good twenty seconds before finally shaking his head. "You're crazy." He said, then laughed. "You're completely crazy! I mean like Rosanne on Ambien kind of crazy! Your elevator doesn't go all the way to the top floor!" Dwayne shifted his weight a little, adjusting his shoulders to make himself more comfortable. "Travis punched that guy because he was grabbing on Travis' girlfriend. If Damon is alive, then he is supposed to be alive. If he weren't supposed to be alive, he'd be dead. What's meant to be happens. There is no *supposed to* or *should have been,* you lunatic! There is only what *is*!" Dwayne was yelling now too, disgusted by the man's delusions. He was using some twisted yin and yang bullshit to justify murder, and it made Dwayne sick.

To his surprise, Tim smiled a deceptively friendly, calm smile, and gave Dwayne a little clap. "You know nothing about the forces all around you. You are nothing but a stupid little boy grasping at the wind. You have no understanding; you have no capacity for it." he sneered at Dwayne in disgust.

"Don't quote Solomon to me, you psycho!" Dwayne spit at him. "Get on with this already! You didn't drug me and tie me up to have a philosophical debate!"

Tim cocked his head to the side. "You're right." He stood up. "I didn't." He walked across the room to the bathroom, disappeared for a moment, then returned holding a red-hot curling iron and a pair of tweezers. "Shall we continue?" he asked brightly, a light finally appearing in his eyes. He sat down and replaced the duct tape over Dwayne's mouth. "Wouldn't want you to scream too loud, now would we? After all, I put a lot of thought into this."

Chapter 13

"Jeez, Starkey! You have your own burger! Leave mine alone!" Travis grumbled from the back seat, pushing the dog away from him.

Randy glanced in the rearview mirror and smiled. "Feeding him hamburgers and french-fries probably isn't the best thing in the world for him."

"He doesn't seem too upset with our current living situation," Travis said around a full mouth.

"You're disgusting," Laura said good-humoredly. "Where did you learn your table manners? A barn?"

"I don't see a table?" Travis said and took another bite. "Besides, not all of us got the silver spoon treatment."

She turned to look at him. "What do you mean?"

"Come on. The way you act, I'm guessing one of your parents is a doctor or lawyer," Travis said, wiping his mouth on the sleeve of his shirt.

"Are you saying I'm stuck up?" Laura asked, hurt far more than Travis would have thought. He wasn't trying to be hurtful, and for the life of him, he didn't know why she took him so seriously.

"No," Travis said quickly. "Not at all!" He leaned forward. "But all of your clothes are brand name, your nails are manicured, and when you speak, it's—I don't know, proper, I just think it's the way you were raised."

Laura looked thoughtful for a moment. "My mother, she's a doctor."

"Is that how you knew how to fix me up?" Randy asked.

She nodded. "I've watched my mom fix my dad up countless times after one of his interventions went bad, and when I got older, I kind of took over."

"Must be useful, being married to a doctor," Travis said.

"Yeah, if you have a choice in the matter, which I doubt you will, marry somebody in the medical profession."

"What do you mean, you doubt I will?" Travis asked.

"Seers can read people. We can read hearts, personalities, even souls if the connection is deep enough. As a result, we fall in love instantly," Laura explained. "We don't get to go through that whole getting to know somebody and slowly falling for them thing. For us, it literally is love at first sight, or rather, touch. It usually takes some sort of physical touch."

"That explains a lot," Randy said.

"Explains what?" Laura asked.

"Nothing!" Travis snapped. He was sure that Randy was about ready to mention his relationship with Sophia and how obsessed he had gotten with her before he had finally convinced her to go out with him. Laura didn't need to know that painful story, and Travis didn't feel like re-living it.

"How come you're not a complete slob?" Laura asked Randy, changing the subject.

"Oh, I am, I assure you," Randy said. "I just tend to be more proper around you ladyfolk."

"Why, Randall James, what a gentleman!" she said, patting his arm.

In the back seat, Travis choked back a laugh. Laura turned and gave him a quizzical look. "What?"

"Shut up!" Randy snapped. "Just let her keep thinking what she thinks."

"What do I think?" Laura was looking back and forth between them, a plastic fork with a cucumber on it held halfway to her mouth.

Travis wiped his mouth, smiling foolishly. "Randy isn't short for Randall."

"What else can Randy be short for?" Laura asked Randy, who was busy glaring at Travis in the rearview mirror. Undeterred by his silence, she grabbed his wallet, which he had left out after paying for the food, and flipped it open. "Randolph?" she said with a smile. "My god, your parents named you Randolph Eugene? Why don't you just go by James?"

"Because I didn't change my name until after everybody knew me as Randy," he said, annoyed.

"Don't feel too bad, Buddy." Travis leaned forward. "I don't even *know* my last name, or my mother's maiden name, for that matter."

"Father's maiden name," Laura clarified.

"What?"

"Father's maiden name, er, bachelor name I suppose," Laura repeated. "When male Seer get married, they pretty much always take their wives' name. It makes it harder to trace them through the system."

"So Nightdale is your mother's last name?"

"Yes," Laura said.

If he had married Sophia, he would have taken her last name. Not out of some need to protect himself, but out of a need to belong to a family. He had loved Sophia's family, and they had loved him. He had no attachment to the name Williams; it was just a name the state had given him.

Travis was thinking about this when something occurred to him, and he leaned forward again. "What makes you so sure that my father was a Seer? You said that one of my parents had to be a Seer, but what makes you automatically assume that it was my father?"

Laura was silent for a moment, chewing thoughtfully. "I guess I just assume," she said with a shrug. "Female Seers are less common than male Seers, and they are almost always weaker, meaning that they have a weaker route. It's more likely that your father was the Seer, but there have been some powerful female Seers in the past, they are just less common."

"What makes a Seer powerful or weak?" Randy asked as he turned into a public park.

"Their route, the path through which they see," Laura tried to explain. "See, there are different routes, the weakest of which is via direct touch. You get an insight into a person's life by physical contact. It's not always bad, as a matter of fact, sometimes it can be a very pleasant exchange. My route is direct contact," she said. "Then there are the more extreme routs, like dreams and visions. Dreams are one of the most powerful because they are the most vivid, and visions are an extremely powerful route too, though they are rare, and both can be very hard on the Seer. Extremely powerful Seers have two routes, but most Seers only have one."

"What if you have all three?" Travis asked as he got out of the car and stretched. Starkey jumped out of the car behind him and trotted over to a trash can to sniff around. Randy opened the driver's door and got out slowly. He was still stiff and sore all over but was moving a little easier. He was putting on a brave face, despite the fact that he was traveling with two Seers who knew what condition he was in no matter what he did to mask it.

"That's impossible. I've never heard of anybody that had more than two routes," Laura said as she came around the other side of the vehicle and handed Randy the bag that had his food in it. As she handed over the bag, she brushed her hand against Randy's and for the briefest moment, her eyes lost focus. Travis always avoided touching strangers accidently, but occasionally, when he came across a person he really liked, he would find ways to come in contact with them because he liked.....liked what?...the feel of their soul maybe? No, that wasn't right. It wasn't their soul he was feeling. It was more like he was feeling *them,* that person in their entirety, everything that was *them.* Before he and Sophia had begun to date and he was simply obsessed with her, he used to find ways to brush up against her in the lunch line, or while turning in papers in class. It wasn't anything sexual that drove him to make contact with her, it was more like an addiction to her. It was just like Laura had said: love at first touch.

He guessed that this was why Laura kept subtlety touching Randy: she liked the *feel* of him. He was certain that Randy didn't notice this interaction between them and hadn't guessed at the reason why. He wasn't sure of the nature of Laura's attraction to Randy. The fact that she liked the feel of him didn't necessarily mean that she loved him in a non- platonic way. After all, Travis used to brush against Momma's hand because he needed to *feel* her affection and love for him.

"What is your route?" Laura asked as they made their way across the grass to a picnic table.

"I have all three," Travis said matter-of-factly as he straddled the bench and shoved a French fry in his mouth.

Laura stared at him. "That's impossible."

Travis shrugged, his mouth full. Randy was busy unwrapping his burger, but he nodded. "It's true, he does."

"But...." Laura seemed like she was having trouble comprehending this fact.

Travis jumped; he had forgotten his phone was in his pocket until it started ringing. He pulled it out and glanced at the caller id. "It's Damon," he said to Randy, flicking the phone open. "Hey."

"Dwayne is in the hospital?" Damon said in a rush.

"What? Why?" Travis could tell by Damon's voice that something was wrong. Beside him, Randy stopped chewing and turned to look at his brother, the sudden change in Travis' voice like a silent alarm.

"He disappeared yesterday. I got a call from one of his co-workers. He never came back to his hotel room after lunch and then didn't show for the conference, either. And he was one of the speakers," Damon explained with panic in his voice.

"Why didn't you call me yesterday? We could have been in San Diego by now," Travis said, trying to keep his voice even.

"You know how he is, man. I was thinking maybe he met some guy and played hooky or something. Dwayne can take care of himself."

"Damnit, Damon! Randy can take care of himself too, and this guy nearly killed him! If he could take out Randy, he could take out Dwayne. You should have called me!"

"I know, I know," Damon said. "I wasn't worried till I got another call this morning. They found him; he was in a dumpster behind the hotel with burns all over his body. He's in the ICU. I'm on my way there now."

A familiar cold chill ran through Travis, and it shocked him to his feet. "No, Damon! No! Whatever you do, don't go there!"

"Why the fuck not! Dwayne is on life support, man! He's all I've got! You know that!"

"And you're all he's got! How is you getting yourself killed going to help him? This guy is waiting for you, Damon. He wouldn't kill Dwayne, but he would kill you. He'd love to kill you."

"Why? If he wouldn't kill Dwayne, why would he kill me?" Damon demanded.

"Because..." Travis was pacing now. "Because he thinks you're not supposed to be alive."

"I don't understand," Damon said. "I know you're physic, man, but what does this guy want with you, and what does it have to do with me?"

Travis took a deep breath. "Damon, I promise, if we live through this, I will tell you everything, but for now, you just have to trust me and not go to San Diego. Please, I know he's your brother, but I'm asking you to trust me."

There was a long silence on the other end. Travis waited patiently. Finally, after what seemed like ages, Damon sighed. "You know I've always trusted you, Travis."

"I know."

"And you promise Dwayne is going to be okay?"

"I do. He won't even scar that badly. In five years, he'll be around to introduce you to your wife."

"How do you know that?" Damon asked a little over a whisper.

"I just do. Tell me you're not going to San Diego," Travis pleaded.

"I'll wait four days, that's it. Four days."

"That's long enough. Thank you, Damon. None of this would have happened if you guys hadn't been helping me."

"Family is family, Travis. Ours may be a little multicultural and cracked around the edges, but it's still family," Damon said and hung up.

Travis pocketed the phone and turned to Laura. "Did you know this would happen?"

"What?" Laura recoiled a bit, stung by the accusation.

"You're a Seer. Did you know?" Travis asked again.

"No," Laura said.

"How could she?" Randy stood, angry at the way Travis had just spoken to Laura. "You went to Damon and Dwayne without even asking her if it was a good idea. She was back at that crappy motel putting me back together, remember?"

"I remember," Travis snapped at him, then turned and strode across the lawn, heading deeper into the park, towards the sound of running water with Starkey on his heels. He hadn't gone fifteen feet when Randy caught up to him, blocking his path.

"That wasn't cool talking to Laura like that," Randy said, keeping his voice low.

"I know, I'll apologize to her later." Travis tried to shove past Randy, but once again, Randy stepped in front of him.

"Nobody is saying this is your fault, Travis."

"Nobody is saying it, but it is. Now can you please just get the hell out of my way!"

"No," Randy broadened his stance, like he thought Travis may shove him. "This is *not* your fault, Travis! Get it through your thick head! You didn't ask for this, you didn't do this. You didn't see it!"

"Why?" Travis asked. "Why do I have to save all these strangers but when it's somebody I love…." He took a deep breath. "Why can't I protect them?"

"Because that's not the way it works."

"It should!"

"No," Randy shook his head, "it shouldn't. If you only protected the people you cared about, well, *that* wouldn't be fair. It's a great big world out there, Trav, and miracles like you and Laura, you shouldn't be caged. You didn't see what happened to Dwayne, what happened to Sophia, or anybody else we knew because you weren't meant to see it. I know that hurts, but that's the way it is, and you can't help it. You can't control it; you just act when fate tells you to act."

Randy took a deep breath. Chasing after Travis had taken more than he expected. "It sucks. It's not fair that bullshit stuff like this is on your shoulders." He looked back towards the picnic table. "But you can't run off right now, man. You can't push us away. We've got to stay together."

Travis was silent for about ten seconds before finally giving Randy a nod. "Yeah, ok," he said, trying hard to get his nerves under control. "I won't run off."

"I think it's time we head into the woods," Laura said the moment they got back to the table. She looked at Randy apologetically, "I know you are still really sore and haven't gotten your full range of motion back yet, but we really can't afford to wait any longer. We need to disappear now. Travis seems to think that the Hunter is still in San Diego waiting for Damon; that gives us a day at least to make sure our trail goes completely cold."

"Can you do it?" Travis asked Randy.

"Sure. We may want to pack a stretcher just in case, though," Randy said, shrugging. "Where is this place exactly?"

"The middle of nowhere. About ten or fifteen miles from where the Klamath and Salmon Rivers meet."

Travis' head came up. "Excuse me?"

"Is there a problem?" Laura asked, perplexed.

"No," Travis wadded up a napkin and threw it at a trashcan five feet away. He missed. "No problem at all."

Chapter 14

There was a mist settling serenely among the tall California pines, shrouding the dense forest in mystery and adding a unique beauty to an already beautiful place. Off in the distance, they could hear the roar of a river, most likely the Klamath, as its age old battle against the bedrock continued. The sun wasn't quite up yet, but already the forest was coming alive, birds were chirping, and somewhere off in the endless trees, two grey squirrels were having an argument.

It was beautiful, breathtaking, with the mountains seemingly piled on top of each other and the trees reaching to the heavens. As the sun slowly peaked it's way over the treetops, the mist that was hovering in the valleys and amongst the pines began to turn purple, then pink, then gold, the kind of scene you would find in a calendar or on a postcard. The kind of moment you would look back on in your later years and know that you had witnessed beauty in its truest form.

It made Travis' skin crawl, and he shivered in the early morning cold, blowing into his gloved hands to keep them warm. Despite the masterpiece all around them, he desperately wanted to flee, to climb back into Laura's little car and drive until he saw the ocean. He could swear there were menacing figures moving about in the mist, and he had the sense of something unholy breathing down the back of his neck.

He was keen enough to know the difference between his Seer sense and his own frayed nerves. The only ghost hiding in the darkness were his own. He had been here before, he knew this but could not remember it, just as he knew that the last time he was here, something had happened. Something so painful, his mind had hidden it from him forever. He did not want to be here.

"Are you sure about this?" he asked Laura, who was double-checking supplies.

"These woods are safe; we have friends here," Laura said, not turning to look at him. She could sense how frightened he was.

"What do you mean by that?" Randy asked.

"The Ohan, the tree people, they live in these woods, and they are friends of Seers. They will warn us if danger comes, even before our own intuition can," Laura explained.

"The tree people?" Randy raised an eyebrow at her.

"You would know them better by the name Bigfoot or Sasquatch. They are kind creatures, ferocious when need be, but they are friends. Are we ready?"

"Bigfoot?" Randy asked.

"Yes."

"Like….Bigfoot?"

"Yeah."

"I don't like it here," Travis said. "We shouldn't be here."

Laura sighed and gave him an understanding look. "The memories of the land are strong here. Bad things have happened near here, a lot of blood was spilt, blood of Hunters, Seers, and Ohan. The land remembers the battles that were waged, and that memory is so strong, even regular people can pick up on it. Hikers steer clear of this area, fishermen too. They don't know why, and for the most part, they don't even know they are doing it. It's one of the reasons we are so safe here.

"As Seers, we feel this more sharply than the average person. As a strong Seer, you feel it so acutely, you want to run. But you must push through this, Travis. Once we are in the valley, you will feel safe again, perhaps safer than you ever have."

Travis nodded, taking her at her word, and bent to grab his heavy pack from the ground. He was shivering all over, and it had nothing to do with the cold. *Push through it*, he told himself, *push through it.*

Randy came around the car to stand next to Laura, reaching around her to get his own pack out of the trunk. "Are you sure about this?" he whispered close to her ear.

Laura barely nodded. "It's time he remembers," she whispered back.

"Are we just leaving the car here?" Randy asked, louder this time.

Laura nodded. "You saw how difficult it was to get down this road. Heck, my poor car could barely make it this far. I think it will be safe here. I'll lock it up tight, though. It's still about another three and a half to four miles to get where we're going. We should have plenty of daylight left to get there and get camp set up."

"Let's get going, then," Travis called from near the beginning of the trail. "We're wasting time!"

***

Tim Harvey turned a page on the magazine he was reading and made a disgusted sound. This was what was considered important these days, what Lady Gaga kept in her bathroom? Who the fuck cares? The photo of the pop queen, looking serious in a hideous shinny dress that was probably considered the height of fashion, seemed a monument to humanity's uselessness.

What really enraged him, though, was the fact that in the same issue, there was a story on human trafficking between Haiti and the United States. Two pages were devoted to one of the worst sociological problems in the modern world, versus the seven pages devoted to Gaga's bathroom accessories and "*.....the one thing that Gaga won't leave home without!*"

He threw the magazine aside in disgust. How he hated these mindless drones, these depthless puppets pretending they mattered.

Nothing mattered—nothing but balance. As a Hunter, Tim knew this. He knew how insignificant he was, how little he mattered. But he also knew that what he *did* mattered. He protected the balance. At the very least, he had a mission, a purpose.

He was currently sitting in a hospital waiting room in San Diego, California, and it was surprisingly peaceful. Hospitals were underappreciated for their quiet. Occasionally, somebody would pass by, or a nurse would stop and ask him if he needed information or if she could help him with anything, but for the most part, people left him alone. He liked being left alone. It gave him time to think, and he needed time to think.

He was thinking about his place in the world, and the places of all those normal people around him. They were dust, nothing else, and he hated them. His father had taught his brother and him to cultivate hatred, and it was a skill he had learned well. At first, in his younger years, it had been difficult and had not come naturally. He used to have regular friends, and still did have a few people he didn't completely despise, but he had risen past that for the most part now. He had let bitterness and hatred take over, and the other emotions, the ones that came more naturally, had been pushed to the back, just as his father had taught him to do.

More than the hatred, Tim forced himself to stop understanding the people around him because understanding lead to empathy, and empathy only got in the way when it came to killing. Despite his efficiency at it, he had never grown to like killing. It was his job, and while he took pride in his work, he didn't relish taking lives. He was unlike his father and brother in that aspect.

He reached down and rubbed his leg. That damn dog! He wouldn't be back to full strength for several days. But that was okay; he had time. He glanced at the clock and stood. Damon, the damaged twin, was not going to come to his brother's aid. Tim had underestimated how much the brothers trusted the creature Travis Williams. Travis must have warned the other man because Damon would have been here by now.

It was no bother to Tim. He was hoping to kill Travis' friend, but it was not a necessity. If he did not find another Seer to hunt after he killed his current prey, he could always circle back around to end the belligerent little punk. His real goal was Travis Williams and the Nightdale family; they were the ones he was after.

But of course, he wasn't in a hurry. He had time to let his leg heal. He knew where the girl, Laura, would take Travis. They were more predictable than they knew. Laura wanted Travis to remember, and that was fine with Tim. He wanted Travis to remember too. He needed Travis to remember.

It didn't feel right killing the boy without him knowing the full extent of why. Killing Seers was his duty, of course, something he had to do, but Killing Travis and the Nightdale family would be his pleasure, and he fully intended on taking his time. Travis needed to remember how much he deserved to be killed, and what he had done to deserve it. So, Tim would bide his time, rest up, and allow his prey to rest up. Travis would wander in those evergreens, and they would do their work. Slowly, his fractured memory would heal, and he would be completely whole again. Travis Williams would die in those mountains, and Travis Nightdale would be reborn, just in time to die.

Chapter 15

Travis stared up at the roof of the tent, his fingers locked behind his head, his breathing steady. On one side of him, Randy was snoring lightly, his back turned to Travis with nothing but a ruffled patch of hair sticking out of the sleeping bag. Randy's hair was so dirty from the hike and setting up camp, it was no longer blond but an odd brown/grey.

On his other side, Laura was sleeping as well. She had French braided her hair tightly with a healthy amount of styling gel before they had departed on this venture, and apart from a few loose strands around her face, it was holding up well. She was smiling in her sleep, having a good dream, and Travis envied her.

They had decided to share a tent for many reasons, the primary ones being that it would be easier to keep warm and safer than splitting themselves up in three separate tents. One tent was also easier to pack into this remote valley. The tent was large enough to accommodate three taller than average persons and one larger than average dog, which was currently stretched out between Travis and Laura.

Before they had even begun constructing the tent, Randy pulled Travis aside and insisted that he sleep in the middle. Travis argued at first. Given his tendency to have night terrors and get violent in his sleep, he thought it would be best if he slept wedged into a corner. But he soon realized what Randy's reasons were and relented. Randy was crushing on Laura worse than he had probably ever crushed on a girl in his life, and his sleeping next to her, even in a strictly platonic fashion, may lead to an embarrassing situation which all parties would like to avoid. So, Travis was lying between his brother and the girl they still barely knew, wide awake.

He stared at the blue canvas above him and wondered why this all felt so familiar. He glanced over at Laura again and fought the urge to shake her awake and demand why she had brought him here. She wanted something from him, and he wanted to know what. But she was elusive and good at avoiding touch when she wanted to. Travis had tried to brush up against her a few times while they were setting up camp to see if he could see anything, but she had avoided him as easily as he normally avoided accidental touch with strangers. She didn't seem to mind letting Randy touch her, though, which Travis was finding increasingly annoying.

Oddly enough, he felt protective of Laura and didn't want to see her get hurt. This was odd because he thought out of the two of them, Randy was the more fragile. Randy had always had a thick wall around his heart, and in pretty much every relationship he had ever been in (which was a lot), he had always played the protector rather than the lover. While a woman needed to feel safe, she needed to feel loved and needed even more. Travis knew this because he was a Seer and had literally seen it in the hearts of nearly all of Randy's former girlfriends. All of whom at some point had realized that there was an intimate line that Randy just couldn't cross and had broken it off with him.

But Randy's interest in Laura was different. She could take care of herself; she had proven it on a number of occasions. She was not a battered woman who needed a champion; she did not need him to teach her how to trust the world again. But maybe, Randy was the one who needed her. It was almost as if Randy expected her to save him, to be his salvation, to teach him how to love on a level that had previously escaped him.

Travis worried that Laura was toying with him, and worried even more that she was not. What if, like Travis and Sophia, Laura had fallen in love with Randy at first touch. What if, when it was all said and done, Randy still was unable to cross that intimate line between protector and lover. What if Randy's deepest fears were real, and he truly was incapable of scaling that wall around his heart? Travis could only imagine what kind of impact such a thing would have on Laura. He knew firsthand how deeply Seers loved and could not imagine not having that kind of love reciprocated.

Travis lay there, staring up at the top of the tent, thinking, until the sky began to lighten outside. He carefully crawled out of his sleeping bag, put on his shoes, grabbed his jacked, and unzipped the tent slowly. He let Starkey out first, then crawled out himself, slowly zipping the tent closed behind him.

He stood and watched the foggy, dense forest all around him. With the toe of his shoe, he scraped a note in the dirt: *Went for a walk.*

He hoped they wouldn't make a big deal of him taking off. He figured Randy wouldn't, but he had no idea about Laura. He tried to tell himself he really didn't care what she thought, but he did. He wondered why it bothered him so much to upset her. After all, she hadn't been honest with them and was yet to tell them the whole truth about anything. He trusted his Seer's instincts, and they told him to trust her.

He took one look around the clearing and took a deep breath of the early, and chilly, mountain air, listening to the creek gurgling some forty feet away and some birds flirting with each other in a nearby tree. The deep forest was calm and serene, and everything about him was peaceful. The apprehension he had felt before had all but vanished once they had entered the valley, and now all he felt was the peace that the forest offered.

The deep green all around him was no longer menacing but inviting as he took off down one of the many deer trails at a slight jog, Starkey running beside him. He loved the way the ice crystals under the dirt crunched under his feet and the way his breath came out in great puffs of steam. He found this fact odd because he had never been one for cold weather. But then, he wasn't overly fond of extreme heat either.

Something about these mountains, and this valley in particular, spoke to him, and as he went deeper into the woods, farther from the creek and the camp, the stronger it got. Laura had mentioned that this Valley had special significance to Seers, and he guessed that was true.

She knows something I don't, he thought, thinking of Laura. *So does Randy.*

Travis was still very conflicted over whether or not he trusted Laura, but he did trust Randy and always would. Whatever they were keeping from him, he was sure they had their reasons, though he didn't have to like it. Slowly, as he wove his way through the woods, his thoughts turned inward, away from the troubling reality and back to more mundane things. He thought about the online role-playing game that he and Randy often played and how his character could best get past a certain obstacle, then he thought about the book he had been reading before fleeing his home and wondered where the plot was going. And he thought of Sophia; he always thought of Sophia. Slowly, he transitioned into thinking of nothing at all and simply observing the natural world around him.

This was how Travis spent the next several days: simply hiking through the valley and nearby mountains and spending as little time as possible at the camp. A couple times, Randy joined him, and Laura tried to join a few times as well, but Travis always shrugged off her invitation and took off before she could argue with him. So, for the most part, Travis wandered, and Randy and Laura hung out together at camp. They spent their night's playing card games and arguing about philosophy and politics, even which cartoon superhero could beat up which. But for the most part, Travis stayed out of the conversations as well.

It was clear something about this place made him uncertain, but not in a good or bad way. If anything, it was in a sleepy way, as if some part of him was waking up slowly and still very much wanted to go back to sleep. There was a side of him buried way back in a far corner of his soul, and this place, this valley, these trees, was desperately offering it coffee. This place meant something to him on a cosmic level, as it meant something to all Seers.

The land remembers…it remembers me.

This idea struck Travis like an icy rain as he was jogging along the creek early one morning shortly after leaving camp. He stopped so suddenly, Starkey ran into his back leg. The land remembered him specifically, and suddenly, he remembered *it.* He stood, looking up the old, worn trail. For a brief second, he saw it differently: not so overgrown, but fresh, with bright sunlight streaming in through the trees, replacing the early morning gloom that had been there only a moment before. This trail he saw in his mind was in late afternoon. It was welcoming, almost loving, and he loved to run down it.

He blinked and the image was gone, replaced by the light fog and darkness of an overcast morning, a trail with overgrown bushes threatening to engulf it, with years of pine needles and leaves covering the once well-traveled earth. This trail before him wasn't welcoming; it was sad. The difference between the image he had just seen in his head and the reality he was now faced with was so stark, he thought the land must be mourning some great loss to look so sorrowful.

Wetness on his cheek brought his hand to his face thinking dew had dripped down from the tree above, but he was wrong; he had begun to cry. Out of pure emotion, he kneeled down and took up some of the loose earth, allowing it to run through his fingers as he closed his eyes. The land held the past. It held the emotions of centuries and just waited for a Seer to come along and listen. Like a ghost haunting these trails, it longed to be witnessed.

As the dirt moved through his fingers, an image entered his mind, fuzzy, but discernable: a man stumbling down this path, exhausted, bleeding from several spots along his arms and legs, and sobbing uncontrollably. It was night, and the stars stood out brilliantly above him, but he wasn't looking at the stars; he was watching the water. As Travis watched through his mind's eye, the exhausted man leaned against a tree, threw back his head and screamed into the night.

"Travis! Travis answer me!" His voice was tight, and the echo that bounced off the mountains was unintelligible. The man paused, waiting for a response that never came, then he covered his eyes with his hands and fell to the ground, curling into a fetal position. For a brief time, he continued to sob, hands still over his face, and his tears drenched the earth beneath his head; the same earth that was currently running through Travis' fingers some ten years later.

After a few minutes, the sobbing gave way to a reserved hopelessness. The man took his hands away from his face and looked up at the stars. "Please," he whispered to the cosmos, "this can't be happening. Please, just let me *see* him, please. I just want to see him." He closed his eyes, waiting for a vision, but one never came. Soon, the tears began again, and the man, too exhausted to stand, was prepared to lie there and freeze, pleading to the woods around him in words made unintelligible by emotion.

****

Travis opened his eyes as the last of the dirt slipped through his fingers and once again, he was faced with the cold dark path before him, the icy fog causing his hairs to stand on end. He stood, pushed aside the branch of an oversized fern and continued up the path, leaving the memory of a grief-stricken father behind. He needed to keep going where the path was taking him. He needed to know why that man, who had pushed himself past the point of collapse looking for his lost son, had never found him.

Travis wasn't thinking. It was too difficult to think, too painful. A part of his mind had shut down, and the automatic part that controlled breathing and movement had taken over. He kept walking up the path, scarcely aware of anything, his hands held out so his fingertips brushed the leaves of the bushes as he passed. He needed that contact with the land. It was his anchor to reality, the here, the now. Without it, he felt like he would float away or disappear entirely. Something was happening to him, something he couldn't begin to understand, but he knew he couldn't turn back even if he wanted to.

There were several areas of the trail that had become so overgrown, it nearly disappeared, but Travis pushed through them with no regard to his own welfare or to Starkey's. He needed to know where the trail went, he needed to know where it was leading him. With every step he took, something deep within him was waking up, urging him onward.

Some two miles later, Travis crashed through some thick underbrush and stumbled into a clearing, and for the first time in close to an hour, he looked around and got his bearings. He was standing in the middle of an old campsite, large enough to accommodate three tents comfortably, with an old and worn picnic table under a pine.

One side of the campsite ended at a small cliff that dropped off to the creek some five or six feet directly below. Travis could hear the creek's steady trickle from where he stood, and the hairs on his arms and neck began to stand on end. He stood at the top of the trail for a moment, just taking in the sight of the camp, and realized that it was a remarkably beautiful place.

A blue jay began calling obnoxiously above, galvanizing his limbs into movement, and Travis began to cross the camp site. He came to the table and stared at it for a moment, sure that this was the table in the picture that Tim had left for him. He hesitantly reached out towards the old, weathered wood, but pulled back, suddenly afraid to touch it. Then, feeling ashamed for being afraid of something as insignificant as an old table, he yanked his hand out and lay his palm down on the smooth wood.

No vision came this time, but a strange feeling began moving up his arm. Travis had never felt anything like it before. It was like a missing piece of himself was being replaced, as if he were becoming whole again. This feeling moved up his arm, then spread across his chest and down his legs. It was like being electrocuted, only without the pain. He imagined this must be what a severely dehydrated person feels when an I.V. is inserted.

He removed his hand from the table as something across the clearing caught his eye. It was just a glint of metal near the base of a white oak that was growing near the edge of the drop-off, but Travis zeroed in on it as if it were a beacon. He moved across the clearing, giving the cliff's edge a wide girth, to kneel at the base of the tree. He brushed a few pine needles aside until he found the source of the light. It was a man's old, silver ring, badly tarnished on one side with a star shaped emerald set into the silver.

Travis picked it up and stared at it, feeling the cold metal rest against the palm of his hand. He was sure he had seen it before.

He stood slowly, still studying the ring, wondering if it could be saved or if it was too badly tarnished, when that damn Blue Jay began screeching again, causing Travis to jump and nearly drop the ring. He glared up at the bird some twenty feet above him in the tree and thought about throwing a rock, when something on the trunk of the tree caught his eye.

It was a bullet, there was no mistaking it. Somebody had shot a bullet into the tree, though it had been some time ago because the tree was well healed. He took a step forward and reached out to touch the wound.

As his fingertips brushed the bark, a jolt went through his entire body, causing him to stumble back and fall to his knees. He hit the ground hard, his left knee slamming into a sharp rock that cut his skin through his jeans. He was unaware of the pain because he was no longer there. Travis Williams was in another place, another *time*, entirely.

Chapter 16

"Okay, now reel it in slowly. That's too slow…there you go! That's it! Perfect!"

Travis smiled at the approval in his uncle's voice as he watched the worm slide slowly across the creek bottom, attracting the attention of several trout. None of them took the bait, which annoyed him to no end. "Good, Travis, that's good. Just keep doing that, and it will drive them crazy."

"These wild trout are so annoying; they don't bite anything! The planters back home are easy to catch!" he complained, watching as a large trout went for the bait, then changed its mind at the last minute.

"That's because the planters were raised in a hatchery, and they are used to being fed," Jeff said, kneeling on his haunches beside his nephew. "Wild ones are a lot funner to catch. They fight like mad, and they taste way better."

"Are we going to eat these?" Travis asked.

"Maybe some of them. If we catch some later this afternoon, yeah, we will. But we can't really freeze them, and fish don't keep that well," Jeff explained, picking up a pine needle and tossing it into the water. He seemed distracted and kept looking up at the ridge, back towards the road. Travis didn't really notice; he was too busy watching the fish, and he was enjoying spending some alone time with his uncle.

Jeff Nightdale lived on the other side of the United States, in Virginia, and only came to the west coast three or four times a year, usually during holidays, to visit his big brother and his favorite (and only) niece and nephew. For him to be spending two whole weeks with them was a rare treat, and Travis intended to take advantage of every moment. Especially since he and his father hadn't exactly been seeing eye to eye lately.

Thinking of his father caused Travis to glance over his shoulder at the tent where his parents were still sleeping. "Hey, Uncle Jeff?"

"Yeah, kiddo?"

"Do you think there's still time to hike up to the reservoir?" Travis reeled in his bait the rest of the way and cast it farther down the creek, hoping to sneak up on the trout.

Jeff laughed and ran his hands through his thick brown hair, once again looking back at the ridge. "Nah, we would have left a couple hours ago if we were going to do that. We were both up in time. Why didn't you say something earlier?"

Travis shrugged. "Dad said we'd go today. He said it would just be me and him."

"Oh," Jeff frowned at his nephew, sure that Travis was more hurt than he let on. He was a sensitive boy. "Maybe you guys can go tomorrow."

"Yeah, right." Travis jerked the pole but failed to set the hook.

"Listen, Trav, I'm sure your dad didn't mean to sleep in. He doesn't get much alone time with your mom these days, and this is the first year that your sister has been old enough to be in her own tent."

"What? Are they trying to make another kid or something?" Travis snapped.

Jeff gave an uneasy laugh and stood, turning towards the ridge and shielding his eyes against the sun. "There are other reasons for adults to want to have alone time, ya know?"

"Whatever."

"Hey," Jeff turned back to his nephew, "you know your dad loves you, and I know you're still upset about the game; he would have been there if he could. We can't help when we have to go, you know that. It's part of being what we are, it's part of the gift and the curse."

"So he can't help running off to do what he does, I get it!" Travis snapped again, looking back at his parents' tent. "But he *can* help not sleeping in after making a promise."

"You're right. He can help that," Jeff nodded. "Sometimes parents do stupid things, Travis, and not keeping promises is one of them. He'll feel bad though, so go easy on him."

"He doesn't want to do anything with me anymore," Travis whispered.

"What?"

"Nothing."

They both turned when they heard one of the tents unzipping behind them, and Travis groaned when he saw his sister crawling through the flap. At ten years old, Laura was a scrawny little kid who seemed to be made of nothing but knees, elbows, and a mouth that never seemed to shut up.

She blinked in the morning light and looked around, spotted her uncle and brother, and skipped over to join them. Travis rolled his eyes and made an annoyed sound. Jeff lightly elbowed him. "Are ya catching anything, Trav'?" she asked, eagerly looking into the water.

"No."

"I thought you and dad were going to the reservoir today?"

"You thought wrong. Isn't there somebody else you can annoy?"

"Why would I annoy somebody else when annoying you is so much fun?" Laura asked with a toothy grin.

"You know, she's got a point," Jeff interjected.

"I bet if I were fishing as long as you were, I would have caught something by now," Laura teased and skipped over to stand next to her uncle.

"You did catch something, and I hope to god it's not contagious," Travis shot back.

"It's called awesomeness, but don't worry. I'm fairly sure Mom and Dad had you inoculated when you were born," Laura said without missing a beat, eliciting a hearty laugh from Jeff. He loved how quick

Laura was with a comeback. She would make a great standup comedian someday.

While Travis was trying to figure out what to say, Laura leaned over and looked at her uncle's hand. "Uncle Jeff, can I look at your ring?"

"No."

"Why not?" she whined.

"Because last time you looked at it, it took over a week to find it again. This ring has been in the family for four generations, Laura. It's not something to play with. It will be Travis' someday. Nag him about it when the time comes."

"Travis never shares anything!" Laura complained.

"I would if you didn't break everything!" Travis shot back.

"Do not!"

"Do too!"

"Travis, I think you caught a fish," Jeff said with a smile.

"Oh!" Travis suddenly began reeling like mad, but the wild trout didn't make it easy. "Wow, you're right, they are funner to catch!" Travis smiled, his whole face lighting up as he finally got the fish up the bank.

"It's so pretty!" Laura exclaimed.

"Yeah, that's another thing about wild trout. Their coloring is quite a bit brighter," Jeff explained.

"Why?" Laura asked.

"I have no idea." Jeff was looking off towards the ridge again, rubbing the back of his neck. Neither of the kids noticed, but Jeff Nightdale shuddered, a spasm that moved all through his body.

"Ah, dang! It swallowed it!" Travis moaned. "Uncle Jeff, can I see your knife?"

Jeff didn't answer; he seemed frozen in place.

"Uncle Jeff!"

"What?" Jeff snapped out of it and turned to his nephew.

"Your knife?"

"Yeah, sure," Jeff dug in his pocket for the buck knife he almost always had on him. "But only to cut the line. We don't kill animals we're not going to eat, not even if they're fish."

"Yeah, yeah, yeah, I know!" Travis cut the line close to the trout's mouth and tossed it back in the water with a splash.

Just then, Jeff spun so quickly, his shoes sent dirt in the air. "Travis! Take Laura and head downstream!"

"What?" Travis looked up, confused by the urgency he heard in his uncle's voice.

"Take the Rope Bridge and head towards the reservoir. Go! Now!"

"I…." Travis began, but then something hot and sticky hit his face, accompanied by a boom that rang in his ears. Jeff Nightdale was falling even as the blood that had struck Travis was still moving through the air.

Everything seemed to be moving in slow motion. Uncle Jeff took forever to hit the ground, and Travis thought he would never forget how misshapen what was left of his head had looked. But of course, he was wrong; some things were so easy to forget.

Laura was screaming, and Allen Nightdale was stumbling out of his tent, having broken the zipper completely. His face registered horror as he saw his brother, but only for a moment before his face turned to his children and he took in a breath to scream at them to run. But Travis had already grabbed Laura's hand. He was dragging her away towards the woods, and they were already in the trees by the time their father had found his voice.

"Run, kids! Run!" Allen Nightdale's voice boomed behind them, sounding contorted in a way neither of them had ever heard.

Laura was still screaming, but Travis kept running, paying no mind to the sticks and ferns that crossed his path, or the gunshots behind them. He needed to get her out of there; he needed to save his sister. It was what his dad had always told him to do if this ever happened. *Protect your sister, son, protect Laura.*

Travis pushed a Manzanita branch aside, not even noticing when it cut his skin, and they burst into a widening of the trail just as a woman's scream sounded behind them. *Mom!* Travis stopped, momentarily torn about what to do. Should he go back or keep going the way Uncle Jeff had told him to? Go back or run? Go back or run?

Laura slumped down in the dirt beside him, hugging her belly as if she had a stomach ache, her long hair sticking to the tears on her face. She had finally stopped screaming but was now sobbing so hard, she was having trouble breathing. Her thin back was heaving with the effort it took to vent her emotion, and the front of her shirt and side of her head was drenched with Uncle Jeff's blood.

Travis kneeled down beside her and gently grabbed her arm. "Come on Laura, we need to go," he coaxed, trying to pull her to her feet.

She violently shook her head and tried to say something, but it was unintelligible. Travis tried again. "Come on, Laura, come on. Uncle Jeff told us to run, remember? We have to run. We have to do what he said. I'll protect you, Lolly. I will, I promise, but we have to go."

"He…he…he…he's de…dead," Laura managed to choke out.

Travis grabbed her face and forced her to look at him. "But I'm not. Lally, I'm not dead. I'm right here with you, okay? Now please get up, please Laura, *please!*"

"Oh, that's so sweet!"

Travis bolted upright at the sound of the voice, so close to them, *too* close to them. He clutched Uncle Jeff's buck knife in his hand, suddenly realizing he was still holding it. He looked around but didn't see anybody, and without taking his eyes off the clearing in front of them, he reached down and pulled Laura to her feet none too gently, pushing her behind him where an enormous pine tree would protect their back. Laura wrapped her arms around his waist, momentarily terrified into silence, and he wished she would just let go. How was he supposed to defend them with her clinging to him like that?

"What a good brother, looking out for his sister," the voice came again, this time with a friendly laugh. He sounded so nice, so friendly, for a moment, Travis wondered if this man really wanted to hurt them.

Finally, he showed himself, stepping out from behind another large pine directly across from them. He was young, couldn't possibly be older than twenty-five, with extra short dark brown hair and a little bit of stuble around his jaw line. He looked like he belonged on a college campus, with his white t-shirt, flannel over shirt and blue jeans, not at all like a killer.

But he was a killer—Travis could tell by the blood smeared across his shirt. Whose blood was that? Travis wanted to know. Mom's? Dad's? Uncle Jeff's? Whose blood?

The killer saw him staring as he sauntered towards them and indicated his shirt with a smile. "Mommy put up a good fight. You should be proud."

Travis took a deep breath and raised his chin a little, disengaging himself from Laura's tight grip. "You stay away from us! We're kids. You can't hurt kids! It's one of the rules!"

"Yeah," the man said with a smile. "And we're not supposed to attack families, either, but...." He indicated the wilderness all around them. "I don't see any witnesses out here, do you?"

"There's always a witness," Travis said, not exactly sure where the words had come from. "Always."

"Well, look at you." The man leaned back and stuck his hands in his pockets, smiling as he surveyed the two. "Your sister here is barely keeping it together, but you, not even a tear. I like that, kid. You've got guts! There's a little bit of Hunter in you."

He took another step towards them, and Travis surprised the Hunter by taking a step forward himself, leading with the knife. "I said stay away from us!"

The Hunter's smile broadened. "Well, well, well, kid, I guess you feel lucky."

"I'm a Seer, jackass. We're always lucky!" Travis said coldly, hearing Laura's sudden intake of breath behind him because he had said a bad word. "Now get away from us!"

"I guess we'll see about that, now, won't we?" The Hunter said and suddenly rushed at them. Travis was preparing for the impact, prepared to fight to the death if he had to, but he wasn't prepared for what happened.

A stone, sticking just an inch out of the ground, caught the Hunter's foot as he charged, causing him to trip and stumble forward, directly onto Travis' outstretched hand, directly onto Uncle Jeff's buck knife. Uncle Jeff had taken pride in his knives and had always kept them as sharp as could be. Travis barely felt a thing as the knife entered the Hunter's lower abdomen, and his own momentum caused the knife to move upwards as his body moved down, until it hit a rib and finally came loose. The knife moved through the Hunter effortlessly, just like cutting butter. Hot, sticky blood was suddenly covering Travis' whole arm. It was so hot, it felt like it was burning his skin and, he jerked back to get away from it.

The Hunter hit the ground with a gasp at the boy's feet, one arm moving to his stomach to try to hold himself together, but the gash was too large, and what was once held in by muscle and skin no longer had such restrictions. Travis stepped back in horror, color draining from his face as he saw what he had done. Behind him, Laura was screaming again, but Travis couldn't hear anything besides the pounding of his own heart and the last words that the Hunter ever spoke.

His smile finally gone, the Hunter looked up from the mess that had once been his gut and met the eyes of his killer, a terrified twelve-year-old boy. "Wow, kid, that was lucky."

***

For a moment, Travis couldn't breathe. There was so much blood! It was everywhere, all over the ground, all over him. He never realized there was so much blood in a person.

He had done this. He had destroyed this life.

He wanted to drop the buck knife, to cast it as far away from him as far as he could, to cover his ears, crawl up in a dark place and scream until he was hoarse. But somewhere in the back of his mind, he knew that there had been two Hunters. He knew that he needed to keep the knife. He knew that he may need to kill again very soon. He didn't want to, though; he would rather die than feel blood on his hands again.

"Travis?" Laura said from behind him, a tiny, scared voice.

Travis blinked and took a breath. They still needed to run. He still needed to protect his sister. They needed to get to the rope bridge. The creek was deeper and faster there. If he cut the bridge behind them, the Hunter would not be able to follow them. Nobody could swim that creek without ending up a mile downstream. If he could get to the rope bridge, they would be okay.

"Come on, Laura!" He grabbed her hand, and they started running again, just as the other Hunter got to the clearing. Travis caught sight of him out of the corner of his eye just before they entered the thicket again. He saw the look of shock on the young man's face, and the hatred and cold fury that filled his eyes when he saw the two fleeing children.

"Come on, Laura, faster!" Travis pushed his little sister in front of him. "Don't look back! Just run! Get to the rope bridge!"

He could hear the heavy footsteps rapidly approaching behind him, hear the Hunter getting closer, closing in on them, and he didn't think he would be as lucky this time. "Dad!" Travis screamed, suddenly so afraid of what he had seen in the second Hunter's eyes. He didn't even know if his father was still alive, but as he heard the bushes being swept aside a mere ten feet behind him, he screamed louder, his voice high with hysterics. "Dad! Please help us!"

"Nobody can save you, boy!" The second Hunter said, so close behind them, he didn't even have to raise his voice. "I'm gonna kill you! Kill you for what you did!"

It was his brother, Travis realized. He had just killed this man's brother!

"Dad! Help us!" Travis screamed again, knowing that the man behind them would never stop, would never give up, would never be able to let it go.

"Daddy!" Laura echoed him, her voice so high, it was almost unrecognizable.

Then, sooner than Travis would have thought possible, they were there, at the rope bridge. They came to the end of the trail so quickly, Laura almost wasn't able to stop in time, and Travis had to grab the back of her shirt to keep her from going over the bank and into the white water below.

"The bridge!" Travis used Laura's own momentum to swing her around onto the single long plank of wood that served as the base of the simple bridge. "Hurry, Laura!" He pushed her hard, causing her to stumble forward. With a tiny squeak, she grabbed the two ropes on either side for support. Travis was right behind her, urging her to move faster. All they had to do was get to the other side and they would be safe. They were so close.

Travis felt more than heard the Hunter behind them and turned to look over his shoulder, wondering if he was going to have to fight again. But the Hunter was just standing at the head of the bridge, looking uneasily down at the rapids, wondering if the bridge was safe.

He's scared! Travis thought triumphantly. The Hunter was too scared to cross the bridge; they were going to make it! They were going to get away!

But then the Hunter did something that Travis had not expected. He reached behind him and pulled out a small handgun, only pausing for a second to remove the safety. The two children, out on the bridge above the water, would make easy targets. They didn't have a chance. The world seemed to slow again as it had when Uncle Jeff had been shot, and Travis watched with muted horror as the Hunter took aim just as Allen Nightdale appeared behind him. Their father would not be able to get to them before the Hunter squeezed the trigger, though. Not even he could be so fast.

There was a resounding boom as the gun went off three seconds before the Hunter was tackled from behind.

The children were no longer there, though, because Travis had cut the rope along the side of the bridge, sending them both into the icy cold water. By cutting the rope, Travis had saved his sister but sealed his own fate. Nothing would ever be the same again—not ever.

The icy coldness of the water hit Travis like a right hook from Cassias Clay and was so shocking, he nearly lost his grip on Laura's arm. He kicked off of a rock and got them both above water just as a wave pushed them under again. For a moment, Travis was confused, not sure which direction was which, but then the blue sky was above him, and he still had a hold of Laura's arm.

"Get your feet in front of you and float on your back!" Travis yelled to her over the rush of the water. "Kick off the rocks the way Dad taught us!"

Their father had taught them how to survive in any number of scenarios over the years; it had been a game for them. He would name a situation and ask them what to do, then he would tell them whether or not what they had proposed would get them killed, always coming back to how to survive. Travis had begun to find this game of their father's tiresome, but now, being faced with a real, life and death situation, he saw the wisdom of it.

Travis managed to push and shove a panicked Laura into the proper position, going under many times in the process. He had no way of knowing where he was along the creek or how far down the water had taken them, it was complete chaos with the water pushing them under, fighting to reach the surface. There was a glimpse of the sky here, treetops there, but there was no real direction to swim in. The best they could do was keep their feet facing downstream, and even that was a struggle. Travis tried his best to keep Laura above the water, but in doing so, he went under repeatedly, and by the time they ran into the tree, he was choking and gasping from swallowing too much water.

The dead tree was stretched out across the water, almost covering the entire creek, hovering maybe two feet above the water with its limbs plunging downwards in what resembled the ribcage of some massive, long dead beast. Laura slipped under the tree, the current moving her past the limbs with ease, but Travis managed to reach out and catch one of the limbs with his free hand. The sudden stop the limb provided instantly pushed him under the water, dragging Laura down with him, and he had to use the limb to pull both of them back up which caused a hot fire to move up and down his arm, so painful, he almost let go of their only salvation.

Despite the pain in his left arm, Travis pulled Laura forward against the current with his right hand, gritting his teeth as pain shot through that arm as well. "Climb, Laura! Get up to the trunk!" He shouted over the roar of the creek, getting a mouthful of water.

Laura got one shivering, bone white hand onto a limb and the other hand onto a higher limb and began to pull herself up, but she instantly slipped. Her brother still had hold of her and pushed her back towards the tree. "Climb!"

"I can't! It's too slippery!" Laura cried.

"Yes, you can!" Travis pushed her harder. "You can, Laura! Now climb!"

She nodded mutely and began to inch her way up the two limbs towards the trunk of the tree, slipping several times but never letting go. "Good! Good!" Travis encouraged, having let go of Laura and holding onto the tree with both hands. "Now get your leg over the top! That's it! Now scoot on your belly towards the shore! You can do it!"

"Aren't you coming?" She whined.

"You need to get out of the way!"

"Oh," Laura said through chattering teeth and began to scoot towards the shore. As soon as Laura was out of the way, Travis grabbed hold of one of the higher limbs and began lifting himself out of the water. Then came a sharp *snap*! At first, Travis didn't know where it had come from, then he was falling back towards the water, the broken limb still in his hand, and Laura was reaching out to him, screaming his name.

That was the last glimpse Travis had of his sister, freezing, soaking wet, clinging to a tree and reaching out for him, screaming his name. "Hang on!" Travis managed to scream at her before he slipped under the water. His legs were no longer in front of him. He could no longer fend off the rocks. There was a sharp stab of pain in his shoulder, then a bright flash of white…then there was nothing.

Chapter 17

Travis didn't know how long he had been sitting at the base of the tree, hugging his knees to his chest, sobbing, and he didn't care. He was so numb, so past feeling, he wasn't even aware of how much he was shivering, how the tears were practically freezing to his face. He had killed a man, felt hot blood cover his arm, and there was no taking it back, no forgetting. Not now, not ever again.

He couldn't get over the look in the Hunter's eyes as the life left him. He kept seeing it again and again every time he closed his eyes. He didn't mean to, and even if he had, it wasn't like he had a choice; still, knowing those things didn't make it any better. Travis felt like he would never be clean again, he would never be able to wash his hands of this one thing he had done; the worst thing a Seer could ever do.

With the return of his long dormant memory came so many other emotions as well, especially sorrow and grief. Uncle Jeff had died here nearly ten years ago, but for Travis, it had just happened, and the shock and horror of it washed over him like a flood, wave upon wave of unbelievable grief. He had lost one of his great heroes, the man he used to call in the middle of the night after having a fight with his father; the man who had given him his first taste of beer and taught him how to skip rocks. That man was gone forever, taken from him in a flash of violence. But what made the loss so much worse was the fact that Travis had *forgotten* him. He had forgotten Uncle Jeff, and not just him; he had forgotten his mother, his father, his sister, his entire life.

How could he have forgotten them?

He was weeping again, sobbing silently into his kneecaps. Starkey was trying desperately to get his head under Travis' arms. He knew there was something terribly wrong with his master, and like a good dog, he was trying to comfort him, but there were some things even a dog couldn't fix.

After the sixth time, Starkey's cold nose touched his ear. Travis leaned back and allowed the way-too-large dog to climb in his lap. He hugged the dog's warm body against him and wiped his tears on his fur. "Sorry, Starkey, I'm sorry buddy. I didn't mean to scare you," he apologized to the dog and finally allowed himself to calm down and think.

He could remember his mother now, and the big mystery was finally solved. He had wondered why the woman who had picked Randy and him up during a snow storm had looked so heartbroken. Her eyes had teared up when Travis had pulled away from her when she had tried to touch him. It had both bothered and confused him then, but he understood now.

"He doesn't like to be touched," Randy had said, excusing his behavior, but still, there had been tears in her eyes. If she had told them she was his mother, how would he have responded? Knowing him, it probably would have been with hostility. Still, he wished he would have let her touch him; maybe this whole mess would have been avoided.

His mother wasn't the only one he had encountered over the years. There had been a man at Sophia's funeral. A man who had spent more time looking at Travis then at the casket. A man who looked just as heartbroken as Travis was. Travis noticed him at the time but didn't care; he had been too shattered, too broken to care about anything outside the fact that his love was gone.

"I'm sorry," the man had said to Travis after the final prayer. "I'm so sorry."

Travis didn't respond to his father then, made no indication that his words even registered, and walked away in a cloud of self-pity and spiteful anger to drink himself into oblivion. His father had been there for him, or at least he had tried to be.

But why, if they had known where he was, did they leave him in that hospital unclaimed? That was the question Travis kept coming back to, the question he couldn't answer. Why had he been abandoned?

Travis rode this train of thought around and around, reliving the events of that day many times, overthinking every moment, crying off and on, sometimes numb, sometimes enraged, until the thumping of Starkey's tail brought him out of the deep hole he had been hiding in. He looked around to realize that the day was coming to a close, and it was already late in the afternoon.

Starkey's tail was sending little puffs of dirt into the air, but he seemed unconcerned, his head still lying in Travis' lap where it had been for the majority of the day. Travis didn't need to guess at who was coming up the trail. Starkey had told him all he needed to know. He wasn't surprised when Randy flopped down beside him.

Randy looked around the clearing, taking in the old picnic table, the drop off to the creek, and without comment reached over and picked up the ring lying between Travis' feet, holding it up for inspection. He was waiting for Travis to talk, but Travis didn't know what to say or where to begin.

After a few minutes of silence, he finally said, "How'd you find me?"

Randy shrugged. "Since when have I not been able to find you?"

It was true. Travis had never been able to disappear from Randy, no matter what obscure bar he had chosen to hide in or what friend's couch he was crashed on. Randy had always been able to find Travis when he was needed. Whenever Travis needed to talk, even if he didn't know he needed to yet, Randy always seemed to walk through the door or into the park; distance had never been much of an obstacle.

"Still, these are some pretty big woods. Did she tell you?"

"Pretty big woods, yeah, and you leave pretty big tracks. Besides, she's gone. She went into town to get some more supplies."

Travis sat up, dislodging Starkey. "You just let her go?"

"Nope. Argued with her for well over an hour about it. She said she'll be back in the morning. We're supposed to meet her at the road to help carry some of the stuff down," Randy said. "Stupid girl is about as stubborn as you are, maybe more."

Travis nodded numbly. "She's my sister."

"Yeah," Randy nodded, "I know."

"You know?" For the first time, Travis turned and looked at his brother, unable to keep the accusation out of his voice. "How? How do you know? How *long* have you known?"

Randy smiled, finding Travis' reaction humorous. "I've known since the first time I ever saw you two together, that night Harvey beat the living hell out of me and I woke up to find Laura putting me back together. Nobody had to tell me, man, it was kind of obvious!" He reached up and took a bit of Travis' hair between his fingers. "There is a *slight* resemblance! Come on! There was no way you two weren't related!"

Travis just looked down for a moment, unable to admit to Randy that he had never noticed. But thinking about it now, they looked a lot alike. So much so, he couldn't believe it had taken him this long to realize it. "Why didn't you tell me?" he asked softly.

Randy shrugged. "What good would that have done?"

Travis thought for a moment. "I don't know, but a little bit of loyalty would have been nice."

"Come on, man," Randy said. "I know you; I know how you think, and some things, you just have to come to on your own."

Travis nodded, knowing Randy was right. "Do you know…what happened here?" Travis asked hesitantly.

Randy shook his head. "Apart from what Laura told the two of us, no, I don't have a clue. I figured it would be wrong for me to know before you did. You don't have to tell me, either. You don't have to talk about it if you don't want to."

"I have to. I can't not talk about it, not after it's been bottled up inside for so long," Travis said.

"Okay."

So Travis told him what had happened, sparing no detail, and Randy sat back and listened, not interrupting him once to ask a question or make a comment. When Travis was done, Randy handed him back the ring and whistled long and low. "Damn, man. So do you think your parents are dead?"

Travis shook his head. "Nah, you remember the chick that picked us up after your freak-out in Mt. Shasta?"

"The emotional lady?"

"Yeah, that was my mom."

"Hmmmm, maybe you should have let her touch you."

Travis laughed. "I thought the exact same thing! Yeah, that was her, and my dad was at Sophia's funeral."

"Why have they stayed away from you this whole time?" Randy asked thoughtfully.

"That's a big question. There are a lot of big questions." Travis said, shifting his weight to increase blood flow before standing up. He hadn't been able to feel his butt in a few hours.

"Like what?" Randy asked.

"That day that the Hunters attacked us, it was in the beginning of June," Travis said, knowing Randy would understand.

"But you weren't found in the river till...."

"Yeah."

"So, where the hell were you for nearly two months?"

"That's the million-dollar question now, isn't it?" Travis said, trying to stand up and instantly falling. Randy pulled him to his feet and brushed some of the pine needles off his back. "Come on, lets head back to camp. I'm freezing and starving!" Randy said once Travis could stand on his own.

"Sounds good," Travis agreed, eager to leave the campsite and never come back. "Oh, guess what? I know my birthday now. It's in April. I'm totally older than you!"

"Yet you're still smaller."

"You couldn't give me this one thing, could you? Not even when I'm in emotional turmoil?"

"I'll give it to you. So, you're older. I'm just saying I'm still taller."

"You're such a jerk."

"Am not!"

"Are too! Hey Randy?"

"What?"

"Don't tell Laura I know, okay?"

Randy turned and examined his brother's face for a moment, then nodded. "Yeah, okay."

Feeling like he needed to say more, Travis tried to explain. "It's just…I don't think I'm ready to have that conversation yet."

"Okay."

They hiked back to the camp in silence, with that Blue Jay following along cawing relentlessly and provoking Randy to throw a few rocks. The bird didn't bother Travis; he was too busy thinking of impossibilities. Now that he remembered what he had been taught, he knew how impossible his very existence was. Powerful Seers had two routes, while Seers with three routes were seen as incredibly rare (mostly thought of as myth). Some had been rumored to exist back in the dark ages when the war between Hunters and Seers was at its deadliest and Flyers and Ohan were being hunted into near extinction. But a Seer like Travis? That was an impossibility.

Travis was an impossibility because he had more than three routes: Direct Contact, Visions, Dreams, and something else he didn't even have a name for. A knowing that until now he had not known was unusual. Sometimes he simply knew things without any reason. When his family had been attacked, he *knew* there had been two Hunters, even though he had not seen or heard anything to make him think that. When Sophia's older brother had graduated high school, Travis had *known* what college he was going to get into. When Randy had graduated community college, Travis *knew* what job he was going to get. He *knew* his neighbor would run out of gas on the way home, and he *knew* that the waitress was a high school dropout. He just *knew* things.

These things—sometimes random tidbits, sometimes incredibly detailed histories—simply came to him without touch or contact of any kind. There was no discernable moment when the knowledge came to him, it was simply his to know. To Travis' knowledge, no Seer had ever had an ability such as this. It was more than intuition. Travis had known several people, Randy included, who had incredible intuition that was so acute, it could appear supernatural to some. But what Travis had was something different; it was fact with no room for error. There was no *might happen* or *probably would*. What Travis knew was chiseled into stone, set, as if it had already happened. He simply *knew*.

But until now, he had not known how unusual his *knowing* was. As a Seer, Travis was without peer, without equal, and that scared him. He was a target, a prize, and he was going to get everybody he loved killed if he wasn't very careful. He hadn't been being careful, not up to this point; he had been making stupid mistakes like using his real name and using his own truck to drive to interventions instead of a stolen vehicle. Any Hunter would have had an easy time tracking him back to his place of origin, possibly leading them to a nest of Seers.

Laura had been right when she said somebody had to have been covering for him to have avoided detection for this long. He was lucky Tim Harvey was the Hunter who had caught his scent, lucky that Harvey had a vendetta against his family, lucky that Harvey hadn't just killed him. He was also incredibly lucky that Randy was even still alive having been so closely tied to a Seer. Randy was special, and now that Travis knew how special, he was ashamed by how often he had put his brother in direct danger.

All this and more went through Travis' head on the walk back to the camp, and he found he could not shut off his brain. He knew too much now, understood too much, and had far too much to process. No matter what twist and turns his mind took, though, he kept coming back to the same three questions. Where had he been for over a month after he went into the creek? Why had his family never come forward? How were they going to get out of this alive?

He found himself contemplating these same thoughts late that night as he lay in his sleeping bag staring up at the roof of the tent. He needed answers, more so now than before he got his memory back, and an idea occurred to him. It was an impossible idea, but maybe not impossible for him, the master of impossibilities.

It was supposedly impossible for a Seer to give himself a vision or control a vision, but Travis had done it before. He had used the crucifix that Sophia had given him, holding it in his hands close to his chest and concentrating, to give himself a vision of her when she was alive and happy…and with him. He had done this when he was desperate to see her again, to hear her voice and feel her touch, and there was nothing more real than a vision save reality itself.

He reached over and grabbed Laura's backpack from where it sat in the corner of the tent, digging around until he found something he could use. In the front pocket, he found it: a man's watch with a broken latch. It had belonged to his father, and his grandfather before him. The watch was a family heirloom. Uncle Jeff had gotten the ring, and his father had gotten the watch.

Travis *knew* that Laura had it with her because she was supposed to get the latch fixed for her father, something she was not able to do because she had rushed to Chico to save Randy and him from Harvey. For a moment, Travis felt uneasy, as if he were about to do something wrong, violate somebody's privacy, perhaps break one of the rules of the galaxy. He began to feel jumpy, physically jerking when Starkey made a noise in his sleep. He shook it off, clutched the watch to his chest and closed his eyes.

***

Travis opened his eyes and blinked. No longer sitting in the tent, he was now standing in the corner of a very clean hospital room, a room in the ICU, by the looks of it. There were machines beeping relentlessly, and a nurse was leaning over a bed brushing the occupant's hair with such care, it made Travis want to cry.

The bed seemed too large for the child that occupied it, with tubes in his mouth and nose and half a dozen machines attached to him. Travis hardly recognized himself. He was so small, so fragile, and so thin. How could he ever have been so vulnerable?

There wasn't much space in the little room; a table near the one window was filled up with flowers and cards of all kinds from people sending prayers to the unnamed boy from the river. Travis still had a few of them, the ones he really liked, and he had read all of them after waking up from his coma. The rest of the space in the room was taken up by the machines, and the nurse had a hard time maneuvering around them. There was one chair where a visitor could sit, and a small space where somebody would stand at the bedside. A curtain blocked off the room from the rest of the ICU.

"There you go, precious," The nurse whispered to him. Her name was Donna. He remembered her because she brought him treats all the time after he woke up, and he got the distinct impression that she wanted to take him home. She had been very upset when they moved him to a foster home.

Donna checked a few of the machines and went to leave, nearly running into a uniformed police officer. "Oh, Charley, I didn't see you there!" she exclaimed, taking a step back. Donna was a funny lady. Travis remembered her little mannerisms still, and how much she reminded him of the old aunty from the Andy Griffith show.

Charley, however, Travis didn't think he had ever seen before. The officer gave Donna a toothy smile, "Sorry, Ma'am, but I've got a man outside who may be the boy's father. His son went missing on a camping trip a month or so before the boy was found. They never found him, and they just returned from staying with family in Europe, getting away from here and trying to cope I suppose, when they found out about the Jon Doe."

"What was their son's name?" Donna asked hopefully.

"Travis Nightdale."

Donna gasped. "Before he went comatose, he said his name was Travis! Oh, Charley, I hope it's him!" She turned and looked longingly at the bedridden boy. "A child like that needs to be loved, needs to at least have a name."

Charley nodded. "So, you're okay that I bring him in?"

"Of course!" Donna followed the officer out, and he appeared a minute later with Allen Nightdale in tow. Allen was a well-built man in his late thirties with messy dark brown hair and day-old stubble on his chin. Not as tall as his son had grown to be, he still towered over the officer at six foot even. His eyes had a sunken-in look to them, and he seemed to have lost about thirty pounds. He was pale, and some grey hair could be seen around the temples. Travis was shocked at the difference between this man and the man that he remembered.

Upon seeing the child in the bed, Allen stopped, his face growing even paler, and he stared with an emotionless face. "I'll give you a moment," the officer said and retreated behind the curtain to the nurse's station.

For a full thirty seconds, Allen stood there, unmoving, then his hand slowly came up to cover his mouth and his whole face seemed to melt as the tears came unbidden; his sobs were muffled by the hand covering his mouth. He reached out with his other hand to clutch the bed rail, his back heaving with contained emotion, and with great effort got himself under control.

"Oh, my boy," he managed to choke out. "My baby boy, I'm so sorry!"

He pushed himself back from the bedrail, standing on his own again with great effort, and reached out to take the tiny hand in his own. Then he froze, his eyes losing focus and his face going blank in an instant.

"What are you seeing?" Travis demanded, his voice silent in the past. Though he had never seen it himself, he recognized the look of a Seer caught up in a vison. He moved to stand directly in front of his father with nothing but the bed and a comatose child between them. "What is it? What are you seeing?!"

In a moment, the vision was over, and Allen blinked several times, shaking himself a little. "No." He whispered, letting go of the boy's hand and taking a step back. "I can't."

"What did you see?" Travis demanded of him, moving around the bed, though it was pointless.

"Forgive me," Allen said, crying again. "Oh god, please forgive me!"

"What did you just see!" Travis screamed at him, mere inches from the man's face yet as insubstantial as air itself.

"Sir?" The officer asked hesitantly, appearing behind Allen.

"I'm sorry!" Allen said, his words barely understood over the emotion in his voice, and turned his back on both the boy and the man that the boy would become. "That's…that's not my son!" He shoved past the officer, sobbing, and stumbled out of the ICU.

"No!" Travis screamed after him, panicking in his vision but not sure why. "Don't leave me! Dad! Come back!" But his father was already gone, and there was no bringing him back, no undoing the damage that had been done.

Chapter 18

Travis was back in the tent, clutching the watch to his chest as a cold numbness swept through him. He didn't want to believe what he had just seen, but there was no denying it. "He left me," he whispered, his voice devoid of the intense emotion he felt. "He left me there."

Travis slipped the watch into his pocket and lay back against his pillow, pulling the sleeping bag back over him, but he could not close his eyes. He kept seeing the look on his father's face as he ran from the ICU, as he abandoned his son.

The coldness Travis felt could not be warmed by the sleeping bag, and despair began to overcome him. He tried to think of Sophia, of her arms around his neck, her lips on his, but he couldn't even picture her face. The only thought he had was that he had been abandoned on purpose. He had been discarded and disowned. *That's not my son.*

But then, in the darkness, a realization dawned on him. Despair was not the only thing he felt; he also felt tension, a strange electricity in the air, like a calm before a storm. He had felt this before, and now he knew what it was. He sat up, adrenaline flooding his system, and smacked his hand down flat on Randy's chest, his eyes on the entrance to the tent as three sharp cracks could be heard from some distance away.

Randy's eyes snapped open, and he looked over at Travis. "What is it?"

"We need to go!" Travis said, rushing to get out of his sleeping bag.

"It's the middle of the night," Randy said.

"We need to go, now!" Travis tossed Randy's boots at him as he fumbled with his own.

Crack! Crack! Crack!

"What is that noise?" Randy asked, beginning to crawl out of his sleeping bag none too enthusiastically.

"The Ohans. They are warning us that a Hunter is near. That's what they do; they smack sticks together three times like that," Travis explained in a rush.

"The Bigfoots? Seriously? I thought Laura was just shitting us about that," Randy said, pulling on his boots.

"C'mon, Randy! We need to go!" Travis hissed at him.

"Where? We're in the middle of nowhere, and Laura has the car, remember?" Randy reasoned.

"Lost is better than dead! Now, c'mon!" He physically pulled Randy from the tent and held the flap open for Starkey.

"What are we taking?" Randy asked, looking around as he shrugged into his jacket. "Nothing. I've got the flashlight, but we can't use it right now. C'mon!"

Randy hesitated a moment, then began following his crazy brother through the dark, frozen woods, still half asleep and very much wanting to go back to sleep. He heard the urgency in Travis' voice, though, and he wasn't about to argue with him about it.

Crack, crack, crack!

"Can you tell them to stop that? We got the message! It's freaking me out!" Randy hissed at Travis, trying not to be too loud.

"What? Are you afraid of Bigfoots now?" Travis whispered back, moving fast through the woods and forcing Randy to jog to keep up.

"Hate to tell you this, man, but I've *always* been afraid of Bigfoot!"

"Ohans are peaceful creatures, but if we need their help, they will help us. Seers and Ohans have been allies for…always," Travis whispered, great puffs of air escaping his lips as he spoke. "It's about the preservation of life. We preserve human life, they preserve the forest—or at least try to. Wherever there are Ohans, the forest flourish, and so we've always been allies."

"Thanks for the history lesson," Randy snapped. Travis just smiled. He could hear it in Randy's voice that he really was freaked out.

***

Crack, crack, crack!

The Hunter heard the sound and was shocked by the fear it evoked in him. This was only the second time he had ever entered Ohan territory, and the first time he had done so after dark. Ohans were most active at night and were very rarely seen during the day, which was why Gene and he had chosen to attack during daylight the last time he was here. Their father had warned them of the dangers of Ohans. While the beasts were peaceful for the most part, they would intervene on a Seers' behalf, and an intervention by a beast the size of an Ohan could easily result in broken bones or loss of life.

It was eerie being back in these woods after so many years, and as he crunched through the pine needles near the road, he felt all those old emotions come flooding back to him—emotions he hadn't felt in quite a long time. The intense love he had felt for his family, the devotion he had felt towards his father, the pain of losing those people who were most dear to him.

Their father had been watching news stories closely and had caught the scent of a Seer somewhere in Virginia. He flew out there from Seattle where the family lived and had been gone some three weeks seeking out the nest. How shocked his father must have been when he realized that the nest was so much closer to home.

Thomas Harvey had been following Jefferson Nightdale for a week when a search of the man's mail led him to the discovery of a nest in Southern Oregon, one state away from their home in Washington. He was very careful to keep his distance from the Seer so he wouldn't set off the Seer's warning instincts and put Nightdale back in the wind. Once he had the location of a nest, Tom didn't think he needed to wait any longer. It was time for the kill.

How it had happened, Tim still didn't know, but knowing his father's habits, he could guess. Tom Harvey often trapped his prey before revealing himself, and he had taught his sons to do the same. Seers were so good at escaping and disappearing, it was essential to cut off any avenue of escape before moving in. This tactic forced a Seer to fight, and Seers were not so good at fighting when that fight happened to be against a Hunter. Their instincts to run often clouded their judgment and sent them into a panic. Against an armed Hunter, they were easy prey, fish in a barrel.

But Jeff Nightdale was half Tom's age, and when forced into a confrontation, he was not as weak minded as the other Seers Tom had faced. Neither son had been home when Tom had called the house to say goodbye; their mother had succumbed to cancer the year before, so the cold voice on an answering machine was his only comfort.

Tim still had the recording of his father saying that he had been badly injured and would not be coming home, that the Seers name was Jefferson Nightdale and that the nest was in Medford, Oregon. He instructed his sons to get to the nest before they were in the wind, that he loved them and was proud of them, and that he knew they were ready.

It was late that night when the boys got home. The first message on the machine was from a police officer in Virginia informing them of their father's death via a severe stab wound. The next message was the one their father had left.

So soon after the loss of their mother, the news of their father's death had devastated Tim and all but driven Gene insane. Gene was only twenty-two to Tim's twenty-four but had long been thought of by their father as the better Hunter, or at least the better pupil, as neither boy had ever been on an actual hunt. Gene was better at suppressing emotion than Tim and better at cultivating hatred and anger. Gene had always been the better student. Even still, the bloodlust he had seen in his brother that day had scared Tim.

By the time the two boys got to Medford, the family had already left on a camping trip that had apparently been scheduled for several months. The family was supposed to be at a campground near the Rogue River, but knowing that a Hunter was possibly after them, they had chosen a more protected area.

Not knowing where to begin to look, the two boys had allowed their Hunter's instincts to lead them to the family. It took them a week to get close enough for the pull to take over. Hunters always had a pull; something akin to the magnetism inside Canadian Geese that lets them know where true north is. Except the pull inside a Hunter would lead him to the nearest Seer.

"Damn, there's kids," Tim had said as he and his brother kneeled on a ridge overlooking the camp. "We should wait till the kids leave or one of the adults is isolated."

But Gene wasn't listening to his big brother. He was too busy taking aim, and then the gunshot was ringing in Tim's ear, and Jeff Nightdale, their father's killer, was falling to the ground. His brother had broken the rules; the one thing their father had told them never to do, the thing their father had always told them would get them killed.

Tim went after the father, who ran off in an attempt to lead the Hunters away from his family, while Gene went after the wife and kids. Gene managed to slash the wife with his dagger before she got a hold of the gun that had been stashed in the tent. It was the only thing that saved him from getting his head blown off. With the slash in her arm, the wife couldn't aim, but still, seeing the gun, Gene abandoned her and went for the children.

It only took Tim a few minutes to realize that Allen Nightdale was planning on skirting the campsite and intercepting the Hunter who was going after his children, so Tim abandoned the chase early on and turned back to re-enforce his brother. Why engage in a tiring chase if you knew where your query was heading?

But as it turned out, Gene wouldn't need help dealing with Allen because by that time, Gene was already dead, gutted by a boy neither of them had perceived to be a threat.

Tim was not ashamed to admit that he had gone crazy when he realized the last member of his family was gone. The anger that ripped through him was so intense, rational thought was completely abandoned. He forgot about the father, the wife, all the other threats that still existed, and the only thing that filled his mind was the boy, mere feet in front of him.

Tim did not want to think about what he would have done to those children had he caught them. He guessed it would have been messy and many rules would have been broken.

His first rational thought came when he was at the base of the bridge wondering if it could hold his weight, then he remembered the gun....

His fight with the children's father had been brief, ending with Tim stumbling through the woods with a large gash in his head, knowing that Allen Nightdale could have easily killed him if he wanted to. It was only the mercy of the Seer that had saved his life and even then, it may not have been mercy but the man's desperation to reach his children. Either way, luck did not favor the Harvey family that day.

"It was your fault!" Tim whispered into the night; his fist clenched at his side. "You never should have broken the rules, Gene, you never should have broken the damn rules!"

It was true, of course; their father had told them as much. *Never break the rules, son, no matter how much you want to. Even if there is nobody else there, fate knows, and fate is the witness to everything! Remember boys! There are always witnesses!*

Gene's bloodlust had cost him his life. Tim knew it was wrong to blame the boy for Gene's death. It was not vengeance for Gene that drove him to annihilate this family but loyalty to his father.

Wiping out this nest of Seers was the last task his father had given him, and with the girl's coming of age, he would soon be able to finish the job and be done with it. He had ten years' worth of hate and imagination inside of him to assist, and he was no longer as unsure of himself as he was then. He would not break the rules this time.

He had been careful, and he did his research. He shot Travis in his home, yes, but the truth was, he shot Travis Nightdale in *Travis Williams* home. He could have done anything in that house, and it would not have mattered.

Footsteps and hushed voices alerted Tim that he was no longer alone, and he smiled, slipping the gun out of the holster at his side. He knew the Ohans would give their warning and drive the three of them right to him; all he had to do was stay near the road and wait.

With a smile on his face, he slipped on his night vision goggles. He could see the Ohan now, three adults, all of them watching him, though only one was close enough to cause him any worry. Next, he needed to locate the dog. That damn dog! He should just kill it, but he would prefer not to if he could help it. He liked dogs, but this one was getting on his nerves.

He frowned. He could easily see the boys, making quick time through the steep woods, but the girl wasn't with them…and neither was the dog. The girl's car was missing from where it had been parked on his previous visits, so it was possible that she had left for some unknown reason. This was fine. He wasn't after the Seers tonight anyway. Laura was not game yet, so why kill her big brother first? Travis had not only killed his brother but also made him look like an inexperienced fool twice. He was the one that Tim wanted to suffer, and there was no greater punishment for a Seer than to lose an Angel that was under their protection.

He was surprised it had taken him this long to realize what Randy *was*. Tim had heard of them but had never encountered one before and unlike Seers, these creatures were completely hidden from a Hunter's natural instincts. They were not members of the third kind.

They were more than that. Tim had no idea *what* they were, only that when discovered, they were to be killed.

Ah, there was the dog! Travis was carrying the animal, probably due to the presence of the Ohans driving the poor thing crazy. That made things easier for him, and it got even better. Travis was a good twenty feet ahead of his foster brother, already climbing the incline to the road with the dog in his arms. Tim smiled; this was going to be so easy.

✳✳✳

Randy shifted his weight from foot to foot, trying to keep warm, as he watched Travis climb the steep incline to the road carrying a less than thrilled Starkey in his arms. They had chosen to go up the incline one at a time so they wouldn't make too much noise.

Randy thought trying so hard to be quiet was pointless with the Ohans smacking those sticks together every five minutes. He shuddered thinking of them.

He remembered watching that old movie, *Bogey Creek,* with his father when he was very young. He remembered snuggling in next to his father as the monster came down from the woods towards the house, remembered hiding his face in his father's shirt. *Those aren't real, are they, daddy?*

Who knows? had been his father's award-winning answer. Randy hadn't thought of that day in a very long time. It was one of the few memories he had of his father sober. His mother had made them popcorn and told his father to turn the movie off because it was scaring Randy, and of course, Randy had denied being scared and insisted on watching the rest of the movie like the stupid little kid he was. He probably scarred himself for life.

It was an absurd idea, but Randy was afraid none the less. A childlike fear had crept into him like a monster creeping out from under a bed looking for fresh prey. He shivered again and gave himself a mental smack. He told himself that he was a grown man and that the Ohans were on *their* side. All the while, his inner child was curled up in a ball with the covers over his head.

Lost in thought, Randy was startled to hear a stick snap behind him, and he jumped, turning towards the noise to find the business end of a handgun inches from his face.

He looked past the gun to see the Hunter's face, blank and emotionless in the predawn darkness, and wondered what he was waiting for. Then he knew. He was waiting for Travis to reach the road and turn around. He wanted Travis to see this. Randy took a deep breath to steady himself, his mind racing, searching for something to say or do. He couldn't help but glance over his shoulder at Travis who was just reaching the road. He knew his friend could not help him. Not this time.

"Don't worry," Tim said softly, too low for Travis to hear, "I won't kill him, at least not yet."

Randy shook his head, amazed by the Hunter's confidence, and even though the other man was holding the gun, holding the power, Randy suddenly saw him for what he was. Tim Harvey was not someone to be feared, not even someone to be hated, but someone to be pitied; a poor soul who had forsaken the purest of virtues like love, friendship, even empathy, for a mission that even he did not understand.

"You don't have to do this," Randy said, but not in the manner of one pleading for his life or trying to negotiate with a mad man. No, Randy did not speak out of fear but with an authority that momentarily stunned the Hunter. Randy had a presence about him, an essence that made the Hunter doubt everything he had been taught. Something in the young man's voice pulled at some buried part of him that he had known long ago. That hidden place he thought was lost forever. The person he was before he made his first kill.

For a moment, something other than cold confidence flashed across Tim's eyes, and in that moment, he saw Randy for what he was: remarkable, and unbelievably, undeniably human. It caused him to take a step backwards, to hesitate, to doubt…and to forget that he was surrounded by enemies.

✳✳✳

Travis reached the top of the incline with both his arms and legs burning. As somebody who had run an average of twenty miles a week since he was fifteen, Travis would have thought climbing a steep incline carrying an eighty-pound dog would be easier. He was out of breath, and his arms felt rubbery as he let the dog drop to the pavement and turned to holler at Randy to start coming up.

His words caught in his throat as his eyes took in what was happening bellow. In the full moon light, Travis had no trouble seeing them. Randy was standing still as a statue, the Hunter only a few feet away, his gun practically touching Randy's forehead. Travis' heart came to a sudden stop, his breath froze in his lungs, and all rational thought ceased. He could do nothing but stare down at what was about to happen.

Then, inexplicably, the Hunter took a step back, and his gun lowered. What was happening? Why had he done that?

No sooner had the Hunter's feet settled into their new stance when a high pitched, bizarre roar erupted from the trees directly to the Hunter's right. It sounded something like an elk call and a lion's roar mixed together with something altogether unheard of. It amplified as it echoed off the mountains, surrounding them with the terrifying strangeness of it. With the roar came the familiar crashing of something large running through the woods, but whatever it was moved in a manner that Travis had never seen from a wild animal. He heard each step as it hit the ground with such impact, they could practically feel it through their feet. Moving fast, heading directly for the Hunter. The moment the Hunter heard it, he turned his gun away from Randy and pointed it into the woods, barely having time to fire off a single sound.

The moment the Hunter's arm swung around to fire at this new foe, Randy bolted, heading up the incline at an angle, not even bothering to look back when the Hunter screamed. Travis was watching, though. He saw the Ohans come out of the woods, two at once, and converge on the Hunter. The largest one grabbed the man by the arm and threw him into the woods like he was a pinecone discovered in their path.

The Hunter landed ten feet back and used his momentum to roll to his feet and stumble into a run, the two Ohan mere feet behind him. Even as he ran for his life from the two beasts behind him, he couldn't resist taking the shot. It was such an easy shot, the boy standing at the top of the incline, silhouetted against the moonlight. Even running as fast as he could on uneven ground, it was an easy shot, especially for a man like Tim Harvey who had been a better than average marksman most of his life.

He fired three shots before turning away from the road and running farther into the woods, narrowly missing running headlong into a tree, and feeling the breath of the Ohan hot on his back. He smiled as he ran because before he had turned away from the road, he saw Randolph James fall.

***

"Randy!" Travis screamed, his voice sounding unfamiliar in his own ears as he ran towards his brother. Randy was slumped at the top of the incline twenty feet away, unmoving. But as Travis approached him, he pushed himself up onto his knees and then his feet, stumbling a little.

"I'ma 'kay!" Randy waved towards Travis. "Let's go!"

"Did he shoot you?" Travis demanded.

"I dropped when I heard him shooting. He missed," Randy huffed. "We need to get the hell out of here!"

"Yeah, that's an idea!" Travis laughed despites the circumstances. His brother was still alive, that was all that mattered to him right then.

Randy suddenly stopped, causing Travis to skid on the dirt in surprise. "Whose do you suppose that is?" Randy asked, pointing across the road to where a red Toyota truck was tucked back under the trees.

"What do you want to bet it's his?" Travis asked, approaching the driver's side door.

"Seems likely," Randy said quietly, coming up on the other side of the truck. Randy sounded strangely out of breath. Travis tried the door and found it unlocked. "Well, well ,well, will you look at this, the keys are in it!" Travis exclaimed.

Randy didn't answer but opened up the passenger door and began to climb in. Taking his que from Randy, Starkey jumped up onto the seat as well and quickly relocated to the extra cab. Travis was still debating—something about this seemed wrong—when a bullet hole appeared in the side of the truck a few feet from him.

"Time to go!" Travis jumped in and slammed the door shut just as another bullet shattered the window next to him, sending little squares of safety glass flying into his lap.

Travis was peeling out onto the main road, sending dirt and rocks flying, by the time the Hunter got off another shot. With his foot to the floor, they were gone in seconds, flying recklessly down the narrow dirt road in the darkness.

"Turn the fucking headlights on!" Randy screamed, both arms stretched out in front of him as if he could somehow slow the vehicle by sheer force of will. The look of terror on his face was so acute, it took Travis off guard for a moment.

"I don't know how," Travis said calmly, narrowly avoiding a large rock near the edge of the road, taking out a low hanging branch with the windshield. Out of the corner of his eye, Travis saw Randy hastily put on his seat belt.

"The button on the steering wheel!" Randy gestured wildly in the general direction of the steering wheel.

"Oh," Travis pushed the button, and the road ahead of them came to life, causing Travis to turn the wheel sharply as they came out onto a paved two-lane road.

"You're out of your mind!" Randy said tightly. He was gritting his teeth, one hand to his neck, the other one tucked firmly under one armpit.

"What did I do, give you whiplash or something?" Travis asked, glancing over at him.

"I'm fine," Randy snapped. "We need to find Laura. Do we have any way of getting in touch with her? We can't let her go back there with that psychopath waiting."

"Um…." Travis thought for a moment. "I can set off a danger beacon. It will warn her, but as for how we would meet up I have no idea."

"We have to…to make sure she's okay," Randy said a little quieter.

Something about the tight, halting way he spoke alerted Travis. "What's wrong with you?"

"Nothing. Let's just get out of here and find Laura." Randy said, eyes ahead.

"What's wrong?"

"Nothing! Just drive!"

"Damnit!" Travis swore and turned on the overhead light. The first thing he noticed was the color *red*. It was covering the seat between them, dripping on the floorboards and glinting wet in the new light. *Red.* Deep, dark crimson red, and Randy was covered in it.

"He shot you," Travis whispered.

"Travis watch the road!" With his free hand, Randy gestured towards the dash, but Travis couldn't take his eyes off of his brother.

"Travis!" The high pitched, panicked quality of Randy's voice snapped Travis out of it and he looked ahead, shouting and jerking the wheel. It was too late; they were going too fast. The truck slid into a spin, then tipped, rolling completely over once to land back on all four wheels just in time to slam into a massive oak tree on the driver's side.

Travis opened his eyes and saw the truck, crushed and still against the tree, and somewhere in the back of his mind, he knew that he had been inside only a little while before. He had not been wearing a seatbelt like Randy; he must have been ejected somehow, possibly through the shattered driver's side window. It didn't really matter.

For a moment, he lay there, not really comprehending what had happened, watching the moonlight sparkle off the frost on the road. Then a small part of him came alive and he tried to stand, but pain shot through him, dropping him to the pavement once more. He lay there until the lights came.

There were two of them, bright white lights, and that small part of him that was awake knew they were the headlights of an approaching vehicle. That same small part of him also realized that he was lying in the middle of the road, but the rest of him didn't care; the rest of him was slipping away into darkness. The approaching headlights disappeared in the darkness, as did the truck and the tree and the pavement and the frost. The last to give into the dark was that one small part of him, that tiny piece that was fighting to remain, to be heard, to be remembered. But then it, too, succumbed to the darkness, and there was nothing left to understand.

Chapter 19

Images appeared before him, real or imagined he did not know, faces, colors, voices in no discernable sequential pattern, always fading back into the darkness only to appear again out of nowhere. Travis paid little attention to these weird moments of half wakefulness. They were just a pit stop between starless night and starless night. He always longed to get back to that place where nothing mattered, nothing existed, where there was nothing at all.

At some point, Travis opened his eyes and realized it wasn't difficult. His mind wasn't foggy, and it felt like he was all there again. He could only remember bits and pieces of drug addled moments and even now, he could not discern what had been real and what had been dream. He stared up at a ceiling that was painted such a light color of green, it could be mistaken as white at first glance. The place appeared to be a motel room of some sort with the typical hotel room layout. There was a laminated list of different channels and local stations printed the same light green as the walls hanging on the wall behind the TV.

The carpets were a pleasant cream color and the blankets and pillowcases that Travis lay on where a stark, bleached white. The color of the carpets and bedding told him that he was in a relatively expensive motel. The cheap ones always had darker colored floors and bedding to hide the stains. Also, the room smelled faintly of vanilla. He guessed it was coming from the ventilation system, and only the classy joints did extra stuff like that.

The next thing Travis took in was his own appearance. He was wearing loose fitting jeans with bleach white socks on his feet. He was shirtless and heavily bandaged around the midsection; he also had a bandage on his left shoulder and bruising over most of his body. The bruising was beginning to fade, indicating that it was at least several days old.

Sitting up slowly, Travis looked over his hands and realized that somebody had trimmed his fingernails and cleaned him up. He was as spiffy clean as he had ever been, and somebody had shaved him. He ran his hands over his face, feeling the baby smooth skin. It was a closer shave than even he was able to accomplish most days. He ran his hands through his hair, feeling that it was not only clean but conditioned.

The loving care that some person had shown him didn't so much touch him as freak him out, and his initial reaction was to shudder painfully. He didn't like the idea that someone yet to be identified had been so intimate with him; especially given his history of not liking being touched.

After a few awkward attempts, Travis forced his sore and stiff body to stand and regarded the two doors in the room. He decided on the one in the far war wall and discovered a sitting room with a desk, a small table in front of a wide window, a loveseat, and two comfy chairs. The sitting room was decorated in pretty much the same as the other, though the paintings portrayed sailboats and yachts. He figured they must be somewhere on the coast.

A quick look around revealed the setup of a small suite; two bedrooms, connected by a bathroom and a sitting room. Travis paid little attention to the bathroom and immediately focused on the second bedroom where he found an unconscious Randy lying on the bed.

Like Travis, Randy was shirtless, but unlike Travis, who was wearing a new pair of jeans, Randy was wearing loose bicycle shorts. Travis guessed that this was to allow room for his swollen right knee. His right wrist was in a brace and appeared a little swollen too. He had a long line of about thirty stitches from the bottom of his right ribcage to just above his belly button, as well as a purple bruise that pretty much followed the path of a seatbelt. The bruise was beginning to fade. There was a cut on his right cheek, incidentally in almost the exact same place the Hunter had cut him with a broken beer bottle several weeks before, and the whole right side of his face was bruised. The right side of his neck was heavily bandaged, and there was a small patch of fresh red blood staining the clean white gauze.

Despite the obvious wounds, Randy's hair was washed to sparkly gold, his face shaven, his nails trimmed. He had apparently gotten the same makeover as Travis had. This did not make Travis feel any better about the intrusion on his personal boundaries. If anything, it made him feel more uneasy.

He lay his hand on Randy's shoulder and gave it a light shake, calling his name a few times. When this failed to rouse him, Travis gave up, not wanting to wake him before he was ready. He figured that like himself, Randy had been drugged, and unlike Travis, who had abused both prescription and illegal drugs in the past, Randy wasn't in the habit of taking even the smallest medications for pain and thus had little to no resistance.

Travis did another, more thorough, search of the suite. He checked the closets and drawers in both bedrooms and the sitting room and discovered little of interest. In the sitting room he found a paper bag sitting in one of the chairs near the table. The bag held four changes of clothes, four pairs of jeans, two in Travis' size and two in Randy's, and four graphic T's. there was also an unopened package of socks and underwear.

On the table above the bag was a note, written on a pad of paper that had the name of a motel Travis did not recognize. He read the note twice and continued to search the place another time just to be sure. Starkey was nowhere in the motel room. Whoever had brought them to this place had neglected to bring Starkey along.

The realization that his dog was not there momentarily frightened Travis, and the ensuing thought that perhaps Starkey had not survived the crash kept him from functioning for several minutes. He sat on one of the chairs and cried for a while out of pure frustration. How had his life gotten so out of control that he didn't even know where the hell his dog was, or where he was, for that matter?

Once the shock and despair had passed, he was able to convince himself that he was perhaps jumping to conclusions; there could be any number of reasons why Starkey was not left in the motel with them. He was deluding himself, grasping at that one small ray of hope. He wanted to believe that his dog was safe somewhere…and unhurt.

He went into the bathroom and examined himself closer in front of the mirror. Cautiously, he peeled back the heavy bandages that covered most of his midsection and discovered three black stitch lines forming a large H. He stared at it in the mirror for a few minutes before carefully replacing the bandages.

It was all falling into place now. He frowned into the sink, a dark mood settling over him. He knew suture marks when he saw them; he had been given surgery at some point after the accident. That, coupled with the grooming both he and Randy had received, pointed to only one person.

Only a mother would pay such close attention to detail. His mother, the doctor, the woman who had fixed up his father on countless nights when he had come home less than whole. His mother had a private practice with a fully functioning surgical unit. If nothing had changed since he was a child, at least half of her staff were aware of her husband's profession. That explained how the two of them had been put back together…and how they had been drugged.

Travis was angry. He went back into the sitting room, put on one of the shirts from the bag and found some shoes, then he settled down on the couch to brood for a while. He was sick of all the lying, sick of the secrecy and the façade. Why did they keep manipulating them like this? Was he their son, or was he a pawn in this Seer/Hunter game of theirs? Was he just something to be used? Were he and Randy just chess pieces, with no way of knowing who was playing the game? When were they going to start being honest with him? Were they ever?

"Hey." Travis looked up to see Randy standing in the doorway, looking drowsy and confused, heavily favoring his injured leg. "Are you okay?"

Of course that would be Randy's first question. It was just like him to think of everybody else first. He didn't even seem angry that Travis had nearly killed him. "Yeah, more or less. Are you?"

"I think so." Randy gingerly touched the side of his neck. "Did I get shot?"

"Yeah." Travis nodded. "I'm so sorry, Randy."

Randy took his hand away from his neck and fixed Travis with a somewhat puzzled expression. "Wait, did *you* shoot me?"

"No." Travis leaned forward; it was his turn to be puzzled. "Harvey shot you. Don't you remember?"

"No, not really," Randy admitted. "Where are we?"

"Not exactly sure. What's the last thing you remember?"

"Ummmm." Randy put his fingertips to his forehead and tried to think. "Laura and I got in a fight. Then I went to find you. Um, I guess the very last thing I remember was going to sleep that night after we roasted the last of the hotdogs."

Travis nodded. "Yeah, that was two weeks ago. I think we were drugged. I did something stupid, Randy."

"Not like that is anything new." Randy shrugged. Travis took a deep breath and told Randy what had happened, sparing no detail.

When he was finished, Randy nodded, taking it all in. "So, what did you do that was so stupid?"

Travis' mouth dropped open. "…I was driving way too fast! You kept yelling at me to slow down. I nearly got us both killed."

Randy shrugged. "Yeah, you had a Hunter on your tail. Laura said that Seers have very strong instincts regarding Hunters, and your instincts are to run. He wasn't holding me hostage this time, you didn't have to engage him, so you were following your instincts and getting your ass out of there as fast as you possibly could."

Travis nodded. "That makes a lot of sense, but just this once, can you not be so logical? Just this once, can you be mad at me?"

"No, I don't think so," Randy said, investigating the contents of the bag on the table and pulling out a pair of jeans. "You punish yourself enough for both of us." He chose a pair of pants from the bag and limped into the bathroom to change. "So, we have no idea how we got here, or who prettied us up?"

"No." Travis said, keeping his suspicions to himself.

"That is too creepy for words."

"Yeah."

"I mean, look at these nails!" Randy came back into the room and held out his hands. "I'm a construction worker! Construction workers are not supposed to have nails like this!"

"Neither are welders. Whoever they are, they left a note." Travis pointed towards the paper on the table. Randy picked it up and began to read out loud.

> Drear Travis and Randy
> You are safe and with friends, please do not try to leave the hotel room.
> There is a chance you are still in Danger.
> We will be back shortly, again, please do not go anywhere.

"Hmmm," Randy made a noise as he set the note back down on the table. "Well that explains a lot now, doesn't it?" He picked up a pen and wrote something down on the paper bellow the other note. Travis got up to read over his shoulder.

> Whoever you are,
> You *CLEARLY* don't know us very well!

Ha!" Travis chuckled and looked up to see Randy grinning at him.

"C'mon, man! Let's go get something to eat. I'm starving!"

"You're the bad influence my mother always warned me about, aren't you?" Travis said.

"Please." Randy snorted, pulling on his shoes with some difficulty. "I'm the bad influence?"

"As bad as they come. After all, you're the one with the criminal record here, not me."

"Oh, you're pulling that card, aren't you?" Randy teased. "Apparently, you don't remember how I got that criminal record."

"I remember. C'mon, let's go." Travis opened the door and stepped outside into the parking lot of a U-shaped motel that appeared to be fairly high end with individual little cabins making up the rooms.

They could hear the ocean from where they stood, and if that wasn't enough to tell them they were close, the salty scent in the air and screech of seagulls definitely was. It was a chilly day, with a ten mile an hour wind coming off the water that added to the cold and caused both boys to shiver.

"Where are we?" Randy asked.

"Crescent City, I think." Travis said. "It has a Crescent City type look to it."

"Where's Crescent City?"

Travis shrugged, "Somewhere along the coast, pretty close to Oregon. I did an intervention here a few years ago. If I remember correctly, there's a little sandwich shop a few blocks up this street near a park by the beach."

"Sounds good!" Randy said and began limping in that direction.

They found the sandwich shop with relative ease and settled down at one of the tables outside on the grassy area overlooking the beach. They were halfway through their subs when Travis asked the question that had been gnawing at him.

"So…you and Laura got in a fight?"

"Yeah."

"Care to elaborate?"

"No."

"Oh, come on! I know how much you like her," Travis pressed. "I just want to know what you guys were fighting about."

Randy sighed. "She said she needed to go into town to get a few things, I said you're not going alone, she said oh yes, I am. She won, I lost. I even offered to go into town and get the stuff for her, but she refused to let me. It was pretty obvious that she was lying about what she needed to do. I called her on it and she ignored me. It doesn't matter now, and it doesn't matter that I like her. I just really hope she's okay. I don't like not knowing where she is."

"She's fine. I know she is," Travis said around a mouthful of sandwich. "Why doesn't it matter that you like her?"

"She's off limits, isn't she? She's your sister. Friends' sisters are off limits."

"No, she's not. Besides, I think the fact that you're my brother cancels out that rule."

Randy set down his sandwich. "Now, when you say it like that, it just seems creepy!"

"It kind of does, doesn't it?" Travis laughed. "Creepiness aside, though, you have my blessing."

Randy sighed again. "You're sure she's okay?"

Travis nodded. "Yeah, I'm sure."

Randy picked up his sandwich again, signaling the end of the conversation. They ate in silence for the next couple of minutes until Randy glanced over Travis' shoulder and mumbled, "seven o'clock".

Travis glanced in that direction without turning his head and stiffened as he saw a tall, broad man crossing the park towards them. He had salt and pepper hair that was longer than how most men his age wore it, and the shadow of a beard along his jaw line. Still in good shape despite the fact that he was pushing fifty, he crossed the grass quickly and came to a stop beside the table where the two boys were eating.

"You left the motel," he said in greeting, his voice a nice tenor.

"Yeah," Randy said nonchalantly, not even looking at the older man. It was the same attitude he had used when trying to piss off a foster dad. "We're not big on being told what to do."

The man nodded. "Are you all right?"

"I've been better, but I'll live," Randy answered, still giving the man the cold shoulder.

Again, he nodded and turned to Travis. "Are you all right? You were thrown from the vehicle and were hurt pretty bad." He reached out to put a hand on Travis' shoulder.

"Don't touch me!" Travis snapped, causing Randy's head to jerk up in surprise. He had never heard Travis sound so cold.

"I'm sorry," the man said, "I didn't mean…I just wanted to know that you were okay…"

"Oh, you care *NOW!*" Travis was out of his chair in one fluid movement and shoved the man hard in the chest. "You care now!" he continued with his assault, the anger in his voice so strong, it made him sound possessed. "Where the fuck were you when I was lying in that hospital, huh, Dad! Where the fuck were you when I was getting the crap beat out of me in those foster homes? Where the fuck were you!!!!"

Allen Nightdale held up his hands in a gesture to calm Travis down. "Travis, please!" he said softly, "Please just let me explain."

"Explain!" Travis yelled, inches from his father's face. "Explain what? I saw what you did! I saw you leave me in that hospital! You left me there on purpose!" Travis was shaking, and he turned away from his father to take a breath, but just then, Allen reached out to grab his son's hand.

"Please!" he begged.

The moment he felt his father's hand on his, Travis whipped around, leading with his fist. He wasn't even sure what he was doing until he felt his clenched fist make contact with his father's cheek; he was lost in a blind rage. The hit was solid, and he felt the bone and cartilage give as drops of blood sprayed from the man's nose as his eyes momentarily rolled back. Travis saw all of this in slow motion, hearing nothing but the pounding of his own heart.

This time, Allen Nightdale was not able to keep his feet. He spun around and stumbled back several feet before hitting the ground with a satisfying thud. "Don't you ever touch me again!" Travis snapped and turned around only to collide with his mother.

Lauren Nightdale had her hands to her mouth, tears brimming from her eyes, shocked over what she had just seen her son do. Laura, who was standing behind her mother, was mimicking her stance. Travis took a step back. He hadn't expected to see her here, and in an instant, his rage was gone, replaced by an emotion he couldn't begin to understand.

Lauren took her eyes off her husband, who was trying to sit up on the grass, and looked at her son, making eye contact for the briefest moment, not sure what to say or do to make her son stop hurting. Travis broke the contact, looked down at the ground, then at his father, then at his mother one last time. "I'm so out of here!" He turned away from them, heading towards the beach.

"Travis!" Laura shoved past her mother. "Wait!"

"Don't, Laura!" Travis snapped over his shoulder, dropping into a trot and then a full run. "You're the last person I want to see right now!"

Laura stopped as if she had been struck and watched her brother storm away. Tears welled up in her eyes as she turned to Randy, a hopeless expression on her face. He wrapped his arms around her, not knowing what else to do, and allowed her to cry into his shoulder. "You said he wouldn't hate me," she said between sobs. Randy smoothed back her hair with his hand and held her as he watched Travis retreating. He knew that Travis' scars ran deep, and some wounds would take a lifetime to heal. He didn't know what to say to Laura. Travis didn't hate her, but he wasn't sure if his brother would ever fully forgive her.

Chapter 20

Travis really wanted a cigarette; he hadn't dealt with cravings for a while, not since about a year after Randy had bullied him into quitting, and the heavy smoke in the bar wasn't helping him at all. He surveyed the almost empty lounge he had just walked into and headed to the bar, sitting at the opposite end as the two chain smokers already three sheets to the wind. He was hurting all over and his midsection where his suture was had been throbbing. Adrenaline had kept him from feeling it at the time but he was likely going to regret every move he had made earlier.

"Man, what happened to you?" The bartender asked.

"You should see the other guy." Travis said. "Can I get a beer?"

The bartender hesitated. "You sure, man? You look like you just went nine rounds. You know it's not safe to mix alcohol with medications."

That was a good point, Travis really had no idea what kind of medication were running through his veins. "Got a non-alcoholic beer, then?"

"Sure man." The bartender said symmetrically and handed Travis an O'Doul's. Travis gave it a kind of disgusted look, but it was better than nothing.

There were too many emotions moving through him at the moment, too many directions for his heart to be pulled in. He was quite sure that if a Hunter had shown up just then, he wouldn't have put up a fight at all. Part of him felt bad about punching his father, while the other part of him thought the jerk had deserved it. Pretty much all of him disapproved of the way he had snapped at his mother, and there was no excuse for yelling at Laura like that. All she wanted to do was make things right, to get her family back, and he had dashed her dreams in a single sentence.

In his heart, he knew that they had to have a reason for this. There had to be a reason for it all. But right now, in this moment, he didn't care what the reason was. His father had seen something in that hospital, something so powerful that he was willing to abandon his only son to protect him. Maybe someday, they would be cool enough around each other to talk about it. But not today, and he was pretty sure tomorrow was out too.

There was a song Sophia had really liked; she used to hum it a lot when she wanted to annoy him because he hated that stupid song. He could still hear it, her soft humming, and it seemed so appropriate to his mood. Terri Clark: *I just want to be mad for a while.* That pretty much summed it up. He didn't care what the reasons were, at least not right then, not tonight; he just wanted to be mad for a while.

He gulped down the last of his beer and signaled to the bartender for another. The bar wasn't that full for what he had learned was a Friday night. There were only about ten people there, and it was a large place. It was dark and smoky, the perfect place for somebody to go when they wanted to disappear for a while.

"Done with that?" The bartender asked.

"Yeah," Travis nodded. "Can I get another?"

"Sure." The bartender looked over Travis' shoulder towards the door. "That the other guy?"

Travis glanced over his shoulder and saw Randy. His brother didn't approach, though, instead he took a seat at one of the tables near the far wall. Giving Travis his space. Travis pretended like he didn't see him and drank is non-beer slowly. He needed just a little more time to brood.

"How do you always manage to find me?" Travis asked, a little annoyed, when he finally joined Randy at the table some twenty minutes later.

"Were you hiding?" Randy raised an eyebrow at him.

"No, but…Will you stop looking at me like that!"

"Like what?"

"Stop it!"

Randy laughed and shook his head. "I'm not looking at you in any particular way, but I do find your paranoia refreshing."

Travis sighed and leaned back in the chair. "So, what happened…after I left?"

"You mean after you laid out your dad most awesomely?" Randy shrugged. "We went back to the motel for a little while, got some stuff worked out. I talked to your dad a bit. He's not mad, by the way. I doubt you care right now, but he's not. He knows he crossed a line; your mom didn't say much, but I got the impression that she's pretty mad at your dad. She gave me a shot in the knee and gave us some pills for the road."

"The road?" Travis leaned forward.

Randy nodded. "Yeah, they left. Five's a crowd, ya know."

"Did Laura go with them?"

Randy shook his head. "No, she and Starkey are back at the motel. Why?" His eyes narrowed. "Did you want her to?"

"No. I didn't want her to go. Is she really mad at me?"

"No," Randy said, "she's not mad, but she's devastated. She thinks you hate her. She's been afraid that you would hate her after you got your memory back for a while."

"I could never hate her. I just…I guess I just want to be mad for a while," Travis said.

Randy cocked his head to the side and smirked, understanding the reference.

Travis pushed himself up with the table. "Let's get out of here…unless you're going to let me get an actual beer?"

"Nope. Besides, your mom said it was a bad idea what with your recent surgery." Randy stood as well and laid a few bills on the table to pay for his coke.

"You just made that up, didn't you?" Travis asked, pushing open the door and stepping out into the bright afternoon light.

"No," Randy said. They began walking up the semi-busy street in silence. It was a nice day, if a bit cold, and the salty air smelled of barbeque and wood smoke.

"Randy?" Travis said after they had gone about three blocks in silence.

"What?"

"If I asked you to do something for me, even if it were really hard, would you?" Randy glanced at Travis with concern and took a deep breath. Something about Travis' voice sounded hollow.

Randy shrugged. "Maybe. Probably."

Travis took a deep breath. "I need you to leave, Randy."

"Really?" Randy said, his voice unconcerned. He had seen this coming a while back. Travis was far too predictable.

"I'm serious, Randy."

"Oh, I'm sure you are. But I'm seriously not going anywhere," Randy said nonchalantly.

"You don't understand!" Travis stepped in front of him, blocking his path and forcing him to stop. "Harvey wants you dead just as much as he wants us."

"Yeah, because you saved me. I know. Laura explained it to me." Randy tried to step around Travis but once again, his way was blocked.

"No, it's more than that," Travis insisted, trying to make his brother understand. "Being saved by a Seer means he can kill you freely. It does not mean he is mandated to kill you. There is something more going on here, Randy, something you don't understand. He is mandated to kill you the same as he is us. Your best option is to disappear."

Randy took a deep breath, trying to be patient. "I'm not leaving you, Travis, and I'm most certainly not leaving *her*. Now, if you're done being crazy, I'm still starving, and Laura said she was going to order pizza."

"No, I'm nowhere near done! Randy, you need to get the hell away from us!" Travis yelled hysterically. Several people in the vicinity began glancing their way, and one person even pulled out their phone. Nervous, Randy grabbed Travis' arm and pulled him into a narrow space between two stores, little more than a walkway littered with cigarette butts and trash.

"You need to calm down," Randy hissed, lowering his voice considerably.

"No," Travis shook his head and began to pace back and forth in the narrow walkway. He was looking at the ground rubbing his hands together in a fidgety manner that Randy had seen a lot in the foster homes with kids suffering from PTSD. Sometimes, a situation would become too stressful, or loud noises would bring uncomfortable memories to the surface, and the kids would have to step back from reality to self-soothe. Randy clearly remembered once when he was fourteen, finding a younger boy hiding in a closet, rubbing his hands together just like that, shaking his head in that same manner. "I…I can't calm down, Randy. I can't. Not until you promise you'll go somewhere safe."

"You know I can't do that," Randy said slowly, watching Travis with a trained eye. There was something more happening here, but he just wasn't sure what.

"You can, you just won't." Travis stopped pacing and leaned his forehead against the cool brick wall, closing his eyes. "You won't, you won't, you won't!" He punctuated each "won't" by slapping the brick wall with the palm of his hand.

"Okay, okay, stop it." Randy said soothingly. He gently grabbed Travis by the shoulders and turned him towards him. Keeping his hands on Travis' shoulders, he carefully examined his brother's eyes. "You just had the two O'Doul's, right? Nothing else?"

"I'm not on drugs, Randy," Travis said, a little annoyed. "I'm just…." He took a deep breath. "I'm scared."

"It's okay to be scared, man. I'm scared too," Randy said, feeling like he was trying to comfort a small child.

Travis leaned against the wall, looking strangely deflated. "You don't understand, Randy. Everything is different now. I know what you are."

"Okay," Randy said, trying to sound soothing. "What am I?"

"You're an Angel."

Randy couldn't help but laugh at that, and it took him a moment to get himself under control. Travis watched him mutely from where he leaned against the wall, wondering how he was going to explain this to a man like Randy.

"I'm sorry, I'm *what?*"

"When I say Angel, I don't mean some celestial being," Travis tried to explain, speaking slowly, and thinking about every word before he spoke it. "I mean… it's what you are." He pushed himself off the wall and began pacing again, but more thoughtful this time, less frantic, talking with his hands. "You know how Laura said that we Seers are more than human? Well, Angels are perfectly human. Angels are everything humanity could be, everything they strive to be, a shining example of the potential of us all. You are perfectly, wonderfully human."

"I'm sorry, have we met?" Randy said, raising an eyebrow at his brother. "My dad murdered my mother a room away from me, and I did nothing. He was so evil that years later, I still couldn't stand up to him! I've beaten up more people than I care to count, including you, whom I put in the hospital!"

Travis shook his head, dismissing what Randy said. "Your father has nothing to do with who *you* are, Randy. Every single fight you've ever gotten into has been to protect somebody else. That's what you are, a *Guardian Angel.* There are different kinds, and you're a guardian, a protector. Don't you see Randy, you are an amazing human being! What kind of person goes through what you have gone through, what happened with your parents, being shuffled from home to home, being beaten and molested, and yet you still became you!

"Randy, every single person you encounter walks away better for having even known you. You call out the gold in people, you repair broken hearts and broken dreams and you don't even know you are doing it. That's the thing about Angels; they never know what they are, or how incredible they are. And they certainly don't know how rare they are."

Randy shook his head. "You're wrong."

"I'm not," Travis said. "Every now and then, humanity produces somebody like you, and fate always tries to wipe you out. Angels are why Seers exist. Not everyone we save is an Angel, they are far rarer than that, but every person we save may produce an Angel someday. It may be generations down the road, but it will happen. And an Angel like you? You guys are like our holy grails! People like you are everything we strive to protect, and everything they strive to destroy. That Hunter knows what you are now, Randy, and I'm not sure if I can protect you this time."

"You're crazy, Travis!" Randy took a step back. "You're wrong. There's nothing special about me."

"There is, Randy. And there always has been. You are not perfect; you are just as deeply flawed as any other human. That's what makes you so extraordinary. You've always been a light in this world." Travis took a deep breath. "You can't help being who you are; you can't help being an Angel any more than I can help being a Seer. That's why you won't leave; a thousand other people put in the same situation would just walk away, but not you because you're a guardian."

"If you know I can't leave, then why did you ask?" Randy smirked.

Travis sighed. "I guess I was hoping I could convince you. I was hoping maybe our friendship was strong enough." He bit his lip. "Is it?"

"No."

"Randy…?"

"I said no," Randy said a little stronger this time and turned around on a heel, heading back towards the street. "This conversation is over. Now pull yourself together before we get back to the motel. I don't want Laura to see you like this."

"This conversation isn't over," Travis said firmly.

"Fine. Stay here and keep talking, then. I'm going to get me some pizza!" Randy said and walked away. Travis hesitated, then stepped out of the dark walkway and followed his brother down the crowded street.

"You're a jerk!" Travis said under his breath when he had caught up to Randy.

"I thought I was an Angel." Randy teased.

"Shut up!"

"You started it!"

"Did not." Travis shot back and Randy was smart enough not to reply. They walked back to the motel in relative silence, watching the people around them in a mixture of curiosity and suspicion. Travis did not sense a Hunter nearby, but that did not mean Harvey did not know where they were. He was in a hurry to get moving, get out of town.

Chapter 21

When they finally got in sight of the motel, Travis felt a sense of dread settle over him. He wasn't looking forward to seeing Laura, seeing that disappointed look in her eyes. She used to annoy him so much when they were kids, it was sport for her, but even when they had wanted to kill each other, she had always looked at him like he was her hero. It was strange how much he wanted that back.

Randy didn't bother knocking. He just opened the door and walked in. Travis hesitated before following him. Laura was sitting in the corner of the loveseat, her knees drawn up to her chest; she had apparently been staring at the door when Randy walked in. She looked pale and exhausted, but other than a little bit of puffiness around the eyes, there was very little evidence that she had been crying.

Starkey was lying on the couch beside Laura, creating a perfect circle of fur, but when the boys walked in, his head shot up and he was off the couch in a blink of the eyes and at Travis' feet, nothing but a swirling mass of tongue and fur, having what appeared to be a seizure of pure happiness. He scratched Starkey behind the ears and under the chin for the next minute before standing up and facing Laura.

"You came back," she said.

"Of course I came back. You have my dog," Travis said, not meaning for it to sound as cold as it did.

"Where's the Pizza?" Randy asked.

"They are running behind, said it would take about an hour and a half, so it should be here in about twenty minutes," Laura answered.

"Good," Travis said. "Can I take a shower?"

Laura stared at him, confused. Travis grunted and lifted up his shirt to reveal the bandages. "I mean is it safe to take a shower?"

"Oh." Laura unfolded her legs and sat up a little straighter. "I'll have to re-bandage you afterwards, and you'll have to be careful not to soap directly over the suture, but you should be fine. It's been long enough since the surgery."

"What was the surgery anyways?" Travis asked.

"I don't know the details, but you were bleeding internally, and Mom had to go in and fix what was torn," Laura said. "You were very lucky you survived. That wasn't exactly a minor accident. You should have been wearing a seatbelt."

I also probably shouldn't have been driving at a hundred and twenty miles an hour, either, Travis thought. "Yeah, I know." He walked into the bathroom without another word.

"That could have gone a lot worse," Randy said, trying to lift Laura's spirits a little. "It's not all you, though. In fact, I'd say you don't even make up ten percent of what's ticking him off."

Laura nodded, not listening. "How is your knee?"

"The walk didn't help it all that much. It's only about three times the size of the other one. Doesn't hurt too much, though." Randy said, sitting down on the loveseat next to her. She nodded and looked down at the floor. "Hey!" Randy said quietly, getting her to look back up again. "Will you stop, please? Travis needs a little time is all."

"He wasn't exactly warming up to me before, if you remember. He was almost always gone when we were camping. He hasn't trusted me since the get go." Laura leaned her head against Randy's shoulder and snuggled into him. "And he *never* lets me touch him. It's a sign of trust among Seers. We let the people we trust brush against us rather than take great pains to avoid contact. Travis will practically pretzel himself to avoid having even the smallest chance of touching me."

Randy sighed and put his arm around her. It was not lost on him how much Laura had been touching *him* lately. None of it was sexual, not even flirty, just simple human contact, but she was right that Travis did not allow any contact with Laura, not even when they were sitting in the car next to each other. He was not at all weary of contact with Randy. They nudged, pushed and shoved each other constantly, but then, Travis had never avoided contact with people he loved and trusted the way he did with other people, the way he did with Laura.

Randy still remembered how surprised he had been when Travis allowed Momma to brush some leaves and dirt out of his hair. It was such a common motherly gesture, but Travis had never allowed any foster parent to have casual contact with him. It had happened before of course, you couldn't completely avoid human contact when living with humans, but Travis had not jerked away in the manner he always had before. For four years, Randy had never seen Travis allow such contact from a foster parent, yet this little old woman had gained his trust. Laura was right. It was all about trust.

"He knew you weren't telling him the whole truth. He knew you were hiding something from him. He knew he couldn't trust you," Randy said.

"I'm not hiding anything anymore," Laura said softly.

"No," Randy agreed. "Things will change now, you'll see."

"You sound so sure," she said wistfully.

"I am." Randy smiled. "That's something I've learned. Reality is in a constant state of flux. Things are bad one day, and then the planet keeps turning and it gets better. You're on your knees, thinking how am I going to survive this situation? Then you blink, and reality finds you standing tall, knowing that you can survive anything. Fights don't last forever; people don't stay mad forever." He took a deep breath. "Right now, we're running for our lives. Travis is pissed off at the world. Both of us are recuperating from yet another near-death experience, and just about every movement hurts. Yet I've never been happier!"

"What? You've never been happier?" She looked up at him with a raised eyebrow.

"Yep!" He smiled down at her. "I'm clean, my hair and nails look great, I have beautiful lady snuggled next to me, and there's pizza on the way. It's all about perspective!"

She looked at him quizzically and burst into laughter. She sat up, laughing so hard that tears came out of her eyes, and Randy realized that he had never heard her laugh before other than in a polite manner. She had a good, strong laugh, the type that filled the entire room and could be heard from outside. Randy's smile broadened; it was nice to see her loosen up a little. She had been so tense for weeks, and suddenly, it was like she was unraveling, like a tightly wadded up straw wrapper after a drop of soda is applied. It felt good to hear her laugh.

The pizza arrived a moment later: a supreme and a beefed-up Hawaiian with bacon, chicken and barbeque sauce. Laura had also ordered two 2 liters of soda and some chicken wings. They were set to pretty much gorge themselves, and Randy fully intended to.

Randy had polished off three slices of pizza, and Laura was just starting her second one when Travis came out of the bathroom.

He was wearing jeans and nothing else with a towel across his shoulders and his hair doing the Einstein. "Hey, Laura?" He asked.

Laura swallowed a bite and turned him, dabbing at her lips delicately with a napkin. "Yeah?"

"Should this be bleeding?" He lifted his arm and turned his side towards her, revealing a thin line of blood flowing from his stitches down his side, already turning the rim of his jeans a dark crimson.

"No!" Laura stood and threw down her napkin angrily. "How the hell did you tear your stitches in the shower?"

"I don't think I did. The bandage was pretty bloody when I took it off."

"Oh," Laura said a little calmer. "You must have torn them when you and Dad had that little tiff earlier."

Travis grabbed a napkin off of the table and held it against his side to catch the blood. "Did you seriously just refer to what happened as a tiff?"

"Well," Laura crossed her arms defensively, "that's what it was."

Randy laughed. "That was more than a tiff! That was awesome! I've never seen you punch somebody like that before!"

Laura turned and glared at him so fiercely, he felt it before he saw it. "Um." Randy paused with his pizza halfway to his mouth. "I mean, bad Travis! Having a tiff with your father! How immature of you!"

"Nice save," Travis said sarcastically. "But I'm still bleeding."

Laura sighed. "I'll go get the medical bag. Wait for me in the bedroom."

***

Laura set the "medical bag", which was actually a tackle box, on the bed next to Travis and opened it to reveal what appeared to be a compact M.A.S.H. unit. Laura navigated through the box like a pro.

"That would have come in handy. Why didn't you have that before?" Travis commented.

"What do you mean?" Laura asked, filling a syringe with saline solution.

"Back when you rescued us in Chico, and Randy was all beat to hell. You had a nice little first aid kit, but nothing like this. Would have really come in handy. I wouldn't have had to go hit up Damon for drugs," Travis explained.

"Yeah, it would have been useful. I didn't really know what was waiting for me when I came to get you guys. I was coming back from a night class when Dad called me and told me to go get you and Randy NOW!" She eyed his torn stitches. "Dad didn't really know what was going on, either. He got an e-mail from Harvey that really freaked him out. When I called him and told him what happened and how badly hurt Randy was, I think he nearly had a heart attack. Lift your left arm for me."

Travis did as he was told, feeling the pinch of the torn suture. Laura balled up a towel from the bathroom and held it against Travis' side just under where the stitch was torn. With her other hand, she took the syringe and sprayed the area with saline, then patted it dry. "Is that really necessary? I just got out of the shower," Travis said, wincing a little.

"I'm just being thorough," Laura said, picking up a gnarly looking hook and threading it. Travis chose that moment to look away; he didn't like to see other people get stitches, let alone himself. "What was in the e-mail?"

"From Harvey?"

"Yeah."

"This is going to pinch a little," she warned, and Travis felt something like a bee sting and then a pull. "The word "Checkmate" and a picture of the back of your house. You weren't anywhere in the picture but Randy was. He was in his bedroom, had his back to the window."

"Was he trying to draw Dad out or something?"

"I think he just wanted to torture him. He knew Dad couldn't get there; he didn't know I could, though. I think he fully intended on killing at least Randy that night, maybe you, too. He just wanted Dad to suffer. He wanted Dad to see Randy in that window, see how vulnerable he was, and know that there was nothing he could do to stop it."

Travis laughed, incurring a hiss from Laura. "Don't laugh! What are you doing! Do you want this hook in your spleen?"

"I'm sorry, I'm sorry!" Travis said, trying to get his mirth under control. "It's just, the thought of Randy being *vulnerable*. The guy is six three and build like Thor! In high school, the football team called him the Wall!"

"Dude took me down with one hit, Travis! Your conversation isn't really helping my self-esteem!" Randy yelled from the next room.

"He's not broad enough to be Thor anyways," Laura commented. "He's also too tall. Thor is shorter."

"I see. I didn't know you were on speaking terms with the god of thunder," Travis said.

"We go way back," Laura said, tying off the stitches and cutting them. "Okay, you're done; try not to do that again."

Travis examined her work. "You're good at this."

"I suppose I have to be," Laura said. "I've fixed up Dad more times than I can count, and Randy and now you."

"Well, thanks," Travis said awkwardly, carefully pulling on his shirt. He walked into the other room without another comment, leaving Laura to finish packing up the first aid box by herself. "Well, I guess that's a start," she said quietly.

***

It was two thirty A.M.; the motel room was silent, save the occasional yip or bark Starkey made in his sleep. Every now and then, a light from a passing car would filter though the closed blinds and move across the wall. The entire world seemed like it had slipped into a coma.

Travis lay on the little couch with his fingers laced behind his head, studying the ceiling with an interest that baffled him, sure that he could see designs in all the thousands of little dots. He was too exhausted to consider that this behavior may not be normal. He tried to close his eyes once or twice for longer than a blink, but the action stung, so he kept them open. If it had been two years ago, he would have called Sophia, and she would talk to him until he fell asleep. If he were home right now, he would go out to the shed and fire up one of the machines, start a new project or work on an old one, or he would go out to the living room and play a video came on mute.

But Sophia was dead, and he didn't have a home anymore, so he lay on the surprisingly comfortable couch and stared at the infinitely fascinating ceiling, contemplating the meaning of life. After some time, he forced his stiff body to stand and nudged Starkey with his foot, rousing the dog. "C'mon, boy."

He threw on a sweatshirt and opened the door, letting Starkey out first before he closed the door behind him. He had intended on going for a short walk, but now that he was out here, faced with the cold, he realized he was too tired for even that. He sat down on the stoop in front of the door instead. At least, outside he had something different to stare at. Starkey settled down beside him and lay his head in his owner's lap.

Travis watched the stars for some time before digging his wallet out of his pocked and opening it to the picture of Sophia and him on prom night. Travis was in a dark blue zoot suit with white stripes and Sophia in a long, blue evening dress that had been worn by her sister before her.

Sophia's hair looked stunning in the photo; so shiny black, it reflected the light back at the camera. She didn't do much to it at all. Her naturally curly hair looked perfect. She was wearing blue eye shadow to match her dress, making her already dark eyes a little too dark for Travis taste, but he never would have told her that. She was sensitive about her looks.

The motel door opened, startling both Travis and Starkey. Laura stepped out and closed the door behind her, taking a seat beside him. "I heard you leave, but when you didn't come back in, I got worried," she explained.

"Did you think I took off?" he asked.

"I don't know, maybe." She shrugged and jerked her chin at the picture he was holding. "I knew you were thinking about her. You always turn light blue when you are thinking about her."

"What?"

"I see people in colors; it's one of my gifts as a Seer," Laura explained. "Usually, I have to touch somebody to see their color, but I have always been able to see yours. I think it's because we're family."

"And I turn light blue when I'm thinking of Sophia?" Travis asked.

She nodded. "Yeah, most people stay one color all the time, but you're a shifter, meaning your color fluctuates." She shrugged. "From what I've seen, most Seer's are shifters. At least I've never met an adult Seer that wasn't."

"What color am I normally? Or do I have a normal color?" Travis asked.

"You are usually a very dark blue. Navy, maybe. With little swirls of dark purple. Like a storm cloud." She said, looking at her hands. "Sometimes, when I walk into the room and you and Randy are joking around and your guard is down, I catch a glimpse of sky blue before you armor up and get dark blue again."

"Huh." Travis thought that was an interesting observation. "What color is Randy?"

"Gold, like polished bronze," Laura said

"He's not a shifter?" Travis asked.

"No." Laura shook her head. "Sometimes he burns brighter, sometimes he dims darker, but he's always gold. Sometimes, he glows."

"Fits him," Travis said. He indicated the picture. "I wonder what color she was."

"Violet, but a very light violet, almost white. She glowed too. When people are glowing, I don't have to touch them to see their colors. They are just there," Laura answered.

Travis stared at her. "How do you know that?"

Laura sighed. "I saw her a couple of times. Mom used to practically stalk you and Randy. Every time she got a weekend off, she was wherever you were. She doted on Sophia and absolutely loved her. She cried for weeks after she died."

"Oh," Travis said, looking away. "I didn't know."

"The first time Mom took me with her, I was fourteen, and we were there all day and hadn't even caught a glimpse of you or Randy," Laura said, looking up at the stars. "We decided to go to *Olivia's* for dinner, hoping that we would at least be able to see Sophia. She usually served at her parent's restaurant on Friday nights. We walked in, and the place was a mess. It looked like every table in the place needed to be cleared. Sophia was the only one working, though we could see her father in the back. She hastily cleared off a table for us and apologized. She said that they were understaffed."

Travis nodded. He remembered that night but did not remember taking notice of Laura or their mother. It had been after the incident in Mount Shasta. If he had looked closer, he probably would have recognized the woman at *Olivia's* as the same woman who had rescued the two of them from bitter cold just over a year before. He didn't spent much time in the front, though. He had been in the back trying to make a dent in the dishes and helping Sophia's father.

"Mom and I were ordering when the two of you walked in," Laura said, her voice distant. "It was the first time I saw you since…and it was the first time I had ever seen Randy. I heard plenty about him and seen a few pictures. I had my back to the door when you guys came in, but Mom's reaction tipped me off. You went right to the kitchen, and Randy grabbed a cart and started clearing the tables. Sophia looked so relieved.

"Randy brought us our drinks and laid on the charm so thick, you'd think he had been doing it his whole life. I almost spilled my drink and he caught it. He touched my hand in the process, and that's when I first saw that he was gold."

Travis was silent for a while, then sighed. "Was that when you fell in love with him? At first touch?"

Laura's eyes widened a little, but other than that did not outwardly show her surprise. "How did you know?"

"I just did." Travis shrugged. "Was it then?"

"I don't know," Laura said. "After that, I couldn't stop thinking about him for months. Other boys would ask me out, and I always found myself comparing them to Randy in my head. I guess that's why I've never had a real relationship. After about a year, I stopped thinking about him all the time. I guess I kind of forgot what his touch felt like. Then after you were shot, I shook his hand at the hospital and…I think that's when I really knew."

Travis nodded. "Do you think he loves you back?"

"Yes." Laura practically blurted.

"That was a quick answer." Travis grinned.

"I know he does." She looked away, blushing.

"How?"

"You know when I said he glows sometimes?" Laura said.

"Yeah?"

"He glows when he's looking at me."

Travis nodded. "Don't hurt him, okay?"

Laura laughed. "I'm your little sister; shouldn't you be giving him this talk?"

Travis shook his head. "Nope. You're way stronger than he is." He sighed. "Randy's always had a wall around his heart. I think it's because he knows it's made of glass."

"You don't give him enough credit," Laura said, offended.

"Maybe." Travis sighed. "So, what happens now? Where do we go from here?"

"Dad's working on a way to get us all out of the country," Laura said.

"Well, at least somebody has a plan," Travis said. "I'm not mad at you, Laura."

"I didn't say that you were," she said quietly.

"You didn't have to. I'm mad at Dad, not you. I'm actually kind of proud of you."

"You are?" Laura's head came up in surprise.

"Yeah," Travis said with a smile. "You've turned into an all right person, which surprises me because you used to be the *sibling from hell.*"

Laura shrugged. "I tried, at least. You weren't exactly the best brother in the world, either, but you were always there for me."

Travis shrugged as well. "I'm going to try to go to sleep." He pushed Starkey off him and stood, offering Laura a hand. "I feel like I should say I love you or something, seeing as we just had some deep conversation, but I'm not going to."

Laura took his hand and stood. "You're not going to tell Randy what I told you, are you?"

"Nah." Travis grinned. "I may start calling him Golden Boy, though. It will be fun to watch him try to figure that one out. What's the use of having a best friend if you can't screw with them from time to time?"

Chapter 22

Tim Harvey took a long drag from the joint he had rolled for himself and held the smoke in as long as he could before releasing it. He hadn't smoked pot in a few years but felt the need to calm his nerves. The Nightdale family and their pet Angel had fallen off the radar again. His ankle was still twisted and swollen from his encounter with the Ohan, and he still had bruises over most of his body. He had given the police a good description of the two young men that had assaulted him and stolen his truck and completely totaled it ten miles down the road. They would be looking for the boys, which may be beneficial to him.

His nerves were raw, but the weed was helping. He needed to end this family, and in three weeks, he would be able to do it according to the rules. The girl was nearly killing age; this would all be over soon. But first, he needed to find them again. Especially before they fled to another state or country; he doubted they would go to another country permanently, but it was possible.

Lauren Nightdale was a doctor, and as such, it was difficult for her to pack up and pick up a new life somewhere else with a different identity. Med school records would have to be transferred to a different name, work history had to be arranged. These things cost money, took time, and almost always left a paper trail. It could be done without a paper trail, but Allen Nightdale lacked those kinds of connections. If they fled, it was likely that they would flee to another country for a few months, then they would enter this country in another area and begin to rebuild.

Allen Nightdale had taken his wife's name when they had married, and his younger brother, Jefferson, had changed his name to Nightdale a few years later after surviving a run-in with a Hunter. Tim did not know their original last name. If Lauren decided to take her husband's name upon re-entry into the United States, this could pose a problem. While a doctor was easier to track, if the name was a common one, it could take months or years for him to locate them again.

No, he needed to end this here, before they had a chance to jump ship. He was sure that Allen was planning on getting them out before Laura's birthday. But Tim wasn't making it easy for him. He had flagged Allen's credit cards as stolen, and for Allen to fix this problem, he would have to come out of hiding and reveal his real home address rather than the ten or so dummy addresses he used. The tracking software Tim used had already alerted him to three attempted plane ticket purchases by Allen, all of them heading to Eastern Europe. The transaction had been halted every time due to Tim tampering with Nightdale's credit cards. If Allen wanted to get his family out of the country, he would have to do it with cash, which wasn't easy after September 11. The FBI watched these things closely nowadays.

He wanted to kill Allen and Travis last, but he also did not want to lose this family. He may have to make an adjustment and kill Allen sooner rather than later or perhaps go after both the men of the family and wait to kill the girl till she was of age. Both scenarios would give him satisfaction. So long as they died, he would be okay with it.

As a licensed private investigator, Tim had any number of resources available to track his prey—most of them legal, a few of them not. He had one of the illegal systems running on his computer screen before him: a facial recognition program that the FBI used. He sat back in his chair with twisted ankle propped up on a pillow, taking long drags from a joint as he watched the computer doing his work for him.

He had hacked his way into one of the leading surveillance companies in the United States, and thus gained access to all of their customer's surveillance footage. The only drawback to the program was that he could not scan for multiple subjects at once. He had to run a new scan for each target. At the moment, he was scanning for Allen. Next, he would scan for Laura. They seemed the two most likely for him to get a hit on.

Blip!

The computer made a noise and the screen froze on the footage from an AM/PM on the coast. The word MATCH blinked in big red letters before disappearing. Tim gently removed his injured foot from the pillow and leaned forward towards the screen. Two patrons could be seen paying with cash. Tim would recognize them anywhere

He grinned and zoomed in on the location. "Well, well, well, Allen, what are you doing in Crescent City? And what did you do to make your wife so upset?"

Lauren was crying in the fuzzy footage, though she was trying to hide it, and Allen had an impressive black eye. Again, Tim smiled; his guess was that young Travis was none too happy about being played with. He wondered if Allen had fought back at all or if he had allowed himself to be used as a punching bag?

He marked the date and time of the footage on a notepad next to his computer. The Nightdale's had made their gas station purchase a little over twelve hours ago. They were probably out of the area by now. He quickly set up another scan, this time starting in the Crescent City area.

Blip!

Tim was surprised; that was faster than he expected. Then he grinned as three familiar faces flashed fuzzily across the screen. Twenty-five minutes ago, at 8:42 AM, Travis, Randy and Laura were at the exact same gas station, buying candy bars and enough caffeine to kill a horse. This day was getting better and better.

Tim dismissed the facial recognition program and selected the AM/PM's individual file. They had an outdoor camera as well. A moment later Tim watched as the little car pulled out of the gas station with that cursed dog's head sticking out of the window like some unfashionable flag. He grinned. It looked like the little dears were heading south.

"Welcome back on the radar, my pretties." He giggled, far more than the marijuana contributing to his high.

****

"Awe, that's adorable!" Randy said, leaning sideways to look at the back seat.

"What?" Laura asked. She was driving and hadn't said more than two words in over an hour, causing Randy to wonder if she was upset about something.

"Check the mirror," Randy said, turning back around in his seat and indicating the rear view. Laura reached up and adjusted the mirror. "Oh my gosh! That may just be the cutest thing I've ever seen!"

"It is, isn't it?" Randy laughed. "Where's Travis' phone? I'm gonna take a picture and set it as his wallpaper!"

"I think he has it."

Travis was sound asleep in the back seat with a sound asleep Starkey curled up next to him, his head on his master's chest, one ear flipped inside out, the tip of his tongue protruding from his mouth. "Use my phone; it's in the cup holder," She said.

Randy snatched up the phone and took some pictures of the sleeping pair. "I think I got it!"

"Good, I'll send one to Mom later."

Randy laughed. "I can't believe he's crashed like that. Didn't he down like three cappuccinos after we left the motel?"

Laura nodded. "Yeah, but he didn't really sleep last night. I heard him tossing around a lot."

"Did you guys get a chance to talk?" Randy asked hesitantly. "I heard him step outside, and then I heard you get up, but I fell back asleep without really registering it."

Laura nodded. "Yeah, we talked."

"Were you guys talking about me?"

"No," Laura shook her head. "We were talking about Sophia. Why?"

Randy shrugged. "I was just wondering if you knew why he was calling me Golden Boy this morning. I can't seem to figure that one out."

"I don't know. I thought it was just one of the bazillion nicknames you guys have for each other," Laura said with a straight face.

"I don't remember that one." Randy said, watching the ocean pass by out the window.

"Maybe it's because you're the only blond in the group," Laura suggested.

"Travis normally isn't that clever with the nicknames," Randy said. "However, he did refer to you as Lolly once this morning. Maybe he's giving us code names."

"He called me Lolly?" she asked softly.

"Yeah, why?" Randy shrugged. "I could give us *way* better code names! Well, actually, as code names go, Golden Boy isn't that bad."

"No, my middle name is Lynne, so Travis used to call me Lolly when he was a toddler. He ran the words together. He kept calling me that as a nickname as we grew up, usually when he was trying to annoy me because he knew I hated it."

"Sounds like a big brother thing to do. Are we slowing down?" Randy asked.

"Yeah, there is a little country road coming up that should connect us back to the five. I don't want to keep heading south. I was going to switch back and head into Oregon, maybe go up and spend the night in Medford, or we can circle around to Klamath Falls and come back into California that way. It will keep our pattern erratic. I don't want to become predictable," Laura explained.

"I'm not really clear on why we are even still *in* California," Randy said. "If we are trying to shake this guy, shouldn't we be making a beeline for the East Coast?"

"We have to keep the family close enough together that when Dad figures out a way to get us out of the country, we can regroup fast."

"Won't that just make us easier to kill?" Randy asked.

"Keep heading south," Travis suddenly said from the back seat, opening his eyes but making no other movement. "We need to go to Fresno."

"Should I ask why?" Laura said, making eye contact in the rearview.

"Shooting at a Walmart," Travis said.

"How quickly do I need to get there? Fresno is a ways," Laura asked.

"By 2:00AM. We should have enough time." Travis closed his eyes again. "If you're worried, let Golden Boy drive. He'll get us there in time. I'm going back to sleep."

Randy turned around and raised an eyebrow. "Okay, what's with the Golden Boy?"

"Nothing, I just thought we could use codenames. Mine is Hawkeye," Travis said, smiling without opening his eyes. "And don't take any more pictures of me!"

Chapter 23

"No." Randy said as he and Travis hastily walked across the dark parking lot.

"What do you mean, no?" Travis said. "You can't say no! I'm the code name guy!"

Randy shook his head. "That's not how it works. You picked my code name; Laura has apparently had hers since she was born, and you don't get to pick your own code name. I get to pick it."

"You didn't write the rules on code name giving!" Travis shot back. "I'm keeping Hawkeye!"

"You look nothing like Allen Alda!"

"I can do that eyebrow thing," Travis said, as if that settled everything.

"No, you can't! You just *think* you can!" Randy argued "I'm picking your code name."

"Fine, what is it, then?" Travis caved.

"Give me a minute, I'm trying to think."

"See? Not so easy, is it?" Travis teased, and turned to a middle-aged man who had just gotten out of a Chevy pickup. "Excuse me, sir?"

"Can I help you?" the man asked, his tone rude.

"If you could pick your own code name, what would it be?" Travis asked, stepping in front of him.

"I don't fucking care!" the man said, shoving past Travis. Travis stumbled back and held up his hands, "Sheesh man! I just wanted your opinion!"

"Yeah! Asshole!" Randy yelled after him. The guy didn't look back but managed to point his middle finger in their direction.

"Well, he certainly was Mr. Sunshine, now, wasn't he?" Randy said as they turned and started walking back.

"Yeah, can't imagine the fit he's going to throw when he realizes I swiped out his loaded Glock for a dummy." Travis said, pulling the gun out of where it had been concealed under his coat. "This thing is heavy."

"What are you going to do with that?" Randy asked, jerking his chin at the weapon. "Turn it into the police?"

"Normally I would, but I think I'll hang onto it for a while. We could use a gun." Travis removed the magazine and checked the chamber before putting the gun back inside his coat.

"Is that wise?" Randy asked, not liking the idea. He had never been a big fan of guns, and while he knew how to use one and was licensed to carry, he didn't much like them anywhere near him. He felt they invited trouble.

"Probably not," Travis admitted. "But you have to admit, there have been quite a few times when we could have used a gun, and unless you want to swing back by the house in Chico and get mine, this one will do nicely."

"You know, I really wouldn't mind swinging back by there and getting some clothes and stuff. My other pair of shoes, toothbrush, ya know?" Randy said wistfully.

"We can't go back there." Travis said.

"Why not?"

"We just can't." Travis shrugged. "It doesn't feel right, okay?"

"That's a vague answer," Randy pointed out.

"It's all I've got." Travis shrugged again.

"Well, I'd like a little bit more then all you've got." Randy was getting annoyed now.

Travis sighed and stopped walking, turning to his brother. "Do you trust me?"

Randy rolled his eyes and indicated the way they had just come. "If I didn't, would I have just walked across a dark parking lot to steal a loaded gun from some psycho off his Thorazine?"

Travis smiled. "Then trust me, something doesn't feel right about going back there. I don't think we should even drive through Chico. It's just…I don't know. It feels like it's cursed or something. If we go back there, our luck will change, and as Seers, luck is one of the only things going for us."

Randy groaned and turned away. "Fine! But I want to get some new clothes soon!"

"Don't like the things my mother picked out?" Travis teased.

"It's not the clothes themselves. It's how few of them we have," Randy shot back. "I've been wearing these jeans for three days!"

"Yeah, we could use some more clothes." He sighed. "I guess I kind of got used to always having money. It kind of sucks not being able to access my bank accounts."

"And you guys are sure that it's not safe to access mine, either?" Randy asked with a raised brow. "I had a fair amount of money saved up myself, you know. Other than gas, food, and clothes, I didn't have too many expenses, and with a job that paid well, I'm not short on savings."

"We risked a lot doing that wire transfer to begin with." Travis said. "Laura has been keeping track of the money, so I'm not sure if we are in trouble yet. We should ask when we get back."

They walked in silence for a few minutes, sweating in the California heat even though it was well into October and just past two a.m. There wasn't too much street activity this early in the morning, and as the two brothers walked through the glow of streetlights, the night fell eerily silent.

Uncomfortable with the seemingly unnatural silence, Randy spoke. "So why did Mr. Sunshine and Therapy back there want to shoot up a Walmart anyways? They fire him or something?"

Travis shook his head. "His ex-wife works there. She petitioned a judge a few years back to have his visitations removed due to the fact that he was becoming unstable."

"Imagine that?" Randy mused.

"The real reason was suicide by cop, though. It's kind of sad. The guy found out he has cancer a few weeks ago. Not much they can do about it. He reasoned that this way, he may be able to get even with his ex. He could pretty much ensure a quick ending, and at least he will get his name in the news."

"That is sad," Randy admitted. "Speaking of sadness, you seem…. I don't know, happier, I guess."

"I do?"

"Yeah, you've been kind of in a dark place for weeks, but right now, I can swear you are almost skipping," Randy observed. "What's up?"

Travis shrugged and grinned. "I do feel happy. Honestly, I think it has something to do with having an intervention to do; it's like a return to normalcy for me. It feels like I'm starting to get back on track. It feels good."

"I thought it may have something to do with knowing who you are for the first time in ten years," Randy suggested.

"Nope." Travis answered a little too quickly. "I'm still pretty pissed off about that whole situation. But give me a nutjob with a gun, and I'm a happy camper!"

"You're a weird guy, Travis."

Travis laughed. "And you're just coming to this conclusion?"

"I think I've been in denial."

"Admitting it is the first step to recovery."

"Good to know."

When they entered their motel room a few minutes later, they found Laura sitting on her bed in her pajamas watching a news story on the television intently. She was leaning forward, her chin resting in her fist and her long hair, still wet from a shower, engulfing her face and shoulders like a tent. She leaned back when they walked in and pushed her hair behind her ears. "How did it go?"

Travis shrugged. "Okay I guess. Picked us up a firearm." He showed her the gun. "What are you watching?"

"Protest in Syria and Egypt." She watched as Travis put the gun away in a drawer next to the other bed. "I'm glad. We could use a gun."

"Seriously?" Randy sat down on the bed next to her and indicated Travis. "You're okay with this?"

"Why wouldn't I be?" Laura asked.

"It's a stolen gun!" Randy emphasized.

"A gun stolen from a suicidal maniac with anger management issues," Travis clarified.

"It's a stolen gun! It's like inviting trouble!" Randy tried again. "We shouldn't go looking for trouble. We should just lay low."

"How is having a gun looking for trouble?" Laura asked.

"It just is!" Randy pushed himself off of the bed and began to pace. "Having one of those things…. it's like waving a welcome banner for the wrong kind of people, people who would otherwise have left us alone."

"Like Harvey, who shot me in my own living room when *you* had our gun?" Travis pointed out.

Randy huffed and sat down in one of the chairs near the television. "I just don't like them."

"Randy is a little superstitious," Travis said to Laura.

"I can see that." Laura smiled at the moody blond. "We're already in danger, Randy. Carrying a gun is a wise move at this point. I don't understand how you can't see that. After all, you were grazed by a bullet just a few weeks ago. I bet you wished you had a gun when Harvey had that rifle to your head."

"I know I sure wished I did," Travis said, still standing next to the door, reluctant to walk farther into the room for some reason.

"No," Randy leaned forward in his seat, "I didn't. I don't understand how *you two* can't see my point."

"Because your point is irrational," Travis pointed out. Randy let out a frustrated groan realizing that this was a losing battle. He decided to drop it but did not want to give Travis the satisfaction of conceding the point.

Travis flopped down on the empty bed and stretched out with his hands behind his head, wincing as his stitches pulled. "Whatever. I would love it if we could go to sleep now. It's like three o'clock in the morning, and checkout is at eleven."

"He always wants to sleep after these things," Randy said to Laura.

Laura nodded. "So does my dad, and if he has two or three in a row, good luck waking him up for the next three days."

"Where's the rollaway?" Randy asked, looking around the room.

"It's in the little cubby hole slash closet thing next to the bathroom." Laura pointed, turning off the television. "Are you sure you're okay to sleep there? I can give you the bed. The two of you are still awfully beat up."

"I'm good, Laura. Besides, I'm too much of a gentleman to take an offer like that. Somebody raised me right. I'm not sure who, but somebody did." Randy said, locating the roll away cot with ease.

He had his back to her, so he couldn't see the sad look that briefly shadowed her face. It was gone by the time he turned around, but Travis had seen it, and he found he could read her expression as easily as when they were kids. She was thinking that somebody like Randy deserved so much more than a psychotic father and meek mother. He had deserved the kind of love he so easily granted to others. His story should not have been tragic, but there was no redeeming the past, only the future.

***

Laura's eyes snapped open with the startling revelation that something was terribly wrong. She blinked in confusion and listened. Then she heard it, a soft yet intense sound, like that of a wounded animal in too much pain to keep silent yet still aware of predators nearby.

She blinked in the gloomy dim light of the motel room, the noise bringing out a primal fear in her that she thought she had left behind with childhood. The kind of fear that arose when the closet door creaked and lead to the certainty that there was a monster hiding in the darkness within, waiting…waiting….

But this noise was no monster, she realized as she suppressed the fear and turned to look at her brother. Sweat had pinned his hair to his face and scalp, and his body was so rigid that at first, she feared he may be in the grips of a seizure. His fist clutching the sheets in a white knuckled death grip. Every muscle seemed to be cramped into a tight knot, even the muscles of his neck. The only part of him that was moving was his head, which he tossed from side to side in a jerky spasm.

It was the look on his face that caused her the most concern. Jaws locked and cheeks hollowed, it wasn't only a look of complete horror, but despair as well. Whatever his dreams had brought him, he did not think he would survive. He was fighting a battle he was destined to lose, yet he couldn't bear to give up the fight.

She sat up, pushed back the blankets and was reaching for him when a soft voice stopped her.

"Don't," Randy said from where he lay on the little rollaway cot against the wall. He was lying on his side with his pillow tucked between his shoulder and head, blankets drawn up to his chin. His eyes were glistening; he had been up for some time, watching his brother. Though it hurt him to see somebody he cared deeply for in so much pain, he had learned to accept that there was nothing he could do. These were Travis' demons. "He may hurt you if you touch him. He comes out fighting most times, and sometimes, he doesn't fully wake up until he's done some real damage. He nearly broke Sophia's arm once."

"I can't leave him like this," Laura whispered, though she was sure that Travis was well past the point that he could be woken by mere noise.

"You can't help him, Laura," Randy said, sitting up.

Laura shook her head, knowing that Randy didn't understand. "Yes, I can," she said and lightly cupped Travis' head between her hands, closing her eyes.

****

She was in darkness, darkness so complete, it was felt rather than seen. It was cold—the kind of cold that drives through you like a thousand knives, drawing the very breath from your lungs. Without conscious thought, Laura knew she was in an iced over lake in the dead of night, and she willed herself upwards, towards the distant surface.

Slowly, light began to filter down to her, soft and blue, yet fractured, moonlight distorted through water and ice. Above her, the ice was as black as the water had been only a moment before. Travis was there, silhouetted by moonlight, pounding his fist bloody against the unbreakable ice, hovering always in that moment of suffocation when one realizes they are about to die, but in the dream, death never comes.

Laura surged up towards her brother, requiring no effort at all. This was Travis' dream, not hers, and thus this world could not hold her prisoner the way it held Travis. As she grew closer, she realized that Travis was not only trapped beneath the black ice, he was watching something take place above, on the surface of the lake.

Above them, a large man beat a small boy with a full beer bottle, and though the child screamed, no sound could be heard above the relentless pounding of Travis' fish on the thick ice. Laura somehow knew that it had been her own thoughts that had caused this image in her brother's mind. As the boy died, broken, alone and forgotten, the scene changed, and they watched as a lovely, young, Italian girl screamed as the headlight of an oncoming truck lit her horrified features. Again, the scene changed, and a small girl clung to a dead tree in the middle of an ice cold creek, her hand outstretched towards the brother who had just let go of her hand and left her alone.

Laura had seen enough. With one hand, she grabbed hold of one of Travis' wrists and with the other, she reached up and touched the ice, which instantly dissolved. In the next moment, they were standing on a hilltop overlooking a valley. It was night, and the stars were stunning, the smell of oleander flowers filling the air.

Laura let go of Travis' wrist before he realized she was there and allowed herself to fade away as a lovely Italian girl walked up the hill to take her brother's hand. She left him there, in the arm of the girl he loved. He did not need to know she had changed his dream. He did not need to know of this intrusion into his mind, so long as he was safe.

She opened her eyes and let go of Travis' face, aware that Randy had leapt from his bed and was charging across the room to defend her. She stood and smiled, seeing the peaceful expression on her brother's face, watching as his clenched body began to relax.

"What…what did you do?" Randy asked, his mouth hanging open in shock.

"I changed the dream," Laura whispered.

"You can do that?" he asked.

She nodded.

"Can all Seers do that?"

She shook her head.

"He was in a frozen lake…." she said, mostly to herself.

Randy nodded. "Yeah…two little boys drowned. He was supposed to save them but…he didn't get there in time."

Laura stepped away from Travis and returned to her own bed. "We should get back to sleep. We've still got a few hours."

Randy caught her hand, and she looked up at him, wondering if he were going to yell at her for intruding on Travis' mind. "Thanks," he said.

She shrugged and began to turn away but stopped when Randy kissed her. It wasn't much, just a soft brush on the lips, but it shocked her into speechlessness. "No, really, thanks for helping him," Randy said and went back to bed, leaving her to lie in bed staring at the roof until well after the sun was fully up.

Chapter 24

"Where are we?" Travis asked, opening his eyes groggily in the back seat where he was curled up with Starkey. He had been unusually sore all over. The kind of soreness that usually came after he had night terrors, but he didn't remember any such dreams the night before. He had gone back to sleep almost instantly after leaving Fresno that morning and guessed he had been sleeping for some time, being as Randy took over driving.

"Pacifica," Randy replied.

"Really?" Travis sat up suddenly, disturbing the otherwise content dog, and looked out the window at the gray and stormy sea. "Awesome! Let's find a beach and walk for a little while!"

"I'm up for that," Laura said with a large yawn. She had been sleeping as well. "I've never been here before."

"You haven't?" Travis leaned forward between the two seats. "Pacifica is awesome! It's all choppy today, but usually, it's incredible! It's nothing but beaches and cliffs and these awesome rock formations."

"It does look pretty," Laura observed, looking out the window.

"Pretty is an understatement, Laura! I'm gonna have to bring you back here in the spring or summer when we survive this."

"I'm up for stopping," Randy said, slowing down as they entered the main street of a small town. "I want to stretch my legs, and I'm sure Starkey would appreciate some exercise. Let's get something to eat first."

A half hour later, the three of them sat on a deserted beach in Pacifica eating to-go baskets of fish and chips. Laura and Randy were engaged in conversation about various Saturday morning cartoons that they watched when they were younger. Travis, who had pretty much avoided the television when he was younger, remained mostly quiet, but, unlike while they were camping, he did not completely remove himself from the conversation. He smiled at the jokes and laughed here and there while watching the slate gray swells roll in.

"It's really nice here," Laura said, lying back against the speckled sand with her hands behind her head. "Cold, but pretty."

"It's really nice in the summer," Randy said. "Frisco should be nice. It's fifty five degrees and cloudy here. Chances are, it's sunny and warm in Frisco. That city never seems to get the memo on weather patterns."

"I've never really been there either," Laura said, "Driven through a few times, but never stopped."

"When I got my first car," Travis chimed in, "Sophie and I ditched school one day and drove to San Francisco. We spent all day on the peer. Momma nearly killed me."

"Travis and I were in a foster home near Frisco for about six months when we were thirteen. The dad, Steve, was really cool and laid back; the mom was a bit of a dictator. Steve would take us out here to Pacifica or into the city on the weekends, just the boys. It was pretty awesome."

"Yeah," Travis said. "I really liked him."

"We'll have to take you to the peer for a few hours, Laura," Randy said. "Get dinner on the Warf, grab a sleazy motel in the Mission District."

"We shouldn't. We're already spending way too long in this area." Laura shook her head.

"I'm with Randy. You need to see the peer." Travis stood up and brushed sand off his jeans. "I'm going to go for a quick walk first, though." He smacked his palm against his leg, bringing Starkey to his feet. "C'mon, boy!"

Laura and Randy watched as Travis began to jog, but then grabbed his side as his body reminded him he wasn't there yet and settles into a walk. "Why does he like running so much?" Laura asked.

Randy shrugged. "I think it's how he resets his mind."

"That must be a nice trick." Laura nodded.

"I'm…uh…I'm sorry," Randy stuttered, looking out at the ocean. "About last night. I shouldn't have done that. I'm sorry if it made you uncomfortable."

Laura sat up and stared at him, Randy would not turn to look at her. Finally, Laura put her hand under his chin, forcing him to turn to her. Then she kissed him. It was not a soft brush of the lips as he had given her, and she knew she had surprised him, but she had been thinking about it for hours.

Neither of them pulled away. In fact, they got closer, and after a few minutes they were both lying on the sand, wrapped up in each other's arms, not caring who saw them. In the beginning, their kisses were desperate and rushed, but after a few minutes, they became softer and more tender. The world had vanished around them, and for that moment, they were the only two people in existence.

Tim turned the knob on the binoculars he held to his eyes, bringing the pair on the beach into focus. He grinned and chuckled to himself, sure that he could kill them both with a single of his rifle. As close as they were, they made an assassin's job easy. But the girl was still underage, and he doubted he could kill Randy without causing unintended damage.

He returned his binoculars to their case and returned to his car. He was not a pervert. He found no joy in watching two young people inspect each other's tonsils, especially too young people he fully intended on killing.

He let them have this tiny bit of happiness before their lives were ended. Why not? It would only make killing the boy that much sweeter. After all, he had thought killing Randy first would be agony for Travis, who loved the Angel like a brother; he hadn't realized that he would be taking something away from Laura as well. His smile broadened. It was going to be a good day.

"Should we be talking?" Randy asked hesitantly.

"We are talking," Laura said.

"No, I mean about…you know, what just happened?" He let go of her hand for a moment to rub the back of his neck nervously. They had been walking down the beach hand in hand, enjoying each other's company but not saying a word. Neither of them had spoken in over twenty minutes.

"We kissed." Laura smiled at him.

"It was a little more than a kiss," Randy pointed out.

"Okay, so we vigorously kissed." She shrugged. "And no, we don't need to talk about it."

"Should we tell Travis?" He reached for her hand again, but she pulled away and turned to him.

"Why would we do that?" She crossed her arms.

"Because he's going to know," Randy said.

"So?"

"He's my best friend, and you're his sister. I don't want him to be mad at me," Randy explained.

"He won't be mad at you; he'll be mad at me." Laura began to walk down the beach again, leaving Randy behind with a puzzled expression on his face.

"Why on earth would he be mad at you?" Randy struggled to catch up to her and took her hand again. The sand was not being kind to his injured knee, though he tried to hide it.

"Because he's more protective of you than he is of me," she said.

Randy didn't respond at first. He wanted to tell her that it wasn't true, but the more he thought of it, the more he realized that is probably was. Travis *was* protective of Randy. Travis was also well aware of how and why all of his previous relationships had ended. He figured it was probably a draw when it came to who he was more protective over.

"Okay," he conceded. "So, we act like it never happened?"

She shook her head. "No, I don't want that, either."

"So…. what?" Randy held his hands out in a helpless gesture. "What do we do?"

"We just be us," Laura said with a smile and turned to continue walking, leaving Randy confused.

"Yeah," Randy said to himself under his breath, "that's not vague at all."

He trotted down the beach to catch up with her, ignoring the pain in his knee. Just as his phone began to ring in his pocket, Laura turned to him, a pleased smile on her face. "Is that the Star Wars theme?"

"Yeah," Randy said, flipping his phone open. "What's up?"

"We need to go," Travis said, the speaker on Randy's phone loud enough that Laura could hear him.

"We're about a mile up the beach. We'll head back."

"I'll come get you," Travis said.

Randy stopped walking. "What's wrong?"

"I think he's found us."

"He can't come get us; I have the keys." Laura pulled them out of her pocket and held them up to jingle.

"He's probably already gotten it hotwired," Randy said just as Travis said, "I've already got it hotwired," over the phone.

Laura sighed. "Of course he has."

Randy hung up the phone and managed to grab Laura's hand before she pulled away. "You okay?"

"Yeah." She nodded, looking out at the ocean. "I like it here; I would have liked to stay another couple of hours."

He brought her hand up to his lips. "Yeah, me too."

Chapter 25

Travis didn't stop driving until well past one o'clock the next morning. He had switched back several times, and at one point, had broken the speed limit by nearly 80mph, prompting Randy to demand he pull over and let somebody else drive. But Travis refused. He wouldn't stop for anything. When prompted, all he would say was, "Got a bad feeling, got a bad, bad feeling."

When they finally did stop, they were in a little no name town in Oregon not too far from Klamath Falls. Travis wasn't happy about stopping. He would have kept driving through the night, but Starkey needed to get out of the car for a little while, and though he wouldn't give in to either Laura or Randy, he really couldn't say no to Starkey's plaintive whines. They woke up a disgruntles front desk man who looked to be pushing seventy at a little family owned inn and booked a room that cost a small fortune.

They slept until nearly eleven the next morning, which panicked Travis. He tried to get behind the wheel again, but Randy wouldn't let him. He was anxious and jittery until they got to Portland, where he finally calmed down.

Once they were checked into a less than clean hotel room and Travis had taken Starkey on a walk through a nearby park that was in desperate need of maintenance, Randy and Laura went to get something to eat. Sitting alone in the hotel room, Starkey sleeping at his feet, Travis held his head in his hands and waited for himself to stop shaking. He wasn't sure why he had been so afraid the day before, but he had felt for sure that Randy was about to die, that he was going to lose his brother, and that Laura was going to know what it felt like to lose the love of her life. As scared as Travis was to lose Randy, knowing what Laura would go through after the fact only made him more determined to save his brother. He didn't know the details, he didn't know the how or the why, but he was certain Randy had come seconds from death.

He could remember how quickly the world had changed that day by the creek. Uncle Jeff had been there one moment, standing strong and tall, then in a blink, Uncle Jeff was gone. Bits of him was filling the air, and Laura was screaming. Travis could remember how warm the blood had felt when it hit him and the smell of it and the way Uncle Jeff's face had....

The more he thought of it, the more he realized why it had been so easy for him to forget.

He had been a child; he could not have protected his uncle; he had done his best to protect his sister. He wasn't a child anymore, though, and he was unwilling to stand by as somebody else that he loved was blown away simply because they existed. He was not going to let Randy die, he told himself, but at the same time, he remembered how quickly it had happened before, how fast that bullet had turned a warm summer morning into a Tarantino film. How could he possibly protect Randy? Or Laura? Or anybody?

He took a deep breath and held it in till it hurt, then released it in a rush. He was letting his mind take him to dark places. He needed to halt the train of thought, throw a cow on the tracks. Self-pity and hopelessness where not the stables of a healthy mind, and they were the abyss of a Seer's psyche. Another deep breath, then another. He smacked his cheeks a couple of times, ran his hands through his hair, stood and paced, then pulled out his phone.

There was something he needed to do, something he had been avoiding.

The woman who answered the phone sounded tired but cheery, a typical nurse who had probably been on her feet for hours and was using all of her strength to muster up a smile. "Can I…" he cleared his throat, "Can I, um, can I please speak to Dr. Nightdale?"

"May I ask who is calling?" the nurse asked.

"This is her son."

"One moment please…" the earpiece was suddenly filled with incredibly annoying classical music that sounded like it was being fed through a dying speaker. Travis held his breath, waiting for that music to stop, dreading the voice he hadn't heard since he was twelve years old.

But instead of Lauren Nightdale, the nurse came back on. "I'm sorry, she's in with a patient at the moment. Would you like her voicemail?"

"Ye-yes please," Travis stammered, feeling like a child.

The voicemail was a generic computerized voice with only the person's name being spoken. *Please leave a message for* Dr. Lauren Nightdale *after the beep.*

"Hi," Travis said, rubbing the back of his neck and pacing the room, hoping his voice hadn't cracked. "Um, hi, Mom, it's…uh…it's Travis. I…uh…I just wanted to let you know that I'm not mad at you, and I don't hate you. I…I don't hate you, Mom." He took a deep breath. "I'm trying to understand, and I really can't right now, but I don't blame you for anything. I'm mad at Dad, and I'm sorry if I made you think that…. that it had anything to do with you. I don't hate you, Mom. It's important that you know that."

He hung up the phone then and wiped at his eyes with the back of his fist, unsure why that had been so hard. He stared at the phone in his hand for almost a full minute, trying to swallow the knot in his throat before finally saying out loud what he couldn't bring himself to say in the message.

"I love you, Mom."

****

"So," Travis said around a mouthful of sausage and eggs, causing Laura to cringe. "I say we keep going north, head through

Oregon, go all the way into Washington, then go east for a while, then south, and enter California through Nevada, or maybe New Mexico."

Randy nodded. "I'm cool with that; I've been wondering why we haven't put more space between us and this psycho's obvious hunting ground yet."

Laura was watching them over the top of her steaming coffee mug, her expression hard to read. Travis knew she was trying to come up with an argument against it. She didn't want to go that far away from her parents. They represented safety for her, and she wanted to be able to get back to them quickly if she needed to. She knew that Travis did not feel this way. To him, their father was not a man who would protect them at all cost; he was not the safe place he had always been for her. To Travis, Allen Nightdale was a man who had failed to protect his family; a man who had abandoned his only son.

She inhaled the scent of her coffee, realizing they were both looking at her, waiting for her reply. She calmly set her coffee down and squared her shoulders. "Yeah, okay, it won't hurt to put some more distance between us, and the Hunter won't be expecting that. He'll be expecting us to stick closer, to be ready to run."

The corner of Travis' lip curled up ever so slightly as he took another bite of his breakfast, and Laura tried to not give him the satisfaction of knowing she saw. He knew he had just won a great victory, perhaps even bringing their sibling rivalry back into play. Randy sat next to his brother, relishing his French toast, oblivious to the great drama that had just taken place.

Driving through Oregon and Washington proved more difficult than they had expected. The early November weather had turned, and they were diverted several times due to heavy snow and rainfall. They never made it into Washington but instead crisscrossed Oregon several times, finally being pushed into the bottom corner of Idaho before dropping down into Nevada. The whole excursion took them about four days, and by the time they hit Reno, Travis was far more relaxed and felt quite a bit safer, confident that for the moment, they were off the Hunter's radar.

They spent the night in Reno and decided to head back into California the next day. But Donner Pass was closed to all vehicles due to a severe snow storm and working under the assumption that most other roads heading that way would also pose a problem, they turned around, heading deeper into Nevada, and decided to go to Las Vegas.

Vegas was not a safe place for Seers. Both Laura and Travis felt very nervous and even close to panic while driving down the strip. They were both acutely aware that while luck favored Seers, it could also turn deadly very quickly. They steered away from the fancy casinos and overpriced motels into a more disreputable section of the city where it was unlikely that any tourist ever went. Here, liquor stores and by the hour motels were prominent, and most storefronts were empty with a splattering of creative graffiti. They found a motel that looked slightly less sleazy than all the others, paid for eight hours, and had a few very uncomfortable moments when all three of them were propositioned on their way to their room.

"Vegas, man!" Randy said, throwing himself down backwards on the bed. "It's not everything it's cracked up to be."

"No," Laura said, pulling a sweater out of her backpack, "we really shouldn't be here. A city like this…it's not a good idea. Reno was bad enough, but Vegas? We should leave first thing tomorrow."

Travis nodded, trying to turn on the television manually before realizing it was broken. "I think you're right."

Randy sat up. "I don't get it. You said luck favors Seers."

"It does," Laura said with a shrug. "But it also *targets* Seers. In a city like this, where games of chance are everywhere—chance itself is everywhere—there is just too much of it, and when there is so much, it can swing both ways. If there is a one in million chance of somebody finding a discarded diamond ring worth thousand, it would happen to us…and if there is a one in a million chance of a single engine aircraft falling out of the sky and hitting one motel room, it would be ours. What's more, it will seek us out, in places like this, where chance gathers like a storm. The air itself is pregnant with it.

Two Seers being here, in the same place, we might as well make ourselves the eye of the storm."

"Ominous!" Randy said. "But bullshit."

"Excuse me?" Laura said at the same moment Travis burst into laughter. Laura glared at both of them in turn before her annoyed expression was replaced with one of curiosity. "Why do you say that?"

"Because luck and chance are archaic, abstract ideas. They are not a force. They have no intention or design. Fearing or placing faith in an abstract idea only takes away your own power of free will," Randy said, standing and warming to the debate. He lived for conversations like this.

"You're half right. It is an abstract idea, but it is also a force of nature. But a neutral force, it can be pushed, manipulated."

"No, it can't." Randy shook his head. "There is no substance to manipulate, which is why it is abstract."

"Once again, you are half right," Laura said. "Try thinking of it in turns of other abstract ideas, like thought. It has no substance, no power, but when it is manipulated, it becomes one of the most powerful things on the planet, a force of nature in and of itself. One person standing on a street corner thinking isn't powerful, but when he compels others to have the same thought, it becomes revelation, it becomes a union march, a revolution, a holocaust. Thought can be dangerous."

"That's not the same," Randy insisted.

"How?"

"Because there is a huge difference between thought compelled by action and action compelled by thought!" Randy sat down at the little table next to the window, moving his hands as he spoke in the way he did when he got excited about a subject. "Thought compelled by action is powerless, because action is the *active* force of the equation. It is the catalyst. People can think about things all they want, but there is no real change, no real power, until they take action. Action compelled by thought is the force of nature, *action is the force!* Thought compelled by action is the opposite. Somebody robs a tourist, and a witness *thinks* to themselves, hey, that's wrong. But if his thoughts do not provoke action, they are powerless. Action provoking thought remains internal, whereas thought provoking action is external and thus powerful."

Laura sat down on the bed and shrugged. "Your very smart, Randy, but things like this, you're using the wrong brain."

Randy cocked his head to the side and smirked. "Did you just tell me to start thinking with my downstairs brain?"

"Stop laughing, Travis!" Laura threw a pillow at him and stood up again. "No, that is not what I meant, but you can't think about the supernatural in the same terms as the natural. The same rules do not apply."

"The natural is all I know," Randy said with a shrug.

Laura smiled at him. "That's not true."

"Well, true or not, I am content to be the voice of reason," Randy said, spreading his arms wide. "And Vegas," he winked at Travis, "Vegas is supposed to be fun!"

"Yeah, well, I can see where this conversation is going," Travis said. "We're not going to convince her to go to a strip club with us, Randy."

"That wasn't...." Randy began to protest.

"I call first shower!" Travis cut him off and headed into the bathroom.

"I'm going to run across the street to that convenience store and grab some food," Laura said, shrugging into a light sweater. Even in the desert, it got chilly this time of year once the sun went down.

"I'll go with you." Randy started to grab his coat.

"No, stay with Travis. I don't want to leave him alone." Laura countered, shooting an uneasy glance at the closed bathroom door. "He's the main target at the moment."

"He's also over six foot and has a vicious hellhound as a bodyguard," Randy said with a laugh. "I think we've put plenty of distance between us and the Hunter."

"Vegas isn't a good place for Seers. I do not feel good here. Please, just stay with him."

"You know I can hear you, right?" Travis yelled from behind the closed door. "And Randy's right, I can handle myself."

"You still haven't recovered from that car accident; you couldn't hold your own in a fight," Laura yelled back at him. Then, in a softer voice, she said to Randy, "Please, just stay here. It's like a block away. I'll be right back."

Before he could give another protest, Laura was out the door and walking across the small parking lot at a steady pace. She didn't like this city, didn't like the feel of it, and knew that she needed to be alone, at least for a few minutes, to calm her nerves. Everything about this city grinded on a Seer's nerves. Chance was everywhere. Everything a Seer was taught to avoid was everywhere. It made her skin crawl.

She cut through a small alley between the motel office and what looked to be a storage building for the motel. Both buildings were made of red brick and seemed out of place among the lights of Vegas, which where bright even in this less than ideal neighborhood. Neon lights seemed to be everywhere. Not the huge ones you would see on the strip, but the smaller ones that seemed to be in every business window. Even the thrift shops up the street appeared to host a single slot machine.

The red and orange blinking lights from the convenience store ahead and blue blinking light from the motel office behind mixed together and flickered against the brick in a strange way that was both eerie and unsettling. Despite this, Laura lingered in the alley for an extra couple of seconds, reluctant to leave her moment of solitude.

But she took a deep breath and stepped out into the light, crossing quickly to the store. To their credit, the teller was not behind class like the motel clerk had been, but there were cameras and monitors everywhere.

The only other patrons in the store at the moment where three men in their twenties throwing straw wrappers at each other over by the soda machine. Laura paid no mind to them, picking up the items she needed as she walked through the aisles.

"Hey, baby." One of the boys walked up behind her. "You're looking real nice. Going someplace special?" His buddies chuckled from across the store.

Laura ignored him and kept moving down the aisle, grabbing a couple cans of soup.

"Hey, lady, what's up? Don't like guy's or something?" The asshole continued to follow her, reaching out to touch her hair. He never got there, though, because Laura dropped her basket and whipped around to grab his wrist and twist it around, digging her perfectly manicured thumb nail into a pressure point near the base of the guy's thumb. With a shriek, he dropped to his knees, tears streaming down his cheeks.

"Shit!" His buddies yelled, suddenly all laughter gone, but none of them raced forward to help their fallen friend.

"Don't touch me." Laura said in an even voice. She held eye contact with him, watching him squirm before letting him go.

"Crazy bitch!" The boy yelled, trying to regain what little amount of dignity he had left in front of his friends. But the tears and snot on his face didn't help his cause much. Only when she turned and walked away did his friends come forward to help him.

"Sorry about that," Laura said to the cashier.

The cashier just smiled and bagged her groceries. "On the house," he said as he handed the bags over. "That was a great thing to see."

Laura nodded and headed out the door. She crossed the parking lot and headed for the alley, moving at her usual, brisk pace. The three boys had moved outside and were smoking near the corner of the building, the younger one supporting his injured wrist in his other hand, his friends laughing loudly.

"Psycho bitch!" he yelled at her as she walked by.

"Sure, I'm the bitch," Laura said her him. "I hate to tell you this, honey, but only one of us is wearing mascara, and it's not me."

"Uppity bitch," she heard one of his friends say as she entered the alley.

Great vocabulary these guys have, she thought. Maybe it had something to do with the downfall of the education system. She was too tired to think about how society was doomed.

She was halfway down the alleyway, looking down at the bricks so the flickering lights didn't hurt her eyes, when a cold shiver moved down her spine. She knew her luck had just turned on her. A shadow fell across the bricks in front of her, and she looked up as one of the boys from the minimart stepped out in front of her, blocking the alleys exit. His two buddies entered the alley behind her.

The boy in front of her cocked his head to the side and grinned. "C'mon, baby, we just want to talk."

Chapter 26

Laura sighed and set her bags down on the bricks. She was not in the mood to beat up three pricks tonight. She just wanted to go back to the motel, get a good night's sleep, and put this wretched city in her rearview mirror.

"C'mon, don't you morons have anything better to do than get beat up by a girl half your size?"

The leader shook his head and smiled, though he was still supporting his injured wrist. Laura rolled her eyes. They should have just camped out in the desert. It would have been safer.

One of the punks behind her grabbed her shoulder, and at his touch she was suddenly in another alley. It was darker, raining, and somewhere close by, somebody was screaming. The flash was too brief for Laura to understand what had happened there, but the glimpse left her with a red-hot rage. She reached back and grabbed the punk by the arm, swinging him around in front of her and slamming him into the brick wall. She used the momentum and weight of the first jerk to spin herself around and land a kick square in the chest of the other guy behind her. Her kick wasn't quite powerful enough to put him on the ground but caused him to gasp and stumbled back several feet.

Laura landed and did a hop-dance to the side to avoid the first punks charge, causing him to overcorrect and nearly run into his friend. Laura hopped to her side again and kicked to her left, hitting the guy she had thrown into the wall in the side of the head and knocking him down again. She didn't kick him particularly hard, just enough to make him think twice about getting up. Despite her anger, she wasn't trying to hurt these idiots. They needed role models, not paramedics.

After the attack on her family, her father had thrown himself into training her to survive in a world of dangers. From the time she was ten years old, she would have her first homework, her schoolwork, and then she would have her second homework, her training. She downplayed her skills in front of the boys, but truth be told, she was far better equipped to take care of herself than anybody realized, and out of the three of them, she was probably the deadliest.

To say that Laura was confident in her ability to handle the three street thugs was an understatement. She was cocky as she danced across the bricks, keeping the three of them from fully getting to their feet and gathering themselves. She had just knocked the ringleader down again when she saw the pride vanish from his eyes and knew he was done. She tried not to take too much pleasure in the victory as she took a step back, just enough to let him get to his feet, then another to let him know she was done hitting him.

But as she took her third step back, her heel stepped on the corner of the plastic bag. Just like that, her luck turned again. Chance worked against her in the kind of inexplicable way she had struggled to explain to Randy. Her foot slipped out from under her, and she was falling backwards before she even really knew what had happened.

She came down hard on the bricks, hitting with first her shoulder blade and then the back of the head. The impact caused her jaws to smack together, cracking a tooth and momentarily lose her senses. She was, dazed, as the world above her was spinning, she could no longer see the alley, the bricks, the neon light, or even where she was any more.

The one thing she was aware of was that somebody was on top of her, and she barely got a scream out before a hand clasped over her mouth.

****

Randy was lying on his back on one of the beds in their trashy hotel room, his hands clasped behind his head, watching the ceiling fan drift in a lazy circle and listening to a weather man on the television talk about a cold front moving in. "So where do you think we should go from here? Back into California?" he asked Travis, who had just opened the bathroom door to let out the steam.

Travis shrugged as he used the towel to wipe off the mirror. "If I had my way, we would be on the east coast by now." He put some shaving cream in his hand and spread it on his face. "Laura's not going to go that far, though."

"She trusts her dad, keeps saying he is working on a plan," Randy said.

"Yeah, well, forgive me if I don't put my faith in the guy," Travis said bitterly. He picked up his razor and paused before touching it to his face. "Either way, you're not leaving her, and I'm not leaving you. I think we are all stuck with each other."

"You forgot Starkey," Randy said, looking at the dog lying on the floor.

Randy sat up, the sight of the dog sending something cold moving down his spine. Starkey was tensed from head to tail, one ear turned back, the other one up, twitching, and he was staring at the door as if death itself was about to walk through it.

"No, I didn't," Travis said. "He counts as an extension of me."

Randy did not answer. Starkey jumped to his feet and emitted a low, brief growl; his head sunk low between his shoulders. Randy was on his feet too, and halfway across the room before Travis looked out of the bathroom to see why Randy had not responded.

Randy hadn't even opened the door a full inch before Starkey shoved his way through the gap and took off running. Randy could feel his breath catching in his lungs as he stepped out of the motel room, ignoring Travis who had hollered after him. The only thought in his brain was that Laura *should have been back by now.*

He stood for only a moment, watching as the end of Starkey's tail disappeared into a dark alley towards the end of the motel parking lot. He was running by the time he heard a man's surprised scream followed by a ferocious snarl from Starkey. He turned the corner in time to see a young man fall back as Starkey hit him in the chest at a full run and bit into the arm that he raised to protect his face.

The man Starkey had just attacked had been sitting on Laura's chest with his hands covering her mouth, while one of his buddies had been trying to remove her pants. The third guy was on lookout duty …and doing a very poor job of it. All three of them jumped away and scattered as Starkey attacked, and the two thugs currently not having their arm ripped apart seemed frozen, unsure of how to help their friend.

None of them saw Randy coming until he was almost on them, and by then, it was too late. The guy who had been standing lookout turned with a deer in the headlights looks, spotting Randy seconds before his fist connected with the guy's jaw. The guy stumbled back but managed to remain on his feet until another fist to his stomach dropped him.

Randy spun around to face the other guy who had circled around behind him. His fist was already drawn back to swing at Randy, but before he could get his hit in, he was tackled by Travis. The two of them hit the bricks hard with the young thug taking the brunt of the impact. The two men hitting the ground next to him momentarily distracted Starkey, who let go of his victim's mangled arm and hesitated, wondering if he should attack the man that Travis was wrestling with or continue with his current prey.

The dog's hesitation allowed his chew toy to stumble to his feet, holding his injured arm against him with the front of his shirt and pants completely covered in blood. He appeared to be going into shock, with his chalk white face covered in tears and snot. He struggled to grab something out of his baggy pants and a moment later produced a gun.

"No!" Randy yelled as the thug pointed the shaking gun at Starkey and fired.

He missed, of course, with his right arm completely useless and his left arm shaking badly.

Randy charged at the guy, not giving him enough time to aim at anyone else. He slammed into him, pushing him into the wall, then drew back to punch him. But Starkey had rushed up and grabbed the guy by the leg, pulling him back to the ground. Randy's fist hit the brick wall with full force where the thugs face had been. Randy dropped to his knees, the impact flowing up his arm and into his shoulder and spine, vibrating his bones. He gasped, his eyes tearing up, and then got back to his feet in time to hear Travis call Starkey off.

The dog obediently released the thug's leg, and he stumbled to his feet, trying to run away but falling several times before finally settling into a half run, half crawl, after his two friends who had already fled.

"Guard," Travis said to the dog, who went on instant alert.

Randy was still holding onto his hand, which was throbbing, but he managed to kneel next to Laura. "Is she okay?" he asked Travis, who was kneeling at Laura's other side. Travis gently lifted Laura's head, trying to determine the extent of the damage. Randy could see that there was a large pool of blood under her head, but they weren't sure where it was coming from. Travis lightly patted the back of her head. His hand came back bloody.

Laura's eyes were open, and she was trying to remain still, but both of them could tell she wanted to get up. She was already shivering as she lay on the cold bricks. Travis moved to where he could make eye contact with her without her having to move her head. "How do you feel?"

"My head hurts, but I don't think I broke anything. My shoulder hurts too. The fall just knocked me senseless, got hit by vertigo, but I think I'm going to be okay," she said, trying her best to downplay her injuries.

"You're bleeding," Randy said. "A lot."

"Head wounds bleed a lot," Travis said. "It feels like there is a cut on the back of your head, but no skull fracture. But we do need to get you to a hospital, though."

"No," Laura tried to sit up but got hit by vertigo again and ended up leaning against Randy. "No hospitals. Just take me to Mom."

"We're taking you to a hospital." Travis said, picking her up in his arms as if she were a small child. "This isn't up for debate."

Chapter 27

"You should get that hand looked at," Travis suggested as he sat down next to Randy. The waiting room that looked both clean, cheery, and mildly depressing all at the same time.

Randy shrugged. "I'm fine." But he was holding his hand like it was hurting him significantly.

"You should at least put ice on it." Travis frowned. "It looks swollen."

"It is," Randy said. "But I think its fine. I don't think it's broken or anything."

Travis nodded and decided not to press it.

"How's Starkey?" Randy asked. "He calm down yet?"

"Yeah, he's good. He got blood all over the back seat, though; he must have done a number on that guy in the alley. Laura probably isn't going to be very happy about that."

"Well, she's put up with the dog hair so far." Randy shrugged. He started to rub the back of his hand and winced. "I would think that a Las Vegas hospital would be more busy."

"The E.R. was pretty packed." Travis said. "This is the baby ward, er, baby wing. Anybody under the age of twenty gets sent here. I guess there aren't too many kids needing x-rays at eleven o'clock at night."

"Must not be a skater town," Randy said. Then, as if it was an afterthought, he added, "You know, Laura and I met in a hospital waiting room. That night you got shot. She just sat with me and talked for a while."

"Yeah." Travis leaned back and grabbed a magazine to thumb through. "You told me that; seems like it was a lifetime ago. It was only about seven or eight months ago, wasn't it?"

"Do you feel better?" Randy asked. "Knowing who you are? I mean, do you feel any different?"

Travis thought about it for a minute. "I guess so. I think I was always me. A part of me always knew. I know it sounds weird, but I think I felt more complete not knowing." He trailed off. Randy was watching him, knowing that there was more to say. "I had Sophia before, she loved me, and I guess because of her, I never really questioned all that much, not the kind of questions I have now. I had you and her and even Momma. Between all of you, I knew who I was. It wasn't complicated, and yeah, I had questions, but they were the kind of questions you ask after reading a mystery novel where some of the strings are left loose. Not the kind of soul crushing questions I have now."

"Like what?" Randy asked.

Travis shrugged. "Why they never came back for me. They knew where I was. Why dad left me in that hospital, hurt and alone." He shook his head. "There are a lot of whys and it's not the kind of thing I can ask Laura about. She was just a kid too. It's not fair to put those kinds of questions on her."

"Think you'll ever forgive them?" Randy asked. "Or your dad at least? He's the one you're really mad at."

"Probably not," Travis confessed. "You ever going to forgive yours?"

"You know," Randy cocked his head to the side, thinking, "I think I have."

"What?"

"I think I have. I mean, it's not like I'll ever forget, but I don't really let it get to me, or define me, anymore. I'm not sure when it happened, but I feel like I let go of something," he struggled to explain it. "I guess I...I don't let the fact that he hurt me keep hurting me anymore. I'm not sure if that is forgiveness, but it's got to be pretty close."

Travis smiled. "I'm happy for you, man. "

"It's kinda freeing," Randy said. "Like, remember when we were training for state, and coach was making us run with ankle waits. It's kina like the way it felt walking after taking the weights off."

"Yeah, I know what you mean," Travis said.

"Mr. Nightdale?" A doctor appeared in the doorway.

"It's Williams," Travis said as he got to his feet and resisted the urge to stretch.

"Oh, I'm sorry," the doctor said, shaking off his confusion. "She said you were her brother, I just assumed...." He trailed off, glancing at the chart in his hands.

"Is she okay?" Randy asked.

The doctor hesitated a moment, not sure if Randy was family as well and thus able to partake in the conversation without a breach of confidentiality. In the end, he answered the question, but addressed his answer to Travis. "Well, the scratch on her head required three stitches, and she has a mild concussion, but her scans are already back to almost normal, so I'm not worried about it. But her shoulder blade, the scapula, was fractured in the fall, which is causing her quite a bit of pain. We're getting her fitted into a sling that is designed to keep her shoulders and arm immobile. We may need to put some bolts in place to strengthen the bone here in a few weeks, but for the time being, there is too much swelling to really do anything.

"We've faxed all of her information to her medical professional in California. She'll be discharged as soon as the sling is in place. She is heavily medicated, so we'll need to bring her out in the wheelchair. Because she is sedated, I'll need you to sign some paperwork. Is that okay?"

"Yeah." Travis nodded. "Do you need my ID?"

"Yes, I'll just have to make a quick copy of it." The doctor, who Travis just realized had never introduced himself, took his ID, nodded, and walked down the hall.

Travis turned to Randy. "Laura gave them her real name; I thought she had an alias set up?"

"She does, but she did have a concussion, and she probably didn't have her fake ID with her when she left for the store. We didn't go back to the motel before we came here, we didn't even drop off the dog. I don't think she had much of a choice."

"We need to make tracks. I'm not sure if we should even go back to the motel. They even faxed her medical information. He's going to know where we are." Travis took a deep breath, trying to calm his nerves and fend off panic.

"We have to go back to the motel," Randy said calmly.

"He knows where we are, Randy!" Travis snapped.

"All of our money is at the motel. If we need to make tracks, then we need gas. It's hard to make tracks when we're broken down on the side of the road," Randy said.

Travis took a deep breath and let it out in a rush. "Sometimes your logic is infuriating."

"So, I've been told."

Despite the doctor's insistence that Laura would be discharged soon, it was still well over an hour later before they finally left the hospital. Randy picked Laura up out of the wheelchair and set her down in the back seat, then climbed in beside her, forcing Starkey into the front seat.

Travis left them in the car as he grabbed their stuff out of the motel room and returned their room key to the front desk. He threw pretty much all their stuff in the trunk, not wanting to linger for very long or go back and double check to ensure that he hadn't left anything. Already, the hairs were rising on the back of his neck, and he knew deep inside that the Hunter had caught their scent and was probably closing in on them already.

By the time he sat down behind the steering wheel, his arms where already covered with goose flesh, and the sense of panic he felt rising up within him was becoming harder and harder to suppress. He locked the doors the moment they were shut and turned to look at Laura, who was barely awake, snuggled in the crook of Randy's arm. "You okay?"

"I want to go home," Laura said sleepily, closing her eyes.

Travis took a deep breath and turned to face the steering wheel. "Yeah, okay," he said, mostly to himself. Perhaps it was time to wrap this thing up, plan for an end game, and face the demons head on. Laura wanted to go home, which was the last place in the world Travis wanted to be. He would rather go anywhere else, even straight to the Hunter if it meant he didn't have to face what had haunted him for years.

But, despite the years they had spent apart, despite all of the mistrust, lies, and everything else that had happened, she was his little sister, he was her big brother, and there wasn't anything he wouldn't do for her. Travis put the car in reverse and backed out of the parking space, already calculating the quickest path to the freeway.

Chapter 28

Travis drove through the night in relative silence. Occasionally, he would make eye contact with Randy in the rear-view mirror, and while his brother remained awake the entire drive, they never spoke. Travis didn't turn on the radio, and other than Starkey occasionally barking in his sleep, there was little to distract him from his concentration.

He needed to feel his way back home, as he had never actually been there. His parents had moved after the incident in the woods, as any smart Seer would. But he could feel them, like the magnetic pull a migrating bird must feel, the kind of phenomenon that science has yet to explain. The closer he got, the stronger and easier it was to feel which direction to take, which road to turn down. He wasn't even 100% sure where he was as dawn approached, just that he was somewhere along highway 44 in northern California, and there were thick woods all around them with dustings of snow here and there.

As the sun was just beginning to peak over the mountains and fully light the sky, he turned off the highway onto a little, curvy country road that wound through the trees. Every now and then, he would see dirt or gravel roads branching off. He assumed most of these were driveways as almost all of them had an address on a post or some other marker. He had gone about five miles when he slowed and turned onto a single car dirt road. Unlike the others, this road had no address to mark it and had been hidden between two fairly large white oak trees. If Travis had not sensed it, he probably never would have seen it.

Going much slower now due to how narrow the road was, Travis was able to look around a little more as the forest began to fill with fresh morning light. He was struck by the beauty of the area. The forest was thick with evergreens, mostly various varieties of Pine and Fir, with Cedar and Juniper scattered about with the odd Oak tree, bare for the winter, twisted in among them..

The new sunlight pierced the trees in thick beams and spread across the frozen ground, illuminating the drops of frozen dew like so many crystals, turning the forest into a sea of golden glitter. Travis couldn't help but smile at the beauty he suddenly found himself surrounded by. No matter how dark things got, the world still found a way to shine.

A half mile down the narrow road, the dirt turned to white gravel, and the drive got a little smoother. With the adage of the gravel, the road also got a little wider, and the trees along the road began to thin.

He was taking Laura home, but these woods held no meaning for him.

He wanted to go to Momma's house, walk up those family steps, pull open that familiar creaky screen door, and walk into a place where he felt safe and loved. The place he was going to now was Laura's home, not his, and he was painfully aware of that. The closer he got, the stronger the Seer pull became. The deeper the pit in his gut got, the sharper the abandonment felt.

Travis was so lost in thought, he almost ran into the gate. It was a simple, white, metal gate, the kind you would expect to see on a ranch, and was attached to a four foot high stone wall that was a property line. Travis pulled up and stopped five feet from the gate. He was about to unbuckle when the gate began to swing open. There must have been some kind of sensor in place.

Once through the gate, Travis was greeted with something that looked a lot more like a driveway than a road, giant white oaks lining both sides for at least a mile. The branches of the oaks from either side locked above the roadway, and Travis guessed that it looked beautiful when the trees were full of leaves and color, creating a kind of natural tunnel. Even with the trees bare for the winter, it was stunning.

The mile-long driveway opened up to a clearing of about a hundred yards that was entirely bare of trees. His parents had created a fire break of sorts to protect the house in case of forest fire.

The large blank space ended with a lawn that lead to a ranch style, single story house with a wraparound porch and large windows to let in the light. There was a big oak tree in the front yard to provide shade, and a smaller wisteria draping itself near the corner of the porch, with vines hanging down like colorful spiderwebs. Large lilac bushes provided shade for the other half of the porch, and a prominent flowerbed along the front of the house sported what appeared to be large rose bushes that were well cared for. It looked like a beautiful place to live, and though he tried, Travis could not swallow the bitterness he felt as he pulled up and parked next to *his* truck.

There it was. The truck that had been stolen the night he and Randy had fled. The truck whose theft had forced the two of them to get into Laura's car. The truck that he just couldn't believe had been stolen at the most inopportune time; that he had been that unlucky.

How long had they been manipulating him?

How far ahead had they planned this?

Had they known that the Hunter was coming for Randy? Had they let that happen?

No!

Travis immediately stopped that train of thought. A Seer could not allow an Angel to be in danger and not act. They would not hurt Randy. They wouldn't let him get hurt. They must not have known. They couldn't have known.

"Is that your…"

"Yup," Travis cut off Randy's question as he got out of the car. He started to walk to the house but could not resist circling his truck a few times, running his hand along the dark blue paint, inspecting the tires. He hadn't realized how much he had missed it until this moment.

After inspecting the truck to his satisfaction, he turned and scanned the yard, listening and trying to feel the air around him in an attempt to discern danger. Everything felt calm, peaceful, isolated and safe.

He approached the house, confident that they were alone and his parents were not home. He had left the car door open so Starkey could jump out of the car and he, too, had gone to inspect the truck, but now, he ran up the porch steps next to Travis, his ears alert, tail stiff as he took in the new smells of the area.

The boards of the porch creaked with a hollow kind of echo as Travis walked across to the door and tried it, finding it locked. Travis hesitated a moment, closing his eyes and feeling the environment around him. He wasn't exactly sure how it worked, but if he calmed his mind, things would just come to him.

He turned to the left and walked down the porch to a swing that was near the wisteria. Attached to the metal on the bottom of the swing was one of those magnetic key holders. Travis removed the key and used it to unlock both the deadbolt and regular lock, then returned it to its place.

Once in the house, he gave the living room a quick glance and headed down the hall, opening the first door on the right to find a large bathroom. The next door on the left appeared to be a guest room, and the one after on the right was Laura's room.

The room was neat and tidy but lived in, and had just a touch of rebellion to it, just a hint that the girl who slept here was far more than a bookworm or a prom queen. The carpet was a dark blue and had curtains on the two large windows to match. The bed was made, but not to the standards that Travis and Randy were used to.

Travis resisted the urge to straighten out the bed as he stepped farther into the room. There was nothing on the walls except a lone poster for a band he didn't recognize. A family photo, over ten years old, sat on the nightstand beside the bed, next to a copy of the book *Where the Heart Is.*

He pulled back the covers on the bed, a light blue bedspread with dark blue sheets. He wondered fleetingly why Laura had surrounded herself with blue. It wasn't her favorite color, he knew that from previous conversations, but there was a pattern of light and dark blue repeating itself through the room. He wondered if had something to do with what she had said about him being blue. Her room was blue because she missed her brother.

Back outside, he opened the car door for Randy, who managed to get out without falling, carrying a still very sedated Laura. Travis led him inside and back to Laura's room without a word and watched as Randy lay Laura on the bed, removed her shoes, and covered her up, tucking her in as if she were a child. Once Laura looked comfortable, Randy lay down next to her on top of the blanket, put one arm protectively around her, and went to sleep.

Travis pulled the door closed as he left the room but did not close it all the way, leaving only a crack so sound could get through. He went back outside and closed the car door, then, finally, he began to look around the house.

There was a wood burning fireplace against the far wall, with bricks to protect the carpet from singeing and a mantle above it that held a half dozen framed photos and a few little knick-knacks. Travis crossed the room to inspect the photos.

He reached up and took the first framed picture down from the mantle and looked at it, wondering how they had gotten it. In the photo, a boy of about seventeen, tall and lanky with his hair a little too long and wearing a track uniform, stood next to a hurtle on a track field. The boy had his arms wrapped around a dark-haired, Italian girl wearing a white dress. It was at the state championship. Sophia wasn't going to be able to come but had gotten her sister to cover for her at the restaurant at the last minute and had driven all night to be there.

Travis closed his eyes, letting the memory flow over him. He could feel the heat of the sun beating down on him, feel the sweat on his skin, smell the freshly cut grass and the rich smell of Sophia's coconut shampoo. That had been a good day; one of the best, in fact. He was glad there was a photo of it.

The next photo was of Laura's high school Graduation, and beside it stood a photo of Travis, Randy, and Sophia at their high school graduation. The photo was taken by Momma, and how his parents had gotten it, he didn't know. Then there was a photo of Laura and their father fishing when she was maybe twelve, and a photo of his parents sitting on the swing in front of the house. His father had his arm around his mother's shoulders, and they were smiling.

The photo after that was the last Family Portrait that had ever been taken with all four of them. Travis was eleven, Laura nine, and in the photo, they looked like a happy family. But then, they had been a happy family back then.

He turned from the mantle and walked across the room to the threshold of the dining room, which had an open floor plan with the kitchen. It was a normal kitchen and dining room, with cream colored tile floors and counters to match, with a large round dining table, six chairs.

Deciding that there was nothing of interest in the kitchen, Travis turned and once again headed down the hall toward his parent's room. Unlike Laura's room, his parent's room was mostly white. White bed, dressers and end tables, with a few abstract paintings to add color.

The bed had not been made, and the sheets were thrown back and messed up in a way that indicated his parents had left in a hurry. One of the dresser drawers was left ajar, adding more fuel to the idea.

He walked across to the dresser, were a stack of books sat. As he got closer, he could see they were yearbooks, one for all six of the high schools that he and Randy had attended while in foster care. Colored notes marked various pages, blue, yellow, and purple.

Travis picked up the first yearbook and began to flip through it. He quickly figured out that the notes were to mark specific pages: yellow for pages that featured Randy, purple for pages that had Sophia on them, and blue for himself. Most of the pages featured all three colors, which was not a surprise, considering how inseparable the three of them were their last two years of high school. While Randy had several girlfriends that flickered in and out of the pictures, Sophia was a staple.

Here and there, in tiny delicate writing, his mother had attached a note. Next to Sophia's senior picture, she had written: *A beautiful, bright girl, fabulous heart, love her to pieces!* Next to Randy's, she had only written three words that seemed to convey a great deal of emotion: *Love this boy!*

There was no note written next to Travis' senior picture, and he tried not to read too much into it. But as his fingertips touched the post it to turn the page, he was suddenly hit with a wave of emotion so strong, he had to fright for breath. The book hit the floor as images flooded his mind's eye.

Lauren Nightdale was sitting up in bed, holding the same family photo that Travis had seen earlier. She held the photo against her chest and began to sob, her entire body reacting to the force of her emotion in great hiccup-like burst. She wanted her family back, wanted desperately to be with her son, to be able to touch him and hold him again.

Lauren Nightdale picked up a shoe from the floor and hurled it across the room at her husband, a cold furry moving through her so fierce, she was capable of murder in that moment. "No!" She screamed at him. "He needs his mother! He needs his family! This has gone on long enough! I swear if you don't let me go to him, I will never *forgive you, Allen!" Then, as if deflated by her anger, she sank to the floor. "I want my boy back." she said, mostly to herself.*

Lauren, sitting at a corner table in the restaurant that Sophia's family had owned, smiling as Travis took her empty plate from her. He was polite but distracted, and she was just another customer to him. "You have a good night,

Ma'am!" As he continued down the aisle, pushing his buss cart, she turned and watched after him, whispering, "I love you, baby boy."

Travis hit his knees, the impact shooting up his spine and causing him to bite the inside of his lip. The pain worked to shock him back into reality, and he reached up to rub tears from his eyes with the back of his hand, gasping for breath as if he had just breached the surface after a deep dive. He was shaking and felt like he had just been punched in the chest. He had a hard time separating his mother's emotions from his own and was dazed for several minutes.

After some time, he managed to climb shakily to his feet, using the edge of the dresser for support. He looked down at the yearbook lying on the floor but did not dare reach down to pick it up. He did not want to risk another venture into his mother's psyche. Instead, he fled the room on wobbly legs and went to the kitchen to sit.

Needing to clear his head, Travis sat at the table for some time, leaning forward with his head in his hands. He tried not to think, not to move, just to let the calm settle over him as he had done time and time again. After five minutes his hands stopped shaking, after ten, his heartbeat began to slow, and by the time Starkey came up and licked his hands, his mind was the only part of him that was not entirely settled.

Travis jerked when Starkey licked his hand and for a moment had to think about where he was. As the reality of the last 24 hours settled on him, he slid off the chair and onto the floor and put his arms around the big dog's neck. As he buried his face in the canine's fur, he realized there were very few things a good dog hug couldn't fix.

Starkey sat perfectly still, used to his master's strange moods by now, and when Travis got up, he jumped up excitedly and followed him into the living room. Emotionally exhausted, Travis pulled the blanket that had been draped over the back of the couch and lay down, covering himself up. Starkey lay on the floor beside him and began to snore almost instantly. Travis reached down and scratched the dog's head before he fell asleep as well.

Chapter 29

Travis became aware of a noise, steady and low, which slowly began to penetrate his dreams. He pushed them aside, not wanting to rise to the world of the living just yet. But the noise became louder, more persistent, and then, just as Travis was beginning to grasp what it could be, a sharp bark shattered his dreams. Instinctually, his hand shot out and grabbed Starkey's collar.

Travis opened his eyes and blinked several times. Starkey strained against his master's grip, still growling at the two people who had just walked through the front door. Allen Nightdale stood in front of his wife, one arm blocking her path in a protective manner. They had stopped halfway through the door the moment they had been confronted by the dog, and Travis guessed that this standoff had been going on for several minutes, until Allen had tried to take a step farther into the house, which had brought Starkey to his feet and had woken Travis up.

Lauren was looking over Allen's shoulder, her eyes on her son rather than the dog, but Allen's eyes were on Starkey as he leaned down and held out his hand palm forward in a soothing motion. "Easy, boy, easy."

"Starkey, chill!" Travis said to the dog as he forced himself into a sitting position and let go of Starkey's collar to rub his eyes. Starkey was as used to the word "chill" as he was to any of the other common commands such as "sit" or "stay" and instantly lay down, though he did not take his eyes off the pair in the doorway.

"Where is Laura?" Lauren asked, stepping around her husband. "I got a phone call that she was hurt."

"In her bedroom with Randy," Travis said.

"Are you okay?" she asked, rushing forward to inspect Travis. Starkey issued a warning growl, which she ignored, as she leaned in closer to Travis, noticing the bruises caused by the fight in the alley the day before.

"I'm fine!" Travis snapped, jerking back to avoid her touch. "C'mon, Stark, let's go for a run." He threw the blanket aside and managed to get up and out the door without making physical contact with either of them. He was at a full run by the time he left the porch, Starkey eagerly keeping pace with him.

Allen watched him go, fighting the urge to run after him, and turned to his wife. "He's still so angry."

She nodded. "He has every right to be."

Without another word, Lauren turned her back on him and disappeared down the hall. Allen took a deep breath and let it out slowly, then closed the door that Travis had left ajar and walked into the kitchen. From a cabinet bellow the counter, he pulled out a large mixing bowl. Cooking had been his meditation for as long as he could remember.

He was getting out the rotary beater when his wife rushed into the kitchen and grabbed a mixing bowl very similar to the one he was using. Without a word, she filled it halfway with ice and water from the dispensers on the fridge. She set the bowl on the table and rushed back out.

She returned a moment later, half dragging a very drowsy Randy into the kitchen. She pulled back a chair and shoved him into it. "Sit here!" she ordered.

"Yes, ma'am," Randy said, just beginning to wake up.

"Put your hand in here." Lauren gently grabbed Randy's forearm and lifted it, guiding his hand into the bowl. The hand was swollen to three times its normal size, to the point that the skin was stretched tight and shiny, reaching the edge of tearing. Randy winced and hissed with a sudden intake of breath as the hand touched the icy water.

"It should have been x-rayed last night." Lauren scolded in her 'doctor' voice. "It's probably broken. But the ice should take down the swelling and then I should be able to wrap it. You're lucky you didn't go into shock!"

"Yes, ma'am," Randy said, looking around the kitchen. "Where is Travis?"

Lauren got a sad look on her face and turned to open a cabinet, searching for the medical bag she kept in there. She had one in just about every room in the house, and she had used all of them at one time or another.

"He ran off," Allen said, pouring the first of the pancake mix into the frying pan.

"And by 'ran off', I take it you mean actual running." Randy raised an eyebrow at them.

Allen nodded. "Do you like blueberry pancakes? If not, I can make something else."

"Pancakes sound fine," Randy said. "That's a good thing, that Travis is running."

"Why do you say that?" Allen asked.

"It means he is feeling non-confrontational. He doesn't want to fight, he just wants his space," Randy explained.

"He runs a lot?" Allen asked.

"Yeah, for sanity, I think." Randy shrugged. "Some people write, some draw or paint or listen to music, some shop, Travis runs."

"What do you do?" Allen asked.

Randy thought for a moment. "I don't know. I guess when I get frustrated with life, I try to find a way to help wherever I can. And if I can't help the current situation, well, maybe I can help a different situation."

"That's a good way to be," Allen said, flipping a pancake. The kitchen fell silent as the conversation ceased but was soon replaced by the sizzling of eggs and bacon. Randy guessed that Allen was making enough food for an army, and the smell of it made his stomach growl.

In due time, Lauren came back into the room and inspected Randy's hand. Once the swelling had gone down to her satisfaction, she gingerly placed the hand in a brace and wrapped it loosely yet securely in a gauze wrap. "We'll have to get that x-rayed later," she said matter-of-factly. "Would you like anything for the pain?"

"No, thank you," Randy said, shaking his head. "It's pretty numb from the ice anyways."

"Well, please let me know if you change your mind." She gave him a motherly smile, and something in her look implied that she wanted to say more, but she turned away as Laura came into the room.

Laura didn't look too worse for wear as she sat down at the table across from Randy. She still wore the same shirt as yesterday with the elaborate sling locking her one shoulder and arm in place. She had changed into Care Bear pajamas bottoms.

"Care Bears? Really?"

"Shut up! Care Bears are awesome!" Laura shot back, unfazed.

"I told you I would help you with that sling." Lauren gave her daughter an annoyed look.

"I'm fine, Mom! I got it!" Laura snapped, giving her mother a look that was a mirror image of her own. This too, made Randy smile.

"How are you feeling, sweetheart?" Allen asked.

Laura started to shrug, then winced and thought better of it. "Shoulder hurts, but I'll live."

"You shouldn't have been in that city. It's not a good place for our kind," Allen said without reprimand.

"I know, but we were tired and needed to sleep. It was just supposed to be for the night," Laura explained.

Randy made an annoyed noise and chose not to comment.

But Laura heard him and smiled. "Randy thinks the whole luck thing is bullshit."

"Is that so?" Allen asked.

"Yes, Sir." Randy nodded. "I just can't get behind the idea of an abstract thought being a tangible force in the world."

Allen smiled and pointed his spatula at Randy. "No, I wouldn't think so. I've always loved that about you."

"You say that like you know me." Randy turned to look at him.

"Oh, son." Allen sighed. "You're kidding yourself if you think you're any less one of my children than Laura and Travis. We've loved you for years."

"Huh," Randy said, not sure how to respond to that.

"Would you like some coffee?" Lauren asked the two of them.

"Yes, please." Randy replied and Laura nodded as Travis came in through the sliding glass door, holding it open for Starkey, who trotted in like he owned the place.

Travis was sweaty and red faced, not used to running in jeans, especially jeans he had been wearing for two days. He was out of breath and ran his hands though his shaggy hair. "It's cold out there."

"Would you like some coffee, sweetheart?" Lauren asked.

Travis hesitated a moment, not sure if she was talking to him or not, but when she continued to look at him, patiently waiting for his answer, he relented and nodded with a meek "yes, please."

Allen produced a bowl of dog food from somewhere and was pouring bacon grease over it. "Here, Boy!" He set the bowl on the floor, and Starkey eagerly began eating. Allen scratched him behind the ears. "I see you like me again now."

"He's probably wondering where his burger is," Lauren said as she carried over a bowl of sugar and a container of creamer and sat them on the table. "When you two were recovering from that accident, your father was feeding that poor dog nothing but burgers for the first three days."

"He didn't complain," Allen said. "Besides, he's a good dog. He earned it." He walked over to the table and held up his hand. "Look at this scar."

Travis raised an eyebrow at him, taking in the fresh white scar tissue that crisscrossed the hand; a dog bite. "Ripped into me pretty good when I was trying to get the two of you away from that crash."

Travis smiled at Starkey but chose not to comment further. He was proud of his dog for protecting him and glad that it had been his father who got bitten and not a police officer or EMT, who may have shot his dog to save time. He guessed it was Laura who had called Starkey off. He liked Laura.

Lauren set a mug of coffee in front of him, and he mumbled a thank you. She poured a cup for herself and sat between Randy and Travis. The room fell into an awkward silence, with the sound of frying bacon and an incredible mixture of smells filling the air. The sensory input brought back a great deal of memories for Travis. He remembered waking up to these same smells every morning as a kid. It was his father's form of an alarm clock. He would just start cooking at six in the morning and let their stomachs entice them out of bed.

His mother had still been in medical school when he was born. She did her internship to become a full doctor when he was two and started her own practice when he was ten. She always worked long hours yet always made time for her children. Travis could not remember ever seeing his mother cook, or ever tasting her cooking. His father had always been the one to prepare the meals for the family and now, sitting in the kitchen smelling the pancakes, eggs and bacon, Travis realized that he truly had missed his father's cooking.

In the foster homes, he scoffed at the fast food they were fed more often than not, though he eventually got used to it. This was something he had never quite understood about himself; after all, most twelve-year-old boys loved having chicken nuggets for dinner every night. But now that he could remember how he had eaten before, he fully understood his reluctance.

He didn't want to give his father the satisfaction of knowing that he had missed it, though.

When he saw his father took out a stack of plates, Travis did something that surprised himself; he grabbed the plates from the counter and set the table. This had been one of his chores as a child, but he had no intention of doing so this morning. He tried to shake it off as childhood indoctrination, but the truth was, he was feeling bad about hitting his father and was willing to make a peace offering, albeit a small one.

"Thank you!" Lauren said, her eyes glistening.

Travis nodded an acknowledgement and sat back down. They ate a family style breakfast, with large plates of food piled in the middle of the table being passed around and over one another. There was little conversation, even from Laura, which worried Travis. When she finally did speak, he realized she had only been thinking.

"Dad?" She waited until her father looked up to continue. "What's going on? You said you were working on a plan? It's been weeks."

Allen swallowed before speaking. "I have new identities and a safe house in Spain set up for the three of you. But it's proving difficult to get your mother and me out of the country. The new identities for you three will only take effect once you get to Spain, which means there would be a paper trail leading to Europe. You could fly into Germany and make your way to Spain from there. That should allow you to disappear with little to no trail."

"What about you two?" Travis asked.

"We may have to relocate in the United States, or possibly leave through Mexico. But as of right now, we can't follow you to Europe," Allen said apologetically. "I have another source lined up that should be able to do the identity transfer on your mother. I hope we can get it done this time. My last source ran into.... complications."

"Complications?" Randy asked.

"Changers and Seers have to adjust their identities often, us because we have to hide from Hunters, and them because they have to hide from each other. The Changer who has always assisted me in an identity crisis was discovered by a rival family and forced to run as well," Allen said, though it was clear there was more to the story. "Without his help, I have been struggling."

Randy nodded, but he wasn't looking at Allen. He was looking at the food on the end of his fork, a melancholy expression in his eyes. Allen studied his expression for a moment, then took a deep breath, as if preparing himself for a difficult conversation. "You didn't ask for this fight, son, and it's not fair to you. You don't have to go to Spain. I have a friend on the east coast that you can go to. There is nothing I can do to keep you here, but I want you to be safe. We don't want to leave you behind, but we won't kidnap you."

Randy glanced up from his food and briefly made eye contact with Allen before looking away. "I'm not going anywhere without my brother."

Lauren made a noise, something between a sigh and a gasp, and looked visibly relieved as she stood up, coffee in hand. "Thank god!" she exclaimed as she walked past him on her way to refill her mug. "Because I *would* have kidnapped you."

"I don't understand why we have to run in the first place. We outnumber him, if it came to a fight. We would have better odds of winning." Randy said thoughtfully.

"We'd have to kill him." Travis said quietly, not looking up at anybody.

"It would be self-defense," Randy said. "I mean, I'm not advocating it, but you would be fully justified in defending yourselves. This guy killed your brother, shot Travis, and beat me to a bloody pulp. At a certain point, you have to do what needs to be done."

Allen took a deep breath and let it out slowly, as Travis often did when he was gathering his thoughts. This similarity was not lost on Travis, who felt a stir of anger knowing he was so much like the man who had abandoned him. "It's not so easy for Seers," Allen said. "To kill, I mean. Even killing in self-defense is extremely difficult for our mental wellbeing. We have nightmares that can be crippling, night terrors that can get extremely violent, and sometimes our brains themselves shut down. We suffer memory loss, anxiety, and that is just the tip of the iceberg. Many Seers kill themselves because they cannot live with it. We are hardwired to preserve life, and to take it…. it's not so easy."

Randy nodded. "That…sounds reasonable," he said evenly, not looking at Travis. Those were the symptoms Travis suffered from to this day. It made sense that his night terrors were due to the killing of the Hunter who had attacked them as children.

"I'm not a Seer," Randy said.

"Could you see yourself doing something like that?" Allen asked, making eye contact with Randy. "Leading somebody into a trap with the intent to kill him?"

Randy thought for a moment, but if he were honest with himself, he didn't have to think very hard. "No, I really can't. It doesn't seem like…me." He leaned back. "But I would do it if it needed done, if it meant that I would be saving the lives of the people I loved."

Allen was still making eye contact. "You'd do it to protect a perfect stranger."

"I'm not so sure about that," Randy said with a shrug.

"I am," Allen said. "You're always willing to be a shield; it's how you were made. If Seers preserve the balance, Angels protect it, fiercely if needed."

"I'm not an Angel," Randy snapped.

"And you're not going to face that monster," Lauren said with a hint of anger in her voice. "Not ever!" She stood and began clearing the table. "And…" Lauren began, but paused a moment, as if she was saying to herself, "nobody else has to die."

"But he won't stop," Randy said.

"No, he won't. But killing in cold blood, it is the worst thing a Seer could ever do. It's the worst thing anybody could ever do." Allen nodded. "Your soul does not need to be scarred with such a thing."

Something in his voice made Travis look up. "Have you ever done it?"

The room fell silent. Even Lauren paused in her gathering of the dishes, and Laura and Randy were staring at Travis, surprised that he had gone there and asked such a direct question. Travis hesitated. "Killed in cold blood, I mean."

Allen sighed, and his eyes went to a dark place for the briefest instant as everybody started eating again. "I have," he said, making eye contact with his son. "The police were there, the situation was under control, I didn't need to pull that trigger. He would have been thrown in jail, tried for murder, attempted murder, kidnapping, and a slew of other crimes. He never would have been released and would have died in prison. I didn't have to kill him…but I did."

"Why?" Travis asked, not sure why he so desperately wanted to know.

"Because…" Allen looked down, gathering his thoughts, then looked back up with the briefest glance at Randy before making eye contact with Travis again. "Because if he had lived, his little boy would spend the rest of his life looking over his shoulder, afraid that someday, that monster would be standing over him again. He never would have been able to sleep soundly at night. If that man would have lived, his face would haunt that boy to his dying day."

Randy dropped his fork, a chunk of pancake still on it. It hit the edge of his plate with a sharp, metal on glass clang that caused both Travis and Laura to jump. As the noise died, Randy looked across the table at Allen with a stricken expression. "Did you kill my dad?"

Allen hesitated and chewed on his lower lip, the lines on his face growing deeper as they revealed a pain that no Seer was ever supposed to feel. The moment seemed to stretch on forever, but then it ended with a silent drop of the chin. The nod in the affirmative revealed Allen's shame. He was not proud of what he had done, but he would not deny it, either.

"I…I thought the cops killed your dad?" Travis said, studying Randy's face.

Randy shook his head. "No, that was the official story, but they were never able to match the slugs to a police issue firearm. They let the press believe that the police had gunned him down, but somebody else took the shot." Randy jerked back in his chair like somebody had smacked him and rubbed his hand across his face. "That musta' been you," He said, gesturing at Allen.

"I'm sorry…" Allen began, but he was cut off by Randy.

"Don't be!" Randy practically shouted. "You're right about everything. He needed to die." Randy picked up his fork and paused before putting the bite of pancake in his mouth. "I'm not sorry he's dead."

"You were never meant to know." Allen said softly. Randy acknowledging that he was glad his father had died that day seemed dark; a stark contrast to the character that Randy had always possessed. The man that everybody knew him to be was briefly replaced by the angry and damaged boy he once was and that would always be a part of him.

Randy's tone of voice was too much for Travis, who pushed back from his chair and charged into the living, red hot anger rising within him and something else he couldn't quite identify. Sorrow? Frustration? He didn't know, but the sudden mixture of emotion threatened to overwhelm him. He stopped in the living room and forced himself to take several deep breaths in an effort to calm himself, but it could not be helped.

Allen jumped up from the table and rushed after him. "Don't…" Randy began, but it was too late. Allen was already in the living room, and Randy was preparing to intervene in what was about to happen.

"Travis…" Allen began, but Randy grabbed his arm, stopping him.

"Give him a little space," Randy warned softly. "Just let him be for a few minutes."

Allen looked back at Randy, weighing his options. Randy knew his son better than anybody. He knew when Travis needed to be alone; knew when to respect that and when to push it. Allen knew that he should listen to him, but he just couldn't bring himself to turn away from his son. He could practically see the pain coming off

Travis in waves, like heat from an oven, and the rational part of him fell prey to the part that just wanted to comfort his son.

"Travis?" Allen said softly, not approaching any closer but subconsciously extending a hand towards his son. "Please talk to me."

Travis took a breath and turned around to face his family, not at all surprised to find tears streaming down his face. "There's really nothing to say."

Randy dropped Allen's arm and took a step closer to Starkey who was picking up on his master's stress and was starting to get agitated. As he looped his fingers securely around Starkey's collar, he shot a desperate look at Laura. She looked back at him, confused and unsure what to do. Despite the weeks she had spent with them, she could not read Travis well.

Randy hesitated. He wasn't sure what had set this off, but he knew Travis hadn't been this close to breaking since the day Sophia died, and it had taken him weeks to recover mentally and emotionally. If Allen pushed Travis too far, the damage may be irredeemable.

"I can't believe you were there," Travis said quietly. His voice was shaking but lacking accusation. Instead of confrontation, his tone sounded pleading, like a small child who did not understand why his dog had to be put to sleep. "I can't believe you let that happen."

"I didn't get there until it was too…" Allen began, but he stopped when Travis held up his hand.

"It doesn't matter," Travis said. "We were scared. I was terrified that Randy was going to die and you…you were there…and you just left, again." He took a deep, shuddering breath and let it out in a rush. "God, how many times did you walk away? How many times did you turn your back on me? On us? Do I even want to know?"

He looked past his father to his mother, who was now crying, and shook his head in dismay. "How could you let this happen? How could you let him leave me?" Lauren shook her head, not knowing what she could possibly say or do that could ever make it right. She began to walk towards him but stopped when Travis took a step back.

Randy took a step forward, still holding onto Starkey, about to suggest they go for a walk or a drive, but he didn't quite make it. The sliding glass door in the kitchen opened and in stepped a tiny woman in a blue dress, so wrinkled she looked more like a raisin than a person.

"What's going on?" Momma demanded before spotting Travis in the living room. "Travis, sweetie, what is wrong? Are you okay?"

Travis looked like he had been shot, and right then, Randy saw what he had been dreading. He saw his brother shatter. Travis shook his head, not taking his eyes off Momma, and whispered "you too?"

Momma didn't have time to answer because Travis turned and rushed out the front door, letting it slam behind him. He jumped over the porch stairs, landing wrong and sending a shooting pain up his leg which he ignored as he ran to his truck. He pulled on the truck door but found it locked. In frustration, he turned, sending loose dirt flying before spotting the keys dangling in the ignition of his father's jeep. He was just jerking open the door when the front door to the house opened and Starkey came tearing down the porch after him. Travis held the car door open just long enough for Starkey to jump in. As he backed out of the drive, he made eye contact with Randy, who was standing on the front porch. Randy made no attempt to stop him, no attempt to ask him to stay. They knew each other too well for that. Despite this, Randy didn't know if Travis would come back.

Chapter 30

Travis sat on the park bench looking out across the deserted lawn. A cold wind blew dead leaves across the ground, and he shivered. He could see his breath and goose flesh covered his arms and legs, but he didn't care. He was numb.

He had been here for hours, just sitting and watching the leaves. He hadn't even been thinking. There was far too much to think about, and the process was far too painful, so he just sat. Starkey had sniffed around just about every inch of the park but was now sleeping at Travis feet.

He had driven for nearly an hour before finding this little park and wasn't entirely sure where he was. He didn't really care, either. His psyche had taken just about as much as it could take today, and he was done with it all. Checking out for a while seemed his only option.

"May I sit here?" asked a kindly, elderly voice that Travis knew all too well.

He looked up to see Momma regarding him. He had not heard her approaching, and Starkey had given him no indication. But still, he wasn't particularly surprised to see her, though she wasn't the one he was expecting. He shrugged. "It's a free bench."

"Thank you," Momma said as she eased herself onto the cold wood and handed Travis the thick sweater she had brought for him.

Travis took it and pulled it over his head. "How'd you find me?"

"Oh, my dear boy, Angels can always find Seers." Momma said, patting his hand. "Why do you think you could never hide from Randy and me?"

Travis nodded but didn't say anything. Momma regarded him for a moment, then reached over and took his hand in hers. "You're hurting. Talking may get it out."

"I can't," Travis said. "I really don't think I can form what I'm feeling into words. How long have you known?"

"Always," she said with a laugh.

"Always?" Travis looked at her, hurt, not sure why she was laughing.

She nodded. "My husband wasn't arrested alone that night, you know. I was with him when those men came to force us out of that restaurant we had no business being in. It was me they really wanted. You may not be able to tell now, but I was a looker in my day, and women didn't have much in the way of rights. Black woman didn't have any at all. If we claimed a white man had forced us, they laughed at us at best, beat us and murdered us at worse. These particular law men thought it would be fun to make my husband watch."

Travis looked away and closed his eyes; he didn't want to hear this. "Your granddaddy, who died before you were born, did everything he could to save us. In the end, he just saved me. You see, the rope broke poor Charles' neck, but not mine. Your granddaddy cut the rope in time. He never quite forgave himself for not saving the both of us. He helped me with the kids, helped me move out here to California. He was a good man, and your daddy was such a sweet little boy."

"I didn't know," Travis said, tears brimming in his eyes at the thought of anybody ever hurting this sweet, old woman.

She patted the hand she was holding. "Oh, sweetie, it was a long time ago. Your mother called me after she picked the two of you up on that road, begging me to do something." She chuckled. "Took some doing too! You two where outside of my district, way outside, but I insisted again and again, and the two of you had moved so much, they finally relented."

"So, you've always known who I was; where my family was," Travis said. It wasn't a question.

"Yes, sweetheart," She smiled at him in a way that made her eyes disappear. "But I didn't need to know your past to know who you were."

Travis nodded and, despite his feelings, returned her infectious smile. He couldn't stay mad at this woman, no matter how much he wanted to. "Do you know why he left me? Why he abandoned me in that hospital?"

Momma sighed and lost her smile. "Yes. I do. It was the hardest thing he ever did. A Seer has his reasons; though they may seem crazy to everybody else." She took a deep breath. "Such a thing is not for me to tell."

Travis moved his foot because it had fallen asleep, dislodging Starkey, and leaned forward to rub at his ankle. "I don't know if I can ever forgive him."

"Nobody is asking you to, sweetheart," Momma said with a soft smile. "It's important that you at least give yourself the chance, though." She looked at her hands as they lay folded in her lap, and her eyes grew distant, as if remembering something. "Anger has a way of eating through you, and if you can replace it with love, you best do it. If I had forbade Charles from joining the good fight with the doctor, he would have been furious with me, but he would have been alive. It would have been worth it for him to see the men our boys became, the women our daughters grew into. I could have been angry, I could have been bitter and hated the world, but choosing to love is the better course.

"Your daddy chose life, Travis. You may never fully understand the reasons, but he chose life. If it meant you would hate him forever, well, he was okay with that if it meant you'd live. Someday, when you open yourself up to understanding, you'll thank him for that choice." She patted his knee and pushed herself up off the bench. "It's a long drive home, and I best get to it."

"I'll thank him for abandoning me?" Travis asked after her, causing her to turn.

She smiled and shook a finger at him. "You'll thank him for saving the lives that he saved."

Travis watched her make her way across the cold grass and climb into her mustang. Part of him wanted to chase after her and demand answers, but he knew he wouldn't get them. He remained on the bench for a half hour longer before he climbed to his feet and began walking towards the jeep he had stolen. His stomach was telling him it was time to eat again, and he desperately needed a change of clothes. There was a GPS system in his father's jeep, which he used to navigate to the nearest convenience store. It was fifteen miles away.

He was still numb as he drove, following the step by step instructions, but deep down, he felt himself beginning to thaw. Somewhere deep inside, he knew there was an obvious answer to his burning question of "why?" He was aware of it, fluttering just outside of his realm of understanding. Even as he was aware of it, he didn't reach for it. He wasn't ready to know just yet.

He pulled into the minimart as a silky female voice he found mildly obnoxious announced he had reached his destination. He parked towards the end of the parking lot and failed in his attempt to keep Starkey in the car as he got out. Not having the energy to fight with the dog, he allowed Starkey to trot along beside him until they were a few feet from the door and commanded him to sit and stay as he went inside.

Travis dug in his jeans pocket looking for the small amount of cash he had with him and fished out a five-dollar bill. That wasn't much in a rural town where prices ran high. He walked the aisles for ten minutes looking for something he could afford. He settled on a fountain drink and a bag of Doritos, which left him with three cents to spare.

As he walked towards the exit, he instantly became aware of a small commotion that was happening just outside. A young boy was sitting with his arms around Starkey, who didn't seem to mind, and was arguing with his father.

"No!" the boy was saying. "This is him! This is the dog!"

The boy's father was trying to be patient, but his voice was showing a little bit of strain. "There are a lot of dogs that look like that, son."

"No! This is him! He's named after a Beatle, which is a rock band and not a bug!"

"That's right!" Travis said as he stepped out of the store, grinning. He recognized the boy instantly, though he had grown a fair amount. "You've got a good memory! Aaron, right?"

The boy jumped up excitedly and pointed at Travis. "I told you!" he shouted to his dad. "I knew it! I knew he was the dog!" Then, as if a switch had been flicked internally, the boy burst into tears. The transition was so sudden, it took Travis off guard and for a moment, he wondered if Starkey had bitten him.

"You saved my life!" Aaron said, tears streaming down his face. "He was going to kill me! He killed lots and lots of other kids and he woulda' kilt me too!"

"Hey," Travis said, kneeling so he was on Aaron's level. "He didn't, did he?"

Aaron shook his head. Travis smiled. "There's all kinds of thing that could have happened that didn't. You're okay." Aaron nodded again and gave Travis a hug. Kneeling as he was, the sudden hug almost knocked Travis off balance, and he had to put out a hand to catch himself, nearly spilling his fountain drink. Once he was steady, he hugged the boy back and patted him on the back.

Aaron pulled back and wiped a tear off of his cheek with the back of his hand, smiling again. "Dad let me get a dog! He's not going to be as big as your dog, though. He's a..aus..Australian…"

"Australian Shepherd," his father stepped in.

"Yeah, one of those. He really likes to run!"

"What did you name him?" Travis asked.

"Leo. Its short for Leonardo, after the ninja turtle," Aaron said excitedly.

"That's awesome!" Travis said as he stood back up. "Those are really good dogs, super smart. One of the homes I lived in growing up had one of them. I think her name was Daisy."

Aaron cocked his head at Travis. "Whadya' mean one of the homes?"

"Oh," Travis said and shot a panicked look at the boy's father. He probably shouldn't have said that. "I...um...I grew up in foster care. Kind of like an orphanage, but you move a lot, so I lived in a lot of different places. I didn't have parents, so I had to go from home to home."

"Oh." Aaron looked down, not quite sure how to process that. When he looked back up there was something familiar in his eyes, something that Travis could now recognize. "When I grow up, I want to be a police officer and protect people. Like the way you protected me. I think…." He glanced up at his dead. "I think I want to adopt too. My Cousin was adopted. If I adopt kids, they wouldn't have to move like you did. They would just have one home, like I do."

Travis smiled. "I think you're going to make one incredible guardian angel, Aaron."

"Aaron, mom's waiting on us," his father said. "Why don't you run inside and pick out the snacks you want. I'm going to walk this guy back to his car. I'll be right there, okay?"

"Okay." Aaron said and turned to give Starkey another hug. Starkey licked the boy's face and wagged his tail. "Thanks for, you know, for saving my life." Aaron said to Travis before running inside.

"He's a good kid," Travis said, watching him run down the candy isle.

"Yeah, he's my whole world," his father said.

"C'mon, Stark!" Travis said, smacking his thigh to bring the dog to his feet, and began walking towards his jeep. Aaron's father fell into step beside him but did not say anything until they reached the jeep.

"I…" The man began, but then something caught in his throat, and he had to stop and take a breath. His eyes were glistening. "I don't know what to say."

Travis shrugged. "There's nothing to say…."

"But there is!" he countered. "There's a lot to say. You saved my boy's life. I wasn't there and you were, and if you hadn't have stepped in…" The man looked on the verge of breaking down.

Travis patted him on the shoulder. He wasn't sure what else he could do to comfort a man who had nearly lost his entire world. "Aaron's fine. Don't dwell on what could have happened, man. Don't let that monster control your thoughts. The worst thing you can do to him is live your life as if he never existed."

The man nodded. "Why did you call Aaron a guardian angel just now?"

Travis shrugged. "It's just something I saw in him."

"That's odd because my wife, she's convinced you were an angel." He made eye contact for a moment before looking away. "The way you saved Aaron and then just disappeared. There were thousands of dollars in reward money that you never even tried to claim. You just vanished, and my wife kept saying that you must have been an angel. Now, meeting you, I think she may be right. I wish there were something I could give you. Something I could do for you."

Travis shook his head. "I'm no angel; I was just in the right place at the right time." He gave the man's shoulder a shove. "Your kid's waiting for you, man."

The father stared at Travis for an uncomfortably long moment before nodding and turning stiffly towards the store. He had more to say but didn't know how to say it. He took five steps back towards the store before stopping and turning back to Travis. "Thank you!" Those two words seemed to sum everything up, and once he had said them, he straightened his shoulders and stood a little taller, giving himself a nod before turning his back on Travis.

Travis didn't waste any time getting out of there. He never liked encountering previous interventions, whether due to Seer instincts or the sheer discomfort it caused, and he certainly didn't want to inadvertently lead a Hunter to that little boy's doorstep. He was breaking the speed limit as he left the parking lot and headed up the road. He didn't get far. Two blocks away, he was forced to pull off the road as realization hit him like a swarm of locus, making his skin crawl with a thousand points of reference that had eluded him. He sat on the side of the road with his forehead against the steering wheel as he took several deep breaths, trying to calm himself. "I was in the right place at the right time," he said out loud. "I was in the right place at the right time!"

***

It took longer to get back to his parents' home than he had originally anticipated due to an accident.

An officer had come along and tapped on his windshield, letting him know that it was going to be several minutes before traffic was moving again, and if he was in a hurry, there was an alternate route to take. Travis had decided to stay the course because he really wasn't sure how to get back if he went any other way. When traffic did finally start moving again, he had been lulled by the radio into a better mood.

He caught a glimpse of the crash as he was waved through, the remains of a blue truck that was crushed like a tin can and a big rig without a scratch, the driver was kneeling beside his truck, an officer standing next to him. The big rig driver looked shaken, distraught, and Travis felt for the man. He doubted anybody could have survived inside the blue truck, and it probably wasn't the guys fault.

For a moment Travis flashed back on Sophia's accident and how angry he had been at the driver of the eighteen-wheeler. He could have murdered that man; but of course, it hadn't been his fault either. Weather can be unpredictable in Northern California, and big rigs can't stop on a dime. The man who had hit Sophia when her car slid into his lane had quit driving after that and, according to Sophia's father, the accident had crushed him. The poor guy had a daughter who had been seventeen at the time, so close to Sophia's eighteen, and simply could not get past taking such a young life, albeit accidentally. Tragedies tended to have a ripple effect like that.

He finally made it back to his parents' house just before dark. There was a biting chill in the air that caused his breath to come out in a puff of steam, and he noticed the distinct smell of ozone in the air; it was going to snow soon. It was nearing Thanksgiving, he realized. It was going to be Christmas soon, and he had never finished that iron rose he had been welding for Momma.

He took a deep breath of the cold air, letting it settle in his lungs, and stared at the closed front door. He wasn't ready to talk, but he was planning on walking through that door and saying that he was. They needed to clear the air. There were things he needed to understand; things he needed them to understand.

He knocked twice before opening the door, though he really wasn't sure why he felt the need to do so. His mother and sister looked up at him as he walked in. They were both sitting on the sofa facing each other, and by the looks on their faces, he was interrupting one of those Gilmore Girls moments. Starkey jumped on the couch between them, practically climbing onto Laura's lap, and she smiled as she scratched him behind the ears.

"You're back," his mother said, sounding as if a weight had just been lifted from her chest. She began to rise from the couch but then, remembering his previous reaction to being touched, thought better of it.

Travis gave her an apologetic smile and looked around. "Where's Randy? I need to tell him something."

Laura was busily scratching Starkey's belly; the dog had rolled over onto his back in her lap and looked like he was about to fall off of couch. "He took your truck and went looking for you, left a couple hours ago."

Travis' legs buckled under him in an instant. Pain shot up Travis' legs and jarred his teeth from the force of his knees hitting the floor. A strange sound filled the room like something that a wounded animal would make, and Travis was too shocked to realize it was coming from him. He was barely aware of his mother and sister leaping from the sofa convinced that he had been shot. In his mind, he saw a devastated man kneeling by the side of the road, a blue truck crumpled like a tin can and a crash he doubted anybody could have survived.

277

Chapter 31

"Travis?"

Travis looked up from his hands to see Laura thrusting a cup of coffee at him. It was steaming and smelled of hazelnut coffee creamer. The smell hit his nose like a sledgehammer and made his mouth water. He took the coffee and brought it to his lips eagerly, but the taste didn't hit him like the smell had. His taste buds had gone numb like the rest of him, it would seem.

"Have you eaten anything since breakfast?" Laura asked as she sat down in the chair catty-cornered from him.

"Stop it," Travis snapped, but there was no bite to his voice.

"Stop what?"

"Trying to take care of me. Mothering or whatever the hell you're doing, please just stop." He set the coffee down on the floor next to his chair and stood to pace the room.

Laura regarded him with eyes puffy and red, her hair pulled back with a hair clip that was only half getting the job done. She didn't look hurt by his words. She had gone numb too. "It's the only thing I know how to do in a situation like this. I'm sorry."

"I suppose you've never been in a situation like this?" Travis walked over to a painting fixed on the wall and looked at it without seeing it.

"No," Laura said.

"I have." Travis turned away from the painting. "When Randy's old man got a hold of him. When Sophia got hit by that truck. Sitting in the waiting room is always the worst part, waiting for days for somebody to tell you anything. Sophia's mom was in the chapel. She wouldn't leave...." Travis realized he was rambling, staring at the floor between his feet. He looked over at Laura who was watching him intently. "She wasn't here when the doctor finally came to tell us she was dead when she got here. Sophie was an organ donor, you see, and they.... They had other lives to save."

"Travis...." Laura began to rise from her chair, but Travis jerked away from her.

"Don't you say it!" he snapped. "Don't you dare tell me he's going to be okay!" He walked back over to the painting, telling himself he was going to look at it this time, but he didn't. "That's what they told me about her."

Travis narrowed his eyes at the painting. No matter how hard he tried, he couldn't bring himself to see the damn thing! It was just colors! He knew that they came together to form some kind of tangible image, but he couldn't focus long enough to see the whole picture. His brain wasn't seeing things the way it normally did. The world wasn't working the way it normally did.

Randy was an organ donor, too.

A sound caught his attention; a faint hiccup that seemed out of place in the quiet waiting room. He looked over to see Laura quietly sobbing. She was trying so hard to hold it in, her whole body was shaking with the effort. She was teetering on the edge of despair, and he was a lousy big brother.

He sat down on the chair beside her and tentatively put an arm around her, pulling her into as tight a hug as her broken shoulder would allow. She deflated into him, and he realized he had never seen her so small. He squeezed her tighter, subconsciously thinking if he held her tight enough, he could keep her from falling apart.

"I'm sorry, Lolly," he said. "I'm sorry this happened." He took a deep breath. "Randy has been broken before; he always seems to come back together." She nodded against his chest, mute with despair, and he realized he would do or say anything to help her hold onto hope a little bit longer. "Please stop crying, Laura, he'll be okay. I promise he'll be okay."

"What happened?" Travis looked up to see his father standing in the doorway, a stricken look on his face. "Have they said anything?"

"No." Laura straightened, brushing away a stray hair that had plastered itself to her wet face. "No, they haven't told us anything."

Allen made a face, something between and grimace and a scowl. He hadn't been at the house when Travis had gotten back, but he was already at the hospital when they arrived here. Travis didn't know where he had been or how he had known what had happened to Randy. Details didn't seem to matter much anymore.

Travis did notice that his father's jeans and shoes were muddy, and there was a fresh cut on the back of his left hand, jagged, like something you would get from barbed wire or a rose bush. He tended to notice such things, and any other time, he would be curious. It didn't matter anymore, though. Nothing seemed to matter at all. His tunnel vision had narrowed to the tiniest pinhole.

Allen ran a hand through his unkempt hair and looked around the room. His eyes landed on his children. "Are you two okay?"

"Do we look okay?" Travis snapped.

"That's fair." Allen nodded. "Can I talk to you? Outside?"

Travis stood stiffly and walked out of the room without a word. He waited in the hallway as Allen said a few hushed words to Laura. When his father stepped out of the waiting room, his shoulders visibly sagged, and he jerked his chin at Travis to indicate that they should walk. Travis fell into step beside his father; the two of them walked in silence.

After they had gone a short distance down the hall, they found themselves in another waiting room, empty with one large window taking up most of the far wall. The view was an unremarkable one, the cream-colored plaster wall of another wing of the hospital. Despite the less than exciting scenery, Travis walked over to the window and looked out, fixing his eyes on a row of pigeons sitting along the far roof.

"Something has been bothering me," Allen began, looking at the same pigeons.

"Really? Only something?" Travis said, his tone neutral.

"You said…." He paused to gather his thoughts. "You said that you saw what I did."

"What?"

"After your accident when you punched me. You said you saw what I did. You said you saw me leave you in the hospital. What did you mean by that?" Allen's eyebrows came together in a pained, thoughtful expression as he searched his son's face for an answer.

"Just what I said." Travis shrugged. "I used your watch to force a vision. I wanted to see what happened…."

"But…Seers can't do that." Allen said quietly. "We can't control what we see. We can't look into the past like that."

"Yeah, well, I can." Travis said. "It gives me a horrible headache, though."

"And you…. have three routes as well?" Allen went on, though now he seemed to be speaking more to himself.

"I think I have five."

Allen's head jerked up, and he met his son's eyes with a shocked and worried expression. "That's not possible."

"All that," Travis waved his hands dismissively, "and I couldn't protect the woman I loved, couldn't protect my brother…."

Allen opened his mouth to speak, but the words caught in his throat. "I'm sorry," he finally said.

"Your brother died twelve feet from you." Travis said, turning to face his father. "While you were sleeping." For the first time he realized that Allen Nightdale may be the only person on the planet that had been where he's been. The only person who had failed as he had failed. It brought him no comfort. "Randy once told me that miracles like us shouldn't be caged. He said that it was a great big world out there, and if we only protected the people we cared about, it wouldn't be fair."

"It's a hard truth to swallow," Allen said. "Especially when you're burying your baby brother." He took a deep breath. "I should have gotten up early. I should have taken you fishing. I never got the chance to say I was sorry."

Travis nodded. "I know why you left me. I know what you saw in that hospital room. You let go of my hand and walked away because of him. You saw Randy."

"Not just Randy, though he was the clearest picture. I saw what you two would mean to each other, the man you would become. I saw the people you would save and path you needed to walk. I saw that you would die otherwise. I didn't like it. I didn't want it to be true. I had already lost you once, and I had to lose you again," Allen said, his voice close to breaking.

"There's a little boy alive today because you let yours go," Travis said.

"There's a lot more people alive than that. A family of five in Mt. Shasta, those kids in that fire."

"Did you see all of them in that hospital room?" Travis asked.

"No, not so much the faces, but the ripple effect that you would have, that Randy would have, spreading like a shock wave. A thousand points of light spreading out from the two of you. Your friend Damon who plays basketball with those kids every Saturday, they won't end up in a gang because of him. It keeps going…. the ripple, the lights that spread."

"Was it worth it?" Travis asked. "Did you know I'd hate you for it?"

"I don't know," Allen said softly. "But I'm okay with being hated."

They stood in silence for the next several minutes. Out the window, two of the pigeons flew away. Travis was the first to break the silence. "How many people have you saved?"

"I've had many interventions, but not all of them were to save a life. Some were to preserve innocence or light. All told, I've saved 63 lives. I have failed fifteen times," Allen said.

"There were two children. They fell through a frozen pond. I didn't get there in time," Travis said. "I still dream about them."

"A father was taking his infant to daycare. His wife always dropped off the baby, and it wasn't part of his routine. She died strapped in her car seat because I got a flat tire. If they had only came out with cellular phones sooner…. She would be Laura's age today."

"Does it ever get easier? Failing?" Travis asked.

"Never." Allen wouldn't lie to him.

"Out of all of the people you have saved, have any of them been a congressman or a senator?"

Allen laughed at the question. "Nope, not a one of them!" He smiled to himself. "Yet, it's amazing the difference that some of them have made. It's incredible the impact that you can make by just letting your light warm the people around you." He made eye contact with his son. "Randy is not going to die."

"How do you know?"

"Because if he does, I'm going to quit," Allen said, looking up into the sky like he was challenging the universe itself. "If that boy dies, I quit."

They walked back to the waiting room without saying another word to each other. Laura was still in the same place they had left her, but she was joined by Lauren who looked as though she had aged another ten years. She was kneeling in front of her daughter, trying to comfort her.

"Mom." It came out a whisper, though he didn't mean for it to.

Lauren stood with a start, knocking over Travis' coffee. She watched the brown liquid slowly spread across the floor but made no effort to clean it up. "Where were you two?" she asked her husband with just a touch of accusation in her voice.

"We were talking," Allen said. "What did you find out?"

Lauren took a breath and hesitated, choosing her words carefully. Travis felt a cold panic begin to move through him, starting at his finger tips and edging towards his heart. Lauren looked at her son with an emotion Travis could only identify as remorse, and her eyes glistened as she took a few steps closer to them. "He made it out of surgery. He's in the ICU."

"But….?" Travis tensed.

"It doesn't look good. He's going to need a few more surgeries but...he's not strong enough to survive them at this point. The next twenty-four hours are critical. If he survives the next twenty-four hours, his chances will go up to 50/50."

"Go *up* to 50/50?"

"Yes." She nodded. "A lot of damage was caused by the metal from his previous surgeries...shifting with impact. They don't even know where some of it went…."

"Please stop," Travis held up his hands, his voice breaking. "I don't need to hear this!"

"I'm sorry, sweetie, I…." Lauren reached out a hand but then stopped, remembering that he didn't like to be touched.

Travis shook his head and rubbed his face with both hands. "He's alive. He's alive. That's all that matters right now is that he's alive."

"Travis..." Lauren still had her hands outstretched, torn between wanting to comfort her son and knowing that he would not allow it. Travis was looking around the room wildly, desperate to avoid eye contact as a mixture of hope and devastation spread across his face. Then he did something that surprised him, and something that surprised her. He stepped forward, into his mother's arms, and put his head on her shoulder, allowing her arms to wrap around him as he sobbed. His world had come crashing in, and he wanted, needed, his mommy.

Chapter 32

Travis paced outside the ICU doors, anxiously waiting for them to open. Only one Visitor was allowed in the ICU at a time, and Laura had gone first. It felt right. Randy probably would have preferred to see the pretty girl he was in love with over a neurotic brother on the verge of a mental breakdown anyway.

There was also the fact that Randy could die at any minute despite the machines that surrounded him, and Travis wanted Laura to have the chance to see him. Travis wished he had gotten that with Sophia; though, even now, he's not sure what he would have said to her.

The door opened with a metallic whoosh that made Travis think of star trek. Laura stepped out and nodded to him before continuing down the hall to the waiting room without a word. She had somewhat pulled herself together in the last couple of hours. Her eyes were dry, and her hair was now in a tight bun, curtesy of a hair tie one of the nurses had given her. She held her head high as she walked down the hall, not staring down at her feet. Travis watched her for a moment as she moved down the hall, struck by the quiet strength she possessed. She was so much like their mother, it hurt his heart.

Lauren had that same, quiet strength. Every time her husband stumbled through the door with a stab wound or a third degree burn, Lauren had never faltered. She would step back, assess the situation, and do what needed done. Never apologizing, never demanding, but simply standing. When her husband didn't show up on some occasion that he was expected, or left her sitting alone at a dinner reservation, his mother had never faltered. He hadn't noticed it as a child, but as an adult, he could appreciate the strength it must have taken to be a Seer's wife, the trust she must have put in her husband to let her child go. Lauren deserved so much better than the life Allen had given her. With an ironic laugh, Travis realized that Sophia never would have done it, even if she knew he was out saving lives.

He turned from his sister and stepped into the ICU as the sudden smell of saline and sanitizer assaulted his nostrils. Randy's room resembled a giant glass box with its own set of whooshing doors. A nurse made him wash his hands all the way up to the elbow and put gloves on before entering Randy's cell in a counter measure against MRSA, a staff virus that would wreak havoc in the ICU if patients came in contact with it. Because his hair couldn't be tied back, one of the nurses fitted him with a hair net. Surprisingly enough, they did not make him wear a face mask.

By the time Travis stepped into the glass box which was Randy's room, he was scrubbed clean, sanitized, and wrapped up like some Christmas gift. But if Travis was a Christmas gift, Randy was the crumpled paper on the floor. He was barely recognizable as a person with the amount of tubes coming out of him, primary among them the breathing apparatus that covered half his face. the other half was a mosaic of blue and purple bruises that probably covered most of his body. Despite being well over six-foot-tall and muscular, he looked so small lying there. The only part of him that was recognizable was his golden hair.

Travis eased into the chair next to him and gently took Randy's hand. For several minutes, he didn't say anything. The machines gave off a cacophony of annoying hums and ticks which drowned out all the sound from outside, giving off a sense of isolation. This was an island within the busy ICU, or a fishbowl, given the clear walls. Annoyed, Travis looked for a curtain to close, but there was none.

"I told you this would happen," Travis said slowly, a hint of accusation in his voice. "I asked you to leave. I didn't want you caught up in this." He leaned back and sighed. "You're such a fucking jerk sometimes. You just had to be noble, had to be a protector or whatever the hell you are. Who are you supposed to protect now, huh?" Travis demanded angrily. "And the really messed up thing is, you're going to break my little sister's heart!" He shook his head, bemused. "A year ago, I didn't even know I had a sister. But I had a brother." He took a deep breath as a wave of emotion suddenly swept over him. "I need my brother."

He looked over his shoulder nervously. None of the nurses were looking his way. He turned back to Randy and lowered his voice, as if it mattered. "I can't do what I'm planning on doing until I know you're going to be okay." He slowly began to pull off one of his gloves. "I have to know if the risk is worth the cost. I need you to show me something."

He slipped his bare hand into Randy's, gave a little squeeze, and closed his eyes.

Nothing.

Travis heart sank. He wasn't surprised, though. He had only been able to force a vision of the past, never the future. The past was concrete, the future fluid, every action sending you down a different path. Travis very existence centered on changing an individual's future with just one action. He was more aware of the fluidity of the future than most. Still, he closed his eyes and took several deep breaths to calm himself as he listened to his own heartbeat. Slowly, the beeping and hum of the Intensive care unit faded away, and a fuzzy image emerged.

It was green—so, so green. Layers and layers of a million different hues, from the grass to the trees, in the beauty of spring. The shores of the Sacramento River in May were stunning, but even they couldn't compare to this level of beauty. With an educated guess from pictures he had seen he assumed he was somewhere in the South Eastern United States, or maybe Ireland.

There was an open meadow in front of him with very closely cut grass framed by trees and flowery bushes. He was standing on a stone path leading to a large white building that resembled pictures he had seen of plantations. A beautiful two-story house with a wrap around, screened in porch.

The front door opened, and his father stepped out. Wearing a tuxedo with a deep crimson tie, he was a handsome image, though he had aged. He held the door open for Randy, who was walking out behind him. Randy was dressed in a matching tuxedo with and equally crimson tie, but he carried his jacket over his arm and was wearing a vest and long sleeve, white undershirt. He was about fifteen pounds heavier, and his hair was a little longer than Travis had ever seen him wear it. He carried a cane which he only used as he descended the stairs to the grass. He was smiling.

Travis stepped off the path as they approached, getting out of their way as if they could see him. They were talking, but he couldn't make out the words. The sound was muffled, as if he were listening to them from under water. Soon, they turned a corner in the path, and Travis saw where they were going. It was a small altar, with an arch lined with dogwood flowers and rows of white chairs laid out before it. Simple but elegant.

A simple, rustic white sign stood off to the side, but Travis couldn't read it as the words were too blurry. Time moved faster now. People began to fill the seat and music began to play. Every face was blurry, except for one: Laura. Her eyes sparkled in a way that only truly happy eyes can sparkle, and she blushed with all the eyes on her, looking stunning in her white, lacy dress.

****

Travis opened his eyes, suddenly thrown back into the coldness of the ICU. The beeping and the humming resumed, and he realized he was crying. Randy's hand felt cold inside his own, and Travis quickly slipped his gloves back on before one of the nurses caught him.

He grabbed a couple tissues from the box on the bedside table and wiped away his tears hastily, blowing his nose at the end.

"Sorry," he said to Randy, his voice tight. "That was really rude."

There seemed like there was a lot he should have been saying, but for whatever reason, he couldn't articulate any of it. It wasn't like Randy could hear any of it in his current condition.

"I'm sorry," he finally continued. "All of this is because of me. It's because of what I am, what I forgot I was." He took a deep breath. "Because I was too damaged to be aware of the danger, not just to me but to you. I can't help being what I am any more than you could help being what you are. The Angel and the Seer. I think the universe made us brothers long before the foster system did. You were a better friend, a better brother, than I deserved. You never flinched, not once." He looked at his hands for a moment as he thought about the time he told Randy what a freak he was….and how Randy had simply accepted it and didn't treat Travis any different. He thought of all the times Randy covered for him or had his back. Randy forcing him to eat after Sophia's death, beating him up after he nearly killed himself with drugs, waking him up during night terrors even if it meant he was going to get punched.

"Thank you for that, "Travis said. "And I'm really sorry for what I'm about to do. I know you're going to be pissed, but there's not a whole lot you can do about it." He gave Randy's hand one last squeeze. "Take care of my sister for me."

He exited the ICU without a word, thankful that nobody in his family was waiting in the hallway for him. He walked past the waiting room, stopped just past the waiting room entrance and leaned against a window sill for a moment, listening to them. He couldn't make out what they were saying, but he could hear their voices, and he reveled in them for a moment. All those years he couldn't remember ever having a family. He wondered if he would ever hear his mother's voice again, ever hear Laura make fun of his eating habits again. Would he ever have the chance to repair the relationships that were broken? He hoped he would, and he was willing to die for the chance.

He pushed himself off the window and continued towards the exit. He had work to do.

Chapter 33

Travis reached inside the front driver's side wheel well of his father's jeep and felt about blindly until he found the magnetic hide-a-key his father kept for all their vehicles in case of an emergency. He took his phone out of his pocket and slipped it through Laura's car window, which she had conveniently left cracked. He did the same thing with his wallet, keeping a couple bills in case he needed gas.

He took the jeep and headed north, stopping periodically to be sure he was followed. He wasn't 100% sure where he was going, but he figured he'd know when he got there. He had been driving for forty-five minutes when he saw a sign for a recreational area and pulled over.

He was in a sparsely populated area just off Interstate 5 surrounded by lush mountains and steep terrain. It wasn't ideal, but it would work. A sign too badly damaged by shotgun holes to accurately read marked the head of a trail that took off towards the sound of running water. Travis turned up the collar on his jacket against the cold and began heading up the trail at a trot.

It was an eerily beautiful area and a marvelous trail that he wished he had found under better circumstances. Pine trees towered over him with trunks and limbs heavy with winter moss. The dirt under his feet was a deep, dark brown, covered in fallen pine needles. The whole area smelled like winter, clean and crisp. Soon, the trail was running along the Sacramento River.

This was not the Sacramento River Travis was used to. The river he was used to was wide and steady, swollen with countless creeks and streams that fed into it. This river was narrow and swift, and it crashed over the rocks with a force. The water was a deep, slate grey color, reflecting the storm clouds in the sky.

After he had gone a mile, the trail opened considerably to reveal a foot bridge over the water a quarter mile ahead of him. Travis couldn't help but see the irony as he climbed the steps to the bridge. It was a sturdy bridge, five feet across with a four-foot railing on each side. The water bellow seemed deeper, with no rocks visible. Travis walked out to the middle of the bridge, in plain view, leaned against the railing, and waited.

****

He didn't have to wait long. Less than a half hour had passed when Harvey appeared at the end of the bridge. He hesitated before stepping out, his eyes scanning the trail along the other side of the river behind Travis. He was waiting, nervous, almost scared. When he finally stepped out onto the bridge and began walking towards Travis, he did so slowly, still scanning the far shore.

"You didn't bring the dog?" he asked, coming to a stop five feet away from where Travis was leaning against the railing. Travis shook his head, and the Hunter seemed to relax a bit. "Good, I like dogs. I would hate to have to kill yours, but the leg just healed."

"I thought it would be best to do this alone," Travis said.

"I can respect that," Harvey said. He faced upriver and leaned against the edge of the bridge as well. "It's pretty here, wild. What made you choose it?"

Travis shrugged. "I just drove. It seemed like a good place to stop. Can I ask you a question?"

"I suppose."

"What you did to Randy, pushing the truck in front of that semi, it seemed…. familiar." He hesitated, his voice catching in his throat a little. "Did you…. did you kill Sophia?"

Harvey sighed and stared down at the water. "No, but I thought it was poetic the way it played out. Honestly, I was trying to track you, and I happened upon him. He never even saw it coming."

"I see," Travis said distantly.

"Would it have made it easier if I had said yes?" Tim asked. Travis didn't answer. "I can understand how hard it would be for somebody like you, who knows so much about the powers that be, to accept that sometimes fucked up things just happen to good people. I researched your history. She was a sweet girl from a loving family, and if there was any fairness in this world, she would still be here today. Why could you save all those other people but not her? Why couldn't you save your brother?"

"The world isn't fair," Travis said at last. "We protect balance, right? That's the ancient line that pits Hunters and Seers against each other. How exactly do we protect the balance when all we do is cancel each other out?"

"The world isn't fair," Time echoed. "My mother was a kind woman, she never really knew what Dad was, what he taught my brother and me to be. She died of cancer when she was still so young. My father died so soon after. His death, I understood. Your uncle was in a kill or be killed situation, and he won. Then you gutted my brother."

"He shouldn't have broken the rules," Travis said without malice.

"No, he shouldn't have. He was a young man who had lost both of his parents. He was angry and brash and wanted to make his first kill."

Travis nodded. "You ever wonder if maybe it's all bullshit?"

"Yes," Tim said. "And maybe it is. There is a story that Hunters tell. That back in the 1890s, a Hunter was tracking a Seer in Europe. He was watching the Seer as he went to save a young girl from a burning building. He had the opportunity to kill the Seer before he saved the girl, but in a moment of weakness, he thought, what harm could letting one little girl live cause? She was just a child, after all. He killed the Seer after the child was saved but did not kill the child. That little girl went on to spawn one of the greatest monsters to ever live. Her seed birthed a holocaust. How many lives would have been saved if the Hunter had just let that little girl die?"

"I know that story. Seers tell it too," Travis said. "We are asked whether we would still save the girl, knowing what her grandson would do. The answer is always yes."

The Hunter's eyebrows came together in confusion. "Why?"

"Because innocence is innocence. She was an innocent child. Her grandson's sins are his and his alone. An innocent life should not be punished because of the future sins of another. If that were the case, not one of us would be clean."

"I suppose if you really think about it, who's in the right and who's in the wrong is in a constant state of flux, good and evil, light and dark. It just depends on which moment in time we happen to be in. A Seer saving an innocent child, a Hunter trying to prevent the horrific deaths of millions. Maybe in that lies the balance."

"Maybe," Travis said. "I guess we have no right to claim the moral high ground, but we do all the same."

Tim smiled. "Seers, always cherishing life, even when if leads to death."

Travis shrugged. "It's our way."

"So, is that why you came out here? To make some kind of deal with me? To sacrifice yourself so that I'll leave your family alone?"

"I love my family.," Travis said. "I love my mother, father and sister. I would die for them, and it sounds like a Seer thing to do."

Tim's smile broadened. "I like you, damnit. I've never met a Seer I liked. But your drive and your fight are admirable. I've never encountered a Seer like you before."

"Thank you for the compliment," Travis said. "But you got one thing wrong. I didn't bring you out here to let you kill me. I brought you out here so that I could kill you."

Tim nodded, not losing his smile. "I like that."

Travis reached into his pocket and produced Uncle Jeff's knife. The Hunter's eyes narrowed as he recognized the knife that killed his brother. "I guess I have a sense of poetry too," Travis said.

The Hunter sighed and reached behind him, pulling a pistol from his waistline. Travis' eyes widened. "I seriously brought a knife to a gunfight?"

"I'm surprised you didn't see this coming," the Hunter said. He looked at the gun in his hand, then unceremoniously tossed it into the river below. "If we're about balance, we might as well respect it," he said as he pulled his own knife from his pocket. "Something tells me you're not going to get lucky this time."

***

Travis took a step back, allowing the Hunter to make the first move. Despite expecting it, Travis was surprised by Harvey's speed. The Hunter swung at Travis with his left fist, forcing Travis to jerk back to avoid the punch, and in the same fluid movement, he kicked out with his right foot. The kick caught Travis full in the knee, and it buckled instantly, sending him tumbling back onto the now swaying bridge.

Harvey wasted no time. Even as Travis was falling, he lunged forward with the knife aiming for Travis' neck. Travis saw it coming and used his own momentum as he fell to bring his good leg up to kick Harvey in the stomach. Harvey fell back, the wind taken out of him, but rolled onto his feet in a single movement and retreated a few steps to put distance between them as he caught his breath. Travis rolled to his feet and steadied himself with the rail. His injured knee didn't want to take his weight.

Harvey was coming at him again, though, and Travis was beginning to regret choosing an unstable bridge as their battlefield. He thought he would have the advantage, being young, fast and sure-footed. But he had been wrong. Harvey was just as fast, if not faster, and just as sure-footed.

As Harvey lunged at him, Travis ducked under the knife and leapt to the other side of the bridge. The sudden movement caused the bridge to buck, temporarily throwing them both off balance but allowing Travis to get behind Harvey and deliver a weak kick to the small of his back. Harvey dropped to his knees but did not give Travis enough time to use his advantage. As soon as Harvey's knees hit the bridge, he rolled to one side and slashed back behind him with the knife, catching Travis across the front of the shin.

White hot pain shot up Travis' leg as the knife cut to the bone. He didn't allow himself to fall again, though, refusing to lose the high ground he had gained. Instead, he brought his own knife down in an almost blind slashing motion that caught the Hunter's side, delivering a five-inch-long slash along his hip.

The Hunter tried to scramble back to regain his footing, but Travis lurched forward, slipping on his own blood, and fell on top of the Hunter. They rolled, bear hugging each other, both trying to get the upper hand, both delivering shallow cuts without either blade driving home. Without the space required for effective hand to hand combat, they resorted to kicking, scratching, and biting.

They rolled around on the now violently swinging bridge, both wrestling for their lives.

Travis kept a tight grip on his knife and brought his elbow up into the Hunter's cheek, rewarded by a spurt of blood before Harvey brought his forehead down onto the bridge of Travis' nose, causing him to temporarily see stars. Blinded, Travis lurched forward, sinking his teeth into whatever was in front of him. He tasted blood and was rewarded by a squeal from Harvey who began elbowing him in the head to get him to let go. Travis bit down harder, until he came away with a mouth full of flesh.

The Hunter jerked back as Travis spit out the glob of flesh he had just taken from Harvey's shoulder, and in doing so, he gave Travis just enough room to extend the arm holding the knife and burry it hilt deep into the Hunter's back. Harvey sucked in a breath in surprise and scrambled away from Travis; his eyes wide and fearful as he realized he had just been fatally wounded.

Travis let him scramble back away from him and made no attempt to stop him. He knew where he had sunk his knife. He knew it was a killing a blow. Harvey's body just hadn't figured it out yet.

Scooting back away from Travis, Harvey tried to reach back to remove the knife from his back, but gave up as he collapsed onto the bridge, blood beginning to trickle from his mouth. He watched as Travis climbed to his feet, using the railing to balance himself.

"I'm sorry." He said to Harvey as he wiped the blood from his chin and a weight the likes of which he had never felt began to settle over him. It was a deep sorrow, a shroud that seemed to block out the sun, and he knew it would be with him forever. Seers were not meant to kill. "I never wanted this."

But to his surprise a smile slowly spread across the Hunter's face and an ironic laugh escaped his lips. He raised one bloody hand and pointed at Travis, laughing even louder. Travis was confused as he clutched the railing with both hands, barely able to keep his feet, and looked down at his feet where blood was pooling.

His shirt was shredded above his stomach and under the shirt his stomach was shredded as well. The Hunter's knife had driven home, several times, and his adrenalin-soaked body just hadn't caught on to what was happening yet. The Hunter wasn't the only one that was dying.

Harvey's laughter turned manic, wracking his body in something close to a seizure as he continued to point at Travis. He was trying to say something, but the laughter wouldn't let him. Travis' eyes narrowed. The world was getting darker and for some reason, he desperately wanted to hear what Harvey was trying to say.

"Balance!" He finally managed to choke out as Travis tumbled over the side of the railing, Harvey's manic laughter following him all the way to the water.

It was dark and cold, and Travis was lost in a world of swirling blacks and blues. He didn't feel pain. Nor did he feel fear. If he felt anything, it was exhaustion, a complete lack of a willingness to go on, and an acceptance that everything was coming to an end.

Then there was sky above him, and he was being pulled towards the water's edge. He was aware of an arm around his chest, pulling him to safety, but its presence perplexed him. He didn't understand what was happening. Then there was ground beneath his back, and little river rocks dug into his skin.

"Travis!" Did he know that voice?

Allen Nightdale's face appeared above him, dripping wet and red faced, bloodshot eyes filled with fear.

"Dad?" Travis choked out, confused.

"Oh god, Travis. Hang on, okay? Just hang on!" He pulled his shirt over his head and pressed it against Travis' shredded stomach. "Hang on! You can't leave, okay? Don't leave." Travis could barely understand what he was saying from the sobs. One hand gently cupped Travis' head, the other applying pressure to his wounds. "Please dear God, don't let him die. Please Travis! We can't lose you again! I can't lose you again."

But Travis wasn't listening. Slowly, his father's voice faded away, as did the rocks and river and the cold and the pain. He felt soft lips on his own and suddenly, he was looking into warm brown eyes, and the scent of oregano and basil filled his nostrils. He smiled. She always smelled like her parent's restaurant. He had missed that smell…

Chapter 34

Randy pushed down on the arms of his wheelchair to slide himself back and winced as a sharp ping of pain moved along his spine. He was used to it at this point. The painkillers didn't do much when your body has been duct taped back together as many times as Randy's. He hated the wheelchair, though; it was uncomfortable and clumsy.

"Damn, man, you look like some kind of android or something," Dwayne said as he flopped down in the chair next to Randy.

"Thanks' man." Randy waved a hand down at the chair. "It's probably accurate at this point, with all of the metal I've got in me."

Dwayne scratched at a fresh, white scar on his cheek and looked down the hall. "We the first ones here?" He had toned up his attire for the somber occasion and was wearing black jeans and a black, collared shirt. His bare arms showed the evidence of his time with Harvey, but for the most part, the scaring hadn't been that bad. The worst scar was the one on his cheek where the curling iron left a third-degree burn.

"Sophia's parents are here, but they are sitting around the corner. Her mom doesn't like seeing me in this chair and wouldn't stop crying," Randy explained.

"That's hard, man," Dwayne said. "Damon should be here any minute. He didn't want to come, but I made him."

"Probate is already started, and once somebody is declared deceased, the will becomes public, so it's not like a will reading is really necessary," Randy said. "Travis requested it, though. I guess he was a little old fashioned." Randy tried to shift his weight again but gave up. Despite being released from the hospital earlier in the week, he was still extremely weak. "It's been three months. I'm surprised they waited for me to be here."

"We all agreed," Dwayne said. "Didn't seem right without you here. Even if you do look like shit."

"Thank you," Randy said. "I'm just thrilled to be able to take myself to the bathroom. How are you holding up? You look good, considering."

"I'm good." Dwayne smiled. "If anything, getting tied up and tortured by a skinny white guy has helped my street cred."

"I'm sorry for what he did to you," Randy said quietly.

"You got the worst of it," Dwayne pointed out, looking Randy up and down. "But you'll be able to walk again, right?"

"Yeah, but it's going to take six to eight months of physical therapy, and I may have to use a cane for a while after that. "

"You were lucky," Dwayne said. "I saw that truck."

"I think I've used up all my luck for one lifetime in the last year. "

Dwayne leaned closer to Randy and dropped his voice. "He is dead, right?"

"Travis?"

"No, skinny white torturing jackass."

"Yes, he's dead," Randy said. "It was the last thing Travis did."

Dwayne leaned back. He seemed satisfied by that. "Good. I wish he was still here, though. Travis, I mean. The funeral was nice. Well. It wasn't really a funeral because we didn't have a body, more of a memorial. But it was very nice. Momma spoke, and it was beautiful. We all put something of him in a little box, and Sophie's parents said they would have it placed in the graveyard with her. I cried. So did Damon."

Randy nodded. "Momma told me about it. She should be here any minute too."

"What are you going to do now that you're rich?" Dwayne asked.

"Pay medical bills." Randy said. "My insurance was through work, and it was dropped when I stopped showing up. There is a chance I may have something left after everything is paid for, but I doubt it."

"That sucks," Dwayne said. "Do you have anyone helping you? You can't take care of yourself yet, can you?"

"I have people taking care of me," Randy said as Damon and Momma entered the hall. Momma was holding onto Damon's arm, and they were walking slowly.

"You can stay with us." Dwayne offered. "We can take care of you."

Randy smiled. "Thank you for the offer, but I think when this is all over, I want to get out of California. I want to start over someplace new."

Dwayne shook his head and began to say something, but Momma and Damon had arrived by their side. "Everyone is here," Momma said patting Randy's shoulder. "Let's get this taken care of."

The lawyer read out the will and the personal messages Travis had left for each of them. It came as no surprise to any of them except Randy, who had still been in a medically induced coma when the probate process had begun. Despite knowing what was in the document, Sophia's mother still sobbed when Travis allotted a hundred thousand dollars for them to open a second restaurant in her honor. Dwayne and Damon were given a hundred thousand each to hire a lawyer to get their mom out of jail. Momma was given half a million to open the youth center she always dreamed of. A hundred thousand was given to the man, not present at the reading, who had found Travis in the river all those years ago.

The rest, an unknown amount due to ongoing assessments, went to Randy. Travis had also written a letter to each person in the room. The letters had already been handed out to everybody besides Randy. The lawyer seemed sad when he handed Randy the sealed envelope. Travis' death had shaken him; that much was obvious. It was the first time he had ever had to do this for somebody so young.

When it was over, Damon pushed Randy out of the meeting room, joking that he finally got to push Randy around. Despite that, little was said. There was little to be said. Momma gushed over how "good" Randy looked despite everything and lectured Damon and Dwayne on their foul language. Sophia's mother hugged Randy and said something to him he didn't understand because she was still crying, and her father shook his hand and said he was always welcome in the restaurant. They gave him some lasagna which had been his favorite meal in high school and told him they prayed for him every night before departing. As staunch Catholics, prayer was their only answer to relief from losing both their daughter and adopted son.

As Dwayne escorted Momma back to her mustang, Damon pushed Randy down the wheelchair ramp. "Dwayne tells me you're planning on taking off?" Damon asked as they reached the bottom.

"Yeah," Randy said. "There's just too much history here. I think I need a fresh start."

Damon kneeled in front of Randy. "Don't do that, man," he said, his eyes searching Randy's face for some indication of what he was feeling. "Don't isolate yourself like that. Don't disappear."

"That's not what I want to do," Randy said.

"Sure? Because that's what it sounds like. Sounds like you want to run away from your pain. Kind of a go to for us fosters, isn't it? Push people away because we never had nobody, and we don't need nobody. But we have family, man. You have family. Please let us be there for you."

"Thank you, Damon. That means a lot," Randy said, trying to convey how much it truly meant to him. "We are always going to be family. I won't go radio silence, I promise. I just need to do this. I don't think I can grieve here, and I don't think I can move on here."

"I get that. I can respect that. But I'm going to call you, so don't change your number on us. We're going to check in, we're going to pester you and ask you if you're okay and make you talk when you need it."

Randy smiled. "I expect nothing less."

Damon stood, towering over Randy like a bodyguard. "Are you going to read that?" he asked, gesturing at the sealed envelope still in Randy's lap. "Yeah," Randy said. "When I'm ready to. I'm not there yet."

Damon nodded. "It's still new to you. Everybody moves through the stages of grief in their own time. Dwayne has hit acceptance, I'm still angry. I think Momma is in denial. Wait till you're ready. Give yourself time to process."

"You will make a good therapist one of these days," Randy said.

"I'm actually going to school for it. I think I want to be a youth therapist. Maybe if I can help some of these inner-city kids process their anger, fewer of them will end up dead in the streets, ya know?" Damon said. "A scarred-up thug like me? Maybe they'll listen. Dwayne told me that Travis may have saved my life once. I figure maybe I should make it matter."

"It always mattered. But I think you're going to do great," Randy said.

"Where am I taking you?"

"Over there, "Randy pointed across the parking lot to where Laura was leaning against the car waiting for him.

Damon grinned. "That pretty little honey going with you? Wherever it is that you're going?"

"Yeah, she is." Randy nodded.

"Damon's grin broadened. "Well in that case, I think you're going to be fine."

"Yeah." Randy smiled at Laura. "I think I'm going to be fine too."

EPILOGUE

Randy stood facing the mirror, his brow furrowed in concentration as his hands moved in an impossible dance with his bow tie. "Son of a..." he growled, pulling the tie off and crumpling it before tossing it on the desk in front of him. He picked up his phone and watched the "how to tie a bow tie" video on YouTube again. He was sure he had just done all of that.

He was also sure he could pull off this suit without the bow tie. He was tall, and he was handsome. Why the heck did he need that stupid thing! He was wearing a deep blue suit with polished black loafers and looked ridiculously proper. The bow tie was a little over the top. His hair was freshly cut and brushed to the side, and he had even gone to a barber to get a close shave.

"What do you think?" he asked Starkey, who was lying a few feet away. "Do I really need the stupid thing?" Starkey didn't respond.

Two years after the accident, his muscle tone had almost returned and the scars had healed. He still walked with a limp and sometimes needed to use the cane, especially when the cold weather hit, but that was something he could live with. The physical therapy had been a pride killing ordeal where he had fought for every step, and every breakthrough had been hard won. He was happy it was behind him and he could finally move past everything that had happened.

He took a deep breath to steady his nerves and took in the scent of dogwood and magnolia. Springtime in Virginia truly was stunning.

He used to think he had seen green before, but he had never seen the shades of green that were found in the south. He loved it here.

"Randy?" There was a tap on the door behind him.

"Yeah!" Randy shouted, picking up the bow tie again. In the mirror, he saw the door open and Laura step in. For a moment, he was caught off guard. "Wow!" he said, turning around. "You look beautiful."

She blushed and looked down at her lavender colored dress. Her hair was curled and pinned back, and she wore one of her mother's gold necklaces that hung low between her breast. "The shoes hurt," she said. "I can't wait to take them off."

"At least you got them on," Randy said with a laugh, holding up the crumpled bow tie. "I can't even get this stupid thing on!"

"Here." Laura grabbed it from him. "Let me." She wrapped the tie around his neck and tied it so effortlessly, he felt instantly embarrassed.

"You make it look so easy," he said, grabbing her hand as she pulled it away and giving it a kiss. "I'll have you know I've been tying my own shoes since I was five."

Laura chuckled. "I'm sorry about this."

He shrugged. "I don't see why it has to be such a big deal."

"It's something about the south. Rehearsal dinners are a big deal, especially if your mother is a doctor and a pillar of the community. Appearances must be kept up."

"We should have eloped."

"We should have."

"Too late now?"

"Too late now."

"Are you sure?"

"Quite sure," she said, giving him a kiss. "I love that you're glowing right now."

"How can I not be? I'm looking at you," he said, stealing another kiss.

"Think he is going to make it?" He asked, turning back to the mirror to inspect the bow tie.

"I think so," Laura said, slipping her arm through his and putting her head on his shoulder. "His flight was delayed, but dad went to pick him up. Remember, you don't know each other."

Starkey's head suddenly came up, and he cocked it to the side, listening. There came another tap on the door. "It's me," Lauren's voice came through. "May I come in?"

"Sure," Laura said, rolling her eyes.

Lauren opened the door and stumbled to the side as Starkey rushed out past her. "OOF! I forget how big he is sometimes," she said, straightening herself. She paused for a moment, taking in the two of them, and put her hand to her mouth. "Oh, you two look so wonderful." She wiped at the corner of her eye with her fingertip.

"Thank you, mom," Laura said, handing her a tissue. She had been crying a lot lately.

"Thank you, dear," Lauren blotted at her eyes and, once under control of her emotions, threw the tissue in a waste basket next to the door. "Randy, dear, can you come with me for a second? There is somebody I want you to meet."

Randy followed Lauren out into the hall where Starkey was making quite a fuss, yipping and whining and twirling around the man who was kneeling and laughing in the middle of the floor trying his best to pet and hug the ecstatic animal. He had shaggy brown hair that had grown out into hippy length, tied back in a ponytail. He was wearing a black t-shirt and jeans and when he stood, he was deeply tanned. His smile was broad as he greeted Randy.

"Randy," Lauren said, for the sake of the reverend who was also standing in the hall, "this is my son, Travis Nightdale. He's been abroad in Spain for the past couple of years. Travis, this is Randy, your soon to be brother in law."

Travis smiled that smile that went all the way to the soul. He had left something behind in that river that day and without it he had been allowed to grow into something he was always meant to be. He had died, been revived, struggled, fought for his life, but had ultimately survived. He had buried himself and resurrected himself and allowed the scars to fade. He had healed.

"It's nice to meet you, Randy." Travis said, taking his hand and pulling him into a hug. "You know, I always kind of wanted a brother."